SAM

SAM

Robin Reid

A Good Reid

First published in Great Britain in 2016 by

A Good Reid

A CIP catalogue record for this book is available from the British Library

ISBN 978-1530583843

First Edition

10 9 8 7 6 5 4 3 2 1

To all my family and Godchildren

Part 1

—— Chapter One ——

The Next Best Thing

Yet another terrorist alert! Richard made his way to the exit of the shopping mall, still empty handed, as the annoyingly loud fire alarm continued to blare out all around him. Honestly, between journalists scare-mongering with non-existent threats and the government forever warning of what might be the terrorists' next move he really was suffering big time from terrorist fatigue. And it must have been years since the last actual incident. Who needs terrorists when our own people get off on striking terror into everyone's hearts, he thought as he reached the street outside. People were pressing against him on all sides. He hated crowds at the best of times but when there was a distinct feeling of panic in the air, it made things all the worse.

Now that he was outside, he thought about extricating his son from the leisure centre down the road just to be on the safe side. Then with a bite of impatience he realised he was catching the paranoia of everyone else. There was no terrorist attack here and there was no point in interrupting Dominic's fun. He continued on his way and was about to turn a corner towards the car park when there was an almighty bang. He looked around in shock. The shopping centre was still intact but there was definitely renewed panic. Then he saw the thick plume of black smoke rising rapidly in the near distance. His heart plummeted. It was coming from the direction of the leisure centre. Please no. He heard a bell ringing as he started running towards the leisure centre. Then there was another bang - several bangs. Not more explosions. These were more of a thumping sound coming from - where? He stopped and looked around. The scene was becoming confused. He thought he could hear someone calling his name…

Richard looked up from his computer with a start. The ringing of the doorbell had by now given way to angry banging. It took a moment for him to realise that he had fallen asleep at his desk. The radio was on, talking about some potential terrorist plot. So, now this hot topic had worked its way into his dreams! Irritated, he switched off the radio and glared at it. No more would he listen to the news. It was always the same rubbish and he'd had enough. The bell rang once more, long and shrill. Richard jumped up from his desk and hurried over to the front door, pausing only to put on a pair of slippers. He flung it open to see the face of his estranged wife looking harassed and annoyed.

"Um, sorry," he said awkwardly, "I, um..."

He forced a brief smile before turning his attention to the eleven year old boy standing next to her, suitcase in hand.

"Dominic!" he cried fondly, stooping down to give him a warm embrace, relieved that he was alive. "It's really great to see you." He tried to expunge the foolish dream from his mind. "It's really great to have you again so soon."

This was an unscheduled visit but definitely very welcome. The two broke apart and Richard gazed fondly at his son who, with a cheeky grin, flicked snow out of his hair straight into his father's face.

"Monkey," Richard said wiping his face. His smile faltered slightly as he straightened up to look once again upon the woman, who clearly did not share his joy.

"Er, do you want to come in for a quick drink?" he asked her civilly.

"No thank you," was her response, her tone as cold as the weather outside. "I told you I've got to get straight off to work. You've already kept me waiting and I haven't got time to be necking bottles of wine with you."

"I meant tea actually," replied Richard softly.

"All the same. I do wish you wouldn't keep trying to get me to come back and spend time in that hovel. You know it drives me crazy."

Richard was determined not to rise to her rudeness.

"So, how long's the hospital on standby for?" he asked, reaching over to take the suitcase from Dominic. "As in, how many days have you got to cover for?"

"No idea. As long as these terrorists keep making tiresome threats, I suppose. I've packed enough stuff to keep him until Sunday night. I'll send you a text or something when I know more."

"OK. Have fun."

"Yeah, whatever. And you," she now turned to Dominic, "make sure you behave." She gave him a swift kiss on the cheek then turned abruptly back to Richard. "Make sure he gets to bed at a *sensible* hour. I don't want him staying up all night on that infernal computer of yours."

"Yes, Amanda," Richard replied with a patient sigh, "I'm sure everything will be fine. Now have a safe journey."

"Yes, well –" She looked as if she wanted to argue but chose not to. "I'll see you in a few days."

"Bye, Mum," said Dominic and Richard closed the door.

The moment she was gone Dominic turned towards Richard with an excited gleam in his eyes.

"Can I play on your computer?"

"Wha-? No, I'm using it. Besides, you heard your mother."

"Oh please, please, please."

"Look, you've only just got in, why can't we just have a nice conversation? Tell me about your Christmas."

"Oh, come on, Dad! Christmas was four days ago. We talked about it yesterday. It was boring without you."

"Okay then, your birthday. How does it feel to be eleven?"

"Dad, my birthday was six days ago. We talked about that as well."

"Fine. How about your journey here: what was the traffic like, which way did you come?"

"Oh please, Dad. I want to play your Cyber Challenge game again. I nearly beat it last time. I just want to have another go. Pleeeeease?"

Richard looked into the imploring eyes of his son and in spite of himself felt his resolve evaporate.

"Oh very well," he said resignedly.

"Thanks, Dad", said Dominic quickly and immediately hurried off to the living room where he knew the computer was kept.

Richard looked down at the suitcase that he was still carrying. Abruptly, he mastered his senses, put down the suitcase and followed Dominic.

"Wait," he said. Dominic was already rummaging around on the PC looking for the game. "First you can take your coat off and hang it in the bathroom to dry. You'd better dry your hair as well; I don't want you catching pneumonia while you're here, I'd never hear the end of it. Then take your case to your room and unpack. When you've finished all that then you can have half an hour on the game before dinner. OK?"

Dominic ceased his rummaging and looked at his father, disappointment etched all over his face. Richard looked back at him, not sternly but with an expression as if to say he thought he was being entirely reasonable. Dominic got the message without Richard having to say any more.

"Yes, Dad", he said and reluctantly walked away from the computer. As he passed Richard, his hand darted out and prodded him playfully in the stomach. Then he ran away laughing. Richard sped after him and caught him in the hallway where he wrestled him to the floor, now also laughing with merry abandon.

Suddenly the whole place was vibrating and there was a heavy thumping noise reverberating through the floor. Richard ceased his wrestling and rolled over onto his back with his hands over his face. The man in the downstairs flat had recently taken to playing his hi-fi extremely loudly if he had heard so much as a fly's footstep through his ceiling. Evidently, Richard and Dominic had been rolling around rather too heavily for his liking and this was his method of telling them. Richard slowly got to his feet and helped Dominic to do the same.

"It'll stop soon if we're quiet," said Richard gently. "You'd best go and unpack."

Dominic nodded and, dragging his suitcase, tiptoed in the direction of his bedroom. The downstairs hi-fi continued to boom its assault.

Richard returned to the living room, half-heartedly brushing carpet dust from his baggy trousers as he went. If he was going to concede use of the PC to Dominic he had better save his work and make a new backup of it all. Not that he begrudged Dominic playing on the PC; at least he favoured intellectual games rather than those that just required you to shoot as many aliens as possible. He felt particularly proud that Dominic had become so hooked on Cyber Challenge, as it was Richard's own invention. However, he could not let him hog the machine for his entire stay as he himself had plenty of serious work to do on it.

The living room was not particularly big and the desk took up a significant part of the room. On it were a flat-screen monitor, a keyboard, mouse, a stack of in-trays and a festoon of paper and mess. On a shelf above the main desk were his printer, speakers and a clutter of pens and other stationery items. The rest of the room sported an old three-seater sofa, a small television set and a dining table that doubled as a secondary desk, currently bearing a laptop computer, a carelessly abandoned wallet, a spent coffee mug and an untidy pile of computer periodicals. On a noticeboard above the fireplace were pinned a photograph of Richard with Amanda and Dominic, taken several years earlier, and a menu for the local pizza takeaway.

Richard opened one of the drawers in his desk and pulled out a box full of rewritable CDs, all carefully labelled. He opened it and riffled through the disks until he found the one marked *Wednesday 4*, which was the disk to use on the fourth Wednesday of his backup cycle. He inserted the disk into the machine and started the backup program.

Half way through the procedure, Dominic returned. Richard looked at him in mild surprise.

"Have you finished unpacking already?" he asked suspiciously.

"Yeah, well I didn't bring that much stuff, did I? Can I have a play now? Please?"

"Let me feel your hair."

"Dad!" Dominic protested as he moved forward for his hair examination. "I know how to dry my own hair."

"Fair enough," said Richard after a quick feel. "You'll have to wait though, I'm backing up my files."

"How long will that take?"

"Oh not long now, a couple more minutes should do it."

Dominic watched the screen for a moment as the progress bar slowly edged towards completion. He knew his father too well to question why he took so many backups of his work, or even why he still chose to use CDs and memory sticks rather than cloud storage. When it came to software, Richard had a deep mistrust of everyone and would never leave his work anywhere if there was even the remotest possibility of someone stealing it.

"Have you been writing a new game?" Dominic asked excitedly.

"I'm afraid not. I've actually been using Brain Stormer to help me refine that adaptive program I told you about. I'm really excited by it now – it's definitely going to be my killer app!"

"Your what?" asked Dominic mystified.

"My killer app - my killer application. Basically, it's going to be so fantastic it will blow the competition out of the water. This is going to change my life forever!" He faltered. "I wonder if I should mention it at that technical symposium, the one in Reading. I'm meant to be doing a presentation on Brain Stormer. In fact, I still need to finish putting that together - although I'm not even sure I can be bothered to go."

"Isn't that like in the next few days? Honestly, Dad, just go. You're always banging on about that Brain Stormer thing. It's about time you showed it to people who - you know - might be interested."

"Yes, yes, I know." Richard sighed in resignation. "But these things can be so tedious. Three long days of listening to geeks going on about some tripe they reckon is so innovative. The only difference this time round is that I'll be one of the geeks boring everyone else. I mean, me? Stand up in front of everyone and speak? Imagine!"

Dominic said nothing. Richard opened a drawer and retrieved a booklet containing details of the event. He liked to remind himself from time to time of what he was letting himself in for.

The technical symposium is a gathering for the purpose of sharing technical innovations with like-minded individuals and to discuss the impact of various technological advancements in computer science and information systems.

His eyes glazed over. He turned the page and began riffling casually through the booklet. Half way through, he paused and shook his head sadly. His eyes had fallen upon the legend "*This page intentionally left blank*" standing alone in the middle of one of the sheets. He sighed.

"One of the great logical paradoxes of our day," he said sardonically, standing up to give way to Dominic. "It makes no sense whatsoever and quite apart from being a total waste of paper, it really does my head in. Maybe you want to try a logical paradox to beat Cyber Challenge. It's the sort of foolishness that makes computers turn their legs up and die because there's no way to work out what on earth you mean."

Dominic chuckled but looked like he might actually consider that such a tactic was worth a try.

The downstairs hi-fi was mercifully silent by the time dinner arrived on the table. It was a simple affair. Richard had not been given much notice of Dominic's arrival and so had not managed to get to the shops to buy anything special. He did, however, manage to rustle up a dish of tuna with pasta and a creamy sauce. It must have been nice, thought Richard, because Dominic remained quiet while he bolted it down. His plate was almost empty again when he abruptly stopped eating and sat quite still for a moment, pensively.

"Dad?" he began and Richard thought he had an idea of what he was going to say. "Why is Mum always having a go at you these days?"

It was exactly what Richard had expected him to ask and he wasn't sure of the best way to answer. It was true that in recent weeks Richard had hardly been able to say anything to Amanda without her snapping at him. It was not surprising that Dominic had noticed. His parents had always had totally different personalities. Whereas she was pretty ordinary, he had often been described as "off the wall". Whereas she had a fairly strait-laced job as a hospital consultant, he worked on what he always described as "extreme software".

It was his fascination for software that had been one of her biggest bugbears and had caused the most arguments. She used to accuse him of loving his computers more than he loved her. That had never been true, as far as he was concerned, although he had to admit that he generally did get on much better with computers than he did with people. And who could blame him? People were so unnecessarily complicated; Amanda herself was living proof of that.

And yet she had loved him once. She had even previously claimed that she loved him with an insane passion, that she would become profoundly depressed if ever he left her. How things had changed.

"I think she simply fell out of love with me," he said. "It happens sometimes. And my being out of work right now doesn't help."

"Do you think you'll ever get back together?" asked Dominic.

Richard played around with some more pasta but did not reload his fork. All kinds of thoughts flooded into his head. Obviously it would be nice to get back together. He had loved his wife very much - or at least he thought he had. If he were honest with himself, he did not really know much about love. However, he had made his marriage vows some twelve years earlier and it seemed only right and proper to stick to them. If only people would behave more like computers. Now that he thought about it, between his desktop PC and his laptop, he had more computers than he had companions. He had no friends to speak of and now that Amanda had left him, Dominic was the only person he really enjoyed being with.

"Dunno," he said with a shrug, still fidgeting with his food. "It would be nice. Obviously. You're a good kid and I love you loads. It would be really good to see you every day again rather than this fragmentary arrangement. And I'd be able to move back into my own house. And... But I don't know, it's been nearly a year already; she's probably grown used to me not being around. Still, who can tell, eh? Maybe when I've finished my killer app and it takes off - hopefully - maybe she'll want to snatch me back. Maybe she'll even warm to the computer a bit more - or at least thaw a little."

Dominic wore an expression that could have been sorrow or sympathy. It looked as though he realised that the conversation had made Richard feel slightly sad. And he himself would undoubtedly be missing the family unit. Since January of that year he had only been seeing his father on Tuesdays and every other weekend. He had learned to accept the situation and there was no evidence that his schoolwork or his general wellbeing had significantly deteriorated since his parents' separation, which he knew was only for a trial period. But wouldn't he fare better in a stable family unit? And this trial period did seem to grow longer day by day.

"I love you too, Dad," he said.

Richard was surprised how much he needed to hear those words. His heart lifted somewhat although he still felt miserable. A few minutes passed in silence, then he put down his fork and stood up, even though his plate was still half full. Dominic dropped his fork with a clatter. He had lost his appetite as well. Richard grimaced and collected the plates. Then with an admirable attempt at disguising his gloom he addressed Dominic more positively.

"Pudding? I have an outrageously scrumptious chocolate gateau just begging to be devoured," he said ostentatiously.

From the look on Dominic's face, the suggestion was most appealing.

The last few days of the year passed in a feast of enjoyment but New Year's Day itself was a haze of fatigue. They had both stayed up to toast in the New Year but the man downstairs had then kept them awake for most of the rest of the night hosting a raucously loud party.

The technical symposium was now just two days away and although he was still not looking forward to it, Richard had made one of his resolutions to use it as a marketing stage for his software inventions, which, he reminded himself, was precisely what it was for. His objective for the year was to accumulate a large pot of money and only then focus on the task of reuniting his family. He had a feeling that Amanda would not be willing to walk full time back into his life if she knew the state of his bank account. He had been out of work for a number of months and had been living off his credit cards, although he was heavily in arrears with them all. The only bills he kept on top of were those that he described as priority debts: his utility bills, his council tax and his rent. He also continued to pay the mortgage on the house where Amanda and Dominic were living, in the hope that one day he would return there to enjoy life with them.

By the time Sunday had arrived, both Dominic and Richard were feeling subdued. Dominic had only just revealed that he had a mountain of homework to complete by the start of the new school term in two days' time, although he had not begun to look at any of it. Richard had given him a token telling off for his lack of organisation but he himself had larger things on his mind. Unusually, he found it a bit of a relief when Amanda returned that evening to pick up Dominic. Normally, their parting was followed by a period of melancholy loneliness, which Richard would too often seek to alleviate with a hefty swig of vodka, always at the ready in the fridge. This time, however, he would be able to prepare himself mentally for his three-day sojourn in Reading.

"Oh," he said as Amanda led Dominic away, once again laden with his small suitcase. They both stopped and looked round. "I nearly forgot. Tuesday. I, um, well I've got to go to Reading for a few days. It's a work thing," he added hastily as she eyed him with suspicion. She raised her eyebrows. "Well, it's sort of work. I, er..."

"Dad's going to meet a load more geeky weirdoes, sell his programs to them and become rich and famous," piped up Dominic. "Isn't that right, Dad?"

"Um, yes, something like that," muttered Richard.

"I assume," said Amanda loftily, "that all this nonsense is your way of saying that you won't be around to look after Dominic on Tuesday and you want me to keep him instead?"

"Well, yeah if that's okay... If you don't mind... And maybe I... Well, I thought that perhaps I could, um, pick him up on Thursday instead?"

He felt himself shrinking rapidly under her quelling gaze. It was like being cross-examined by a school headmistress but he stood his ground. He had, after all, just completed a similar favour for her. He had looked after Dominic for three additional days because she had been unexpectedly called into work. It was perfectly reasonable, therefore, to propose a one-day swap in return. Amanda must have thought so too because she pursed her lips and consented, albeit grudgingly.

"I will do this for you this once," she said. "But in future if you want to alter the arrangements I will expect rather more notice. Dominic, let's go."

And without any further backward glances she swept Dominic towards the stairs.

Richard watched them for a while from his living room window as they got into Amanda's red Toyota and drove away. Already he could feel his spirits sinking. But there was no time to mope. He had just a few more hours to make last minute adjustments to his symposium presentation and to make sure that he had packed everything that he was likely to need. He crossed the room to his computer and copied his work onto a USB memory stick. Then he checked the Internet for directions to where he would be going the following day. Naturally, he would be using his satellite navigation device for the journey but one could never be too careful and he printed off several instances of the map currently on his screen, at differing levels of zoom.

When he was finally satisfied that he was as ready as he would ever be, Richard decided to go to bed, figuring that an early night would be prudent. He checked for new emails one last time before shutting down the computer. Normally, he would leave this running all the time but there would be no need for it over the next few days while he was away. At last he was in bed. Just before turning out the light his eyes fell on a photograph of Amanda that was standing on his bedside cabinet.

"This is all for you," he said to the photograph and switched off the light.

Whatever she may have thought, she and Dominic were the most important things in Richard's life. In their absence, his love of software was the next best thing. But one day, he would have the best of both worlds. One day – he just knew it – he would be reunited with his family. And if his computer software could somehow help him to achieve that goal, then all the better.

—— Chapter Two ——

The Symposium

"Thank God for satellite navigation!" thought Richard as he manoeuvred his car down the narrow side streets of Reading in a desperate bid to avoid the traffic. Despite setting off in good time he was still behind schedule, thanks to the immense tailback on the M4. He had considered a last minute decision to make the journey by train, which would have been especially convenient, as his destination was so close to the station. However, the breaking news just before he had left his flat was that as a result of a security alert in London all public transport had been halted in and around the capital. No tubes, no buses, no trains. He guessed that this had been the major contributor to the motorway madness he had just escaped from. He was now making steady progress, blindly following the instructions from the machine mounted on his windscreen. Considering that he had not wanted to attend the symposium in the first place, he now was very keen to arrive soon. Every minute that went by filled him with ever increasing anxiety. It would be embarrassing if he arrived late, particularly if he happened to be the first speaker. In truth, he had no idea of the running order; his information pack had merely said that the agenda would be supplied on arrival.

"Just ahead, turn left onto the A327 (Shinfield Road)," said the navigator on the windscreen.

Richard obeyed and a few moments later he was on Whiteknights Campus and the Palmer Building made itself known to him. Richard recognised its distinctive shape from the photograph in his information pack. His heart was beginning to thump with nervous anticipation as he drove around looking for somewhere to park. Although the car park seemed ample he struggled to find an available place. Round and round he went in a fruitless search. He felt heat build inside him and even a few drops of sweat on his forehead. If this conference was supposed to be attended by such innovative minds why couldn't someone invent something to direct drivers straight to an available parking spot?

He was back where he started at the entrance to the car park. He sighed deeply and looked around frantically. He wondered how safe it would be to park on the road. Then he spotted a disabled spot in the corner. He hesitated for a second then made a beeline for it.

"Sorry but needs must," he muttered aloud as he manoeuvred into the spot.

He considered sawing off one of his legs to legitimise his decision, remembering some daft comedy sketch he had seen on the television some time previously. Smiling to himself, he switched off the engine, jumped out of the car and locked the door. He looked around briefly to get his bearings then began hurrying over towards the building. Suddenly he stopped and headed back to the car. He opened the boot and withdrew a laptop bag. He wouldn't get very far without that! He opened the pouch of the bag and withdrew a half bottle of vodka. He took a quick swig from this to try and calm down his agitated nerves. Then he replaced the bottle, once again secured the car and hurried back towards the building. He knew he was already late yet he would have to freshen up before joining the event.

A woman was sitting behind a reception desk. Judging by the lack of anyone else Richard knew that the conference had already begun. He walked up to the reception desk and the woman greeted him.

"Good morning, sir. Are you here for the symposium?"

"Er, yes," he replied. "I'm supposed to be giving one of the talks."

"Lovely. And your name is?"

"Richard Neilson."

The woman ran her finger down a list of names until she found Richard's. "Ah yes, sir, you're giving the talk on Analytical Creativity? You're not on until this afternoon. Two o'clock."

"Oh okay," Richard was relieved. "Has it actually already

started? The symposium, I mean." He was rather hoping that it had been slightly delayed, perhaps because of the traffic, and that people would still be settling in.

"About ten minutes ago but not to worry. You grab yourself a coffee from the machine and just go right in." She handed him a folder. "This contains all the information you'll need for your stay. There's a map of the campus with details of accommodation and dining facilities. You'll be staying in Windsor Hall with most of the other delegates, not too far from here. There's also an agenda and a pad and pen for making notes. If you do have any queries then I or one of my colleagues will be here to help you."

"Right. Um... Okay." Richard was looking distractedly at the information the woman had just handed to him. "How many delegates are there, as a matter of interest?"

"I've written that down here somewhere." The woman consulted her list of names again. "Ah yes, three hundred and eleven."

"How many?" Richard's eyes seemed to burst from his head in shock. He had expected perhaps thirty or forty, fifty at the outside. But over three hundred! He had certainly never in the past spoken in front of so many people.

"It's always nice to have a decent sized audience when you're speaking," said the woman with a broad smile. "Is there anything else I can help you with?"

"Er, no, thanks. Er, yes. I need – Is there a – Where're the gents?" Richard was now feeling even hotter and sweatier than before.

"Just along the corridor behind you."

"Oh okay, thanks." He turned and left.

Whoever it was that thought it a good idea to have the entrance to a lecture theatre right at the front of the room ought to have had his head examined. These were Richard's thoughts as he joined the conference a further ten minutes later having made himself look presentable and availed himself of the coffee facilities. It did not help matters as these were not the quietest of doors and as far as he was concerned there may just as well have been a loud klaxon announcing his lateness. He staggered clumsily into the room, his laptop over his right shoulder, a cup of coffee and a couple of biscuits in his right hand. He stood framed in the doorway for a while looking up the steps, daunted by the sea of faces above him as his eyes scanned the rows for an available seat. He was still looking when the door came swinging back on its hinges and collided with him sending his coffee flying. He caught it just in time and the only damage was to some now very soggy biscuits. The clatter, however, had caused even those who had not previously noticed him now to look inquisitively at the source of the intrusion. Indeed, even the lecturer broke off from his ramblings and turned to face Richard who could feel the heat building up inside him all over again. He half expected the lecturer to shout at him for disturbing him mid-flow or to cast him out for being late and disruptive. But he merely indicated the front few rows of seats, all of which were available.

"Plenty of seats down in front," he said genially. "Don't be shy."

In fact, Richard had always been shy of front seats, which is why he had not seen them in the first place. Nevertheless, he muttered something inaudible, tried to smile and made his way to an empty seat in the middle of the row, feeling thoroughly exposed. Once he was seated he tried valiantly to focus on what the current speaker was saying but he didn't take in a word of it. He was still unsettled, still hot and bothered. But there was nothing he could do about that right now. The lecturer was standing at a lectern equipped with a microphone. Loudspeakers ascending the walls on either side carried his voice to his audience. Behind him an enormous white projector screen relayed the image on his laptop which showed a demonstration of something undoubtedly fascinating.

Richard consulted his agenda again. Each of the three days began at nine o'clock and continued until four thirty with an hour off for lunch from twelve o'clock. He imagined the lunch hour to involve a buffet with hundreds of geeks standing around with plates of fatty food talking loudly about some unimaginably tiresome subject. He really was not looking forward to it. Why had he even bothered to come? Why had he spent large amounts of money registering for such an event? Well, as Dominic had said, it was time he showed his software to people who might be interested. He had so far made very few sales of Brain Stormer, which was a shame because he was very proud of that work. And now he had created an even smarter tool. Realistically, however, he did not think that standing up in front of this crowd of misfits would generate any further sales of his products. Indeed, given his unforgettable entrance he was probably already doomed to failure.

He was to be the second speaker after lunch. He went over in his mind once again what he would demonstrate. He had prepared some additional material to fill in time in case his audience became so numbed by what he had to show them that no one had any questions to ask. Half an hour could be a long time to fill with nothing to say. Wait a moment - *half* an hour? He peered at the agenda again. He was on from two until three - a whole hour. He began to panic. He had not prepared a whole hour's worth of material. He now imagined a mass of stern faces looking down on him expectantly when he had dried up after only twenty minutes. Perhaps some of them would even demand a partial refund from him. With an effort he forced his mind to focus on the current presentation. Maybe if he was clever enough he could somehow link his own talk into all those that went before him. Then he would shamelessly be able to reiterate vast swathes of other people's sessions as part of his own. With that in mind he began to take notes furiously, amazed at his own brilliance.

Time passed and two further speakers had been in the spotlight. By lunchtime, Richard had scrawled down several pages of notes, although in his haste to get as much onto paper as possible he had missed the essence of all the talks so far. All he knew was that none of them particularly fitted in with anything he wanted to say that afternoon. He decided to use the break to refine his presentation still further, perhaps to get some new idea of how to pad his material to fill the scheduled time. Unfortunately, he kept getting distracted by overfriendly geeks enthusing to him about some of the talks that had already occurred. He wondered if people were descending upon him in particular because of his high-profile arrival but mercifully no one mentioned that at all.

Richard glanced at his watch. To his horror there were only fifteen minutes left before the afternoon period was due to begin and he still had not even eaten anything. He consulted the information he had in his folder to find out that lunch was to be held in the Cedar Room some fifty yards from the Palmer Building where he currently was. He set off gloomily to sample whatever remained, resigning himself to the fact that his presentation would be humiliatingly substandard.

When he arrived at the university restaurant he was not surprised to find that there had indeed been a buffet although by now most people had dispersed. Most of the food had also vanished and he was left to pick at the few remaining scraps of the selections on offer. Two sandwiches and half a pork pie later it was five minutes to one o'clock and the afternoon session was almost about to begin. Determined not to make another foolish entrance, he gulped down a small glass of orange juice and hurried off back towards the Palmer Building.

On the way back he paused off at the coffee machine where he overheard a couple of delegates talking about an item of news they had just received. It sounded like Heathrow Airport had been temporarily closed because of a suspected terrorist threat. He did not hear the details of the conversation nor did he feel that he had the time to consult with them to get more information. Indeed, he suddenly realised that he had very little interest in the affair. Getting home without too much inconvenience was all that concerned him.

He arrived back at the lecture theatre to find that most people had already returned. There was a buzz of excited talk, which made Richard feel rather alone in his lack of enthusiasm. He could not explain to himself why he felt the way he did. Perhaps it was just his nerves. However, he definitely hoped that no one shared his mood when he himself got up to talk.

The last few people drifted in and took their seats. Then the chairman approached the lectern and silence fell at once.

"Ladies and gentlemen, welcome back. I just want to say before we carry on what a great privilege it is to be in the presence of so many talented and vibrant minds. Some of the things we saw this morning simply blew me away. And I've seen a lot in my day!"

Richard looked at the scrawled notes he had taken during the morning sessions and wished he had paid more attention to the details of what had been said instead of worrying about his own presentation. He had not learnt anything new. The chairman continued.

"Well, we still have a lot to get through so I'll get off and we can carry on. There is a slight change to the programme. We were at this time supposed to be hearing from Mike Evans about New Ideas in Artificial Intelligence. Sadly, he's had a technical hitch with his presentation so that's being put back to last thing tomorrow in place of Jon Byrnes' talk on Four-Dimensional Graphics which we'll have last thing today instead. Meanwhile, we'll skip ahead to our next talk on Analytical Creativity. So if I'm not imposing on you too much could I ask Richard Neilson to take the floor please, if you're ready."

Richard sat stunned. Why had nobody warned him that the plans had changed? As if in answer to this, the chairman, who had been looking around the room waiting for Richard to identify himself, now seemed to guess who he might be and addressed him directly.

"Very sorry to put you on the spot like this. I was trying to find you at lunchtime to let you know but no one seemed to know where you were. Are you able to do your talk now?"

Richard nodded feeling utterly numb.

"Of course," he said bravely and got to his feet.

His brain seemed to go into overdrive working out how to begin. He picked up his laptop and sidled along his lonely row and walked down the steps towards the lectern, rather like he was making his final march to the gallows. In his dazed state he heard, as if from a distance, applause coming from behind him. It did not make him feel any better.

He reached the lectern and without looking up began to set up his laptop. The chairman was helping him but in his detachment Richard failed to notice. The laptop was switched on, cables were plugged in and buttons were pressed. At last everything was ready and it was time to begin. The chairman took his seat leaving Richard feeling quite alone.

Richard finally looked up and gazed around the room assessing his audience. It was almost alarming how stereotypically geeky most of the people looked with their long unkempt hair, goatee beards and pizza paunches. There were some women too, almost indistinguishable from the men, although most did not have beards. Dotted around the room was a handful of people looking smart, some even wearing suits. These were typically the older ones, perhaps those who had evolved into managers, having outgrown the attraction of cutting edge technology.

Richard cleared his throat. The noise resounded unexpectedly through the loudspeakers. He took a moment to collect his thoughts together. How should he begin? What should be his first sentence? Should he perhaps say hello? How had the other speakers begun? His mind was blank. He no longer knew anything.

"Um," he heard himself say through the loudspeakers. It was disconcerting to hear his ineptitude magnified in this way. Why couldn't someone invent a microphone that muted such hesitations? A Falter Filter – now that would be a good idea!

"Um," he said again and just managed to stop himself from

cursing himself out loud. He took a deep breath and plunged on at random. "Okay, I thought I'd show you - this talk is called Analytical Creativity but before I get onto that I thought I'd show you how I came up with the project."

That was the introduction out of the way. Now onto the more interesting, hopefully easier, bit.

"Some of you may have heard of Brain Stormer. Brain Stormer's a software package I designed about eighteen months ago and it does exactly as you might expect – brainstorm. It's funny but when I gave the first demonstration of the system it became clear to me that not everyone knows what brainstorming is. So I'll just spend a few moments discussing that for the benefit of anyone who might be in the same boat."

He was beginning to relax a bit more now and his words were flowing with more confidence. He had not planned to talk about brainstorming as such but he now realised that this was a superb opportunity to flesh out his talk so that it would last the prescribed hour.

"If you've got a problem to solve or even if you just want to generate new ideas one thing you can do is to get a group of people together into a room and have everyone shout out possible solutions spontaneously. All the ideas get written down without judgement, no matter how bizarre they might seem at first. Ideas generate new ideas and before you know it you've got the basis of a pretty inventive solution.

"When I first came across brainstorming we wrote everything down on flipcharts. Nowadays, there's a whole load of software out there that will help you capture your ideas and will present them in all sorts of amazing ways. Brain Stormer does all that but the big difference with Brain Stormer is that it will do the actual brainstorming for you as well. So it doesn't just capture your ideas but also generates its own. It does this by recursively abstracting and extending the initial requirement, taking it to a new level at each iteration. It presents these ideas to the user as a mind map with the original problem in the centre and umpteen initial ideas radiating out from this and further ideas radiating from each of those, and so on. You can use Brain Stormer as part of your brainstorming group of people but I find it's most effective if you leave it to its own devices and check on it from time to time to see how it's doing. That way you're free to do other things."

As he continued with his lecture, Richard became aware of the total silence amongst the audience. There was no feedback whatsoever: no nods, no frowns, no raised eyebrows, no murmurs, nothing. He could not tell if this was because everyone was too numbed by tedium or too enthralled by what he was saying. It unnerved him a bit and he floundered once or twice but proceeded valiantly. After a while, however, he decided that it was time for a change of tack.

"It's probably a good idea for me to show you a quick demo of what the software can do."

This is where it was bound to go horribly wrong. A live demonstration in front of over three hundred people was not what he would have described as plain sailing. He turned to his laptop and started tapping in a command. Soon his application had started. On the screen appeared a window with a single edit field and a button labelled *Go*. Richard looked up.

"Let's take a really simple example to demonstrate the program's capabilities. Let's say we want to think about what to consider when, say, going to the zoo. Um. Before we start, perhaps we can simulate a real life brainstorming session right now with all of you as the participants. Just shout out your ideas on what you think should be considered when going to the zoo, and I'll write them up on this flipchart."

He began walking across to the flipchart, which was just a few feet from the lectern. The last few words of his sentence died as his voice parted company with the microphone but his listeners seemed to have got the message. He looked at them expectantly. For what seemed like an age no one said anything and Richard's confidence began to waver again. Then gradually people became alive and began to shout their ideas down to him.

"Decide which animals to see."

"Decide up front what order to see them in."

"Allow enough time to see them."

"Take something to feed the elephants."

"Take something to feed yourself."

"How to keep the kids amused if all the animals are in hiding."

"Don't get your hat eaten by the giraffes."

"Where's the nearest pub?"

It went on in this vein for about ten minutes. The audience even seemed to enjoy being part of the experiment. The ideas rained down, most fairly similar to one another, others downright ridiculous. Richard wrote them all down on the flipchart, admirably keeping up with the speed of delivery. But soon it was time to stop and return to the talk. He walked back to the lectern, having filled two sheets on the flip chart.

"Well, anyone who didn't know what brainstorming was before should have a pretty good idea now. That was very interesting, thank you. Now let's see what the machine can do. If I just type in here..."

He entered the phrase "Going to the zoo" and clicked the *Go* button. There was the briefest of pauses before the screen cleared. Then instantly a multi-coloured diagram began to appear with boxes radiating from other boxes, each with a word or phrase inscribed, the centre box being labelled with the input phrase "Going to the zoo".

Richard felt the need to give a commentary while the program worked.

"So this is doing alone what we've just done in community. And interestingly, it's thinking about methods of actually getting to the zoo - something none of us here mentioned. As you can see it's considered driving, which in turn might involve traffic queues - rather like this morning - and petrol costs. It also considers whether the car's big enough to take the whole family so it obviously recognises this as a family outing. Interesting! As for the zoo itself, it mentions feeding time, hunting patterns, survival of the fittest, the law of the jungle, habitat... So you can see it's considering making the visit a bit of an educational trip. Oh, and look, it's come up with some rather controversial entries here under animals: circus, cruelty, vivisection, riots... Struth! And all this in just a minute and a half! We had ten minutes and came up with not getting our hat eaten by the giraffes."

He now clicked the *Stop* button.

"I'll terminate this for now; I think you've got a flavour of its potential. Obviously, this was a very simple example so it didn't take long to analyse. More complex situations can take it quite a lot longer, especially if the requirements are vague. When you terminate the program, it leaves the mind map on the screen and you can see from this one how each idea flows into another series of ideas."

Richard wound up his demonstration by showing how Brain Stormer collated all the information in its mind map to formulate new ideas. There were some fairly obvious ones such as *Take coach to safari park*, as well as some that were quite abstract, including one which suggested *Train in taxidermy*. But somewhere in between gave rise to the most inspiring concepts, such as *Go on conservation tour*.

"You probably had no idea what sparks could be generated just from the initial idea of going to the zoo! But there's something even more special I want to share with you today. However, before I continue, are there any questions on Brain Stormer?"

There was a blur as scores of hands shot into the air at once. The questions came thick and fast but not through any lack of understanding. The audience had been so enraptured by what Richard had to say and what he had shown them that they wanted to know more. Some, to Richard's great delight, even wanted to know how they could obtain their own copy of the software under licence. It was a shame to have to interrupt the flow of questions; Richard was in his element answering them all but time was running out and he really wanted to demonstrate his newest product. When he had once more got their attention he proceeded.

"You've seen how Brain Stormer can take an idea and enhance it to form new ideas. Well, I recently had a brainwave how to revolutionise the IT industry by automatically implementing the best ideas into software components. What I came up with is what I call the Super-Adaptive Module or SAM for short. This is an intelligent program that will analyse an existing piece of software and automatically enhance it for you, opening up all sorts of possibilities. All you need to do is to expose the software to SAM by placing it in its hunt zone - that's like a domain - and SAM will modify any compatible software it finds inside it. You also need to write a short abstract so that it understands the purpose of the software. And then you're away.

"SAM uses the same word association subroutines that Brain Stormer uses but it has built-in termination points so that you don't end up with a completely unrecognisable program. For instance, you'd want a chess program to stick to the rules of chess no matter how much you enhance it. And we can all rest assured that because it remains within constraints none of us should be made redundant by this tool."

A chuckle went round the room perhaps mingled with a hint of relief.

"Again, a demonstration will illustrate the point."

He went into an edit window and typed in a four-line program.

"This simple program will be familiar to all of you, I'm sure. All it does is display the phrase *hello world* and then exit."

He compiled the program and ran it. He continued to type as he spoke.

"Now if I copy the code into SAM's hunt zone... And I'll just write the abstract as 'Small talk'. And we can begin..."

He clicked a button labelled *Begin* and waited.

"This might take a little longer than Brain Stormer but shouldn't be too long really. Incidentally, if you don't use a hunt zone, SAM will go into Trawl Mode and enhance any program it finds on the computer, including your operating system, which may or may not be desirable. A hunt zone restricts its search to the programs you specify. So in this case it only finds my *hello world* program. Internally, it's generating a similar mind map based on the abstract I entered. Normally, the abstract would be rather more detailed than this one, more akin to a high-level spec. But this program's so simple... And it looks like SAM's already made its first enhancement! Let's see what changes it's made. Remember, it modifies the source code but it recompiles it for us so we can just run again without further ado."

He ran the program again. This time, as well displaying *hello world* it went on to display *how are you today*. There was a definite gasp from members of the audience.

"And it will continue to enhance all the time until I tell it to stop." Richard felt almost triumphant. After several more minutes, he ran the program once more.

"Hello," it displayed. "I hope you are well. What is your name?"

Richard typed in his name at the prompt and pressed the enter key.

"Hello, Richard. My name is - JOB ABORTED."

"Ah," said Richard slightly abashed. "Well, it's still in its infancy and has a few teething problems."

But the audience were completely overawed. They burst into spontaneous applause and cheers.

"That's the software to rule the world," shouted someone near the back of the room.

A camera flashed from somewhere. Richard blushed but was really very pleased indeed. Despite being most reluctant to attend the symposium, he was now really glad he had done so. He may not have concentrated as much as he ought to have done in the morning but he was certain that none of the other talkers had enjoyed such a rousing reception. He again revelled in answering the barrage of questions that greeted the end of this demonstration. All in all, he had thoroughly enjoyed himself, as had his listeners. As he powered down his laptop and resumed his seat, blissfully unaware that he had overrun by half an hour, he thought to himself that, despite being as yet incomplete, SAM just might be his road to riches.

—— Chapter Three ——

William Barber

Instead of availing himself of the evening meal provided in Windsor Hall, Richard had ventured into town to seek out a restaurant where he could be alone. He was aware that this was not the best financial decision as food on campus was likely to be subsidised whereas anything he ate in town would have to be paid for in full from his own diminishing pocket. He had already finished his starter and was now waiting for his main course. He was really hoping that this would be a generous portion; now that he had started to eat he realised just how hungry he was. Breakfast had been some twelve hours ago and had consisted of a bowl of cereal and a cup of tea. Apart from a few soggy biscuits the only other thing he had eaten since were the scraps left at the lunchtime buffet.

Richard let his gaze wander around the restaurant while he was waiting. It was dimly lit and fairly busy. Mood music played gently in the background as waiters attended to their customers, many of whom were sitting alone. Richard guessed that most of these people were also away from home on business. Some of them might even have been at the same symposium that he himself had spoken at. He wondered if anyone would recognise him and felt both anxious and excited by the thought.

His contemplation came to an abrupt end when a voice spoke from over his right shoulder.

"Richard Neilson?" it said.

Richard looked round expecting to see a waiter while at the same time wondering how a waiter would know his name. A man, perhaps in his late fifties, stood before him immaculately dressed in a light grey suit. Richard simply stared at the man, not knowing what to say.

"I loved your talk on Analytical Creativity," said the man. "And I have a proposition for you. Do you mind if I join you?"

For a brief moment of confusion, Richard actually thought that the man's request to join him was his proposition. Then he realised with a growing thrill that he might be about to make a sale.

"Please do," he invited, gesturing the man to the chair opposite. "Er, I've already had my starter. I'm just waiting for my main course now. I hope that's all right."

"No problem," said the man looking at a menu. "I'll just launch straight in with the main."

He summoned a waiter and placed an order of venison steaks along with a glass of Champagne. Richard knew that this would delay his own main course and tried to stifle a rumble of his stomach.

"So, is your room okay?" asked the man conversationally. "Where are you staying, Windsor Hall?"

"Er, yes. Yes, it's fine. I checked in not so long ago. You?"

"I'm also in Windsor. Nice place! They tend to put most delegates in there. How was day one for you?"

Richard had been waiting for the man to introduce himself but he seemed in no hurry to do so.

"Um, yes it was good, very interesting. Sorry, but..."

"I'm sorry," interrupted the man, "I haven't introduced myself yet, have I? I'm William Barber. I run an innovative company called Automated Services. I doubt you will have heard of us because we've not been going for long. We specialise in new technology such as electronic components that don't burn out and batteries that never die. I'm hoping to get us on the map in the next few months. And I believe you can help us."

Before he could elaborate the waiter arrived with his Champagne. He set it on the table and then left without a word.

"Your glass is almost empty," observed William. "Would you like another? What is it? Lager?"

William was about to summon back the waiter but Richard

managed to stop him in time.

"No, please, I have to drive back and this is quite strong stuff."

"Very wise," said William with a smile. "No use taking unnecessary risks."

He took a sip from his own Champagne and sighed pleasurably before continuing.

"Yours was by far the best talk today and I'll tell you why – you came across as very genuine. I got the impression that a lot of the demonstrations we saw today were put together to show us only what the demonstrators wanted to show us. Hacked together, in other words, hard-coded. But you, you obviously believed in yourself and your abilities to the extent that you were prepared to give us a genuine live demonstration of your products. I don't think you yourself knew what was going to happen when you clicked that *Go* button. That takes confidence but not misplaced confidence. That tells me that you take great pride in what you do, that you're very thorough and won't ever be satisfied with mediocrity."

Richard muttered an embarrassed "thanks" and waited for William to make his proposition. William took another sip from his Champagne and then turned back to Richard with a sudden air of business.

"SAM – your Super-Adaptive Module. I was particularly taken with that. Astonishing functionality! And I suspect that its practical potential far outstrips your own imagination. I can already see how several of my company's applications can benefit from its implementation, not just in the business world but also in the domestic market. Have you sold many licences yet?"

"Well, not yet," Richard said defensively. "Today was its first unveiling. I've not finished writing it yet. Still a few more tweaks to do."

"That's good," said William bracingly. "Because I'd like Automated Services to acquire exclusive rights to it, to knock out any competition before it starts, and to give us a unique position in the marketplace."

This pronouncement knocked Richard for six but before he had any time to recover William proceeded.

"Starting from now, or as soon as you're able, I'd like to offer you the position of Technical Consultant at Automated Services working on SAM to complete it. We have a major campaign that needs to be rolled out in time for next Christmas. The finished product needs to be the number one best seller in the domestic market and with you and SAM on board, I'm certain that we will realise that goal. I'll assign you a team to work with you and I'll pay you handsomely for your expertise. What do you say?"

The words resounded in Richard's head like a gong. William's tone was level, his face benign, but there was something of the predator in his eyes that made Richard wary. Such an offer was not something he had anticipated but he was sure that it was one he could not accept. Although it was rare to be offered such an opportunity out of the blue he did not like the idea of granting exclusive rights to one company. If William could be so impressed with an incomplete product that he had only briefly experienced, it stood to reason that several other companies would be interested in the finished article.

"It's an intriguing idea," he said diplomatically, "but I think I'd rather sell separate licences. I don't really like the idea of being tied to one company."

"Oh, don't think of it as being tied. Think of it as being freed. Automated Services gives all its engineers a lot of leeway to express their technical expertise. And because we specialise mainly in the domestic market we can, with our cutting-edge technology, add quality to the lives of ordinary, *appreciative* people. The company's already quadrupled in size in the short time that it's been going. We have an extremely prudent finance director who's managed the books very well indeed. We plan to float on the Stock Exchange in the next few years when the time is right."

It was as if he had been rehearsing this speech for days. He spent several minutes chipping away at Richard's defences, trying to make him see that engaging with a company of experienced people was far better than going it alone. And that Automated Services was the logical choice to make.

"We look after all our engineers very well indeed. They're all busy on projects that they want to work on, learning new skills all the time and all are assured that their efforts are put to good use. I appreciate you wanting your products to reach as many clients as possible; we can help you achieve that. It's a tough market out there. It doesn't matter how good a product you have, it will be doomed if you can't get it to the right people at the right time. You need to have very good marketing skills. Perhaps you do?"

"Some," Richard lied. "I think I'll do all right."

William raised his eyebrows. "Have you sold much business software? A product such as SAM will turn out to be a major tool and will require an entire company to maintain it. Businesses generally prefer to deal with other businesses rather than individuals. Now supposing you get a decent customer base. Even if you do all the software development yourself you'll still need people to help you: there's your sales team, your marketing team, your support team. You might want a finance person, perhaps someone to help with all your legal bits and pieces, maybe someone to train your users, someone to write your documentation... And with all that personnel you'll need to consider some sort of human resources function. It all costs money - even if you choose to outsource everything. Believe me, I know too many people who tried to go it alone and ended up on the bread line. I don't want that to happen to you. Your product is too good to waste like that and we have the infrastructure to help it get to where it needs to be."

"I have sold some business software," Richard replied, this time truthfully. "There are a few licences out there for Brain Stormer."

"But do those few licences pay the mortgage? We all like to do interesting work but at the end of the day we need to pay the bills, right? That's why so many people end up getting stuck in jobs they hate. I'm offering you a rare opportunity to have the best of both worlds: a very generous income and a stimulating environment full of like-minded people."

Richard was still not convinced.

"The problem is that at the moment I own all the rights for SAM whereas if I come and work for you on the same project, I'd lose those rights. I wish to retain the intellectual copyright on all my creations regardless of who I'm working for at the time. Otherwise, I hand it all over to you, then at some time in the future you make me redundant and next thing I know I'm not even allowed to continue developing what I invented in the first place. I've been down that route before and it's not one I mean to travel again."

"I sympathise entirely with that and I'm sure we can come to an arrangement about the copyright. Automated Services is not like any company you're likely to have come across in the past. We do things differently. We employ top class engineers us and we need to make sure we keep them happy and give them what they want. What sort of company are you with now?"

Richard hesitated. He did not want to admit to this man that he was currently out of work. He knew that would be playing into his hands. He considered pretending he was still at his previous company but knowing his luck William would know someone he used to work with and would easily find out that he was lying. Instead, he chose to fabricate a company.

"It's a company called, er, DSO. They do data-warehousing for marketing purposes."

"Hmm, yes, I think I've heard of them. Where are they based?"

Richard's heart sank.

"Er, this is probably a different one. It's not *the* DSO. This is an American company. I've only been there a few months. It's okay, I guess."

"And it was DSO that sent you on this symposium?"

"Er, yes, well no, not really. Well they gave me the time off but I came independently."

He felt the blood surge to his head and was convinced that William knew he was making it all up. William, however, made no more mention of it. Instead, he took out a business card and gave it to Richard with another smile.

"Here, take this and think about my offer. It seems we need you more than you need us so think also about how much it would cost to persuade you to come to us. Everyone has his price."

Richard took the card and gazed at it, not entirely sure what to do. Just then the waiter arrived balancing a tray bearing their main meals. Richard pocketed the business card as a fresh wave of hunger swept over him. During the course of the meal, the conversation steered away from business onto more relaxing topics. They ended with a lavish portion of hot chocolate fudge cake with vanilla ice-cream after which William absolutely insisted on picking up the entire bill. It had been an interesting evening with good food and had given much food for thought.

The second day of the symposium turned out to be less interesting for Richard. There was no pressure for him to stand up in front of everyone and deliver a seminar so he was able to relax a lot more. Unfortunately, none of the speakers in the morning session were particularly charismatic and Richard found his mind wandering several times during their talks. Dozens of times he considered William's proposal to work for Automated Services but each time he dismissed the idea as a non-starter. As far he was concerned his days of travelling to an office each morning and being forced to get embroiled in tedious politics were long gone. He wondered how he would have felt if the offer had been made as a temporary contract instead. At least then he would know there was a definite end date when he could once again leave the corporate life. However, there would still be the bigger issue of the intellectual copyright. He was far too possessive about his work to let anyone else take ownership of it. If he were honest with himself he would rather not show anyone else the source code at all but forever keep his algorithms a closely guarded secret.

Ideas began to chase themselves around in his mind about the best way to market SAM to big corporations. Before long, he was completely lost in his own thoughts and had no regard for where he was or what was going on around him. SAM would definitely be a boon to businesses around the world. Even government projects, notorious for being late, over budget and flawed, would benefit from its approach to continuous improvement. He'd have to finish writing it first and perform hundreds of rigorous tests before he was satisfied with it. There were also the issues to think about that William Barber had mentioned over dinner the previous evening, issues such as documentation and after-sales service. But it was the initial marketing that was causing him the biggest concern. In fact, his problems were twice as large because he had two products to market, Brain Stormer also being an excellent business tool. And then an idea flashed into his mind. It was such an obvious idea that he wondered why he had not considered it a lot earlier than now. He would use Brain Stormer itself to help him come up with a strategy to maximise his sales and hence to maximise his profits. Now he realised that since he had two products to market, his chances of success were immediately doubled.

Best get started then, he thought and was about to reach for his laptop when he remembered where he was. He was still stuck in Reading, surrounded by hundreds of geeks listening to someone spouting on about nothing. He suddenly felt restless. There was work to be done and here he was wasting precious time at this symposium. His lack of enthusiasm for this event was even greater now than it had been before he had arrived. This was largely down to the fact that despite his positive reception after his talk the previous day not one person had approached him to arrange, or even discuss, a licence for either of the tools he had demonstrated. He had to remind himself that most of the delegates were engineers so although they were suitably impressed with the products - a great compliment in itself, given the calibre of the people - they were not necessarily in a position to negotiate a purchase. Hopefully, however, they would report back to their managers on their return to work and convince them that both products were unconditional requirements.

Time seemed to slow to a crawl as lunchtime approached. Richard had already decided that he would at that point retire from the symposium and return home to work on his new ideas. This move would have the added benefit that he would be able to escape the clutches of William Barber, just in case he had any more ideas about accosting him while he was trying to eat. Then a wild thought occurred to him. It was Tuesday and on Tuesdays he normally had Dominic. It would be nice to spend time with him when he got back and tell him about his stay in Reading. He, after all, had been the one most keen for him to go. Added to this, it was Dominic's first day back at school after the Christmas break. Perhaps he had some interesting news to report of his own. He knew it was a long shot and that Amanda, having agreed to take him this Tuesday in the first place, would not be happy about changing plans again. But, he thought, if you don't ask you don't get. With that in mind he took out his mobile phone to discuss the idea with her via text. To his dismay the battery was totally flat. This was not one of those new-fangled smartphones that scarcely lasted five minutes before demanding to be plugged in. No, he would normally expect to get a good five days' use from a single charge and he had charged it on Sunday night precisely so that he would not have this problem. He wondered briefly if William Barber's immortal batteries were available for mobile phones. Dismissing the thought, he made a mental note to replace the phone at the earliest opportunity; he had no time at all for unreliable technology.

The morning's final lecture finished at last and people began to disperse for lunch. Richard collected his belongings and hurried out of the room after the crowd. Instead of going to the Cedar Room, however, he wandered back to Windsor Hall to retrieve his remaining possessions. He had not brought much for the few days' stay but on entering his room he noticed that somehow everything had managed to spread itself all over the place. He was glad that the cleaners had not been round to witness the mess he had made. Nonetheless, it did not take him long to gather everything together and soon he was packed and ready to go. He opened the door to make his final departure but paused and looked back at the bed. Should he strip the covers? Where should he put the dirty linen? Was there a checkout procedure? After a few more indecisive moments he stooped down and started rummaging in his bag for the information pack. Perhaps it said something about what state to leave the room in. He stopped abruptly and stood up. This was insane. Here he was on the brink of a major technological breakthrough and he was worrying about whether to strip a bed. He snatched up his bag in irritation and left the room with no more backward glances.

As luck would have it he came across a payphone in the foyer and remembered that he wanted to arrange with Amanda to pick up Dominic. He fumbled in his pocket for some change, scarcely recalling how to use a payphone let alone knowing what to say when she answered. He inserted his money and dialled her mobile number. His heart thumped in anticipation as the ringing tone purred in his ear. After a short time, a voice answered.

"Amanda Lewis," it said.

Richard suddenly felt winded as if he had been punched hard in the stomach. For a moment he could say nothing.

"Hello?" said Amanda's voice.

"How long have you been using your maiden name?" Richard managed to croak at last.

"Richard!" She sounded startled. "How come your number hasn't shown up on the phone?"

"My mobile's dead, I'm in a call box. So, how long have you been using your maiden name?"

"Not long. Only since... Oh what does it matter?"

"It matters a lot to me. This was *supposed* to be a temporary separation. You've allowed it to drag on for a year already and now you've gone back to using your maiden name. Sounds like you're trying to make it a permanent arrangement."

"Don't be silly. I've always used my maiden name for some things. Anyway, I'm busy. What is it you want?"

Richard knew there was no chance of Amanda granting his request to have Dominic and now he was in such a bad mood that he was no longer receptive to the idea himself... although, he did usually feel happier when Dominic was around.

"I'm on my way back from Reading," he began tentatively. "I've decided to come back early. It was a bit dull. Anyway, seeing that it's Tuesday I was wondering if I could pick up Dominic on the way. A normal Tuesday, in other words."

"Richard," it was clear from Amanda's tone what her answer was going to be, "we've talked about this before. You can't expect me to change my plans at the last minute just to suit your whims and fancies."

"And do you actually have any plans or are you just being awkward as usual?"

"As a matter of fact we do have plans. We're going out."

"Oh yeah, where're you going?"

"Out! You can pick up Dominic from school on Thursday as we agreed. Now if you'll excuse me I have some work to do."

The line went dead. Richard stayed where he was, still holding the receiver and trembling with rage. Was he crazy to harbour any hopes that he and Amanda would ever get back together again? And if she had no intention of ever making their relationship work why was he the one losing out on everything? It was she who had decreed that they have a trial separation yet he had agreed to move out of the luxury house into some tiny flat with noisy neighbours, although he continued to pay the mortgage. It was she who had initiated the split yet he had agreed to let her have primary access to Dominic. If she was going to end the relationship permanently and even change her name then it was time also for him to change. It was time to make things difficult for her.

A tone sounded in the telephone earpiece and ended Richard's plotting. He slammed the receiver back onto its cradle, snatched up his bag and stormed out of the building. His car was parked nearby. He threw his luggage into the boot, being a little reckless with his laptop, then climbed into the driver's seat and started the engine. Once his satellite navigation system had come online he floored the accelerator and skidded away, rock music blaring loudly from his music system in an effort to overpower his rage.

The journey home was no better than the journey outbound. As soon as Richard got to the main road he was snarled up in traffic. No amount of detouring alleviated the situation and his mood went from bad to worse. On the M4, the traffic was at a standstill. The loud music had little beneficial effect.

"Why isn't everyone at work?" Richard asked himself angrily. "Like I've got nothing better to do than sit here growing old!"

As if in answer, the travel news cut across the rock music, commandeering the airwaves.

"Well, yesterday's security alert still having devastating effects on all roads into and out of London. Police are using powers under new anti-terrorism laws to conduct random searches of vehicles on several roads including motorways. So expect big tailbacks if you're travelling anywhere near the London area. Worst affected is the M1 southbound where traffic's at a standstill from just south of junction 11 all the way down to junction 7. Also, extremely heavy traffic in both directions on the M4, M20 and M25. Avoid those roads if you possibly can. If you're already stuck in traffic, police are asking drivers to be patient while they conduct their investigations..."

Richard heaved a deep sigh of frustration. He still had no idea of the exact nature of the security alert he had briefly heard about the day before. All he knew right now was that the congestion was not helping him to calm down. He switched off his loud rock music in favour of a rather more soothing classical music station.

According to his navigator the journey from Reading to home should have taken a little over one hour. It took nearly four. To make things worse, the weather had deteriorated and rain was now beating down relentlessly onto the roof of his car. He switched off the engine wearily and sat still waiting to see if the rain would at least slow down. It did not. All that happened was that the car windows became so steamed up that he could no longer see out of them. Eventually, when the only evidence of a world outside was the continued beating of the rain, Richard resignedly got out of the car into the deluge. In seconds he was drenched. He quickly unloaded his boot, locked the car and hurried indoors into the warmth.

When he got into his flat he was irritated to hear music coming from downstairs. It was not the usual assault Richard now associated with what he called "revenge racket" but it was obtrusive all the same. He swore out loud and went to the fridge to pour himself a large mollifying glass of vodka. Returning to the living room he slumped into the sofa and placed his glass on the floor in front of him. For a few moments he simply stared at it, too exhausted even to drink. Before he knew it, he had fallen asleep where he was.

He dreamt that a policeman had flagged him down on his way to a prospective client. The client was very keen on buying ten thousand licences for SAM but would only go ahead with the deal if

Richard could meet him at exactly nine o'clock, which was only five minutes away. He tried explaining this to the policeman but he wouldn't listen. Then the policeman turned out to be William Barber in disguise. He shouted at Richard for not putting his dirty sheets into the laundry as he had asked and said that it was precisely that sort of unreasonable behaviour that had made him decide to change his name. He added that if he had any decency he would hand over to him all the source code for SAM as it was rightly his.

Curiously, it was the sudden cessation of the downstairs din that made Richard awaken with a start. Realising where he was, he reached out and swallowed his vodka in one gulp. Then he forced himself out of the sofa and went to his proper bed, ready for a good night's sleep.

—— Chapter Four ——
Project Neptune

Over the next few weeks Richard busied himself on his computer refining his Super Adaptive Module while at the same time sending letters to countless companies whom he thought would benefit from its abilities. He was finding the process extremely difficult and frustrating as most companies did not even have the courtesy to reply to his communications and those that did clearly did not like the sound of software that would modify their own work, however beneficially. For some reason he had taken to pinning up his rejection letters onto the noticeboard above the fireplace. They were by now quite numerous. He did not want to admit it but he knew that William Barber had been correct when he said that good marketing skills were needed to sell a product. And no matter what he had said to William, Richard knew very little about marketing.

When he had told Dominic about his conversation with William in the restaurant and his subsequent decision to decline William's offer of employment, Dominic had called him "a nutter" because as far as he was concerned his father had thrown away a golden opportunity. Richard had reacted with uncharacteristic ire at this and had yelled at his son for his rudeness, adding that he knew nothing about the situation. He had regretted his outburst ever since for Dominic had carefully avoided getting involved in any more discussions on the subject, although Richard did value his opinion.

February arrived, bringing with it still more miserable weather. As each new day dawned and faded away with no success, Richard could feel the pressure building inside him ever more relentlessly. Not only was he failing to stir any interest in either of his products but also his money was fast running out while the bills poured in remorselessly. As well as the bills, Richard knew he was going to need money for a completely different reason. On the Thursday following his early return from the symposium he had picked up Dominic from school, as arranged.

"So, what did you get up to on Tuesday night?" Richard had asked him, wondering if Amanda had manufactured the outing that she had insisted they were having.

"Oh, we just went round for dinner at Dave's," Dominic had replied.

"Dave? Who's Dave?"

"Dunno. Some chap Mum's been seeing for a while. She wanted me to meet him. It was a bit boring really; they just kept going on about that bomb thing on Monday."

The mention of a bomb had completely failed to have any impact with Richard, even though this had probably been the cause of his delays to and from Reading. Far more arresting had been the news that his estranged wife had started seeing someone else. This revelation, coming so soon after the one that she had changed her name, had so affected Richard that he had resolved to stop co-operating with her altogether. His resolve was strengthened still further when it also transpired that she had been hiring a child minder to look after Dominic while she swanned off to spend time with her new fancy man. Richard's plans now were to reacquire his house and to become the main custodian of his son. How he would achieve these goals he had no idea but he knew that they would both involve substantial expenditure in legal fees, which he could only fund if he achieved several successful sales of his software.

He thought about what Amanda would say if she knew what he was plotting. No doubt she would dismiss the plans as more of his "all mouth and no action" ideas. But he'd show her. He helped himself to another sip of wine from the glass on the desk. Just then, he realised that he could begin putting his plans into effect immediately without even having to move from his seat in front of the computer. With vindictive pleasure, he logged into his bank account and cancelled the direct debit for the mortgage on his old house. No more would he fork out for a property he was not even living in. He considered sending Amanda an email to let her know what he had just done but he figured it would have more impact if she found out the hard way when the mortgage company started sending her nasty letters threatening her with eviction.

A rattle at the front door announced the arrival of the post. Still feeling grimly satisfied with himself, Richard got up from his desk to pick up what was bound to be the latest batch of rejections and bills. He saw a pile of envelopes on the floor. Squatting down, he picked them up and began sorting through them.

"Bill, bill, statement, bill," he muttered to himself as he did so. "Hey, what's this?"

He had picked up a manila envelope with a hand-written address upon it. This neither looked like a bill nor a bank statement. It also did not look like it was from any of the companies he had written to. He made his way back to his desk and tossed the unopened bills into his in-tray where they joined an accumulation of other neglected mail. Then he ripped open the manila envelope and withdrew from it a hand-written letter. With mounting curiosity, Richard began to read it.

Dear Richard,

It was a pleasure to meet you at the symposium last month and to talk business with you over dinner. I am now writing to invite you to lunch at my house on Sunday 13th February from 1pm. My wife and I both enjoy cooking and like to have guests round to taste our creations. I hope that you have had time to consider the business opportunity we discussed. I really need to bring you on board for Project Neptune, which is already underway.

Please let me know if you can make it on Sunday week. You can contact me via any of the means at the head of this letter.

Here's hoping you are keeping well.

Sincerely yours,

William Barber

Richard sat frozen on his chair. How on earth did this William Barber know where to find him? He had definitely not given him his address. And why was he hounding him in this way? Had he not already made it clear that he was not interested in the business opportunity being proposed? And what was all this about Project Neptune? Richard was far too familiar with management vocabulary to get at all excited about this. No doubt it was simply a fancy name for a boring project. In a fit of pique he screwed up the letter and dropped it in the wastepaper basket under his desk. The last thing he needed right now was to be stalked by some demented old man who had taken a shine to him.

His eyes fell onto his in-tray and the pile of bills. They could wait. He averted his gaze as if to put the bills out of his mind. His eyes instead fell onto the noticeboard where a mass of rejection letters leered back at him. He heaved a heavy sigh and bent down to fish William's letter back out of the bin. Perhaps it was, after all, time to open his mind to other possibilities. Perhaps he should put aside his ideals for now and find out exactly what Project Neptune was all about. If it was going to make him some real money then it could not be all that bad.

Before he could change his mind, he decided to send an email of acceptance to William. He found the address at the top of the letter, as stated. Then a thought occurred to him. He was due to have Dominic that weekend and there was no way that he was going to ask Amanda to rearrange their schedule. He wondered whether he should postpone William's appointment but then concluded that it would be quicker to accept it nonetheless on the understanding that he could bring Dominic with him. He was certain that Dominic would raise no objections and he did not honestly care what William thought of the idea. Accordingly, he composed his response. It took him several iterations before he was finally happy with the wording.

Dear William,

I gratefully accept your kind invitation to Sunday lunch on 13th February. I hope it will not inconvenience you if I were to be accompanied by my son Dominic, as he will be staying with me that weekend.

Looking forward to seeing you and to hearing your thoughts.

Yours

Richard

That ought to do it. It placed the ball firmly in William's court should he wish to rearrange the engagement to a Dominic-free weekend. At last satisfied, Richard clicked the Send button.

William Barber's house stood imposingly on the corner of Lancaster Gardens and Lancaster Road. The drive was wide and sweeping with separate entrance and exit gates, each flanked by impressive stone columns. There was also a double garage adjoining the house that would easily have accommodated the large Mercedes parked on the drive. Not wanting to be too forward, Richard opted to leave his own car on the street. He switched off the engine and sat quietly for a moment, steeling himself for what he expected to be a fairly stressful afternoon.

"Are we going in?" asked Dominic.

"I suppose so," replied Richard resignedly.

William had responded by return to Richard's email and said that Dominic would be more than welcome to come along. Richard was glad about this not only because Dominic would provide some moral support for him but also because Richard would be able to use him as an excuse if he wanted to leave early.

They both stepped out of the car and made their way towards the immaculately polished front door of the house. Dominic rang the bell. Almost immediately the door swung open and before them stood a handsome, elegantly dressed woman.

"Hello," she said, extending an arm to shake hands. "You must be Richard. And this must be your charming son Dominic. I'm Marilyn, William's wife. Please, do come in."

She stepped aside allowing Richard and Dominic to pass into the large entrance hall. There was a mouth-watering smell of cooking wafting from the kitchen. Dominic's stomach rumbled audibly.

"Dinner will be ready very soon," said Marilyn. "Let me take your coats and I'll introduce you to the others."

Richard was just wondering who the others might be when a boy of about eight poked his head round one of the doors and then immediately retreated back inside.

"That's our grandson," explained Marilyn taking the guests' coats. "He's pretending to be shy but he's not at all really. We've got our daughter and her family staying with us for a few days. But don't worry, they won't get in the way of your business talk. Come."

She led them to the living room where the boy sat on the floor under the watchful eye of his parents. He was playing with a toy robot that was making happy cooing noises as if thoroughly enjoying the attention. Marilyn did the introductions.

"This is our daughter Yvonne and her husband Robert. Yvonne, Robert, meet Richard and his son Dominic. And this," she added, indicating the boy on the floor, "is our pride and joy Marcus, our only grandchild."

There was plenty of hand shaking and pleased-to-meet-yous during all of this. Then Marilyn made to leave the room.

"I'll put these away," she said indicating the coats she was still carrying, "and see how William's doing."

She left, leaving in her place an awkward silence. After a short while that seemed to last an age, Richard turned to Yvonne and Robert.

"So, how far did you have to travel to get here?" he asked conversationally.

"From Devon," replied Yvonne. "We didn't make it for

Christmas, which disappointed Daddy something awful so we're doing a sort of Valentine's visit instead."

She let out a false laugh, which Richard returned, feeling foolish. Robert attempted to fill the new void.

"You managed to get here without being held up by terrorists then?"

Richard looked blankly at him.

"Well," explained Robert, "it was last time you met Bill that there was that awful bombing attempt, if you remember."

The mention of this reminded Richard of what Dominic had said in passing some weeks earlier. He realised only now that in all the time since the symposium, which was some six weeks, he had not seen, heard or read the news anywhere at all. He had been so wrapped up in his own affairs that World War III could have been declared and he would be none the wiser.

"Oh yes," he mused, "someone planted a bomb at Heathrow or something, didn't they?"

For a fleeting moment there was a look of astonishment on both Robert's and Yvonne's faces and Richard knew at once that he had betrayed dreadful ignorance. Very professionally, however, the couple quickly fixed their faces back to polite smiles.

"Interesting," said Robert. "I was saying to Yvonne only the other day that there wasn't much else reported about that incident. It's all they talked about for the first few days but then silence. There were just the six bombs in the end, all over London. The Heathrow one turned out to be a hoax, of course. Still caused mayhem though. Imagine the chaos if any of them had exploded!"

"Shocking," said Richard piecing together all this new information. "They should all be shot," he added. "The terrorists, I mean."

"Well, I guess there're plenty who'd agree with you but it is a tricky business," said Robert doubtfully. "Besides, many of the bombers kill themselves in the process, don't they?"

"With all the Intelligence we have these days," persisted Richard, "we should be able to round up the suspected perpetrators before they have time to act. Like the Americans do. Lock them up and throw away the key."

"Well," Robert was still not convinced, "you say that but the Americans are allegedly holding a lot of innocent people."

"Seldom do you find smoke without fire," said Richard doggedly.

"This is a very deep topic for a Sunday afternoon," observed Yvonne after a pause.

She was right. Richard had been in the house for only a few minutes and in his anxiety had already committed the cardinal sin of talking politics. They probably now thought he was an opinionated fascist and would not want William to do business with him after all.

Another awkward silence ensued. Richard chanced a glance at Dominic who had been paying no attention whatsoever to the conversation. Instead, he was gazing inquisitively at the robot on the floor with Marcus. It seemed almost alive with its mannerisms and was still making bleeping noises, sounding very happy. From what Richard could see, it looked like a fairly complex piece of machinery, not necessarily designed with children in mind.

"Er," he began and Robert seized on the opportunity.

"Meet Mickey the Mini-Mechanoid, one of Bill's creations. He's only a prototype but he's scarily realistic. He can see and hear you and was even enjoying the smell of the cooking earlier on. Bill only gave him to us on Friday and I've fallen in love with him already."

"He didn't give it to us, dear, he gave it to Marcus," corrected Yvonne.

"Well, he'll be part of the family though, won't he?"

"And it's not a he, dear, it's only a toy."

"He's no ordinary toy," insisted Robert. "He's almost human. He can do way too much to be dismissed as an ordinary toy. You've seen the way it interacts with people. Hey," he turned back to Richard excitedly, "if you get two of these things together they can communicate with each other *telepathically.*"

"Boys and their toys!" muttered Yvonne under her breath but Richard was fascinated.

"Where can I get one from?" he asked. "How much are they?"

"Not yet available," replied Robert. "You'll have to wait for next Christmas, I'm afraid. There're still some features to be added."

"Can't wait to get the finished one," Marcus joined in.

"Well, we can't promise anything, sweetheart," said Yvonne. "It's bound to be expensive."

"Could I have a go?" asked Dominic and was delighted when Marcus invited him to join him on the floor with the robot.

Instinctively, Richard also sat on the floor in the hope of having a play himself but at that moment William Barber entered the room and he scrambled back to his feet again.

"Richard," William greeted warmly. "So glad you could make it. Hello, young man," he called down to Dominic who was too engrossed with his new friend to have noticed his arrival.

"Dominic, say hello to Mr. Barber," said Richard reprovingly.

Dominic looked up with a start and muttered a quick hello before returning to the robot.

"It's William, please," said William. "Or Bill. Calling me Mr. Barber always sounds frightfully formal." William looked down again at the boys on the floor with the robot. "I see you've met Mickey."

"Just," said Richard. "Robert was telling us about him - er, it - shortly before you arrived."

"Yvonne had words to say about it, did she?" William smiled.

Yvonne merely pursed her lips and looked away. Abruptly changing the subject, William spoke again.

"Dinner will be ready in five minutes so you might like to freshen up and make your way into the dining room. Robert will show you where everything is. Marcus, time to wash your hands. You can bring Mickey to the dining room but I don't want him sitting at the table, okay?"

He left the room.

William had obviously gone to some trouble to prepare a most sumptuous meal to impress his would-be employee. The starter - a luxurious game terrine - had already gone down very well and they were now tucking into a delectable dish of roast lamb served with honey-drenched parsnips and a variety of other vegetables. Richard, who had been concerned that the food might not be to Dominic's liking, was very pleased that his son was lapping it all up with rapacious gusto. The adults accompanied their meal with the most delightful Champagne that Richard had ever tasted, poured into expensive looking crystal flutes. Not to be left out, the two boys each had a sparkling apple juice served, rather bravely Richard thought, in the same crystal flutes.

Conversation had been a little stifled. This was not Richard's forte at the best of times and the current setting made him feel even more intimidated than usual. The boys, however, seemed to be having a whale of a time communicating with each other non-verbally and struggling to control fits of giggles. When this happened for the umpteenth time, Yvonne rounded on her son with an admonishing glare.

"Marcus!" she snapped.

But William held up a quelling hand.

"Let them be. It's nice that they've made friends so easily."

On a cupboard against the wall Marcus' robot bleeped and was swinging its arms nonchalantly while gazing around the room in apparent curiosity.

"So," said William to Richard, "what do you think of Mickey?"

Richard, who was still looking at the robot, nodded his head fondly.

"I like him. He's kind of cute. I was asking Robert earlier when they'd be available in the shops but it seems like I have to wait to the end of the year."

"The plan is to hit the shops by September and make it the number one best-selling toy for Christmas. By then it will be available in all sorts of other shapes and sizes - dogs, cats, dinosaurs, aliens - to appeal to a wider market. The characteristics will change for each type of model but the low-order functions will remain the same."

Dominic was now listening with rapt interest. It was clear that he would dearly love to have the robot in any guise.

"Diversifying the outward form, however, is not the only thing left to do," William continued. "By far the greater task is to make this machine blow the competition out of the water. You must have noticed that there's a bewildering assortment of toy robots on the market already. Well, ours has to be better than all of the rest. And that's where you come in."

Richard raised his eyebrows. He knew that he had wanted him to work for Automated Services but he could not see how he would be useful in the field of robotics or toys as he knew very little about either. And if all William wanted were some ideas on how to achieve his number one goal then he could simply buy a licence for Brain Stormer. He was about to say as much when Marilyn stood up and started clearing away the plates, all of which had been wiped clean as every last morsel had been eaten.

"I'll go and fetch the dessert," she said, now carrying the pile of plates and cutlery out of the room.

"I'll come and help you," said Yvonne, springing to her feet and following Marilyn out of the room as if anything would be more interesting than talking about robots.

"Project Neptune," continued William, "is the code name for the development of Mickey the Mini-Mechanoid. I must ask you not to talk about this beyond these walls because it is strictly confidential. We have just over six months to complete the project, including testing, before we start our aggressive marketing campaign. One of the key things we would like to implement is an ability to adapt and learn. And I don't just mean remembering a few neat tricks either. Indeed, we would like Mickey to possess the most advanced learning capability ever seen in a toy. When you demonstrated your Super-Adaptive Module back in January, I knew I had found both the perfect tool and the perfect man for the job."

Robert was beaming encouragingly at Richard but Richard found no comfort in this.

"Um," Richard began hesitantly. "Well, SAM's really meant for business software. It enhances *business* software. It's not actually a learning tool at all. I don't know how well it would work on robots. I mean, I don't know anything about them really."

"That's fine," said William undeterred. "We only need it to enhance the sophisticated algorithms our engineers have already created. That should be sufficient to make the machine almost infinitely adaptable. We'd like this thing to grow with its environment, to develop as part of the family. You'll be guided by top engineers who know all about the systems, who know all about robotics. They'll help you every step of the way. You won't be left alone to flounder."

"I provided some of the funding for the start of the project," piped up Robert. "If you agree to come on board then I'm sure I can arrange a handsome payout for you."

Richard felt at a distinct disadvantage. This was not simply about the money, as he had already tried to explain. How best was he to walk away? As he saw things, he was not only vastly outnumbered by the opposition but he was on their territory. In addition, he had just been fed an abundance of the most delicious cuisine and felt a little ungrateful in flatly refusing to entertain the suggestions being put forward, even though nothing new was being said.

"What I'd like," William persisted, "is for you to come with me to have a look round Automated Services. Now I don't pretend to know you very well but from what I've learned of you so far I'm sure you'll love the place."

Both William and Robert were grinning enthusiastically now and Richard felt his resolve beginning to buckle. He was still not interested in returning to a corporate lifestyle and he was still insistent that he should maintain absolute control over his software tools. Yet, in spite of himself he found himself nodding his agreement.

"Okay, I'll take a look at it," he sighed, "but I'm not promising to come and work there. When were you thinking of showing me?"

"That's my boy," cried William. "How about going this afternoon once we've finished lunch?"

"What, today? But - but I've got to..."

"I know," interrupted William, "you need to take Dominic to his mother's by 6pm. We'll be back long before then. Don't worry."

"Yes, we'll need to be. She's very fussy about... Hang on, how did you know that?"

"Daddy does a lot of research on his candidates before meeting them." Yvonne had just re-entered the room closely followed by Marilyn. Each was carrying a tray laden with bowls of meticulously presented profiteroles drizzled in a chocolate sauce. "Some people find it a little unnerving but I think it's really rather nice. It shows an interest."

Richard was nevertheless taken aback that William's research would have gone into such detail as his private family arrangements but he chose not to pursue the topic.

"Marilyn," said William, "Richard and I are going to pop over to the office for a bit after coffee. Would you mind holding the fort?"

"You're driving to the office?" asked Marilyn in an accusing tone. "But you've been drinking. I'm not so sure that it's a good idea."

"I just had the one glass. I was anticipating the trip."

He winked at Richard who was not sure how to react.

Dessert was over and everyone had retired to the living room.

They were all drinking coffee apart from the two boys, who were play-fighting exuberantly on the floor with Mickey nearby as always. Yvonne looked like she would dearly love to tell Marcus to simmer down but she seemed to content herself with pursing her lips again when she realised that he had the upper hand in the battle and was merrily pummelling Dominic on his chest. Richard watched for a moment before deciding that his son was quite safe. Then he resumed drinking his coffee. He could not be certain but he thought he could taste a liqueur in his drink. He had not asked for anything fancy and he wondered if William was trying to dull his senses to get him to sign a contract absent-mindedly. It did taste exceedingly pleasant though. He would just have to stay alert and on his guard.

"Security's very tight at the office," said William between sips, "so it will just be you and me, I'm afraid."

"Oh, you mean I can't take Dominic with me?"

"Sorry. They don't allow kids at all."

Richard thought about this for a moment and considered rescheduling the appointment for another time when he would be alone. But he rather preferred to get everything over with now.

"Dominic," he called over the boys' noise. Dominic made no response. "Dominic," he shouted.

The boys promptly ceased their wrestling and Dominic turned to look at his father with an expression indicating that he had completely forgotten that anyone else was around. Richard explained the situation to him.

"I'm going to have to take you to your mum's a bit earlier than planned. As you probably gathered during lunch, I'm going on a quick tour of William's work place."

"Can't I come?" asked Dominic in mild disappointment, trying to fend off Marcus' renewed attacks.

"Apparently not."

Richard was not particularly happy about the policy but knew it would be pointless to argue.

"He's quite welcome to stay here," said Marilyn. "He'll be no trouble."

"Yeah, can I stay here?" asked Dominic eagerly. "I don't want to go to Mum's just yet."

This statement lifted Richard's spirits considerably. Perhaps Dominic was growing weary of his mother's company. Maybe he actually preferred to be in his father's charge. Richard smiled his first genuine smile since entering the house.

"Of course you can stay," he said. "You enjoy yourself."

"Yeah!" cried Dominic. "And now I'm gonna get you," he added to Marcus and launched himself forward to pin him to the floor.

Instantly, there was a dreadful cacophony coming from the general direction of the boys. All the adults looked round at them in alarm but it was neither of them making the commotion. It was the robot. It was howling angrily and waving its arms around manically while advancing on them. Dominic and Marcus, who had promptly ceased their antics, were looking a little frightened. Yvonne, however, was beside herself.

"What's happening?" she screamed. "What's it doing? It's trying to attack my baby."

"Nonsense," said William rising from his seat. "It can't attack anyone."

He picked up the robot and held it aloft smiling. The robot continued to wail and flay for a while before gradually calming down.

"Get rid of it," yelled Yvonne. "I don't want it anywhere near him."

"Yvonne," said Robert placatingly, "I think perhaps you're overreacting just a little."

"I don't care," she screamed, "get rid of it."

"Yvonne!" said William sharply. Yvonne abruptly stopped her screaming and turned to look at her father through her veil of tears. William resumed his normal gentle tone. "It was coming to Marcus' aid. It thought Dominic was attacking him and it was trying to defend him."

"And what would it have done to Dominic?" asked Richard indignantly.

"Nothing. Look at it. It's a piece of plastic scarcely two feet tall. How much harm do you think it could cause?" William smiled again. "See how it's calmed down now that they've quit fighting?"

He placed the robot back onto the floor next to Marcus, his eye on Yvonne.

"Your son has his very own protector," he said.

The robot purred contentedly and walked over to Marcus and stroked his arm affectionately. Marcus in turn stroked Dominic's arm so that the robot could see.

"This is Dominic," he said to the robot, "and he's my friend. We were playing."

The robot cooed and walked over to Dominic and also stroked his arm. Yvonne chuckled and dried her eyes.

"Cool!" said Dominic impressed.

"There you are," said William. "Those engineers are something else!" He had a proud, wistful look in his eyes. "They put in that behaviour themselves. It wasn't in the original design specs. It's a classic example of how the team will go the extra mile to produce a world class product. The robot can see, hear and smell, as you know, and there's a complex recognition circuit that enables it to identify faces and objects. But the engineers have gone a stage further and slipped in this bodyguard feature as well. I like it. It doesn't matter that all it does is make lots of noise and get into a flap. It's that sort of attention to detail that could make all the difference between a good product and a great product."

Richard said nothing. Inwardly, he was very excited about the idea of working on the robot. He knew it would be a most rewarding experience. And if he could somehow integrate SAM into its circuits to enhance the already intelligent software, then that would yield magnificent results. He still had some reservations but as his eyes flicked round the room they fell on Robert, whose look of quiet optimism indicated that he had detected a sizeable chink in his armour.

— Chapter Five —

Automated Services Ltd

The journey to William's place of work was smooth and uncomplicated. Apart from a couple of Sunday drivers the traffic was very co-operative. The car was luxurious, the ride comfortable, the background music soothing. And yet there was a sense of unease in the pit of Richard's stomach. He still had no desire to return to a corporate lifestyle. He was quite content to persevere with trying to market his products alone. He just hadn't tried hard enough so far, that was all. Why had he allowed himself to be talked into coming on this ominous visit?

William seemed completely oblivious to Richard's anxiety. He spoke quite normally to him throughout the twenty-minute journey. The most Richard could manage was a smile, a nod, a "yes" or an occasional "hmm". He would much rather have been at home working on his computer in familiar surroundings.

The car halted in front of a set of solid-looking gates. William fumbled in his pockets for something, muttering to himself.

"Now where did I put my… Ah, here it is."

He pulled out of his jacket pocket a plastic card bearing his name and photograph. Then reaching out of the open window he waved it in front of what was evidently a card reader. The gates clanked into life, sliding open very slowly, driven by what looked like an ancient system of chains and pulleys.

"As I said, we're very hot on security here," William informed Richard. "A little too hot sometimes, if you ask me. But you'll see why when you look around."

William parked the car and they both got out and began walking towards the main entrance to the building.

"There're no reserved spots in the car park," continued William. "Well, we have a few visitors' spots round the corner and a couple of disabled spots in pole position but for the rest of us it's all for one and one for all."

"Does everyone manage to get a space?" asked Richard, feeling that to say something might help to calm his nerves.

"Oh yes," replied William holding open the entrance door for Richard. "But if you're very late it means you have to go all the way to the far end, and if you're lazy like me then you won't want to walk all the way back - especially if it's raining."

William then put his car keys up to his lips and spoke to them. "Secure," he snapped and Richard instantly heard the distinctive click of a car's central-locking system. He looked back at William's car in time to see the hazard lights going out and the driver's window closing by itself. He guessed that the alarm system had just been armed.

The reception area was welcoming with plush leather sofas and a large top-of-the-range television. Two security guards sat behind a sweeping, curved desk. On the wall behind them written in large letters were the words

AUTOMATED SERVICES

Embracing the Extreme.

One of the security guards addressed William.

"All right, Bill," he said jovially, "Coming to keep an eye on the troops?"

Richard was a little puzzled by this greeting. It was Sunday after all and he doubted that there would be many troops to keep an eye on. Indeed, he thought it quite extraordinary to find the desk manned by two guards rather than just one.

"Just sign in, would you," continued the security guard indicating a register on the desk. "Fire regulations, you know. Oh, and your guest will need a visitor's pass as well".

William signed in and then passed the pen for Richard to do likewise. Meanwhile, the other security guard scribbled in a different register holding a visitor's badge in his hand. Then he passed the register and the badge to Richard.

"Just sign for the badge, would you, pal," he said, rather informally Richard thought. "You have to wear it in a prominent place at all times. And make sure you're accompanied wherever you go. Yes, even to the gents'."

Richard signed and handed back the register. Then he clipped the badge to a belt loop on his trousers.

"Cheers, mate," said the guard. "Guess we'll see you later, eh, Bill?"

"Indeed", replied William. Then he turned to Richard. "Welcome to the world of innovation!"

Richard followed him to the inner door and waited behind him. William was bent down over something but Richard could not see what he was doing. He did, however, hear him muttering to himself again.

"Cards, codes, prints. They'll be wanting a blood sample next."

Finally he straightened up and held open the door for Richard. Beyond was a corridor lined with more doors on either side.

"That's the most secure entrance," said William pointing over his shoulder to the door they had just entered through. "You need to swipe your card, enter a security code and do a fingerprint scan before it even thinks about letting you in. A bit of a bind if you're carrying a hot cup of coffee. These other doors are just card-operated proximity sensors. They're not too bad because the readers are quite sensitive so as long as you're wearing your card in a sensible place you don't need to do too much."

With that, he effortlessly pulled open the first door and stepped inside. Richard followed and was astonished to see so many people and so much activity going on. The atmosphere was quite relaxed though obviously busy. There was a background of noise from individuals frantically typing on computer keyboards or else discussing potential solutions to technical issues.

"This is the main development office," said William, "where most of our systems start their lives."

"How come it's so busy? I mean it's Sunday. How come... why isn't everyone at home with their families?"

William smiled proudly.

"Because they love their work. They love their families too, naturally, so we're very flexible here with working hours and most teams have adopted a nine-day fortnight. You may have heard of such a scheme. Normally it means you work longer hours during the week and have every other Friday off. Well this lot redefined it to mean you can work *any* nine days within the fortnight and then have the other five days off. So a lot of people choose to work across one weekend and then have a five-day weekend the following week. If they're happy with that then it's fine by me. These are some of the best engineering minds I've ever come across. We only take the best and these people take to the most demanding challenges like a duck to water. So it's up to me to maintain a stimulating and flexible environment that's good for everyone. If it's good for the workers then it's good for business."

Richard looked around him. The atmosphere had exactly the sort of 'techie' ambience that he liked. Ahead of him a man evidently in deep thought sat reclined in his chair staring into space with his eyebrows creased in a frown, his hands folded across his protuberant belly. On another person's desk was a model Triceratops that would intermittently let out a resounding roar while raising and lowering its horned head threateningly. No one except Richard took any notice when it did this, as if it were a perfectly normal thing to have in an office. Nearby, a woman in bare feet sprung out from her desk and hurried over to a printer to pick up a large wad of paper before tutting and throwing the entire lot into the bin.

"Bill," said a voice that cut through Richard's musing. A man wearing a T-shirt bearing the slogan "The Greek Geek" was walking towards them.

"Manny," greeted William. "How's the darkbulb coming along?"

"Hey," replied Manny, "I give you demo, yes?"

"Not just now, Manny, I have a visitor. This is Richard who, I hope, will be joining us quite soon. He has the ignition key that will really launch Project Neptune. Richard, this is Manny."

Manny shook Richard's hand.

"You'll love it here. 'Tis very nice place."

"Manny's been developing a darkbulb," William filled in, "a sort of lightbulb only in reverse - turn it on and everything goes dark."

"We thought it come in useful for er, how you say - slide show?"

"Presentations", offered William. "You get a better image from a projector if you dim the lights. But imagine if you need the same effect in broad daylight. Well, not everywhere you go will have blackout curtains so instead why not take along your very own portable darkness? No more sun reflecting on your screen!"

"An interesting idea," said Richard, taking the concept in his stride.

"Trouble is," continued Manny, "it kills projector light as well. So no good."

"A bit too successful," smiled William. "We based the idea on our Noise Abater, a useful little device for cancelling out excessive noise. Can be used in all sorts of places: roadworks, helicopters, airfields, noisy neighbours."

"I could do with something like that," muttered Richard, thinking of the incessant boom from his neighbour's hi-fi.

"We don't make it now," said Manny. "'Tis done."

"It's just a phase inverter," said William, "Easy enough to make, old technology. And now there's an outfit not too far from here that makes similar devices for the commercial market. We prefer to stick to newer ideas. It's what sets us apart from our competitors. In fact, one of our biggest challenges is knowing which of our new ideas are actually new. We have a team dedicated to that very task." William turned back to Manny. "We're pretty sure there're no darkbulbs out there though. And now if you'll excuse us, we have to get on. I'll look forward to your demo tomorrow."

"OK. And I hope to see you, Richard, with us soon, eh?"

William led Richard back to the door, pressed a security switch to release the lock and then stepped outside. They continued to walk along the corridor with William pointing out what lay behind various doors.

"That's where we burn our software into chips. We'll not go in right now, it's not that interesting to see... That's just the cleaning cupboard... Over here are our top-security toilets," he added with a wink. They passed a door bearing a large red notice saying DANGER OF DEATH. William, who had evidently seen Richard looking at it, dismissed it with a wave of his hand. "That's just the plant room where we've got our backup generators, air conditioning control units, that sort of thing. Nothing interesting really." Then he opened another door. "In here is where we test our proofs of concept."

Richard followed him through the door into a spacious room. This room seemed almost as busy as the main office with people talking animatedly over the particular item that they were testing. William led Richard to one group of people huddled around what looked like a fairly ordinary wine rack, apart from the fact that it had wires coming out of it.

"Gentlemen," William addressed them, "Sorry, and lady," he added noticing the one woman amongst them. "How's it going?"

"We're getting there," replied one of the men. "It's still more suited to the committed dipsomaniac but we reckon we're more or less on track."

"Will you be ready for field testing on schedule?" asked William.

"Yeah, yeah," said the man with an air of forced confidence. "Well - yeah, should be," he added in a rather less convincing tone.

William raised his eyebrows at the man. "Full field testing in two weeks?"

"Trust me," said the man now not meeting anyone's eyes.

Still looking sceptical, William turned back to face Richard.

"This is the perfect utility for wine lovers. It looks like your common or garden storage unit so won't look out of place wherever you'd normally put such a thing. Space for up to fifty-four bottles, each of which can be individually temperature controlled. So you can set it to chill your favourite Chardonnay while keeping your Cabernet Sauvignon nicely at room temperature. And when you're running down on stocks it can automatically hook up to the Internet and order some more from your usual supplier. As Andy suggested, we're still being challenged by that at the moment as it keeps over-ordering, so unless you can get through several bottles a day... But the team's working on it. And I have every confidence in them."

He gave the team a meaningful look and then moved Richard on to another crowd of people who were examining children's shoes.

"These people are developing our Clever Clogs range - tracker shoes for kids. Each shoe has a tiny GPS chip in the heel that relays its whereabouts to a handheld controller that the parents keep. If the child strays beyond a predetermined perimeter then the controller instantly alerts the parents by means of a great deal of noise, on-screen co-ordinates and frequent SMS messages, emails and everything short of carrier pigeons. We're hoping that child abductions can become a thing of the past."

"And it's not just kids it protects," piped up one of the engineers. "We intend to put these trackers into everything - wallets, mobile phones, handbags, laptops, suitcases. So no more lost luggage when you go abroad."

"How does the chip see the satellite if it's buried inside a shoe?" asked Richard interestedly. "My old satnav doesn't even work inside a building."

The engineer looked at William who gave him a nod as if to say he could divulge more information.

"We've developed this technique that can catch reflected satellite signals and triangulate its position from there. As a fallback the unit can also use mobile phone technology to interpolate its position. We're still perfecting it all but it's looking pretty good so far."

William smiled and thanked the man. Then he took Richard to a quiet area of the room where there were no people, just a toy robot lying inert on a test bed.

"And this is Mickey the Mini-Mechanoid," he reminded Richard. "You've already seen it in action, I know, but like I said there's still plenty of work to be done on it. This is what you'll be enhancing as part of Project Neptune should you decide to come and work for us."

Richard examined the machine. It was undoubtedly a very technologically advanced toy, covered in sensors, but he could not see many people being able to afford it. It was bound to be expensive.

"The company's still in its infancy," William said before Richard could voice his thoughts, "just coming up to two years old, very much an unknown. Yet I'm convinced that if we can launch Neptune in time for Christmas, complete with your adaptive algorithm, we will shoot to the top of the leader board. It will be just the break we need. As you can imagine most of our research and development is very expensive so we could do with a good best-of-breed product to make us a realistic contender in the marketplace. We'll sell it as cheaply as possible, get everyone interested and get ourselves on the map."

Richard hesitated. If he were honest with himself he liked what he had seen of the place so far. He had even imagined himself working there. But something was still troubling him.

"The thing is," he began uncertainly, "I... er... I really don't think that corporate life is quite my style. I work best alone, you see, with no one to report to – just me and my work."

"What if I were to say that you could still do that? We have a number of employees who do just that. Some people we don't see for days but we know they're producing results. We recognise that different people have their own preferred way of operating and we try to accommodate their desires while still enabling them to interact with the rest of their teams. As I said, it's a very flexible environment. You've seen several people here today, Sunday afternoon. That's their own choice, nobody's making them do it. And if anyone works lots of extra hours they can take all the extra time off in lieu."

Richard wasn't sure why he was still resisting. It was exactly the sort of environment that he worked best in. And William seemed like an ideal boss: patient, understanding, trusting.

"What about the intellectual copyright?" Richard now asked. "I nearly lost Brain Stormer because the company I was with at the time tried to claim it as their own. I used it once to help them out of a situation and next thing I knew I was facing a legal battle over ownership. It was only because I was able to prove that I had developed the whole thing in my own time and on my own machines that I was able to rescue it. Even then I still felt the need to leave the company."

Richard was aware of the bitterness in his tone. He was quite sure that William would also have spotted it even though he showed no sign of having done so. They were in the corridor again and continued to walk in silence for a few more steps.

"We're hoping to float in a couple more years," William said coming to a halt. "You get in now and when that time comes you'll never need to work again, I'm sure of it. Think of all that extra time you'd be able to spend with your family. When the money starts rolling in I'm sure you'll all be a lot happier."

Richard considered this for a moment, unsure how much William already knew about his family situation. But then his mind returned to the matter at large.

"What will you pay me in the meantime?" he asked.

"You name your price. We very much would like to buy your services. And where your talent is concerned, it's a seller's market."

Just then, something streaked past their heads. Richard looked round in time to see what looked like a miniature UFO crash into the wall. A man in beige corduroys, sandals and a Star Trek top came running from a nearby room after it. He looked to be in his early thirties and he had a wispy beard and lank, greasy hair.

"Charlie," said William reprovingly, "is that yours? Careful, we've got visitors."

"Sorry," panted Charlie, "The antigrav's still a bit skew whiff. It's affecting the guidance system."

"Richard, this is Charlie. He's the technical lead for Neptune. Charlie, this is Richard. We're hoping he's coming to work for us."

"Oh yeah?" said Charlie looking appraisingly at Richard. "Hey, you're gonna like it here, it's real cool."

"Richard is the technical genius behind Brain Stormer," added William.

Charlie's eyes lit up with a manic enthusiasm. "No way! Brain Stormer? That is some seriously cool shit! I tell you what, I knew this chap; he was a greengrocer or something. And for some reason he got onto that Brain Stormer as a demo. And all he did, quite literally, all he did was type in the word 'greengrocer' and this thing started coming up with all sorts of stuff such as fruit 'n' veg, food marketing, the Internet. It even suggested branching out into fruit bowls and crystal and all sorts of things. And I'm telling you, no word of a lie, this man is now running a successful online business reselling tableware." He said all this very fast as if carried away by awe. Then he added sincerely, "Hey, if you did that Brain Stormer we want you here."

William smiled at Charlie.

"Why don't you take Richard on the rest of his tour? I have a couple of calls to make."

"Hey, I almost forgot," blurted out Charlie, "Johnson phoned you about half an hour ago. Said he'd like you to call him back as soon as."

"Thank you. I shall tend to him first. One of our most important clients," he added to Richard and he strode off.

"So you do have some clients then?" Richard asked Charlie who was retrieving the remains of his UFO.

"Prospects really. No one's signed on the dotted line yet for anything. Surprising really 'cos they've been tinkering with that Internet wine cooler since before I joined and I've been here nearly a year. I mean it's not exactly frontline technology. We do waste a lot of time developing dead-end products. We spent months doing this Super Smart Card, 'your programmable plastic pal'. Supposedly it was to help people with their car immobilisers. You know, the sort where you've got to insert a card before your car will start. Well, people are always losing them so the idea was that you could insert a blank Smart Card and it would do some whacky thing with the card reader and next thing you know you've got yourself a replacement card. Ingenious the way it worked - and ideal for crooks and spies. Turned out it also worked in ATMs, security doors, you name it. It was withdrawn when we found that it even opened the main gates here. Quelle surprise!

"We're quite hopeful about this robot thing though. Bill's really quite excited about it. So am I actually. I've been working on various components of it for the past eleven months. I designed the so-called 'psychic communications module'. It's just a radio link really but Bill wanted me to build in all sorts of extra stuff with microwave transmissions and crypto and everything even though I can't see any of it being used. I think that Johnson chap on the phone's something to do with all that. He keeps asking for all sorts."

They entered another room that looked to be some sort of recreational centre. There were all kinds of games in here including pool, table-football, pinball and a couple of video games. Charlie casually put his UFO with its remote control on top of a pool table and continued walking towards a refectory area where light snacks were available.

"You want to get something to eat?" Charlie asked. "I'm starving.

I completely forgot to have lunch."

"Um, actually I've just eaten. I had lunch at William's house."

"Aw, call him Bill, everyone else does. Wanna coffee? I recommend the mocha. Really nice! Or have you ever tried a zebra? It's basically mocha with the addition of white chocolate. To die for! You've got to try one. I'm buying."

He steered Richard to a table and they both sat down. Richard had no idea what to expect next as there was no one behind the counter and apparently no one serving. Yet the moment they sat down a machine glided towards them, bleeped and stopped right next to Charlie. It was some four feet high and made from white plastic with a domed head that was riddled with sensors. In some ways it reminded Richard of Marcus' toy robot. He gazed nonplussed at the machine but Charlie spoke to it as if it were an old friend.

"Get us two zebras, one carrot cake," he turned to Richard, "You sure you don't want anything to eat?"

Richard shook his head.

"And, er," continued Charlie, "what sarnies have you got?"

The machine bleeped again, this time in a different tone that Charlie evidently understood.

"Sandwiches. What sandwiches have you got? Jeez, you'd think they'd invent voice control that understood a few colloquialisms, don't you think?" he added to Richard rolling his eyes to the ceiling.

The machine rolled away and came back a few seconds later clutching a menu in its artificial hand. Charlie took it and studied it, all the while emitting a long "er". Finally he made up his mind.

"I'll go for... Get me a lamb and mint in default bread."

The machine bleeped and glided away.

"It's one of our service units," Charlie said in answer to Richard's unspoken question. "They're prototypes supposedly for the domestic market. They'll do anything for you. Can't see them catching on, to tell you the truth - far too expensive for most people's pockets. And they can't even climb stairs, for crying out loud. I mean, what's the point of that?"

"All right if you live in a bungalow", said a voice behind Richard and another man came and sat beside him, munching on a bag of crisps.

"Dog!" cried Charlie in surprise. "Didn't expect you here today. I thought you were off to Donegal to see your folks?"

"That was last week. Glad to see you missed me. I got back yesterday. What're you doing here anyway? Have you got that wretched drone to fly yet?"

"Kind of. It just doesn't avoid walls very well. This is Richard, by the way. He's gonna be working for us soon."

Richard did intend to correct this assumption but got distracted by Charlie's next introduction.

"Richard, meet Dog. He's management but he's really a techie at heart."

"Dog? Why do they call you that?" enquired Richard shaking the man's hand.

"Because he's barking mad", said the man.

Charlie laughed, "That's quite witty for you."

"My name's Dillon," said the man firmly.

"His name's Dillon O'Grady," persisted Charlie. "Check out the initials."

There was a familiar bleeping from behind Richard and the service unit glided back into view carrying a tray containing their order. Charlie took the tray and flashed his identity card at the machine, which then rolled away apparently satisfied.

"It will add the cost to my tab," explained Charlie to Richard. "It's programmed to recognise ID cards. I'll get a bill at the end of the week."

"Are you not eating?" Dillon asked Richard observing that he only had a drink while Charlie was gnawing away at his sandwich.

"No, I had quite a lot to eat not so long ago."

"You mean yes," said Dillon correcting Richard who hadn't a clue what he meant. "I asked if you were *not* eating and given that you're obviously not, your answer should've been 'yes you are not eating'. Otherwise you have a double negative."

"Don't worry about him, he's like that," said Charlie dismissively to Richard. "He could pedant for England."

"I think you'll find that the word 'pedant' is a noun," said Dillon tartly.

"See what I mean?" retorted Charlie. "They're all a bit like that in SSS. That's his department. Full of weirdoes! What does SSS stand for this week, Dog?"

"Strategic Security Services. And as far as I know it's always stood for that."

"So it's not Strategic Software Security any more? Or Software Security Systems?" Charlie evidently enjoyed teasing Dillon. "It'll change again next week, I'm sure. They change the name every time someone makes a security cock-up, don't they? Who was it last time? Was it that Hicks kid again?"

"There was no cock-up. And besides, we have a no-blame culture in our department."

"Yeah, that's probably his fault, an' all."

Richard grinned at Charlie then turned back to Dillon.

"Are you in charge of all the swipe cards then?"

"Amongst other things. We do all the software security as well: firewalls, the VPN, failovers, audits, that sort of thing. We're also in charge of health and safety - personal security, if you will. We monitor ergonomics, organise the fire wardens, test the fire bells..."

Charlie gave a loud affected yawn. Dillon ignored him but changed the subject.

"So when do you start here?" he asked Richard.

"Er, well, I'm not sure if..."

"He hasn't agreed a start date with Bill yet," interjected Charlie, "but you can bet it'll be soon."

"Well he obviously likes you," said Dillon. "He wouldn't let you out of his sight if he hadn't already decided to hire you. You can be sure of that. He'd at least have one of my lot tailing you wherever you went." Then as if to indicate that he himself did not have the job of tailing Richard he finished the last of his crisps and abruptly stood up to go. "Well, I'd best leave you to it. And I expect I'll see you again when you start," he added to Richard.

"See you later, Dog. Woof!" said Charlie.

"For Crissake," muttered Dillon and he left.

It was strange. Everyone behaved as if Richard was already an employee of the company. He quite liked it - it made him feel comfortable. And everyone seemed to be a character, albeit all slightly mad. He quite liked that as well - he seemed to get on best with eccentric people. But there was still a nagging doubt in his mind.

"Let's say I do agree to join the company and develop my module for your robots, how can I guarantee to keep control of it? I want to have the freedom to use it elsewhere without getting into any mayhem about intellectual copyright. In fact, I'd rather no one else saw any of the code at all. I'm really possessive about this particular work."

"I wouldn't worry about that if I were you," replied Charlie reassuringly. "Bill's really flexible and provided you grant him a decent licence to use your software as he wants then there shouldn't be a problem. And as for hiding the code, the best way of doing that I've found is by encrypting it into a standalone chip. We've got the framework for it already so it should be a piece of cake. Well, relatively anyway. All you really need to do is get a sufficiently strong crypto algorithm and apply it to your system."

"I don't know much about encryption."

"Nor do I but I know a man who does. I've had to use some pretty strong encryption myself recently and I used some revolutionary technique I got from this chap Dr. Azis. That man's the

Crypto King! He devised this incredibly strong crypto technique that not even Dog's lot could crack. If you give me your email address I'll send you his details. He's quite well known in this organisation although I don't know anyone who's actually met him. I only ever spoke to him over the Net; he's got his own secure messaging system and everything and... Well, you'll see. Drop him a line and if you mention my name he'll probably be quite willing to help. And he can explain to you how to embed the encrypted software into a special crypto-aware chip so that it can still be interpreted by the operating system. He's fantastic! Bill knows of him as well. In fact, it was he who put me in touch with him in the first place. Don't know how he knows him but I'm glad he does."

It seemed that Richard's last excuse was in tatters. He could no longer think of a reason not to accept the invitation to join the company. He could think of plenty why he ought to. He began to feel quite excited. He scrawled down his email address on a napkin and passed it to Charlie.

"What's the pay like?"

He really wanted to ask Charlie how much he personally was on but knew that would be extremely rude.

"If Bill really wants you, as he clearly does, then the ball's in your court. Just name your price and he'll pay it. Don't be too outrageous but don't sell yourself short. And make sure he gives you some shares as well. Then when this company floats in two or three years... Oh boy!"

"Thanks, Charlie, this has been a really useful talk. I guess I'd better find Will... er, Bill. I'm sure he'd want to see me again."

"Yeah, I'll take you to his office."

Charlie finished the last of his drink and then led Richard back out, up the corridor and to the door of another room.

"This is it," said Charlie. "I'd better scoot myself but I know I'll be seeing you."

"Cheers, Charlie."

Charlie went back along the corridor. Richard took a deep breath and knocked on the door. It was immediately opened and there appeared the benevolent face of William.

"Come in, come in," he said stepping aside for him. "Take a seat."

Richard entered and sat down in front of William's desk. William also sat down.

"Did Charlie show you the rest of the site?" asked William.

"Er, well, we just went to the canteen really. But we had a good chat though," he added quickly.

William smiled. "I might have known. That's his favourite stomping ground. It's a wonder he stays so skinny given the amount he eats."

Richard said nothing. William continued.

"So have you had a chance to think about what it would take to get you here?"

"Charlie said I might be able to keep the copyright on my software and encrypt it within your systems?"

"If that's what you want. I can even put you in touch with a man called Dr. Azis, who's developed some encryption methods specially for us in the past."

"Yes, he mentioned him." He paused. "And, er, will I get some shares? I mean how many shares will I get? As part of the package, I mean."

"You'll have the opportunity to buy some shares at a nominal cost. It's a bit too complicated just to hand them out as remuneration. It messes up the tax accounting, unfortunately. Is there anything else? Have you decided what basic rate you'd require?"

"Yes," replied Richard decisively although in reality he did not feel he had given this matter adequate thought at all. He had been taking home three and a half thousand pounds per month after tax in his last job. He thought that had been quite good but he wondered if he dared push the boat out further and demand five.

"I'd like ten grand a month," he heard himself say. "After tax."

William's face was inscrutable. For a moment Richard thought he had blown his opportunity by being greedy. But then William smiled and said,

"I think we can stretch to that."

Richard could hardly believe his ears. To be paid such a large amount of money to work on what he did best in an environment that he felt comfortable in was more than he could ever have hoped for.

"I'll have a word with Personnel," continued William, "and we'll get some papers sent out to you in the next few days. When's the earliest you can start?"

Richard shrugged numbly. "Whenever."

"Welcome aboard." William seized Richard's hand. "Now I suggest I run you back to the house and let you celebrate with that charming son of yours."

They left the office, Richard completely unable to believe what had just transpired.

Richard dropped off Dominic at his mother's house at precisely 6pm according to the town clock, which had just begun chiming. Dominic was ecstatic about his father's good fortune and seemed reluctant to leave him, preferring to go back with him to celebrate, as William had suggested. Finally after much laughter and many hugs, Richard persuaded him to leave the car and make himself known to his mother before she blew her top. He then made the journey home alone.

When he arrived back at the flat, he poured himself a glass of wine and logged onto his computer. An email was waiting for him from Charles Cassidy detailing how to contact Dr Azis.

"Fast worker," said Richard to himself. "Still, no time like the present to contact the Crypto King."

And he clicked on the *Create Mail* button and began to type.

—— Chapter Six ——

Key to the Crypt

Although he still had not officially started work, Richard had set his alarm clock to sound at 7am so that he could gradually get used to the early starts during the week. It was still quite dark when he awoke and he felt no inclination to get up. He rolled over and started to drift off to sleep again. Before he was completely away a frantic and penetratingly strident clamour came from the far side of the room. Richard was shocked into wakefulness and shot out of bed like a bullet. The noise was coming from his backup alarm clock strategically configured to be so annoying that he was forced to get up and cross the room to silence it. Once out of bed there was no point in returning. He stretched and rubbed his eyes with a moan.

Suddenly forgetting his fatigue Richard hurried over to his laptop on the chest of drawers, eager to see if Dr. Azis had responded to his hail. He had left the machine switched on overnight, as was his wont, so there was no need to wait for it to boot up. To his disappointment, however, he had received no emails at all. Even at the best of times he hated not receiving emails as it made him feel worthless. But now there was big money at stake. He quickly sent himself a test message to satisfy himself that his email delivery system was actually working. This arrived almost immediately and he was forced to resign himself to the fact that Azis simply had not yet responded. He was undoubtedly a busy man and in all fairness, Richard had only contacted him a few short hours ago.

He switched on the radio to listen to the news. After his embarrassing display of ignorance at the Barbers' the previous day he was determined to stay abreast of what was going on in the world. Unfortunately, he was too late and the news had already finished. He decided instead to check the headlines on the Internet. Nothing grabbed his attention.

"And that's precisely why I lost interest in the news in the first place," he said to himself.

Leaving the radio switched on he made his way to the bathroom to get ready for the day ahead.

Richard was just finishing his morning coffee when he heard his brand new mobile phone announce the arrival of a text message. Remembering that he had left all his contact details with Dr. Azis he raced across the room to pick up his phone to retrieve it. He looked at the display.

1 message received.

He pressed the *Show* button and read the text. He reread it several times, thoroughly bewildered. It was not from Azis at all but from Amanda.

Thanx 4 the flowers but really u shouldn't have.

What was that supposed to mean? He certainly had not sent any flowers to her or to anyone. Why should he have? Then it dawned on him. Today was Valentine's Day. Of course! This must be her way of sending a sarcastic Valentine's greeting. "Thanks for the flowers you didn't bother to send." Richard felt anger surge inside him. Who did she think she was? Why should he send her anything after the way she had behaved? Was it not she who had walked out on him? Was it not she who had already formed a new relationship with someone else?

He pressed the *Reply* button and stood for a moment trying to work out how to phrase "boil your head" so that it would have maximum impact. He was interrupted by the announcement of another message, this time from his PC. He hesitated, wondering if he should expect further arrogance from his estranged wife in the form of an email. He stomped over to the machine feeling decidedly bitter but when he reopened his email program he found something far more satisfactory than more sarcasm from Amanda. His mood changed instantly as he realised that Dr. Azis had just sent his response. He opened it eagerly.

Hi,

Thanks for your email. I can certainly help you with your cryptography. I devise new algorithms all the time. However, before we proceed I should point out that I don't like to discuss security issues over email. Instead I use the attached tool. It's basically an instant messaging app except all conversations are strongly encrypted across the ether to prevent eavesdropping. You can also see when I'm online. Just double-click the icon and follow the instructions; it should install on most systems. Before beginning any conversation send the code phrase "Chlorine drains" so that I know it's you. My authentication phrase is "I'm in a Lotus". Email me directly only if you have a question about the attachment.

Regards,

Dr. Azis

Several years of working with computers had taught Richard to be cautious so he performed a quick virus scan of the attachment. Then he searched the Internet for any indication at all that it could be malware. Only when he was sure it was safe did he double-click it as instructed. The installation program fired up at once and began copying files to his computer's hard disk. It asked him no questions, gave him no warnings and did not insist that he restart his PC afterwards. The ease of installation made Dr. Azis immediately shoot up in Richard's esteem.

Once installed and running, Richard was able to see all other users who were logged into the system. At present there was only himself and one other person. The label associated with the other was *Dr. Azis – private location*. With some excitement Richard double-clicked his icon. A message window, split across the middle, appeared on his screen. The lower part contained a blinking cursor and was evidently where he was supposed to type his side of the conversation. The upper part looked to be where the entire conversation was recorded. He began to type:

Hello. I've installed your application, as you can see.

He paused, waiting for some acknowledgement. Nothing happened.

Hello? Anybody there?

Still no response. What was wrong? He was evidently still connected to the Internet because he could see the other person - unless this application always showed Dr. Azis as online.

I'd like to talk to you about encryption. It's Richard Neilson here.

By identifying himself he finally realised what, in his excitement, he had forgotten to do. He rechecked the email he had received from Dr. Azis and then typed in his code phrase.

Chlorine drains.

At last something started to happen.

>>> *I'm in a Lotus*

Richard whooped.

At last! I thought I'd never get through.

>>> *I think you just have.*

"Yes!" cried Richard. "Now down to business."

So can you help me with my encryption?

>>> *Before I get into that, how are you today?*

Very well, thanks. You?

>>> *A bit queasy. Probably something I ate.*

Sorry to hear that. What have you been eating?

>>> *Oh some green stuff. Do you think that might be the problem?*

This was not at all the sort of conversation Richard had expected but at least the Crypto King seemed human and sufficiently down to earth. Richard decided to be likewise.

Could have been, I suppose.

>>> *You don't seem too certain.*

I'm not a doctor. You are though :)

>>> *Of course you're not.*

Anyway, I drink peppermint tea when I have stomach ache.

>>> *I'll take your word for it. Do you like Hawaiian punch? I'm drinking one now.*

What's in it? I've never had one before.

>>> *Hold on, that's the phone. BRB...*

Richard was not particularly au fait with text-speak abbreviations but he had recently learnt from Dominic that "BRB" meant, "[I'll] be right back". He sat on tenterhooks waiting for Dr. Azis to return. His first impression was that he was dealing with someone rather off the wall. But it was only his knowledge that Richard sought and he did not care how weird he happened to be.

>>> *I'm back. That was the garage. It's time for my car to be serviced.*

Is it a Lotus?

>>> *It's a Honda Civic.*

Nice.

>>> *Yes, quite nice. So what's the weather like where you are?*

It was taking Richard longer than he had anticipated to get to the point of this conversation.

I've not been out but it looks okay from the window.

>>> *Well, appearances can be deceiving. So, have you planned your holidays yet?*

Er... not yet.

>>> *Hey, guess what.*

Richard sighed.

What?

>>> *I went fishing yesterday.*

Really. Did you catch anything?

>>> *Only a cold.*

Richard was beginning to find this conversation a little too random and trite so he tried to steer it back to business.

OK. What encryption services do you provide?

>>> *Well, when it comes to encryption I'm definitely the expert.*

Good. I need a really strong, unbreakable cipher.

>>> *Don't we all.*

It has to be original, never used before. I'm told you're quite accomplished at doing this?

>>> *Indeed.*

Richard really had no idea how to articulate over this system what he needed and Dr. Azis seemed to be waiting for some more information.

OK. Let me try to explain. I have an extremely confidential computer program that I need to integrate into a much bigger system. My program must be strongly encrypted so that no one can ever see how it works. What do I need to do to achieve this?

>>> *You're a computer programmer! What languages do you know?*

It's written in a mix of languages. Is that a problem?

>>> *Yes, I think it is.*

Oh. Can you overcome it?

>>> *Yes, I'm sure that together we could.*

At last the conversation became more coherent. It still was not easy work. Richard found it cumbersome to discuss his technical requirements over this medium. Meanwhile, Dr. Azis was intent on trying to return to small talk and seemed to want to know every minor detail of Richard's life, from his family tree right down to the colour of his socks. More than two hours later Richard felt just as far away from a decent encryption algorithm as he ever was. Yet he felt that some progress had been made just by the very fact that he and Dr. Azis did at least seem to get on well with each other.

Next morning, Richard rose even earlier, having been woken up by the sound of hailstones smacking noisily against his window. He peered through the curtains into the darkness beyond and, seeing the weather, decided on the spot that this was a day to remain indoors. Yawning, he dragged his feet to the living room and sat at his desk to check for emails. There was nothing interesting, only the regular spam. In the absence of any true correspondence he knew that the sensible thing to do right now was to get ready for the day ahead. Instead, he found himself irresistibly drawn to his SAM program. There was still much work to do on this, quite aside from hiding it behind an encryption shield. Everything was in hand but it was going to take time. He had spent the whole of the previous day at the computer without leaving his desk once. This sort of behaviour was common practice with him and he never considered such days wasted. If this really were to be his killer app it needed to be perfect.

At 7am his alarm clock sounded in his bedroom. Slightly startled, Richard jumped up out of his seat and went to switch it off. In anticipation, he also switched off his annoying backup alarm clock at the other side of the room. Now that he was on his feet he thought he might as well pay a quick visit to the bathroom, recognising that there may be several hours before he gave himself another opportunity. When he came out again, he crossed the room and turned on the radio just in time to catch the end of the news.

"Today's main story again. Twenty-six people have been confirmed dead and over three hundred wounded by last night's bomb blasts that rocked the capital. In a co-ordinated attack five bombs were detonated in restaurants around the city while couples were enjoying a Valentine's night out. The attacks bear the hallmark of the group calling itself The Real Jihad and are thought to have been carried out by suicide bombers. On 3rd January this year, police foiled a plot to detonate six bombs around London designed to go off as people returned to work after the Christmas break. The country's been put on the highest state of alert, meaning that another attack is imminent. We'll keep you updated on developments throughout the day."

Richard hurried back to his computer and accessed the BBC news website, baffled as to how he could possibly have missed this story last night when his radio had been on all day long. He supposed he must have fallen asleep before the event, not being used to the new regime of early morning starts. There now before him were all the details with pictures of mangled restaurants and panicked faces. He read in horror how the restaurants were apparently chosen for their locations "as if to trace Cupid's burning arrow through the heart of London". Each of the bombs had exploded within one minute of each other at 8:35pm when all five of the restaurants were at their busiest.

"This is a mad, mad world," said Richard sadly to himself.

Swapping applications he opened his new instant messaging system and was pleased to see that Dr. Azis was already online. He felt the need to talk to someone.

Chlorine drains

>>> *I'm in a Lotus*

Morning.

>>> *Hey. What's up?*

I've just been catching up with the news.

>>> *Is that so?*

Did you hear about the Valentine's Day bombings? Terrible business!

>>> *Terrible indeed but could be worse.*

Richard paused, wondering how much worse things could be. Then he remembered 9-11 and other terrorist attacks that had occurred on an even bigger scale.

Well yes, I suppose so but isn't it a mad world?

>>> *That's what people say.*

The war on terror doesn't seem to be going too well, does it?

>>> *Well, now that's a deep subject.*

Richard paused again. Why was he talking to Dr. Azis about the news?

You're right. Let's not get too depressed.

>>> *Hang on, my toast is burning...*

It was extraordinary but despite this being a very brief exchange Richard was already feeling better. There was something about Dr. Azis' offhand tone that cancelled out his own gloom. He speculated that had Azis reacted to the news with gloom and despondency then they would probably both be utterly maudlin by now.

>>> *I'm back but can you believe I'm out of butter!*

Oops!

>>> *Oops indeed.*

Sorry to interrupt your breakfast but have you had any more thoughts on my encryption program?

>>> *No, I can't say that I have.*

Is there a problem? Do you need some more information from me?

>>> *Well, it would certainly be helpful.*

It was going to be another long struggle to express his requirements. Useful though it was to have this instant messaging system, Richard could not help thinking that it would be far easier to meet face to face. However, when he suggested this, Azis became quite defensive and refused to reveal his location. Richard would have found his reaction absurd if he himself were not also being secretive, in his case about his software. He did not want to give away too much information about SAM and Azis seemed to need a lot of details that he was not prepared to impart. Consequently, the conversations were long-winded and convoluted, made even more so by Azis' penchant for small talk.

The hours ticked by and as expected Richard did not move from his desk even for a bite to eat. When he wasn't talking to Dr. Azis he was applying enhancements to SAM, some of which were ideas generated by Brain Stormer running on his laptop. His concentration was only broken in the middle of the afternoon when his mobile phone started beeping piercingly. He was still getting used to the sound of his new phone but he knew that this was definitely not its usual ring tone. Neither was it the announcement of a new text message. Richard got up from his desk at last, stretched and walked over to the dining table where the phone lay, still assaulting his ears. He picked it up, then looked at his watch in wide-eyed shock. It was 3pm and his phone was reminding him to pick up Dominic from school. He had completely lost track of time, not to mention the day of the week. And he was still in his pyjamas.

For several precious minutes he stood irresolute, trying to decide on the best course of action. The obvious thing to do would be to drag on some decent clothes and hurry out immediately before it was too late. But he knew he must look very scruffy and felt the need to shower and shave before going out, even though he knew that that would take up even more valuable time. Perhaps if he was really quick he might just be able to make it. Making up his mind he reset his mobile alarm clock for ten minutes' time then dashed into the bathroom hoping against hope that he was doing the right thing.

It was approaching 4:30 when Richard pulled up outside Dominic's school. By the time he had dolled himself up to his satisfaction it had become clear that he was not going to arrive in time for the end of the school day and that Dominic was going to have to wait for him in one of the allocated classrooms. He knew that Dominic would be used to this; turning up to anywhere on time was a rare occurrence for his father, who liked to quote that punctuality was a virtue of the bored. Even so, today he was much later than he had ever been in the past and once they had finally met up, he apologised over and over again for his tardiness.

"I'm really, really sorry. I just got carried away at work, completely lost track of time. If it hadn't been for my alarm clock, I'd still be..."

"Dad," said Dominic in exasperation the fourteenth time he said this. "I told you, it's all right. It just means that I was able to start my homework a bit earlier, that's all. Honestly, it's no big deal."

Richard gave Dominic a one-armed hug in gratitude.

"Thanks, mate. You're a great kid. And, um, please don't..."

"No, I won't tell Mum. I don't tell her everything, you know."

"Of course you don't," said Richard feeling a lot happier.

"So, does this mean you've already started your new job?"

"Yes, I've been - well no, not really, not officially. But I've managed to contact Dr. Azis - that's the Crypto King I mentioned on

Sunday - and we've been discussing how best to protect my software. We're getting there - slowly."

They walked along the deserted corridors, out into the courtyard and back to the car.

"You know you've been doing all that crypto stuff?" asked Dominic as he fastened his seat belt. "Do you still get paid for all that?"

"No, I wouldn't have thought so, not before I've actually started. It's still useful though," he added quickly. "It means I'll be able to hit the ground running when I do start. It's a bit like you beginning your homework early, making the best use of time."

The streets were just beginning to get busy as the rush-hour traffic started to build up but they arrived back at the flat before there was any major congestion. As they got out of the car Richard decided to ask Dominic something that had been on his mind since the previous day.

"So," he began, trying to sound casual, "Did your mum receive many Valentine's cards yesterday?"

To Richard's surprise, Dominic flushed a brilliant shade of red and did not reply. At first Richard thought that this probably meant that Amanda had indeed received some cards or even gifts, although he was not sure why Dominic should look quite so embarrassed about this, given that Richard already knew about Dave. Then his face split into an impressed smile as a shrewd realisation dawned on him.

"Or was it *you* who got all the cards? Have you got an admirer?"

"Dad!" Dominic was less than amused by his father's teasing.

"Aren't you a dark horse!" Then Richard's tone hardened. "Hey, just don't go getting too dependent on her, okay. They're a dangerous lot, women, with their feminine wiles. They hook you with their venomous talons then chew you up and spit out your spent husk. Just give them half a chance, that's what they'll do."

"Dad, would you just drop it. Please!"

"All right, all right. Just giving you some fatherly advice."

He did not bring up the subject again although inwardly he was intrigued to know who Dominic's apparent admirer could be.

The evening passed quietly with Richard back at the computer in conversation with Dr. Azis, and Dominic busy with the remainder of his homework, the two of them only stopping briefly for a light supper at seven o'clock. It was only after Dominic had retired to bed that Richard realised that he had squandered their short time together in favour of furthering his relationship with his cold, passionless machine and a strange man at an unknown location on the planet. With a tinge of guilt he understood why Amanda had grown to despise his computers and why she had eventually walked out of their marriage. He thought about reconsidering his decision to fight her for the house and for custody of Dominic, not that he had yet done anything about either. In his life he had never set foot in the legal jungle and he felt a great inertia for doing so now. It was so far removed from his field of expertise. Subduing his remorse he returned determinedly to his computer. What he was working on now was short term. Once he had completed it and made his fortune then he could return to normal family life. All everyone needed was patience and it was unjust to expect otherwise.

As the days continued to roll by, Richard began to wonder if William's letter formally offering the position at Automated Services had got lost in the post. William had seemed pretty keen to get him started as soon as possible so Richard had expected the letter within a few days of his meeting with him. Unfortunately, the postman only seemed interested in bringing more bills, which Richard tossed, unopened, into his in-tray. Finally, on the Friday of the following week, nearly two weeks after his visit to the company, a thick A4 envelope thudded to the floor with the morning's post. It was clear whom it was from since it bore the Automated Services logo upon it.

Richard picked up the envelope and unceremoniously ripped it open. Inside there was a very brief letter along with two thin booklets. Richard examined the letter.

Dear Mr. Neilson,

Please sign both copies of the enclosed contract on the first and last page and return one copy to me at the address below. The other copy is to be retained by yourself for future reference.

I would like to take this opportunity to welcome you on board and to wish you the very best of luck with your new assignment.

Yours sincerely

Mary-Anne Dawkins

pp William Barber (Chairman)

The address for Automated Services appeared at the bottom of the letter. Richard then turned to the booklets. They were identical. From the first page he realised that his assignment was on a temporary basis for twelve months. That was better than being permanent, as he had expected. And he would continue to own the rights to SAM, offering it on licence to the company. The start date was 7th March, ten days from today. He was expected to work an average of forty-five hours a week, typical office hours being from 8am to 6pm with an hour off for lunch. The rate was £650 a day. Richard hurried back to his computer to do a quick calculation to satisfy himself that the amount was near enough what he had agreed with William Barber. It was plenty, even taking into consideration extortionate tax rates. There was no capacity for overtime payments but he was quite happy with that. Yet it was the final clause that clinched it for him. He was only required to attend the actual site of Automated Services for a minimum of one day every fortnight. At all other times he was permitted to work from home provided that all company material was kept strictly confidential and that verifiable progress was being made on the project.

It was satisfactory for Richard and without bothering to read the nitty-gritty details of the rest of the contract he picked up a pen and signed where required. Then after writing a quick covering letter he put the whole into another A4 envelope and prepared to post it when he next went out. He sat for a while smiling contentedly to himself. With the funding from Automated Services and the freedom they were offering he at last felt ready to take on the world.

—— Chapter Seven ——

The First Morning

The next few days were a bit more stressful for Richard. Now that he had a firm start date he felt the need to make as much progress as possible with both the development of SAM and with its encryption. He worked late into the night and even occasionally felt guilty for preventing Dr. Azis from going to bed, although Dr. Azis always maintained his usual cheery persona. After four days and nights of burning the candle at both ends Richard reminded himself that he had not yet started at Automated Services and most of what he was doing could be done under contract when he would actually get paid for his efforts. After this realisation he learned to relax rather more and enjoy his few remaining days of unemployment.

It was Monday 7th March. Richard's alarm clock rang at 7am, as was now customary. He was very pleased that he had been getting up this early for the past few weeks as it was no longer a struggle for him. He got up immediately and switched on the radio to listen to the news. Nothing interesting was happening - at least there was nothing that Richard felt he had not already heard a hundred times before. He went into the bathroom to shower and shave then prepared to get dressed for his first day at work. Nothing had been said about a dress code but judging by his one visit most people wore casual clothes. He was aware that his visit had been on a Sunday so it was quite possible that no one had made any special effort to look smart on that particular occasion. He decided to play it safe and wear something that could pass for smart without going over the top and wearing a tie. After all, it was not as if he would be client facing where presentation was considered important. And even then he fully recalled a previous job where the clients expected the techies to have a dress sense bordering on the scruffy.

Several minutes later, Richard inspected himself in front of the mirror. His shoes would have benefited from a good clean but he was out of polish. Otherwise, he wore a pair of loose-fitting trousers, an open-necked shirt and a tweed jacket whose pockets bulged with an assortment of rubbish. He nodded at his reflection, satisfied that he looked the bee's knees.

After wolfing down a bowl of cereal he was ready to leave. He snatched up his briefcase and set off. In fact, there was nothing in his briefcase, not even a packed lunch, but he had always taken it to work with him and now was not the time to break the habit. He jumped into his car and programmed his satellite navigation tool to take him to Automated Services. Then he stopped and remembered something. He shot out of his car again and went back inside the flat to retrieve his letter of acceptance and contract terms. He did not want to get to work only to find that there had been a big mistake and that no one was expecting him. While he was at his desk his eyes fell on a memory stick that he had been using to back up his SAM code, in addition to the array of CDs he used to back up the machine. It would be a good idea to take that with him as well although he had no intention of copying any of the contents onto the computers of Automated Services.

Considerable time had passed by the time Richard was finally on his way. Fortunately, the traffic had not yet started to build up and he had a clear run. The journey took just over fifteen minutes and at 7:55 he came to rest before a set of solid-looking gates. He opened the driver's window and pressed a button on the card reader attached to the gates. After a few seconds a voice crackled over the intercom.

"Hello, can I help you?"

"Er, yes. I'm here to see William, er, Bill Barber."

The gates clanked into life and very slowly slid open. As soon as they were sufficiently wide, Richard drove through and parked in a nearby spot. He then took a deep breath, got out of the car and headed for the building.

There were two security guards behind the reception desk. They were different from the ones Richard had met previously and seemed to be eyeing him with suspicion.

"Er," said Richard as he approached the desk. "I'm starting work here today with Bill Barber."

They continued to look at him without saying anything. Richard felt himself flush.

"Do you think you could, um, call him for me? Please. My name's Richard Neilson."

"Ah," said one of the guards at last, now consulting a memo on the desk. "Richard Neilson, new starter, reporting to William Barber. Got any id on you?"

"Oh," Richard was taken aback by this. He had not been told to bring any id but now that he thought of it, William had warned him how hot they were on security. Reaching inside his breast pocket he pulled out a plastic wallet packed with cards. He began rummaging through them until he found what he was looking for.

"Yes I have," he proclaimed triumphantly, pulling out his driving licence.

"Have you got your offer letter with you?" asked the guard taking the licence from Richard and examining it as if determined to find something wrong.

"Actually, yes, it's right here."

Richard praised his own paranoia as he opened his briefcase and pulled out the letter of acceptance. The guard inspected this as well and cross-referenced the name and address with the licence before handing both back to Richard.

"Sign here," he said, now also passing him a register.

Richard signed and the guard handed him a visitor's pass.

"Make sure you wear this visibly at all times and hand it back on your way out."

"Thanks," said Richard fastening the pass to a belt loop in his trousers.

"All right," said the guard. "Just take a seat and I'll have Bill come to meet you."

Richard sat on one of the leather sofas and watched the television. The BBC news was on but nothing new was being reported, just more on the Valentine's Day bombing several weeks ago. Instead of calling it news they should call it olds, thought Richard and he chuckled at his own wit.

After a few minutes William appeared in the doorway.

"Richard!" he called happily. "It's good to see you."

Richard got up and walked over to William without looking at the security guards. William waved Richard into the corridor beyond and let the door close behind them.

"You will need a permanent security pass at some point. And you'll need to record a fingerprint scan for the main door. I'll get Mary-Anne to sort everything out for you later on today. Did you find the place all right?"

"Well I used my satnav so yes it was fine, thanks."

"Good."

William led Richard into the main office, which was already a hive of activity.

"I'll show you where you're sitting and then hand you over to Charlie who's the technical lead on Project Neptune. I know you're not planning on being in the office very much but I've given you a fixed desk anyway with your own PC and telephone. Also, it would be nice if you could come in every day for the first couple of weeks just so that you can settle in and people can get to know you."

Richard nodded but immediately thought of a potential problem.

"On Tuesdays I've, um, got to pick up Dominic from school. So I'll need to leave here by 3pm – if that's all right."

He felt slightly embarrassed and was sure that William would see these early departures as skiving. William, however, was perfectly content with the arrangement.

"That's absolutely fine. Family comes first; it's the reason why most of us work. Just make a note of it in your Calendar so that people don't book you for meetings at the same time."

Richard felt relieved. Then he saw a familiar face ahead of him, which made him feel unaccountably happy. Charlie was sitting in the far corner of the room eating a croissant. He leapt to his feet when he saw William and Richard approaching and held out his right hand.

"Richard! Great to see you."

"Hi," said Richard shaking his hand.

"Hey, did you ever manage to get in contact with Azis?" Charlie launched in without preamble.

"Oh yes, I've been speaking to him every day for quite a few weeks now."

"Isn't he ace? Did he give you a copy of that messaging app he likes to use, with a passcode and everything?"

"Yes, that's right. He is good although he's a bit, I dunno..."

"Oh, he's completely nuts but I think that's what makes him so brilliant."

"I'll leave you gentlemen to it," said William with a smile as he prepared to depart. "Richard, I'll speak to you later to see how you're getting on."

"Okay, thanks," said Richard.

"Yeah cheers, Bill," said Charlie.

"So," said Richard turning back to Charlie, "when you were dealing with Dr. Azis did he keep straying off the subject?"

"All the time. He loves his small talk and he seems to want to know everything about you. But be patient, give him a few more weeks and Sam will be impenetrably encrypted."

"Don't get me wrong, I think Azis is off the wall but I do like him and we are making good progress. The other day, he put me in touch with a load of hacker sites and I downloaded some of their tools. Then I wrote a simple program to test out a prototype of his encryption routine. All bar one of the hacker tools failed to crack it. And the one that succeeded didn't do it very well; there was lots of binary rubbish in amongst the text. But he reckons he can sort that out."

"Well, we've got a couple of hackers working here – or crackers as they prefer to be called. They use this neural network tool they call CLEFT – that means Constantly Learning Encrypted File Translator. If anyone can break through a cryptogram, they can. They test out our security systems so we'll see what they make of the doc's final algorithm. It does sound like you're almost there. What about SAM itself, how's that coming along? Have you finished it yet?"

"Almost. Just a few more tweaks to make it perfect."

Richard knew that he would never be entirely satisfied with SAM but was certain that it was already of marketable quality. He would use the remaining time while he was dealing with Dr. Azis to put the finishing touches to it.

"Sounds good. There are a few things you'll need to build in as well – you know, things to enable SAM to integrate with the rest of the system. Then we've got our coding standards to adhere to. I don't mean to tell you how to code but there are some standard tools that need to be included to help with audit, debugging, that sort of thing."

The office continued to fill up as they spoke. Richard estimated that this room alone would seat a hundred people in blocks of desks holding four apiece. No one else had yet joined his own block. On his desk were a PC, a telephone and a welcome pack. He had just reached for the welcome pack when Charlie spoke to him again.

"Wanna take a walk? Let's go for a quick coffee."

"Yes, I could do with a coffee," agreed Richard and they both got up and walked back towards the door.

They went to the breakout area where refreshments were provided by robotic service units. Soon after sitting down at an empty table they were greeted by one of the units, which bleeped and waited for them to place an order.

"What are you having?" asked Charlie civilly.

"I'll get them this time," insisted Richard.

"No can do. You haven't got your badge yet and it's all cashless in here. Don't worry, you can owe me. So what'll it be?"

"What was that drink we had last time, the black and white mocha?"

"Oh you want a zebra? Good choice. I might join you." He turned to the machine. "Get us two zebras please and - do you want anything to eat?" he added to Richard.

"No, no, honestly."

"And a fruit doughnut."

The machine bleeped in acknowledgement and glided away.

"So those machines," said Richard, "Are they anything like - is the programming the same as for Mickey the Mini-Mechanoid?"

"The low-order functions are identical but Mickey's control module is way more sophisticated. The technology behind Mickey's sensors is similar to these things' only on a much smaller scale, so both types can see, hear and smell. They can also both understand what you're saying although the service units don't have as good a vocabulary as Mickey. Mickey doesn't speak but it's great fun when he understands you. And when SAM's aboard - well, then we'll be motoring!"

There was another bleep and the service unit returned carrying a tray containing two drinks and a doughnut.

"Thanks very much," said Richard to the machine as he took the tray.

"Don't mention it," responded Charlie, flashing his card at the machine.

"So how many people are working on Neptune?"

"Including you, that's four, although we all work closely with other teams to build the different components. For instance, these days I mainly work on the comms module from a software point-of-view but there's another team that produces the actual hardware that makes the communications possible. There's another chap – Patrick Arnold – who works solely on the control modules to enable free movement. He spends most of his time with the cybernetics team in the engineering room. I'll show you all the machine rooms later; they're quite interesting. Then there's another Patrick – Patrick Roberts – who's more on the business side of things: market liaison or something like that, more of a clerking role."

"Will I get to meet all these people?"

"Yeah, I'll take you round after this." Charlie suddenly lowered his voice, "Hold on, I recognise those dulcet tones."

Charlie glanced behind himself and then turning back to Richard rolled his eyes. Richard looked and saw an extremely fat man sitting at a table some distance behind Charlie. He had evidently just placed an order and a service unit was gliding away from him.

"He's in charge of the machine rooms," Charlie explained in a whisper. "We call him Circumference."

Richard could guess why, judging by the man's girth, and he laughed out loud.

"He always orders these two massive pork pies for breakfast," Charlie went on, "And he can be a right pain if you need him to do anything for you. Hence, the formula Two-Pie Arse."

Richard thought about this for a moment and then, remembering his trigonometry, laughed even louder. Sure enough, a few seconds later a service unit had glided up to the man carrying a tray containing two pork pies the size of side plates. Richard stared incredulously at him. It was no surprise that he was so large if that's what he had for breakfast each morning. The man opened his mouth wide and effortlessly bit off an enormous chunk of pie. Richard continued to stare transfixed. The man looked up and saw him watching him.

"What?" he said, spraying his table with crumbs.

Richard came to and broke his gaze.

"Sorry," he said. "I- I thought you were someone else."

"This is Richard," said Charlie turning round again. "Just started today. I'll be bringing him round to see you at some point if that's all right."

"Have you made a Calendar appointment?" asked the man through another mouthful of pie.

"Well no, I was just going to introduce him quickly and show him the machine room and..."

"You can't just go waltzing into the machine room whenever you feel like it," snapped the man. "You need to raise a ticket requesting access and you need to put forward a legitimate business case."

"Fine," sighed Charlie, "I'll do that."

"And if he's a new starter," ranted on the man, "I hope you've already filled in the required security access request forms if he needs to be set up on any of the machines, remembering that it takes three working days to ratify all such requests before the necessary work can be carried out."

"Thanks for reminding me," said Charlie dully and turned back round to face Richard. "See what I mean? A real bureaucrat! He loves rules. He uses them to sap the efficiency out of people."

"He kind of reminds me of someone," said Richard. "There was some jobs-worth chap at one of the places I worked who was very similar. He actually set up a project to confiscate all mouse mats that weren't of corporate design and expected the offenders to write a full report on why they found it appropriate to contravene company policy."

"You are kidding! What happened?"

"He got sacked. He was stupid enough to challenge the CEO, whose mouse mat had a photo of his family on it. Still, it's crazy stuff like that that turned me off corporate environments."

"Drives you nuts, doesn't it? This place isn't generally too bad but I guess every place has its weirdoes." He finished the last of his zebra. "Let's get back if you're done."

They stood up and left.

Instead of returning to the main office, Charlie took Richard further along the corridor to some of the other rooms.

"This is the engineering room where we burn our software onto chips," explained Charlie as Richard followed him through the door. "It's a restricted area so not all swipe cards will work. You will need access eventually and you'll need a special type of chip that can cope with your encryption. Sorry to say, you'll need to liaise with Circumference nearer the time to get that sorted out."

Richard looked around him. There were only three other people in the room, none of whom turned out to be his teammate Patrick Arnold. Ten desks, each with an ordinary computer terminal on top, stood in a row against the wall. At the far end of this room there was a second door with its own card reader. Through the frosted window of the door, Richard could see another room containing rather more interesting-looking machinery and a few people who were apparently wearing white coats and hats.

"That's the room," said Charlie, following Richard's gaze, "where the chips are actually made. It's a clean room so we can't go in; they're worried about dust and static discharge."

Richard was not familiar with the conversion process of software to solid state and would quite like to have had a tour of the machine room. However, Charlie was already heading back to the exit door.

"I can't show you the computer room either, I'm afraid," he said as they made their way back to the main office. "I haven't filled in the required forms! It's a shame because I wanted to introduce you to Justin; that's the chief infrastructure architect. I call him Justin, as in Justin Case, because he's the most paranoid person I've ever come across. He works with Dog in SSS. Builds contingency into everything! He's set up the systems so that everything – and I mean *everything* – is duplicated. Massive redundancy! Each machine has five copies of its disk so if one of them crashes we don't lose any data. But there're also two copies of each machine, partly to improve performance but mainly as a backup in case one of the machines goes belly up. If that's not enough we've got another site about a hundred miles from here with an identical set-up - duplicated machines, each with five duplicated disks. That way, if this place suffers some major disaster we can all traipse over to our backup site and continue running from there. Must cost a fortune to run."

"Sounds like he's got a pretty resilient set-up," said Richard approvingly.

"Yeah, I suppose," conceded Charlie. "It's just a bit of a pain when we have one of our random disaster drills and we've got to put the business continuity plan into operation. We've got quite slick at it now."

They had returned to their desks. Charlie continued to give Richard a general overview of the company and some of its employees and Richard learned a great deal. According to some brochure, which Charlie found lurking at the bottom of one of his capacious drawers, there were one hundred and twenty-four full-time employees and a further forty-seven part-time, most of whom were engineers. There were comparatively few non-techies - or as Charlie put it, 'clerks' - on the books. The youngest paid employee to date was a seven-year-old boy whose task had been to test out a new game for children. Apparently he had become bored with it after only a few minutes so it had never gone to market.

The company had also achieved several ISO accreditations, not least because of its extensive use of formal procedures. Charlie showed Richard an enormous manual containing all the procedures that needed to be followed when doing various tasks. There was a procedure for almost everything, ranging from how to requisition a new computer system, all the way down to how to dispose of waste products.

"Believe me," said Charlie, "someone only the other week was reprimanded for throwing a plastic cup into the rubbish bin when it should have been put into the cup recycling bin. I think it comes under ISO14000 or something like that, I get confused by all the numbers these days."

Richard swooned and mentally kicked himself for accepting a job like this one, laden with politics. Charlie must have spotted his reaction because he reassured him that he was not expected to memorise the entire manual.

"Don't worry about it, most of it's common sense," he said. "But to make things even easier for you I've got a list of the less obvious rules summarised here."

He produced a much smaller document, having somehow managed to condense the entire manual into a page and a half of A4.

"I'll email you a copy," said Charlie as Richard examined the summary. "There is a separate document for coding standards. It's not quite as thick as the general manual but it's still full of obvious stuff that really doesn't need to be written down for anyone who knows how to program. I've got another summary here which I'll also email to you."

He produced another sheet of paper with just two bullet points on it. The first dictated that all code had to make calls to a certain in-house subroutine that provided a verbose trace of instructions executed. The output was written to a file called captains.log and Richard had a shrewd idea that Charlie himself was involved in the implementation of the rule.

"It's really useful for debugging and stuff although I think it might also be used for interdepartmental cross-charging."

He pulled up on his computer an example of an output file that he had produced earlier. It contained information such as the date and time that each command was executed, the process id of the job that was running and an English text string describing the command. The example looked like it was from one of Charlie's comms tests. Richard saw such phrases as

Broadcast message received from host 192.168.15.22:5280
Status is ready

Transmission complete.

Most of the log made little sense to Richard but he was sure it was all perfectly clear to Charlie.

"The only other thing you need to be aware of," said Charlie firing up a new application on his machine, "is how to integrate your application into the rest of the system. We have this tool called Interface Builder to help you do just that. I'm not sure how well it handles encrypted code but I'll give you a demo of it this afternoon."

Richard glanced at his watch and was shocked to see that it was already after midday.

"Crikey!" he exclaimed before he could stop himself. "Where's the time gone? I thought it was about ten o'clock."

"Do you want to go for lunch now or leave it for a bit? I normally go one till two. That way the afternoon doesn't seem so long."

"Yes, one o'clock's good," agreed Richard still stunned at how quickly the morning had flown by.

"Great. In the meantime I'll let you set up your PC. There ought to be something in the welcome pack telling you your username and password. We use Linux boxes here so I don't know how familiar you'll be with..."

"That's what I use at home."

"Superb, another home Linux user! You and I are gonna get on just fine. Anyway, you'll need to set up some basic admin stuff so I'll show you how to connect to the email server and that. You'll also need to publish your Calendar so that everyone can see your appointments."

By the time Richard had logged on, changed his password, set up his email account, read the dozen or so emails already waiting for him and set up his first Calendar entry - a recurring appointment labelled School Run every Tuesday from 3pm until 4:30 - he was ready for his lunch. His stomach gave a loud rumble at exactly the same time as Charlie's. They looked at each other.

"Time to go," they said together and promptly left their desks.

—— Chapter Eight ——

The Quest

Richard's afternoon was largely spent doing administrative tasks. There were forms to fill in making him promise to keep all the company's secrets strictly confidential. Then there were photographs to be taken, both for his personnel record and also for his security card which he received from Mary-Anne Dawkins, William's personal assistant, who also did his fingerprint scan. And there were more people to meet. Richard was not sure that he would remember everyone's name but he did at last get to meet another key member of his team Patrick Arnold, the cybernetics guru.

Patrick was some years older than Richard and seemed rather more strait-laced than Charlie. He was very enthusiastic with the work he was doing although he seemed convinced that the engineers in the cybernetics team were not properly focused on the correct objective.

"They waste lots of time and money building things to the wrong scale," he complained. "We've got very strict specifications for the robot and all the dimensions have been calculated with very little margin for error. Mickey's only supposed to be twenty-two inches tall. So what's the point of building joints big enough for a hip replacement on a full sized man?"

"Does Bill know what they're up to?" asked Richard.

"Well I've told him but he's too laid back. Tells me to let them get on with it, that it's all useful research. But these are kids; some of them are still in their twenties. They need firm guidance but my hands are tied."

Richard did not meet the other Patrick, the last member of his team, until the Thursday of that week. Patrick Roberts spent most of his time off site but even when he was in, he was usually engaged in some meeting or other and was seldom at his desk. Richard otherwise spent the day reading manuals and familiarising himself with some of the in-house software tools such as Interface Builder. Charlie had been quite right to question whether it could cope with encrypted software because it turned out that it could not.

"It'll be another job for Azis," said Charlie resignedly. "You're going to have to modify Interface Builder to bolt on an extra layer so it will know what it's reading. I'm afraid that means you're going to have to read some more procedures. Sorry, I didn't think you'd be modifying any existing code."

"Hang on though," replied Richard. "Didn't you also use encryption? How did you manage then?"

"My code wasn't encrypted, only the data it transmitted."

So Richard not only had to learn how to *use* Interface Builder but he also needed to understand how it was written. And that meant liaising with the software development team.

"Normally," the lead developer explained in a strong Geordie accent, "we do all the software changes. And if you want us to change anything then you'll need to raise a Software Change Request, attach the requirements spec and provide a high-level test plan. After that it will have to be scheduled in amongst all the other changes that are happening."

"How long will all that take?" asked Richard bewildered.

"It depends on the size of the change. Interface Builder is one of our central components so that could take about nine months to get through change control."

Richard could only gawp in astonishment and wonder if this chap was in some way related to Circumference. When he reported this hurdle to William in one of their regular catch-up meetings William pointed out that he had forgotten to use the magic words "Project Neptune". And magic they seemed to be. He used them on a repeat visit to the Geordie developer and before he knew it, the source code had been released to him for his personal attention.

As Friday afternoon marched on, Richard observed that most people continued busily focused on work with no slacking off for the weekend, as had been the case in his previous job. Then he remembered the nine-day fortnights that the staff liked to use. This was an interesting idea but not suitable for Richard on this particular weekend as he would be looking after Dominic, necessitating another early departure to pick him up from school. He had already seen him on the Tuesday when he had told him about his first two days at work but Dominic was keen to hear about the rest of the week. He seemed to think that the whole place was one big comedy club, having laughed himself hoarse at the story of Two-Pie Arse. He was now most eager to hear more hilarious tales about some of the other characters.

Richard related anything he thought Dominic would find interesting, adding one or two embellishments to keep the tone light. He told him about William Barber, who was known by some of the staff as Benevolent Bill. You couldn't help but trust William and Richard would confide in him whenever appropriate. Charlie, on the other hand, was down to earth and easy to get on with. Richard confessed that he felt comfortable with him and was certain that the two of them alone would make a perfect team.

"You just have to be careful when he introduces you to someone because he's forever giving people nicknames," said Richard. "The other day he introduced me to this chap he called Kettle. At first I wasn't sure if he called him that because he whistled a lot or because he was always in hot water. So, I ask the chap, quite jovially, 'why do they call you Kettle'? And he rounds on me and says 'because that's my bleeding name' and stomps off."

Dominic roared with laughter.

"Anyway," said Richard once they had both calmed down, "how was your week at school? Learn anything new?"

Dominic simply shrugged.

As the weeks ticked by the laughter became less. Richard was now working from home more often than not, still having long, rambling, online conversations with Dr. Azis. The encryption tool was now ready for testing but he needed to engage his expertise further in order to make Interface Builder understand the encrypted code. Although Project Neptune had allowed Richard to bypass some of the more rigorous procedures, he was still having to follow strict standards in his development. Having to read the related documents slowed down his progress and he found himself becoming increasingly stressed. Then towards the end of the month, to make matters much worse for him, he received an unwelcome text message from Amanda.

Don't forget we're all away for Easter so you won't see M until 1st Apr. Happy Easter.

"What?" snapped Richard aloud. "What do you mean 'don't forget'?"

This was, in fact, the first time he was hearing anything about Dominic being taken away for the holiday period. Enraged, he dialled Amanda's mobile number at once. There was no ringing tone. Instead, a recorded voice spoke in his ear.

"The cell phone you are calling is unavailable at this time," it said.

Richard dialled her home number even though he knew that no one would be in. The phone rang and rang and rang but there was no answer. Frustrated and angry, Richard hung up. He tried to send a text back to her to express his displeasure but he was trembling so much that he could not get the keyboard to write any sense at all. He yelled loudly and hurled the phone across the room. Fortunately, it landed on the sofa and was not damaged. However, his yell had disturbed the man downstairs who instantly retaliated with a thumpingly loud assault with his hi-fi.

The rest of the day was unproductive. Richard trawled the Internet to find anything that might explain his rights to him. There were lots of pages but most pertained to laws of other countries or were otherwise blogs posted by people who did not necessarily know what they were talking about. What he needed was someone to talk to. The only people he could think of were Charlie, who was single, and William. He supposed that William could be quite helpful but he really wasn't ready to drag his private family life into work.

Impulsively he stood up, put on his coat and went out. He jumped into his car and drove directly to Amanda's house to wait for her return. When he arrived he switched off the engine and waited in the silent car as if on a surveillance exercise. Hours passed. For all he knew, they had already set off on their holiday and he had no idea where they had gone.

It was completely dark when Richard finally decided to abandon his mission but just as he was about to start the engine two figures appeared, walking side by side towards the front door of the house. Richard bolted out of the car without hesitation and made an aggressive charge towards them.

"Where's Dominic?" he demanded loudly.

"Richard," said Amanda startled. "What are you doing here?"

"Where's my son?" Richard bellowed even louder.

"He's at the child minder's. We're going to pick him up soon."

"What's all this about you taking him away for Easter?"

"That's right. We're going tomorrow."

"You're going tomorrow? And you're only mentioning it now?"

"Don't be ridiculous. I mentioned this to you months ago. If you can't be bothered to..."

"It was the first I heard about it when you sent that text."

Curtains in the surrounding houses were being pulled back as neighbours investigated the commotion. The man with Amanda, who Richard assumed to be Dave, had adopted a protective stance close behind her. He was much bigger than he was but Richard did not care.

"Easter weekend is *my* weekend with Dominic," he insisted. "You had him at Christmas, I've got him at Easter. And that's not going to change."

"Oh the great loving father is going to deprive his only son of a holiday he's been looking forward to for months. How can you be so selfish?"

"Don't you call me selfish, you..."

"Oh give me a break! He doesn't even like coming to stay with you. He hates that flat of yours. He says it's cold, messy, pokey and noisy. And if you think he'd rather sacrifice ten days in the sun for a weekend with you in that hovel then think again!"

With that she turned on her heal, opened the front door and disappeared inside leaving Richard face to face with a smug-looking Dave who stepped forward threateningly.

"Don't come round here again, little man."

Richard stood his ground and looked him straight in the eye.

"This is *my* house," he said in a quiet voice that shook with a dangerous tremor. "That is *my* wife and we were talking about *our* son. None of this is *anything* to do with you so I'll come round whenever I see fit - *little* man!"

He turned and strode back to his car where he sat breathing deeply for several minutes before driving back home.

It turned out to be the worst Easter Richard could remember. He spent most of the weekend fuming and got very little work done. Several glasses of vodka failed to calm him down so he looked around the flat for something else that might distract him from his negative thoughts. All he saw was lots of mess. There were piles of computer periodicals stacked in every corner of the living room. His desk was festooned chaotically with loose bits of paper and envelopes. His noticeboard was still bedecked with his old rejection letters. And the place had not had a good clean for months. Was there some truth in what Amanda had said? Could it be that Dominic really did not like coming to stay? Or was Amanda just being vindictive? Indeed, was she poisoning Dominic's mind against him? Richard knew that he would have to redouble his efforts to keep his son close to him. He would also need to motivate himself to fight for primary custody of him although from what he had read on the Internet so far, it seemed highly unlikely that a court would rule in favour of him in his current situation. No, difficult as it may be, for now he would continue to focus wholeheartedly on SAM.

"In one year I'll be free," he told himself. "Then shall I have my revenge!"

It was several more weeks before Richard had managed to regain control of himself sufficiently to return to work in earnest. Although Dr. Azis commented that it had been a long time since last they had spoken, no one at Automated Services seemed to have spotted his absence, nor that he had not been into the office for over three weeks, despite his agreement to be present every fortnight. In his now weekly one-to-one meetings with William, usually conducted over the telephone, Richard was able to assure him that he was making good progress and that he would be ready for integration testing by the end of June, as planned. The truth was very different, however. What with his unscheduled Easter break, the extra work he had to do to enhance Interface Builder, and all the ISO-approved procedures he was required to follow, Richard thought he would be very lucky indeed to finish all his tasks even by the end of September when the product was due for launch.

April turned into May bringing with it some very warm weather. Richard, however, spent most of his time sitting indoors slaving away in front of his computer. He sometimes wished he had a garden so that he could work outside using his laptop, although if he were to do that the garden would need to be enclosed by enormous walls to prevent passers-by from seeing his work and stealing his ideas. Instead, he continued to sit at his desk, scarcely moving save for the occasional visit to the bathroom and the odd trip out to deliver Dominic to or from school. Even when Dominic was in the same room as him, Richard was spending less and less time with him so that he could progress with his work. Dominic never complained about this. He would quietly get on with his homework and then watch television or play until bedtime on whichever computer Richard was not using.

"Sorry to ignore you," said Richard one Saturday when Dominic was staying. "Not much longer now and I'll be able to lead a normal life."

"Are you rich yet?" asked Dominic innocently.

It was only then that Richard realised that he had been with Automated Services for two months and he had not once checked to see if he was being paid.

"That's a good point," he said and was about to check his bank details online when the question that had been on his lips since his confrontation with Amanda came spilling from his mouth. "Do you like coming to stay here?"

Dominic looked at his father in astonishment.

"Yeah, course I do."

"But you'd rather stay at your mum's, I suppose."

Dominic continued to look puzzled.

"Well, I mean I like staying there as well, yeah but... Why are you..."

"Your mother and I were having a discussion a while back and she seemed to think that you didn't like coming over to stay."

Dominic sighed.

"That's not what I said."

"What did you say?"

"Dave had been asking me which place I preferred and I said that the house was nicer. But I didn't mean I didn't want to see you."

"So if I managed to get back the house then you'd prefer to spend more time with me?"

"Oh, come on, Dad, you know I want to spend more time with you. I want to spend more time with you *and* Mum. Together!"

Richard was dumbfounded. It had been quite some time since he had harboured any real hope of rekindling his relationship with Amanda. There had been a number of unpleasant developments since then and he was no longer sure that she would continue to feature in his life after Dominic had grown up.

"What about Dave?" Richard asked. "What do you think of him?"

"Dunno," Dominic shrugged. "He's all right, I suppose."

"You don't sound too sure."

"No, he seems okay. Well, he hardly ever talks to me but Mum seems to like him."

"He seemed a bit full of himself to me."

"Have you met him?"

"Unfortunately yes. I went round just before Easter. It appears they both forgot to mention that to you, just as you all forgot to mention that you were all going on holiday together."

"I didn't know about that holiday myself until a few days before we left," said Dominic defensively. "They said it was a surprise. I thought they'd told you not to say anything."

Richard glowered. So they would use Dominic as their pawn to mess him around.

"They think I'm daft," he muttered to himself, "but we'll see who has the last laugh."

As time continued to tick by, Richard took to working well into the small hours to make as much progress as possible with all his tasks. Dr. Azis had by now provided him with a seemingly uncrackable encryption algorithm, which he was using on SAM, and a subroutine that he was able to add to Interface Builder so that his encrypted code could work in the rest of the system. All that was left to be done was to integrate all the components together, do lots of testing and burn the software into chips. He was always extremely fastidious with his testing and SAM would be no exception.

He was now attending the office in person for at least part of every day; although he was still relatively early into his contract it was a critical stage in the project and he recognised the need to communicate easily with the rest of the team. There were progress meetings every morning led by Charlie but often attended by William. By the middle of June the meetings became increasingly upbeat. Charlie reported that the communications module was complete and integrated perfectly with the master control module. Patrick Arnold had completed the build of the mechanical body, boasting twenty-six degrees of freedom. Richard reported that SAM was not only complete but also encrypted with an algorithm so powerful that not even the resident crackers could break it using their neural network tool CLEFT. Meanwhile, Patrick Roberts, who had made a rare trip into the office, reported that his marketing campaign was going very well indeed and that interest in the product was already growing despite the fact that nothing yet existed to sell.

Over the next two weeks Richard did so much testing on his SAM module that he would have taken it as a personal slight if the testing team found any bugs. He had painstakingly exercised umpteen scenarios and picked his way through thousands of lines of output in captains.log, which he had implemented in accordance with the coding standards. By the end of the month, therefore, he felt quite happy to hand over his work to the testing team for their initial assault. Meanwhile, he and Charlie turned their attention to getting the software burned into the chips. Richard's requirements were slightly more demanding than Charlie's because of the special chip he required, designed with the help of Dr. Azis.

At 2pm the following Monday, Richard made his way to the systems administration team at the far side of the building where a technician was sitting alone at a bank of desks. The technician looked up as Richard approached and seemed amazed to see human life in his vicinity.

"Yes, can I help you?" he asked in an almost mystified tone of voice.

"Er, yes. I'm looking for –"

Richard faltered. In truth, Charlie had made an appointment on his behalf to see Circumference about burning SAM into the special crypto-enabled chip. Now that he was here, however, he realised that he had no idea what Circumference's real name was.

"Yes?" asked the technician in response to Richard's inane gape.

Fortunately, Richard was spared any further embarrassment as the man in question returned to his desk at that moment, carrying two Mars bars, a packet of crisps and a large cup of Diet Coke.

"Ah," said Richard in relief, "the very man."

Circumference, however, took no notice of Richard who was then forced to try and gain his attention without using his name.

"Er," he said approaching his desk. "Excuse me."

Circumference looked up, munching noisily on his snack. Richard proceeded.

"I, er, have an appointment with you at 2pm."

"Did you send a Calendar appointment?" asked Circumference brusquely.

"Yes. Well, Charlie did."

"Did I accept it?"

"Um. I don't know. Charlie arranged it. He didn't say."

"Hang on."

Circumference put down his food impatiently and began riffling through windows on his PC until he found his Calendar program. He studied it for a while, disappointment beginning to spread across his fat face.

"Meeting to discuss crypto-chip," he conceded grudgingly. "For an hour and a half."

"That's right," Richard confirmed.

"Have you raised a ticket to get access to the chip room?"

"Er, I don't know. Well, no, I haven't but Charlie might have done."

"I neither remember seeing nor actioning any such ticket and as such your access will be denied and there's little point in us having this meeting. However, I can point you in the direction of some extensive documentation that will tell you all you need to know once your ticket has been raised and resolved."

"I should say," said Richard remembering his trump card, "that this is for Project Neptune."

"Be that as it may," barked Circumference obstinately, "you can't gain access to the chip room until you've raised a ticket, had it ratified and had your request carried out by myself. It's a secure area and we need to maintain appropriate levels of control."

It was useless to argue. The project might be put into jeopardy but this man had made a name for himself for rigidly following rules with no exceptions whatsoever. Even William Barber himself reputedly had had difficulties with him in the past.

Richard walked dejectedly back to his desk and told Charlie of his failure. To his surprise Charlie simply laughed.

"Two-Pie Arse - what did you expect?"

"But..."

"Don't worry about it. I've already spoken to Dog and told him the urgency of the situation. He says you'll have access within the hour."

Richard felt both pleased and annoyed at the same time.

"But what's the point of that slob anyway? All he seems to do is eat."

"Yeah I know, he's a pain but believe it or not he actually does do a good job on the machines - he's just no good with the people who need to use them."

September arrived. The last couple of months had been fraught with stress. The software had been burnt into the chips, the chips had been built into the robot, full system testing had been undertaken and bugs had been fixed. It had been a frustrating time but finally William had some good news. He called the entire company together for a rare all-staff meeting.

"Today is a very exciting day. Today Mickey the Mini-Mechanoid goes into mass production! And it's already well on its way to being the number one best-selling toy this Christmas. I would like to thank everyone who's worked on Project Neptune this past year - and most of you have been involved in some capacity. It's been a tremendous challenge and I appreciate all the extra effort people have made to make the project a success. I would especially like to thank Charlie, who's led the team unwaveringly through difficult times, while producing sterling work himself. And Richard whose very individual way of thinking has brought us on leaps and bounds. I'm very sure that SAM is going to make Project Neptune put us on the map. And Patrick Arnold, who has not only completed the original mechanoid shape but also many of the animal shapes planned for the future. I'd especially like to thank Patrick Roberts for his outstanding marketing. We may have the best product in the world but without a good marketing team it would fail. Patrick's found us sponsors, won us some free advertising and very early on managed to get a list of prospects as long as my arm. Thanks to his efforts we'll be able to offer the product at an extremely competitive rate. And it won't be very long before its popularity spreads around the world. Finally, and by no means least, I'd like to thank the rest of you for being such a fantastic can-do team. You've all pulled together to make this project successful and you all deserve to give yourselves a round of applause."

There was much clapping, cheering and whooping following this speech. Richard felt slightly embarrassed, especially when a man he had never spoken to threw his arms round him, congratulating him in a tidal wave of emotion. The door to the office opened and six service units glided in, each carrying a tray laden with Champagne. The machines came amongst the people and everyone took a glass. Then William spoke again.

"A toast – to Project Neptune, to Mickey, and to all you guys who made it possible."

It was a proud moment. Richard looked around the office and saw unrestrained joy on everyone's faces. Even Circumference had a smile on his face. And it was not surprising that he did, Richard thought; if the project really did succeed and the company really did float as William had planned, then many of these people would become very wealthy indeed. As he sipped his Champagne, Richard thought about what he personally had achieved in his first six months in the company and felt very pleased, at last, that he had decided to accept the job.

— Chapter Nine —

Family Additions

The launch of Mickey the Mini-Mechanoid all but took over Richard's life. Dominic had begun secondary school on Tuesday 6th September but even the momentousness of this occasion had been overshadowed by Mickey. Patrick Roberts had done such a good marketing hype on the product that by the time it hit the shops later in the month, it was reported to be the most eagerly anticipated toy ever.

"Order early to avoid disappointment on Christmas Day," said the news reporter, standing in a shop in front of an enormous queue of people all waiting to buy Mickey. "That's the message from Automated Services, the manufacturer of this incredibly lifelike robot. But the company will continue to churn out the toys as quickly as possible so that supply can meet the fierce demand and so that no one is left frustrated for the festive season.

"At a recommended retail price of just £49.99, including an all-risks five-year guarantee, this seems like extremely good value for money. It will be an obvious must-buy for children up and down the country but with advanced features such as its audio-visual sensors and an incredible ability to smell, it's easy to see how this toy would appeal to many grown-ups as well. In fact, the sheer adaptability of this product means that even the most mature of adults should get a great deal of enjoyment from it. Indeed, Automated Services is gearing itself up in the full expectation that by early next year, every household in the UK will have adopted one of these lovable robots as part of the family."

Internet online reviews also provided extremely positive feedback even from the most hardened of robot enthusiasts.

So you think your existing robot can do everything you could ever dream of? Think again. Mickey the Mini-Mechanoid far outstrips the capabilities of any other robot I have ever seen in my life. I have not ceased to be impressed by this toy ever since I got it out of the box. Previously, the best robot I had owned was a Cybersentinel 1200DS. I had always been very pleased with Sentinel's functionality but it now seems like a cheap toy by comparison. Mickey is the closest we've come to creating a mechanical human being. Its movements are really lifelike and smooth, and its interaction with people and other robots is unbelievable, even to the extent of responding to your voice commands. Tell it to sing, walk, dance or fight and it eagerly obeys. But I was completely bowled over when I managed to teach it a brand new dance the other day and was totally stunned when it remembered the routine the next time I played the same music. I would recommend this toy to anyone.

As the weeks rolled by and the Christmas merchandising became ever more prevalent, there were more and more reports of Mickey's performance. All of these were superb but what really astounded Richard was the vast increase in the amount of coverage devoted specifically towards SAM. It was almost as if the reporters believed that Richard had programmed the entire robot single-handedly. It gave him a pleasant feeling, mingled perhaps with the merest hint of guilt.

He was still required to report into work at regular intervals, even though he now had very little actual work to do. Charlie somehow seemed to keep himself constantly occupied, making all sorts of tweaks to various subsystems and liaising with other teams. However, he seemed reluctant or simply too busy to discuss what he was actually doing, describing his activities, rather tersely, as "special projects".

It was money for old rope, thought Richard as he considered how much he was being paid for doing so little. He had finally got around to checking his bank account online and was very happy to see a tidy sum sitting there. Other than his own financial ineptitude he now really had no excuse at all why he should not take himself in hand and pay off all his bills. It was time to start afresh, time to put the old Richard behind him and create a new dynamic self, one that would remember the world outside his computer. And yet, even as he reached for his first credit card statement, a thought distracted him. What would it be like to have a completely different personality? How would it feel to be someone else? He supposed that this must be how actors felt when they "got into character". Could he possibly hide away from all his personal problems if he could pretend to be more like, say, Bill, ever attentive to other people's needs? Could he perhaps actually become more like Bill if he kept up the pretence for long enough? Certainly, Bill was still happily married and even had a grandson. Richard considered him enviously. How did he, how did other people conduct themselves in the privacy of their homes? If he could understand that, maybe he would integrate better with other people. Maybe he would not be sitting in this uncomfortable flat by himself but would be in his cosy house with his own wife and child? There was nothing for it; he would have to learn to change his ways. Was there such a thing as a course on social skills?

The bills could wait. Right now, he had a greater cause - to come up with a strategy to reunite his family under the one roof of his old house. Quite how he would achieve this with Dave still on the scene he had absolutely no idea. Furthermore, a lot had happened since they had separated; many events had arisen to drive an ever-deeper rift between them. And yet, although his emotions towards her these days often teetered on the edge of hatred, somehow there endured a significant part of him that compelled him to give the relationship another try.

It was sufficiently close to the end of the year for him to make a resolution to have reclaimed his life by the same time the following year. Then he remembered with some melancholy that he had made much the same resolution for the current year. "Always making grand plans and then not seeing them through." Amanda's accusation rang tantalisingly in his head. At least he had accumulated lots of money and that had been the other part of his resolution. He would get up to date with all his bills, paying them all off at the beginning of January. There was, after all, little point in paying them off right now only to run up new debts for Christmas. His mind made up he finally turned his attention to Christmas itself and what to buy Dominic as his main present. There was only one choice for that and without any further ado he began composing an email to Bill requesting a staff purchase of Mickey the Mini-Mechanoid.

Snow was falling as Richard tramped his way round the shops looking for stocking-fillers for Dominic. He had decided to get Charlie a present as well, although he usually made a point of not providing gifts or even cards for work colleagues. This year, however, Richard had casually invited him for dinner and he had accepted. Dominic would be spending Christmas Day with Amanda, and Richard had not been looking forward to spending another Christmas alone.

As he continued on his way, Richard got the impression that people were watching him surreptitiously, even talking about him amongst themselves. He tried to ignore this but became increasingly self-conscious, wondering if he had left his flies undone. It was only when he got to the main shopping mall that he realised what was going on. A sizeable crowd had gathered in the centre of the mall where exhibitions usually took place. A tall man, dressed from head to foot in silver, spotted Richard passing by and hurried over to greet him.

"It is you, isn't it?" he said, his face gleaming with enthusiasm. "You are the creator, aren't you?"

Richard looked at him nonplussed. Then he looked towards the crowd. There were some other people dressed in silver as well as far too many people looking like geeks.

"What's going on?" Richard asked tentatively.

"I'll show you," said the man and without waiting for consent grabbed Richard by the arm and began to propel him towards the crowd.

As he got closer and more people noticed him, one by one they turned to gaze at him in awe and slowly moved in to gather round him. Some even whipped out their mobile phones and began to take photographs of him.

"Er," said Richard uneasily, "I'm sorry but I still don't know what's going on."

"But you must know," said the man in disbelief. "This is the SAM Convention - the first ever, as far as I know. I had no idea you'd be coming in person. This is really exciting."

SAM Convention? Richard remained baffled. Previously round this time of year the centre of the mall had been host to a splendid assortment of animatronic penguins, polar bears and reindeer, all leading the way to Santa's grotto. This year, however, due to a combination of a lack of funds and industrial action, no such display had been erected. The omission had caused a public outcry amongst residents but the council had refused to budge on the issue. An even bigger outcry was then raised when permission had been granted for a computer fair to take place instead. Now, as the crowds parted to afford Richard a better view of the arena, it appeared that the idea of a computer fair had given way itself to a spectacular exhibition of scores of toy robots. Many of these were in the standard shape of Mickey the Mini-Mechanoid but there were some animals as well, not quite the festive reindeer but mechanical dogs, cats and dinosaurs.

As he looked on, many of the robots performed a variety of acts, including synchronised dancing, acrobatics and a most impressive martial arts display. Others sat at small tables playing chess either against each other or against human challengers. The robotic animals also did their own stunts, chasing their tails, jumping around on their hind legs and enacting a seemingly choreographed battle between a Tyrannosaurus Rex and a Triceratops. Richard was amazed but his fascination was interrupted by a small throng of geeky children jostling for his autograph.

Completely bemused, Richard took a pen from one of his eager fans, along with a programme for him to sign. He was about to apply his signature when he stopped dead. Staring up at him was a photograph of himself, one that he had no recollection of posing for.

"I took it," said another man, correctly interpreting Richard's puzzlement. This man was also dressed from head to toe in silver and was standing with one of the children queuing for autographs. "I took it at that symposium where you first talked about SAM. I hope you don't mind. A lot of the people here today attended that event and your stuff was really wow! But what a twist to use it in a robot! Brilliant idea! I would never have thought of that. Awesome! Truly awesome!"

Wondering if his autograph was really for the man and not the child he was with, Richard read the title beneath his picture: *Richard Neilson – the robot god.* This is absurd, thought Richard. He knew nothing about robots other than what he had seen in movies, where they would invariably go wrong and plot the destruction of mankind. But there was nothing more about him in the programme, nothing to describe his actual involvement in the building of the machines. Yet somehow everyone here seemed to hail him as the master and behaved as if SAM was the be all and end all of Mickey. He was not sure how he felt about this.

Trying to keep everyone happy, he signed as many autographs as he could, while still keeping one eye on the exhibition in the arena. It seemed to last forever but was so enthralling that he found himself quite unable to walk away from it. Occasionally, a robot would break away from the main group and wander out of the arena back to its owner. It was surprising at first that the robots would always find the correct owner amongst so many people. Then Richard remembered their built-in recognition circuits, along with the fun add-on of a bodyguard subroutine. With so much advanced technology, he simply could not understand how Automated Services were willing or able to sell the toy for so low a price.

Charlie arrived at 11am on Christmas morning carrying a bag containing a present for Richard, a present for Dominic, a large Christmas pudding and a bottle of Champagne. Evidently, the man downstairs also had guests; Richard could hear their raised voices over the raucous sound of Christmas song.

"We get free entertainment in this place," said Richard bracingly. "I never need to keep on top of the pop charts because he provides everything for me."

"Sounds like a good arrangement," smiled Charlie reaching into the bag and pulling out the Champagne. "I didn't know if you'd already sorted out drinks for dinner but I thought I'd bring this along anyway. You can never have too much. You might want to whack it in the freezer for a couple of hours, let it chill for a bit."

Richard took the Champagne and Charlie followed him to the kitchen, where a delicious smell of roast turkey met their noses.

"Wow!" said Charlie impressed. "It smells like you're one hell of a cook."

"I'm all right when I turn my mind to it," replied Richard modestly, reaching for a bottle of sherry and two glasses. "You're not driving, are you?"

"No way. I anticipated a drop or two of the old juice so I walked here."

"You walked here all the way from Croydon?"

"It's not that far, only five or six miles. It took me about an hour and a half. And I'll walk back as well. Should help to clear my head for tomorrow."

"Why, what's happening tomorrow?"

"Oh nothing much, just something I'm doing for Bill."

"You're back at work tomorrow? On Boxing Day?"

"Not officially but it's an excellent time to get things done without people distracting you all the time. I'd be working today if you hadn't invited me over. I don't normally bother with Christmas. It's for kids really, isn't it?"

"So what are you actually working on that's so urgent?"

"Now, now," said Charlie wagging a finger. "Special projects are on a need-to-know basis. You know that."

Richard shrugged and began filling the glasses with sherry.

"Hey, did you hear," said Charlie suddenly, "some rival company were trying to buy the rights for SAM from us?"

Richard almost dropped the sherry bottle.

"What company?"

"Oh I don't know, it had some funny name like Intelligent Intelligence or something like that. Don't worry, Bill told them it's not for sale. He used the word 'sacrosanct' and warned them against approaching you directly. He's almost as protective over it as you are."

Richard felt decidedly uneasy about this news. Had he done the correct thing to forfeit his rights for the exclusive benefit of Automated Services? How many other companies would be denied the right to use his products? And would William keep his word about allowing him to retain the intellectual copyright to his work? Charlie could see how the news had affected him and sought to distract him from it. He reached into his bag again and withdrew an enormous Christmas pudding. It would easily satisfy a family of eight, although Richard was pretty sure it would be all gone by the time dinner was over.

They walked back to the living room with their glasses of sherry and Charlie was at last able to offload his bag of presents. He gave Dominic's present to Richard, who placed it safely under a tiny tree in the corner of the room, from where he recovered a small present from himself to Charlie.

"I didn't know what to get you," he said sheepishly. "So I, er..."

They swapped gifts. Both were about the same size, more of a card than anything else. Simultaneously, they tore off the wrapping to reveal two identical vouchers from Automated Services for a "Wise Witch".

This voucher entitles the bearer to the latest in wine storage technology from Automated Services – the Wine Integrated Storage Environment With Individually Temperature-Controlled Housing (Wise Witch). Coming soon!

"Thank you," said Richard.

"Likewise," said Charlie. "Great minds and all that. Don't know when they're going to finish it though; they've been working on it for years. Still, I'm sure it will be worth the wait."

Dinner was superb. The turkey was always going to be too large even for Charlie's appetite but that was fine because Richard was to enjoy another Christmas meal with Dominic the following day. Despite second helpings of everything they did indeed manage to finish the entire pudding and still had room for a mince pie. Sherry, Champagne, port and liqueurs flowed in abundance and the afternoon passed in lethargic indolence. At six o'clock they managed to squeeze in a turkey sandwich and a slice of Christmas cake, after which Charlie took his leave and insisted on walking off his indulgence back to Croydon. It had been a good day, thought Richard, marred only by one nagging doubt - how could he prevent William from misusing SAM? In his struggles with Amanda he had demonstrated to himself his inability to put up a decent fight. If William refused to abide by the agreed rules, what would be his course of action?

As far as Richard was concerned, Christmas did not properly begin for him until Boxing Day, once he had picked up Dominic from his mother's house. In sympathy with him, the weather had turned decidedly wintry and a thick frost had descended overnight to give the illusion of an idyllic Christmas card with the ground and the leafless trees adorned with their white dressing.

Richard was almost beside himself with giddiness to be with Dominic at last. The previous day had been pleasant enough but it just wasn't the same without him.

"So, how was Christmas at your mum's," he asked?

"It was all right," Dominic shrugged.

"Only all right?"

It was not the response that Richard had anticipated. However, Dominic made no further reply so he swiftly changed the subject.

"Here, have I got something for you," he said excitedly and hurried into the lounge.

Dominic followed him with considerably less enthusiasm. On the floor next to the television plinth stood the tiny tree with its twinkling lights. And at its base was a small collection of presents, now all for Dominic. Richard passed these to him in the order that he wanted him to open them. He began with Charlie's, which turned out to be a copy of the remote-controlled antigravity drone he had been playing with during his very first visit to Automated Services.

"Oh wow," exclaimed Richard, restraining himself from taking the drone from Dominic. "I wonder if you can fly it any better than he did."

"I bet I can." Dominic at last seemed to be warming to the here and now. "I'm going to be ace at this. Have you got any batteries?"

As Dominic checked the box for the battery requirements, Richard's heart sank. He must need batteries to power the robot but he had completely forgotten to buy any. Nor did he have any in the flat.

"Never mind," said Dominic, correctly reading his father's expression. "What else is there?"

"Er, yeah, open this one," he muttered distractedly and passed him a smaller package.

This was an MP4 player, which was going to be equally useless with no batteries. In fact, everything that Richard had bought him was electronic but it had never occurred to him to buy batteries for any of them.

"Why don't they just include these things as part of the product," he snapped in irritation.

Finally, feeling despondent and utterly annoyed with himself, he passed over the last package. This was not wrapped in Christmas paper but in laminated foil with the slogan "Happy Birthday" printed all over it.

"It's not every day your boy turns twelve," said Richard still sounding glum. "Sorry it's a few days late but I'm sure you'll- well, I think- well, I hope you like it anyway."

Dominic ripped off the paper with gusto and an expression of disbelief filled his face. There was his very own Mickey, gleaming white in a beautifully crafted presentation box. He opened the box with trembling fingers and untied the robot from its mount. And at once, both father and son were united in happiness as the robot looked up into Dominic's face and bleeped with joy.

Part 2

— Chapter Ten —

Rise of the Machines

By the middle of January Richard had satisfied the first part of his resolution and had at last paid off all his credit card bills. The pile in his in-tray had become so large that there was no way he was going to painstakingly examine each bill in turn. Instead he used the Internet where possible to find out his current balance. Even this had proved difficult because a number of his card issuers had frozen his account for non-payment and as a result he was not able to log in. He therefore had to make a number of humiliating phone calls and explain why he had allowed his accounts to get so out of hand. Telling barefaced lies was not usually Richard's style. However, in this case he figured that any semblance of the truth would simply preclude him from all hope of credit in the future. Not that he expected to need it any time soon. Even so, he decided on a cock-and-bull story, the more outlandish the better.

"Mr. Neilson," the customer services woman was saying at the end of the telephone line, "I'm looking at your account and it seems that you've not made any payments at all for fourteen months."

"No," replied Richard solemnly, "Sorry about that. I've been stuck in hospital all this time undergoing reconstructive surgery to my left foot. It was trodden on by a camel."

"By a what, sir?"

"A camel," he reiterated with a convincing sigh. "I was on holiday in Morocco and a policeman was leading his camel on the pavement and it collided with me and somehow managed to crush my foot. The policeman didn't even apologise."

This story received mixed reactions but with Richard's detailed embellishments, it was ultimately believed by everyone. In sympathy, some companies even reversed the penalty charges levied on the account for non-payment.

The next stages of his resolution were bound to be much trickier. How was he to convince Amanda to let him back into his house and to come back into his life? It would be nice to get both aspects resolved while he was still with Automated Services in case he could use his substantial income as a bargaining tool. This, though, would give him very little time as his contract with them was due to expire in a matter of weeks. He brooded on this for a fair while but in the end it was Amanda herself who made the first move. At the start of February Richard received a text from her out of the blue.

You'll be pleased to know that you can have the house back. I'm moving in with Dave at the weekend.

Now what? Richard stared hopelessly at his phone re-reading the message over and over again. Okay, so without trying and against all odds he had won back the house. But he wanted back his wife as well, to start over, perhaps to renew their marriage vows. It seemed highly unlikely that this would happen if she moved in with another man. He pressed the *Reply* button and began to type.

I want...

He paused, thinking it would sound wet to say outright that he wanted her back. He returned to the phone and modified his approach.

I want custody of Dominic as well.

He pressed *Send* and waited. There was no reply.

Richard was not going to turn down the opportunity to move out of his godforsaken flat. Even as he packed his belongings the hi-fi downstairs blasted its hellish beat. He wanted as short a time as possible to get moved and settled in so he was making use of Automated Services' nine-day fortnight scheme. He knew he was being a bit ambitious to expect a five-day weekend to be adequate to do everything but would feel no guilt if he had to take off a bit more time because there was not much work for him to do these days anyway. It was going to take him a few trips to complete the move as he was using his car as the only form of transport. This in itself was not such a bad idea as, being furnished accommodation, he had nothing large to move. Dominic was round the following Tuesday to assist with the last few bits and pieces and to help him unpack at the other end. He did this without complaining but he seemed not to be particularly happy.

"So, what do you think of the new arrangements?" asked Richard bracingly when they were taking a break from unpacking to have some supper.

Dominic shrugged and said nothing.

"How's Dave's place?" Richard probed.

Dominic shrugged again.

"It's all right."

"Well, I told you I'd have the house back by next Christmas. It's a little earlier than expected but as I always say, no time like the present, eh."

Dominic mumbled something inaudibly. Richard desisted. At least Mickey's feeling at home, he thought as he watched the little robot wandering around the room by itself. Perhaps Dominic was just beginning his teens a year too early.

Richard had Dominic for the whole of the following weekend. He went to some efforts to prepare a lavish meal for his arrival but Dominic seemed to take no interest. He had also bought a large state-of-the-art television that stood proudly in the corner of the living room, constantly broadcasting even when no one was watching it. But Dominic spent most of the weekend confined to his own room supposedly to focus on his homework. It was obvious to Richard that living with Dave had unsettled him somewhat and he intended to use this to his advantage when he spoke to social services, if it came to that.

Towards the end of the weekend Richard decided to approach Dominic directly. He was beginning to fear that he was drifting away. Richard went upstairs to his son's bedroom and tapped gently on the door. There was no answer. He opened the door ajar and poked his head inside. Dominic was lying on his bed idly playing with his robot, which bleeped maniacally as Richard entered.

"Hi," said Richard tentatively, stepping into the room properly.

Dominic merely grimaced in reply. Richard quickly glanced round taking in the familiar features. It was a large room with a single bed in the corner, a chest of drawers, a wardrobe and a free-standing full-length mirror by the window. Otherwise there was plenty of floor space – at least there would have been had it not been for Dominic's ongoing construction. Dominic had for some years been building a model something in his spare time out of pieces from a wide assortment of disparate model sets. He had pooled all the pieces together and had constructed from his own imagination what appeared to be some sort of military base spanning many centuries. The centrepiece was a medieval fort complete with a number of token knights, but there was also a Desert Storm tank and a World War II bomber lending their support. Also, for no obvious reason other than the fact that there were plenty of pieces left over, a cargo train circumscribed the perimeter of the castle grounds.

"Have you finished all your homework?" Richard asked.

"Yeah," Dominic replied without looking at him. "Ages ago."

"Why don't you come downstairs?"

"Dunno," Dominic shrugged.

"Listen," Richard said deciding to get to the point, "I've sorted out my finances at last and was thinking about starting legal proceedings to get primary custody of you."

Dominic stopped playing with his robot and looked warily at Richard. Richard continued even more tentatively.

"So I, er, thought I should find out, you know, what you thought about the idea and if you wanted me to go ahead."

Dominic rolled over on his bed so that his back was now towards Richard.

"Doesn't seem to make any difference what I think," he said grumpily.

This reaction took Richard quite by surprise and he was not sure how to react.

"What do you mean? Your opinion's always been very important to me. You know that."

Dominic made no reply.

"Why don't you talk to me? You've been cooped up here all weekend. What's wrong?" Richard struggled to keep the hurt out of his voice.

"Is it time to go back yet?" asked Dominic brusquely, getting up and consulting his watch. "You know how Mum goes mental if I'm late."

With that he put the robot into his bag, which was otherwise already packed, and put on a coat ready to leave. Richard watched, unable to speak for the swelling in his throat, as Dominic swung the bag over his shoulder and walked past him out of the room without a backward glance.

The next day, being Monday, should have been a working day for Richard. However, he had realised only the previous day that he needed to transfer his broadband account to his new address. As far as he was concerned this should have been straightforward as he was using the same account as when he was living in the house previously. When he spoke to the broadband company, therefore, he was not happy to be told that an engineer would have to come round to "do some magic with the wires" before he could be connected. And there was no engineer available until Thursday, nearly two weeks after he had moved in.

Richard had tried to make do with using his phone as a router but was forced to give up when he blew his mobile data allowance. He chose instead to take another day off to continue settling into his new - or rather his old - home. He was still feeling rather depressed about Dominic's new behaviour and made a mental note to research the Internet properly for articles on "winning back the affections of your child", which was the string he had typed into the search engine when he was still online. It had returned several gems of advice on that subject, although at first glance most of it seemed to be referring to teenagers.

It was not until mid-afternoon that the house really started to look decent. Most of the boxes were now unpacked, clothes were hanging in the wardrobe, dishes had been put away, and his collection of techie books had filled the shelves he had previously erected in his office, which was the third bedroom. There were four bedrooms altogether: two large ones, a medium sized one and a box room. Richard had elected the first time he was living here that the box room was best left to guests and the medium sized room was just right for a decent sized office. It seemed that Amanda had never got round to reverting it to a bedroom and the desk and shelves were still exactly as he had left them.

By late evening, Richard had settled in the house a lot more. He slumped into the sofa, tired but rather pleased with the progress he had made in turning the place back into his home. He sat in front of the television to catch up with the latest news but started flicking through the channels after he realised that it was all the same as yesterday's. There was nothing on that caught his attention and he was so tired that he decided to have an early night rather than fall asleep where he was.

Tuesday dawned cold and miserable. Richard got out of bed with an inexplicable sensation of foreboding. Trying to ignore this, he had a shower and got himself ready for the day ahead. He had considered going into the office today to fulfil his fortnightly quota but he really could not be bothered since there was still nothing at all for him to do. At least by working from home he could use the prolonged slack periods for his own personal needs. He still did not have broadband but there was some work that he could do without the need to connect to the machines at Automated Services.

It was a little while later that Richard understood why he was feeling so apprehensive. Indeed, there were two reasons. Firstly, it was Tuesday so he would be looking after Dominic that evening. He sincerely hoped that Dominic would be in a much better mood than he had been of late. He considered getting him a special treat but knew better than to try to buy his affection. He would just have to take each moment as it arrived. Secondly, today was Valentine's Day and, recalling the previous year, he wondered if Amanda would be sufficiently brazen to send him another snotty message for not sending her any flowers. Well, if she did he was going to give her a serious piece of his mind.

He tuned the television to the news channel. He was not sure why he still felt the need to be up-to-date with what was going on since he could guess most of the stories in advance. Sure enough, the reports turned out to be much the same as his predictions: conflicts in the Middle East; disagreements over what and how to teach children in schools; deranged politicians unnecessarily interfering with people's daily lives. In this bulletin alone, one MP was calling for a total ban on spicy food on the grounds of health and safety, while another was demanding free sun-block for his fair-skinned constituents. Richard was just recalling the blissful days of his ignorance of the news when something appeared on the TV screen that made him sit bolt upright. Above the caption *'The Future of Security?'* was a photograph of what looked like a small army of robots rather like the one that Dominic had.

The newsreader spoke, "Well, Mickey the Mini Mechanoid may be everybody's cute family friend but could its big brother be the solution to global terrorism? As the nation remembers the victims of last year's Valentine's Day bombings, Mickey's adaptive learning abilities are being adopted by our security forces. Gillian Clark has the story."

The picture cut to a reporter standing with a microphone outside the gates of none other than Automated Services.

"This is the company that brought us our robotic friend Mickey but they've now completed production on a full size model incorporating the same enhanced learning abilities. It is believed that the robot's capabilities could be used as a weapon for the security forces in the ongoing War on Terror. Since the September 11th attacks on the United States the British government has created several additional security taskforces with special powers under the new anti-terrorism laws. Most operations are understandably covert. This latest initiative, however, is the highest profile and the most technologically advanced of all. Each of the new robots will combine mobile CCTV, sound recorders and sniffer devices, while remaining in constant communication with a secret Intelligence taskforce. Initially, a hundred of these machines are set to hit London's busy streets from as early as next week in what has been described as the biggest challenge to terrorism to date. If this initial trial is successful, it is expected that hundreds - possibly even thousands - more robots will be released onto the streets in months to come.

"The robots are programmed to apprehend any suspects they may encounter and hold them until the police arrive. And it's hoped that the so-called Super-Adaptive Module - or SAM chip - that's built into all these machines will help to identify patterns and infiltrate sleeper cells before they have a chance to come into full and deadly operation. But what if something goes wrong? Well, it sounds unlikely. Each robot is fully voice controlled by key personnel in Special Forces and a rapid response unit will be on emergency standby, equipped with manual control devices to subdue any machine in the unlikely event that it goes berserk. A spokesman for the Home Office insisted that 'the security of our future depends on the future of our security'. But the idea has not met with universal approval. Opposition parties have expressed their displeasure that the new measures were forced through Parliament with little or no consultation and have accused the government of 'selling out the nation for thirty pieces of silicon'. Gillian Clark, BBC News."

Richard was no longer hearing what was being said. If he had understood that news report, the adaptive algorithm - *his* adaptive algorithm - was being used in a new breed of machine without his permission. He had agreed with William Barber that he would retain the intellectual copyright of the technology and yet now he was hearing people announce to the whole world that his ideas were being wilfully usurped. It was exactly what he had feared.

He got out of his seat angrily and went straight to the telephone to contact William. His number was programmed into his mobile phone but he used his landline to dial. He listened for a short while to the ringing tone before a female voice answered.

"Good morning. Automated Services. How can I help you?"

"Hello, is that Mary-Anne?"

"It is, yes."

"Hi, it's Richard here - Richard Neilson. Is Bill around?"

"Oh hello, Richard. Yes I have seen Bill today. One moment; I'll try his office."

There was a few moments' pause during which Richard tried to control his breathing as, in his anger, it felt - and probably sounded - like he had just run a mile. Soon, he could hear William's gentle voice at the end of the line.

"Hello, Richard. How are you settling into your new home?"

"Bill. Yes, fine thanks," replied Richard.

He was about to launch directly into his complaint but got distracted by a thought. How did William know he had moved house when he had not yet told anyone? Amanda had moved out so unexpectedly that he had not got around to it. He was on the point of voicing this when William spoke again.

"I was talking to Charlie the other day, I don't know if he mentioned it. As part of ISO9000 we need to have a record of your development approach as proof that you followed all the procedures. Charlie should be emailing you the location of the spreadsheet so you can start filling..."

"What's all this about my SAM chip being used in a load of security robots?" Richard cut across unable to contain himself any longer. "I've just seen it on the news."

There was a slight pause before William replied.

"I announced this via email to all members of staff yesterday morning. Today we've gone public. Is there a problem?"

Richard, however, had not received any such email because he was avoiding the Internet until his broadband was back online. He chose not to admit this, however, in case William developed any suspicions about him skiving work. He had not, after all, officially booked any holiday and he had every intention of charging the company for his time.

"I – Yes there is a problem," he said resolutely. "You promised me that I would maintain control of SAM and how it was used and now you're using it in new developments without my permission."

There was another pause. Then William spoke again just as gently.

"I was unaware that we needed permission to reuse our products in any way..."

"*Your* products? *Your* products? SAM is *my* product," Richard exploded. "That was the agreement. I wrote it, I own it, I'm keeping it!"

"I suggest," said William now sounding firm, "that you reread the terms of your contract. Perhaps then you will realise that as long as you're working for us we can deploy the products you make for us in any way we see fit. And after you leave we can continue using the products in the same way as when you were under our control. We don't need your permission unless we want to use SAM in any further new developments after you've gone."

"Is that so?" said Richard sceptically.

"That is so," said William decisively. "It's always wise to read contracts properly before signing them. Now if you'll excuse me I'm due in a meeting. I'll get Charlie to email you the location of that spreadsheet. Please make sure you complete it."

And with that, he hung up. Richard wasted no time. He went to his office and found the original booklet containing the contract he had made with Automated Services. This was still in his briefcase from his very first day at work. He sat down and painstakingly read every word of every paragraph. It did not take long for him to confirm that William was correct. He slammed the booklet closed and cursed himself out loud for failing to spot this in the first place. Then his eyes fell on the front page outlining all the benefits of the contract, in particular the flexibility to work from home and the £650 daily rate. And was it not telling that of all the chips that could have been mentioned it was his SAM chip that the news reporter had chosen to highlight. SAM was supposed to be his killer application so why was he getting so upset that people wanted to use it?

His anger had ebbed away by the time he returned to the living room. The news had by now moved on to a different, far less interesting, story. Richard sat down on the sofa thinking about the security robots. He supposed that somehow the service units he had seen at Automated Services would be upgraded and brought into operation in a security capacity but he was not sure how effective they would be. After all, as Charlie had said they had some pretty restrictive limitations, including the inability to climb stairs.

The doorbell rang, somewhat startling Richard. Who might that be? He was half way to the front door when he stopped dead, remembering that it was Valentine's Day. Had Amanda sent him something to try to make him feel guilty for not sending her anything at all? Well he would have to make sure her plan backfired on her if she had. He marched to the door and swung it open. Before him stood two large men. They regarded him for a moment as if they had not expected to find anyone at home.

"Yes?" prompted Richard.

One of the men held up an identity card.

"We're from the county court and we have possession of this property. Have you made any arrangements?"

"What?" asked Richard in puzzlement.

"You were served with an eviction order for non-payment of your mortgage."

Richard gasped in realisation. He had frozen his mortgage payments a year ago but Amanda had never said anything. Naturally he had assumed that she had adopted the payments herself and he had long since forgotten about the incident.

"I didn't get any order," he said breathlessly.

Both bailiffs wore the same sceptical expression.

"The order was served by hand on the thirtieth of January," one of them said.

"No, you don't understand," Richard protested. "I wasn't living here then. My- My wife, well she's not really my wife, well she is my wife but we've separated and she was living here then, she should have been paying but she's moved out now and said I could have it back but never mentioned anything about..."

"Sir, we're under instructions to take possession of this property, cut off the gas, drain the taps and change the locks so that it can be on the market tomorrow. Now we can help you to move out your possessions if you wish..."

"But I haven't got anywhere else to go," shrieked Richard frantically.

This was not entirely true, as he still had a couple of weeks remaining from the notice period he had given on his old flat, although he had no idea if the place had already been promised to a new tenant for when that period had expired. Besides, he had no wish to return to that pokey place when he had just started to get used to the luxurious space of the house.

"Look," said Richard rubbing his hand through his hair, "how much arrears is outstanding on the mortgage? I'll pay it all off now."

The bailiffs looked at each other and then back at Richard.

"You're going to pay off twelve months' arrears in one go, are you, along with all the additional charges? The repossession order alone costs an extra ninety quid."

"How much do I owe?" demanded Richard.

One of the men produced a pad and glanced at it.

"£9,094," he said. "There's a detailed breakdown in the van."

"Fine. I'll write out a cheque right now."

"No can do, I'm afraid."

"What? Why not?"

"Listen, there's no way I'm accepting a cheque from you for over nine grand. Now I suggest you start packing up your stuff and moving out or we're gonna have to resort to enforcement measures."

"Okay, I'll give you the cash. Just let me go to the bank and I'll withdraw the cash. I'll even give you a little something for your troubles."

The bailiffs looked at each other again.

"Where's your bank?"

"Just ten minutes down the road."

"Right, we'll take you in the van but I'm warning you, if you're wasting our time..."

"I'm not."

It was an unpleasant trip. Richard felt extremely intimidated by the sheer size of the two men but he did take some comfort in their agreeing to stay his eviction if he came up with the goods. He had had visions of having to pick up his head from the floor for not co-operating exactly with the men's demands.

Fifteen minutes later, Richard proved as good as his word. He had withdrawn a round £10,000 and given it to the men, who in turn gave him a receipt for the arrears cancellation. Richard had told them to keep the change without even calculating how much he was giving them. He had just parted with a whole month's income but at least he was being allowed to keep the house. The bailiffs even had the goodness to give him a lift back home, while Richard himself felt extremely bitter towards Amanda for what she had failed to tell him. Any resolutions he had been harbouring about trying to get back together now evaporated completely.

The rest of the week was far more satisfactory than that morning. Richard picked up Dominic from school much later on and although he was still a little introspective, seemed much more like his old self. Richard suspected that he was making a special effort after he had told him about the stresses of his day. On Wednesday Richard was pleasantly surprised to find that his broadband was working a day ahead of schedule. And by Friday he was happy to report to William that he had made good progress on the rather tedious task of documenting the evidence that he had followed ISO procedures to develop and implement SAM. He was also pleased to find that William was being perfectly friendly towards him despite his earlier outburst.

The following week there were several news reports dominated by the recent launch of the new security robots. These had appeared in Central London amid some controversy, as not everyone agreed that they were either safe or necessary. It was only two days after their launch that Richard heard about their first arrest. He was half-heartedly watching the television, while enjoying a glass of red wine, when the programme was interrupted by a news flash. Behind the newsreader appeared the caption *'Vicebot'* along with a picture of a robot. This was nothing like Mickey; this was a full size model with a strange dome-shaped head. What was more, this model had legs, not at all like the service robots Richard was more familiar with. The newsreader spoke.

"The first true test of the new mechanised security patrol has been hailed as a success even though their action had nothing to do with counter-terrorism. David Skinner sent in this report."

"This is the house in Soho that experienced the first ever robot raid. Two so-called mechanoids - which have been dubbed Security Sam by locals - arrived at the house in the early hours of the morning. It's been said that at first the robots used the doorknocker rather aggressively and then, when no one answered, forced their way into the house. Inside they found stockpiles of chemicals sufficient to make enough Ecstasy pills to give a street value of nearly forty million pounds. Police were called to the scene where they arrested three men. Questions have been asked how the robots seemingly knew about the stockpiles. Government officials have put it down to superior technology but not everyone's convinced."

The television picture now flicked to various ordinary people living in different parts of London, all of whom had an opinion on the rise of the robots.

"I don't like the idea of these huge machines - and they really are huge - barging into people's houses in the vague hope of finding something slightly illegal. I mean, at the end of the day they are only manmade machines and they're putting people in danger."

"I think the new security idea has proved itself with this raid and if it can really be used to stop terrorists as well then I'll feel a lot safer; I'll be able to sleep at night."

"Anything that can help the police fight terrorism and vice is to be welcomed."

"I reckon it was a police plant, you know what I'm saying. 'Cos they want us to believe that them robot things are capable of doing their detective work for them, right, so that the real police can, like, spend more time catching speeding drivers or something, you know what I'm saying."

Far from being angry at this news report, Richard could not help feeling rather proud that he had been involved in developing the machines that were set to clean up the nation. It had long been his ambition to develop a super-intelligent computer system. He had not bargained on a 'mechanised security patrol' but it gave him an additionally warm sensation to know that people were nicknaming the robots Sam after his super-adaptive module. It told him that this was the feature that impressed people the most. Certainly, not everyone was going to like it but the government clearly did, which meant that the machines would be around for the foreseeable future and he could watch how his program influenced their behaviour. With that happy thought he poured himself another glass of wine, looking forward to the coming weeks when he could see his life's ambition unfold before him.

—— Chapter Eleven ——

SAM – The Self-Adapting Mechanoid

Over the next few weeks the new mechanised security patrol made the news almost every day. Interestingly, Richard did not mind this repetitious story appearing over and over again as it was always nice to watch how each iteration of its telling had developed from the last. It was particularly satisfying to hear the robots' success stories. So far, as well as the drugs raid they had reportedly foiled an alarming number of terrorist plots, exposed an organised fraud gang and dismantled a multitude of secret gatherings that promoted illegal sexual practices. They had also been instrumental in the capture of a number of more run-of-the-mill criminals such as tax evaders and shoplifters. Certainly, not everyone was going to welcome the new patrols but as far as Richard was concerned the biggest protesters were those who had the most to hide.

Richard had, by now, completed his contract at Automated Services. He had been half wondering whether it would be extended for a bit in order for him to lend some support to the new project but on balance he was pleased that it had not been. He had felt a little tied down since the launch of Mickey back in September as there had been comparatively little for him to do since then. Now at least he was free to do whatever he wished. With the continued publicity of SAM it would probably be a good time to renew his marketing assault on Brain Stormer, which had not sold any new licences for several months.

There was also the matter of obtaining primary custody of Dominic. He had had an initial meeting with the Citizens' Advice Bureau, who were supposed to guide him through the process. After this meeting, Richard was left with the impression that fighting for custody would be an immense uphill struggle, not least because he was a single parent who was now out of work. He fully expected

Amanda to be as obstructive as she could – and her stunt with the eviction order demonstrated just how conniving she could be. The adviser had suggested that Dominic's recent behavioural change may well have something to do with his parents' prolonged separation and that changing the custody arrangements would not necessarily help him to settle any better. She recommended that he waited a few more months and observed Dominic's development before deciding whether or not to proceed. Richard was far from happy about the delay but chose to follow her advice so as not to risk alienating Dominic any further.

Richard had been sensibly keeping on top of his bills since the start of the year, paying them off as they came in. Occasionally, there were transactions on his credit card statements that he did not recognise, and since he hardly used any of his cards these days he was a little mystified by this. He let the first two occurrences pass, assuming they were down to his own financial ineptitude, but when it happened again in April he contacted the card company to find out what was going on. The company confirmed that three unknown transactions had been made from his card, one in January, one in February and one in March, each more expensive than the last, each purchased over the Internet. The credit card company eventually agreed to cancel the card and refund the fraudulent expenditure. They also agreed to monitor activity on the cancelled card in an attempt at tracing the culprit.

The days grew longer and warmer and summer was definitely in the air. People in Central London had become used to seeing mechanoids on street corners and minor crime had significantly dwindled. The robots had apparently been meticulous in enforcing the law and one of them had even scared a teenage girl witless when it detained her for dropping a crisp packet onto the ground.

"Good," said Richard to the television as he heard this reported on the news. "Deal harshly with petty offences and the major ones will soon cease."

Living out of London, Richard himself had not seen any of the new robots. However, as the small contingent in the capital continued to be hailed as a success, it was announced that more of the machines would be rolled out to Greater London and the Home Counties before expanding nationwide by the end of the year. The public still had mixed opinions about their presence, with many feeling safer on the streets and others feeling intimidated. Richard watched with interest as the Home Secretary was interviewed on the news one afternoon.

"Let us not forget," he was saying, "that our nation is under constant threat from The Real Jihad and other terrorist groups and we remain at the highest state of alert. The mechanised security patrol has already helped us to uncover as many as *thirty* plots to attack key installations in London - plots that we otherwise may not have detected until way too late, until there was carnage in our city. The patrol is doing an extremely good job behind the scenes as well as assisting the police in their day-to-day tasks."

"What do you say about allegations that innocent people have been menaced by the mechanoids?" the interviewer asked.

"Well, I can't comment on individual cases but if people feel that they've been wrongfully arrested then they can rest assured that we do have an outstanding judicial system in this country, one of the best in the world. Anyone detained will be entitled to a fair trial just as they would be if they had been detained by the regular police."

"Will the young lady who allegedly dropped an empty crisp packet be receiving any kind of compensation for her ordeal?"

"As I said, I can't comment on individual cases but everyone is entitled to a fair trial."

"But a crisp packet! Come on, even you must see this incident as heavy handed?"

"I'm afraid I really can't comment on individual cases. We'll just have to leave it for the courts to decide."

"Is there any truth in the rumours that the United States Senate voted overwhelmingly to reject the introduction of similar mechanoids because of fears of dangerous instability in the SAM chip?"

Richard now listened with heightened interest. This was the first hint of any negativity towards his invention. And how come he had not been consulted about exporting his SAM chip to the United States?

"The British government are entirely satisfied that the British people are much safer now that we have the mechanised security patrol on the streets. Remember that the security of our future depends on the future of our security. If we don't keep ahead of the terrorists then they will get ahead of us. And I'm confident that that cannot happen under the new regime."

"Home Secretary, thank you."

There was much in that interview for Richard to ponder. Quite apart from the suggestion that the United States had been in talks about acquiring his SAM chip it was still sounding as if the media considered that to be the *only* chip operating the mechanoids. On the one hand, it was nice that his invention was getting all the recognition despite the vast array of other technology in the robots. On the other hand, he did not want it to be blamed for any strange behaviour experienced in the machines, especially as he himself had not been involved in their production. In any case, he had been so thorough in his testing that he was absolutely confident that SAM, to all intents and purposes, was totally bug-free.

It was almost the end of the summer term and Dominic's first year at his new school was drawing to a close. Richard went to pick him up one Tuesday in mid-July only to find that he was not around. He was not unduly worried about this; Dominic had expressed an interest in making his own way home from school, as most of the other students did at this new place. However, they had not agreed to an immediate commencement of this arrangement and indeed Richard figured that they may as well continue as they were for now and start afresh in the new term in September.

After ten minutes of waiting by the gates Richard ventured into the school. Most people had evidently been in a hurry to get home and only a few stragglers lingered. He found his way to the administration corridor and tried to find someone to help him. It seemed that everyone had already gone, however. He considered conducting a search of every classroom until he found him but this was such a large school that it would have been impractical, not least because he had not yet learned the lay of the land. Besides, he was not convinced that he was permitted to wander around the school unaccompanied.

He decided to return to the car and wait a few minutes longer before fretting. He was just on his way back there when he saw a lone figure ahead of him dragging his feet towards the exit gate.

"Dominic," he called.

Dominic turned round.

"Oh hello," he said casually.

"Where have you been?" demanded Richard irritably. "I've been waiting half an hour for you."

"I got detention. Didn't do my homework."

"Isn't it customary to give notice of detentions so you can warn your parents?"

"What? Oh yeah, I was given it yesterday."

"Well?" Richard was beginning to feel quite angry.

"Well what?" asked Dominic bemused.

"Why didn't you tell me?"

"I forgot," said Dominic in a tone suggesting that this was obvious.

"You forgot! And why didn't you do your homework?"

"I forgot," said Dominic again, shrugging and looking at the floor.

"So you *forgot* to do your homework and you *forgot* to tell me about your detention?"

Dominic shrugged again. Richard fought the urge to give him a slap and chivvied him forward.

"Hurry up and get to the car. You're going to have to buck up your ideas, young man."

Not for the first time there was a chill in the atmosphere that evening. Richard sat unfocussed in front of the television feeling depressed that he no longer knew how to talk to his own son. Dominic, meanwhile, had taken himself off to his bedroom where he could be alone.

"This is ridiculous," Richard said to himself out loud and resolutely got up and climbed the stairs to see Dominic.

He knocked on the door.

"Yeah," called Dominic wearily.

Richard looked in to see Dominic lying on his bed playing with some handheld computer game. His robot was wandering around the room by itself but looked round and bleeped happily when Richard entered. Richard watched it as it now made a bid for freedom, sauntering straight passed him, out of the bedroom and into his office. Dominic, engrossed in his game, paid no attention.

"Hello," Richard said to him.

"Not now, Dad, I'm just finishing level nine," said Dominic in an almost panicked voice.

"Have you done all your homework?"

"Yes," replied Dominic without looking up from the game.

"Are you sure?" probed Richard.

"Yes," snapped Dominic. "We didn't get much."

"Do you mind if I see what you've done?"

"Dad, I'm trying to..."

The sound effect of an explosion issued from the computer game followed by some lamenting music.

"Oh Dad!" shouted Dominic angrily. "You just made me blow up my own battle cruiser. Now I have to start all over again."

"Sorry, I'm sure," said Richard unconcernedly. "Now can I have a look at your homework?"

But Dominic had already restarted his game and did not respond. Richard's instinct was to stride over and pluck the game from his grasp but he decided on reflection not to be too authoritative at this stage. Instead he gazed at his son plaintively for a moment before retreating to the door.

"I'm always here for you, son," he said.

Dominic made no response.

As time went by, it became increasingly clear that Dominic's behaviour was not Richard's only problem. The robots on the streets of Central London had also begun to behave more and more erratically and there were many calls from the public for them to be withdrawn from service. So far the government had refused to do this, insisting that the good they were doing far outweighed the bad and that the SAM chip would improve any behavioural glitches over time. However, it was precisely this SAM chip that was raising the most concerns. People feared that it was turning the robots into monstrous machines with minds of their own. By September, there were demonstrations protesting about the use of the robots, many unions were calling strike action, refusing to work in a city "overrun by metal menaces", and a few schools had sent their students home early, supposedly for their own safety.

"'SAM is safe', says the Prime Minister amidst growing fears that the mechanised security patrol is dissolving into chaos."

Richard was watching the latest developments on the news.

"There have been several confirmed reports of robots attacking members of the public for very minor offences and in at least one case for no offence at all. A spokesman for the Home Office has called for patience and has sought to play down fears that they have lost control of the situation. But for many people enough is enough."

"We've given notice to our landlord," said a member of the public on camera, "and we're moving back to Yorkshire. Those machines have been on the street for about seven or eight months and in that time it's been absolute hell. It really has. They've gone completely mad. Supposedly they can easily be brought back under control by the security forces but there's never anyone around who can do it. It's like something from a horror film. There was one Asian gentleman walking home the other day, minding his own business, and a robot came out of nowhere and pinned him against the wall until the police arrived. No reason was given, it just accosted him and pinned him by his throat. It was horrible to watch. He was gagging and writhing. He was terrified. We were all terrified. I thought he was going to die. And there was nothing anyone could do to help him."

The camera cut back to the reporter.

"There appears to be no discernible pattern for the attacks. Men, women and even children, of any nationality, all seem to have an equal chance of being aggressively apprehended by these machines with no apparent motive. Yet the government has insisted time and again that there is nothing to be afraid of as long as citizens remain within the law. However, a spokesman for Automated Services, the company that built the mechanoids, has suggested that there's no room for complacency."

Richard sat up in surprise as the spokesman appeared on his television set. It was Dog, the security chief at Automated Services. He was even more surprised to hear what he had to say.

"We're helping the security services with their enquiries. There is a slim chance that something's gone wrong with the machines but we're told that the security services have the situation largely under control. We're satisfied that all the robot components that were built in-house are functioning correctly but the SAM chip itself was outsourced and there is a chance - only a slim chance, mind you - that it's modified something that it shouldn't have done in the programming."

The camera cut back to the reporter again.

"SAM - or self-adapting mechanoid -"

"That's super-adaptive module," corrected Richard impatiently.

"...is designed as a self-learning machine that continually adapts itself to improve its own efficiency. Critics have lambasted the decision to deploy them on the streets of London, describing it as 'woefully negligent'. Some have gone so far as to say that it is only a matter of time before someone is seriously injured, or even killed, by the very patrol intended to protect us."

As the allegations of robot violence persisted it became clear that it was not just the news that was implicating SAM. One day late in October Richard received a telephone call out of the blue from Charlie.

"Listen," he said with some urgency, "you might have guessed by now that something's gone horribly wrong with the security bots."

"Tell me about it," said Richard bitterly. "All I'm hearing these days is that my SAM chip's terrorising the people."

"Believe me, you haven't heard the half of it. Bill's been having to liaise with all kinds of government bodies lately and he's asking me all sorts of questions about SAM."

"Why, what's going on?" asked Richard intrigued.

"Those robots are supposed to be under government control but apparently they're no longer communicating with them - not updating them with day to day findings, not responding to voice commands... they're doing their own thing. I don't know the ins and outs but the government are a lot more concerned than they're making out on the telly."

"Do they - do you - does anyone know how to bring the situation under control?"

"I need to meet you. I don't want to do this over the phone. Do you want to meet for dinner? What're you doing this evening?"

"Er, yes, I guess, um, yep that's fine."

"Great. Do you like Indian? How about the Bengal Brasserie? It's not far from Automated Services."

"Oh yes, I know the one. It's quite good. Okay. Um. What time?"

"I'll book a table for 8pm."

That evening, Richard prepared to go out experiencing an unusual level of excitement. He had got on with Charlie very well when he was with Automated Services. He had been the first person in a long time who had similar thought processes to himself. Yet he had neither seen nor heard anything from him since his contract had expired at the beginning of March. It would be nice to see him again, even if the main reason was to talk about the growing crisis in London. Perhaps he could get some better understanding of the situation in technical terms without SAM being blamed for everything that was wrong.

At precisely 8pm Richard entered the Bengal Brasserie. It was not particularly full and Richard spotted Charlie at once standing at the bar. As he sauntered over Charlie looked round and saw him.

"Richard," he cried, extending his right arm.

"How's it going?" asked Richard cordially, shaking Charlie's hand.

Charlie looked a lot older than Richard had remembered him, as if he had undergone a lot of stress in a short time.

"Hey," Charlie looked at his watch. "You're on time. You haven't caught punctuality, have you?"

"No," said Richard with a chuckle. "Just hungry."

"Let me get you a drink. What're you having?"

"Oh, thank you. I'll have whatever Indian lager they've got."

Fifteen minutes later, armed with their drinks, Charlie and Richard were sitting at a table, munching their way through their starters. Richard was having two large meat samosas, which somehow reminded him of someone.

"So is Circumference still there?" he asked.

"Unfortunately yes," replied Charlie. "Still eats two massive pies for breakfast, still an arse."

Richard laughed.

"And how are Bill and the rest of the team?"

"Bill's feeling a bit stressed, poor chap. So am I for that matter. Patrick Arnold left the company back in April. He wasn't happy about being kept in the dark about the security bots. His team were building full-sized body parts right in front of his nose and he never cottoned on to what they were up to. Meanwhile, Patrick Roberts is still doing his marketing stuff so I don't get to see him much. Last I heard he was launching a new offensive trying to drum up some interest in those service units. Can't see even him being successful with that one!"

"Why did Bill keep the security project so secret? I didn't know about it, Patrick didn't know about it. Why not just come clean?"

"Well, I knew about it, of course; I was its chief engineer although I worked mainly on the comms unit."

"How come you never mentioned it? You must have been working on it ages before I left."

"Yeah, sorry, but I was sworn to secrecy. Some of our projects are classified, usually so that competition can't get wind of the idea, but when they're classified we're not allowed to talk about them even to other teams within the organisation. And seeing what we've produced, I can understand why it was classified." He looked suddenly morose. "You can imagine now, though, how much I wish I'd had nothing whatsoever to do with it. When I think about all the victims... I'd never written software before that attacked people! I'd do anything to get rid of that horrible sense of guilt."

The conversation continued to flow freely as the main courses arrived. Richard told Charlie about what he had been doing over the months since they last met but managed to upset himself when he realised that he had actually achieved very little. He mentioned his troubles with Dominic and Amanda but Charlie, having always been single, could not really relate to these topics of conversation. Finally, over coffee their talk turned to the reason for their meeting. It had been such a good evening that Richard had quite forgotten why they were there. Charlie now brought him back down to earth.

"You may have noticed that the extra bots were never released round the country," he said. "We're having a big, big problem. I think Automated Services might be in a lot of trouble. I think -".

He paused, looking at the table as if not wanting to meet Richard's eye.

"What?" Richard prompted.

Charlie now looked directly at Richard, his face a picture of anxiety.

"You need to watch your back. I'm really sorry to have to tell you this but I've heard your name mentioned a few times back at the office and - and no one was saying anything nice. At first, people were saying that you've got serious bugs in your code. Now they're saying you somehow managed to tamper with it after it was released."

Richard stared at him in utter amazement.

"Why on earth would I want to do that?" he demanded.

"They're saying," said Charlie hesitantly, "that you objected to SAM being used in the security bots so you somehow changed the programming and are now controlling them via a back door."

"Via a back door?" said Richard incredulously. "There is no back door."

Charlie held up his hand.

"I'm not accusing you, mate. But a lot of people seem to think that you're doing this to teach the company a lesson. Some people even supported your action in the beginning but now they, er, well they think it's gone a bit too far. I even overheard someone the other day suggesting that you be prosecuted. I know they're all talking rubbish," he added quickly, seeing the look on Richard's face. "I'm sure you wouldn't have deliberately sabotaged the project, even if you didn't agree with it. But as for the bugs, well..." He sighed. "Bill decided not to use a hunt zone for SAM. Both with Mickey the Mini-Mechanoid and the security robots, he wanted SAM to operate in Trawl Mode so that the entire system would benefit from its enhancements. It made it a difficult system to test with SAM potentially changing every line of code all the time."

"What are you saying?" Richard asked with growing suspicion. "You think SAM is ultimately responsible for all the attacks?"

Charlie looked as if he was feeling very uncomfortable but he stood his ground.

"Unfortunately, well, the logs leave us in little doubt that SAM is at fault. We've more or less proved that conclusively. Sorry."

"More or less... Look, SAM's working perfectly well in Mickey the Mini-Mechanoid so I don't see why it should suddenly start malfunctioning in your new machine. It's obvious to me that there're bugs in that system. So why not start from there?"

"Yes, we've already exhausted that route. It all checks out but the code – all the code – is constantly being modified by SAM."

"Well, I'm not convinced," said Richard mulishly. "And let's face it, even if the problem is with SAM, I was not involved in the building of those new machines so either way it's not my problem."

"Oh please don't be like that," said Charlie imploringly. "The situation's getting right out of hand and we really need you to help us."

"I'm not sure how I can." Richard was dismissive.

"Can SAM be disabled remotely?"

"I don't know. You're the Comms King."

"Okay, let's say we manage to make contact with one of the robots. Could SAM then be disabled? Is there a self-destruct?"

"A self-destruct? Of course there isn't a self-destruct. Why would there be? Is there a self-destruct built into the comms module?"

"Well, the main control module does have one. When activated it wipes out the system's Sector Zero, completely blitzing all the software, rendering the machine useless. Bill was reluctant for us to implement it because each machine cost a small fortune to build. But he was glad in the end that we did."

"So why don't you use it? Wipe out the machines entirely. Seems to be what the public wants. And maybe then I'll stop getting nagged."

"We've already tried."

"And?"

"It didn't work. We believe SAM's disabled the subroutine."

"Oh give me a break! It probably failed because you can't communicate with the machines any more, that's all. You can't issue the actual command for them to self-destruct. It's nothing to do with SAM."

"No, it was logged as disabled even before we lost comms."

"Listen, SAM only ever makes tiny enhancements. What you're describing are major changes." Richard was beginning to feel quite resentful towards Charlie. "If I were you I'd check out the comms module. It's obviously faulty."

Charlie sighed deeply and massaged his brow.

"So you won't help us," he said bitterly, "I told Bill I'd try to talk to you. I thought..." He paused, then went on almost pleadingly. "Couldn't you at least get the robots to obey my commands as well?"

Richard stood up angrily. It was as if Charlie had not heard anything he had said.

"Tell William," Richard searched for an appropriate response. "Tell him that I'll come back on board to help him out only if he agrees to pay me as before *and* pays for a SAM licence backdated to March for each robot roaming the streets."

And without another word he stormed out of the restaurant leaving Charlie alone to pick up the bill.

—— Chapter Twelve ——

The Uninvited

Richard arrived home shortly after 11pm thoroughly disappointed by the way the evening had turned out. He parked the car on the drive, switched off the engine and sat there for a while pondering. SAM had proved itself in Mickey the Mini-Mechanoid, which was just as popular now as it had been on day one more than a year earlier. He was certain that he would have heard of anyone complaining of strange behaviour in the toy but to date no one had done so. It was blatantly obvious, therefore, that the problems with the security patrol were caused by some new software that had undoubtedly been implemented without proper testing.

Richard had just got out of the car when he noticed something odd about the front door to his house. He moved in for a closer look and the floodlight came on affording him a better view. He stared in disbelief at what he now saw. While he had been out someone had taken it upon themselves to adorn his front door with graffiti in the form of a series of apparently random, spray-painted squiggles. He quickly looked around at the neighbouring houses but none of them had been similarly targeted. All kinds of thoughts flashed into his head. Who would have done this? The first thing he considered was that an opponent of SAM had been round to perpetrate the vandalism. It was common knowledge from the launch of Mickey that Richard was SAM's author but how could anyone have found out where he lived? Was the vandal living right there in the neighbourhood, ready to strike again?

Richard hurried inside, returning shortly afterwards with a damp sponge, which he began to work vigorously on the hideous marks. They showed no sign of coming off. After several unsuccessful attempts at scrubbing them with different substances Richard gave up and angrily marched to his telephone to call the police. He was even angrier after his phone call, however, as they did not seem particularly interested in his troubles. They simply gave him a crime reference number and told him to contact his insurance company. What else they should have done Richard could not say but right now he was in no mood to be relegated to a mere statistic. He went to the kitchen to pour himself a large glass of wine to help him calm down before going to bed. It had little effect and he spent most of the night awake, racked with anger and tension.

The next morning when Richard woke up it took a moment for him to remember why he was feeling so miserable. Then it all came back to him. It seemed that he was being made a scapegoat for the government's mishandling of the robot crisis on the streets of London. Charlie reckoned that he could prove that SAM was the cause of the problem. Dog had been on television and more or less announced to the world that SAM was the cause of the problem. And now the public had begun what would no doubt turn out to be a ritual hounding of him personally.

It was already quite late when Richard got up but he still felt very tired. He reminded himself that as yet there was no evidence whatsoever that the person who had vandalised his front door had done so in revenge for the robots. It could equally well be run-of-the-mill mindless youths. He took heart from this and made up his mind not to worry unduly about anything. The opinion of the people at Automated Services was less important to him and he was quite sure that whatever they might say in public, deep down they had to acknowledge that he could not possibly be to blame.

The best thing for his door, Richard concluded, was probably going to be a lick of paint. It was a bright, crisp day and looked unlikely to rain. What better day to get started. He left the house and drove to his local DIY store. He knew he was completely ignorant when it came to decorating and figured that the sensible thing to do would be to buy as much equipment as possible so that he could get the entire job done that day. An hour and a half later he was driving home laden with three large tins of paint, brushes of various widths, two rollers, plenty of white spirit, a scraper, every grade of sandpaper available, and a blowtorch. That ought to be sufficient, he thought to himself. He felt much happier now that he had a plan of action.

He busied himself for most of the day scraping at the door to peel off the old paint, rubbing it down with sandpaper and applying fresh paint to the newly stripped surface. He listened to the radio as he worked and when he had finished much later on, he was not at all unhappy with the results. He even considered going the whole way and repainting the window frames as well, which were now looking a little tired against the renewed freshness of the door. However, he did not finish working on the door until late in the afternoon by which time the light was beginning to fade. Perhaps he would reprise his newly discovered talent another time. Meanwhile, he cleaned his paintbrushes and rollers and stored all his materials in the garage, amused that he had somehow managed to use everything he had bought that day.

It was after 5pm by the time he had cleaned himself up and was making himself a cup of tea. He was in a much better mood now than he had been at the start of the day, a feeling enhanced by the fact that for once no mention had been made on the radio of SAM or the security robots. He had worked non-stop throughout the day, completely forgetting to eat anything at lunchtime. He was just considering where to go for a quick snack when he was interrupted by the ringing of his landline phone. Leaving the teabag to steep, he hurried to the lounge to see who was calling.

"Hello," he said announcing his presence.

The person at the other end said nothing. Yet there was definitely someone there. Richard could hear breathing.

"Hello?" he said again.

There was still no answer. Richard was about to hang up when all of a sudden a furious tirade assaulted his ears.

"Get your bleeding killing machines off the streets, you raving psycho!" It was a woman's voice but Richard did not recognise it. "You don't own the place, you know! What right have you to go setting robots onto innocent people?"

"Er. Who is this?" Richard was completely bewildered.

"Who made you lord of the land? You're nothing but a sad, egotistical lunatic and someone ought to shoot you!"

Richard hung up the phone. For several minutes he stood where he was, trembling and feeling utterly stunned. There was no getting away from the fact that whoever that person might have been she was definitely accusing him of being responsible for the mechanoid attacks. Would anyone believe he had nothing to do with them? He thought again of the graffiti on his front door. Perhaps it was not mindless youths after all. Maybe he was correct in the first place that someone had it in for him because of all the negative media coverage of SAM. Might the mysterious caller and the mysterious vandal be one and the same person?

There was another ringing, this time from his mobile phone. Still trembling he automatically picked it up to check who it was, wondering if it would be another verbal assailant. However, it was Amanda's name on the display. He pressed the green button on the keyboard and lifted the phone to his ear.

"Hello," he said numbly.

"Have you got Dominic?" Amanda sounded quite hysterical.

"What?" Richard asked blankly.

"Dominic! Is he with you?"

"Um. No. It's Thursday, isn't it? He's supposed to be with..."

"He hasn't come home from school. I've not heard from him. I've no idea where he could have got to."

"Well, knowing how he's been lately I'd say he's just forgotten to mention a detention to you."

"Don't you think I've already been in touch with the school?"

snapped Amanda. "They say he left at the normal time, which means he should have been home ages ago."

Since the start of the new term Dominic had been making his own way to and from school, as previously discussed. This arrangement was primarily at Dominic's behest but Richard had found it much more convenient as he no longer needed to plan his Tuesdays round school. He had assumed that Dominic preferred the idea because he would feel more mature travelling in by train rather than being shepherded around by his parents. Richard now wondered if the real reason was that he would be freer to get up to mischief with his friends after school without adult interference.

"Okay," said Richard, "I'm going out to look for him. I suggest you do the same. Take your phone with you and keep in touch."

"Please find him," said Amanda now sounding tearful. "I'm so worried about him with all these attacks going on."

Richard was not sure if he detected a hint of accusation in her voice but he chose to ignore it all the same.

"I have every intention of finding him safe and well," he said.

There was a beeping in his ear, indicating that there was another call waiting on the line.

"I'll speak to you in about half an hour," he finished off and hung up.

The news of Dominic's disappearance had driven the previous landline phone call out of his mind. Now he remembered it and looked cautiously at his ringing mobile, unsure whether or not to answer. There was no number being displayed. Then bracing himself for another onslaught he pressed the green button.

"Hello," he said tersely.

"Good evening," said a polite voice. "Could I please speak with Mr. Richard Neilson?"

"Yes, speaking."

"Mr. Neilson, my name is Naresh Mistry and I'm calling to discuss your Visa credit card with..."

Richard hung up. Now was not the time to be entertaining new marketing opportunities for credit card companies. He put on his coat and hurried out, ignoring the renewed rings from his phone. He jumped into his car and began driving, not knowing even where to begin his search. He switched on the radio in case Dominic's disappearance had made the headlines, although he knew it was far too soon for that. There was a current affairs phone-in programme on and they were discussing SAM. It sounded like the point being discussed was whether or not there should be a public enquiry over the deployment of the robots. From what he could gather, the general consensus was that the robots might have been safer if the SAM chip had not been installed within them. One person claiming to be an employee of Automated Services went so far as to say that the inventor of SAM was a political extremist and had always planned to use the chip to terrorise the nation. Fortunately, the presenter appeared not to be impressed by this caller and Richard was pleased that he cut him off in his prime. Nevertheless, he decided to change radio stations. He was growing weary of him and SAM being dragged into the ongoing crisis, which was wholly of someone else's making.

The last of the autumn sun sank below the horizon. Richard had been driving around aimlessly and had made little progress in terms of distance. He parked at the side of the road and got out of the car for a quick look round. Nothing caught his eye round here. He was in the town centre but very few people were around as most of the shops were either closed or closing. Across the road was a large development site for a new "futuristic shopping arcade", separated from the area by a tall wooden fence. It was one of those projects that had burst both its budget and time scale and Richard could not help doubting that he would ever see the finished product.

It was time to phone Amanda.

"Any luck?" they both said together once contact had been established.

"No, not yet," they both replied.

"Right, I'm calling the police," said Amanda resolutely.

"Okay," said Richard slowly, "although..."

Something now caught his attention. Somewhat amplified by the general quiet, he heard some odd electronic sounds coming from nearby, accompanied by children's voices. Normally Richard would have thought nothing of this but under the circumstances if there was any chance at all that Dominic was amongst the noise makers then it was worth investigating.

"Hold off for now," he told Amanda. "Give me ten minutes and I'll call you back."

Richard knew that there was little logic behind his reasoning but acting on his hunch he began to trace the source of the sounds. It was coming from behind the fence on the development site. He stood outside it listening. The voices were intermittent but he was certain he had just heard Dominic. Or had he started experiencing auditory hallucinations? There appeared to be no way of getting to the other side of the fence, apart from climbing over. No doubt if he were to examine its entire length he would find some sort of gate but he did not have time for that. Instead, he deftly hoisted himself up and pulled himself over the top of the fence before landing ungainly on the other side.

Three boys, who had evidently been playing some sort of handheld computer game, interrupted what they were doing and gawped at him, each looking stunned, though none more so than the youngest.

"Excuse me, gents," said Richard politely as he approached them. "Dominic, a word please."

He put his arm behind Dominic's back and steered him away from the other two boys. As they walked, the machine in Dominic's hands played some jolly music and an electronic voice announced,

"Ha ha! Game over. You lose, I win!"

Richard stopped some distance away from the other two boys,

one of whom was now smoking a cigarette. He turned to face Dominic.

"What the hell have you been doing?" he demanded.

From the little light that was around, Richard could see Dominic form a nonplussed expression on his face.

"What do you mean?" asked Dominic innocently.

"What do you mean what do I mean?" snapped Richard suddenly angry. "Your mother has been frantic with worry about you. It's well after six, you haven't gone home, you haven't called her. I mean what are you playing at?"

"It's all right, I didn't get any homework."

"You didn't get– You're supposed to be at home not wandering around building sites with god-knows-who!"

"They're my mates," said Dominic almost defiantly.

Richard grabbed Dominic's shoulders and gave him a brief but violent shake.

"Now you listen to me, young man," he said now trembling with anger. "You're getting really stupid and I'm sick of it. I'm under enough stress as it is without you acting all Jack the Lad. You need to remember that there are lots of loonies out there, both human and mechanical, and it really would be no laughing matter if you were attacked by any one of them. In future you will come home directly from school without dawdling and if you're going to be unavoidably late you will make every effort to contact your mother or me. Do I make myself clear?"

Dominic nodded, looking quite shocked at his father's outburst.

"Good," said Richard in finality. "Right, you're coming home with me now."

"B-but I'm supposed to be with M-mum," stammered Dominic.

"You - are - coming - home - with - me - now!" shouted Richard. "Now where's the gate out of this place?"

"Um, it's over there," said Dominic pointing, still looking shocked.

"Let's go."

As they walked towards the gates the other two boys shouted after Dominic.

"See you later, Dom. Try and get us some more of those games, yeah?"

Richard turned round and walked up to them.

"If you come anywhere near my son again, I'll..."

"What're you gonna do, set your machines on us?"

The boys laughed foolishly. They had clearly been drinking though neither looked quite old enough to do so.

"Just stay away from him," said Richard and turned back to join Dominic.

They walked through the exit gate and started making their way round the enclosing perimeter fence back to the car. All the while Richard continued muttering phrases to himself such as "worried sick" and "no consideration" and "hanging out with layabouts". Then he spoke out loud to Dominic.

"So what do those boys know about my involvement with the robots?" he demanded.

"Only that you're the SAM author," Dominic replied sounding far more respectful. "They were quite impressed."

"They didn't sound that impressed to me," said Richard with disdain.

"They're not normally like that," mumbled Dominic. "They took some stuff earlier and started acting all weird."

Richard was not surprised to hear this but was concerned over the welfare of his son.

"So have you been drinking and smoking as well?" he asked in an accusing voice.

"No, Dad, honest," said Dominic earnestly.

"And have you taken any *stuff*?"

"No! I told them they were jerks for doing that."

Richard believed him and felt considerably better for it.

"Well I don't want you mixing with them any more. They look like trouble."

"But they're my mates."

"Well they're not your mates any more, understood?"

Dominic scowled and did not reply. Richard stopped and turned Dominic round to face him.

"Is that understood?" he demanded.

"I suppose so," said Dominic at last, avoiding all eye contact and looking mutinous.

"Good. Now get in the car."

They both got in and Richard phoned Amanda.

"I've got him," he said looking straight ahead. "He was larking about in the town centre... No he seems fine, just a bit sulky... Well I'll take him home and I'll see you shortly."

Richard drove them back to his house in silence. Dominic continued to scowl for most of the journey although a couple of times he looked up as if he wanted to say something but chose not to.

When they got back to the house Dominic sat in the lounge on the edge of one of the armchairs looking anxious. Evidently he knew he would be in even bigger trouble when his mother arrived. Richard watched him from the hall, no longer feeling angry with him but very concerned, wondering what had gone so wrong with the boy why he insisted on behaving in the way he was. After a minute he entered the room and stood an unthreatening distance from him.

"Are you all right?" he asked.

Dominic looked up at him but made no reply. Richard now walked right up to him and squatted next to the armchair. He felt a desire to express his deep affection for him but did not know how to do this without provoking a hostile reaction. In the end he simply gave him a gentle pat on his shoulder and stood up again.

"I'm always here for you," he said in a melancholy voice and began to walk away.

"Dad?" Dominic called after him.

Richard stopped and looked round. Dominic appeared more anxious than ever.

"What is it, son?"

"Nothing," said Dominic, dropping his gaze to his knees. "Is Mum going to be really mad at me?"

"Probably." Richard approached the armchair again. "Listen, I want you to understand that although she and I may not see eye to eye, we both love you absolutely. There's nothing at all we wouldn't do for you. Unfortunately, we can't always give you exactly what you want, although I for one..." He blinked and swallowed. "I'd really like to turn back the clock a year or so. You and I have changed the way we are towards each other and I'm not sure I like it. We used to have laughs. We used to be open with each other. We used to help each other along. But now, we never seem to talk unless we're rowing. We need to give each other a lot more support. I'll try to be a better father to you but it would be really useful if you would occasionally point me in the right direction and help me to be the father you'd like."

Dominic seemed unable to make eye contact with Richard and continued to look down at his knees.

"Sorry, Dad. I've been a right dickhead," he said quietly.

The language was not what Richard would have liked but he was pleased to hear some remorse. Instinctively he bent down and kissed Dominic on the top of his head. Dominic did not pull away.

"Of course I forgive you. Let's start afresh this weekend."

Dominic looked up still apparently concerned.

"Dad?" he said tentatively. "I've got something to tell you."

But just then the doorbell rang.

"That will be your mother. You'll have to face the music, I'm afraid, but try to be good for her, okay?"

Dominic nodded mutely and resignedly got out of his chair.

The moment Richard had answered the door he felt something

hard hit him in the face and chest. Temporarily blinded he heard childish laughter and pairs of feet running away from him. It only took a moment for him to realise that he had just been pelted with eggs on his own doorstep. He wiped the yolk from his stinging eyes and saw Dominic standing there looking appalled.

"I'm getting sick of this," he muttered and started heading towards the bathroom to clean himself up.

Just then, however, Amanda did arrive at the still open front door. As soon as she had seen Dominic she swooped upon him in a tight embrace. Then she let go, seized him by the shoulders and glared at him.

"You just wait till I get you home, my lad," she said furiously. Then she turned to Richard, ignoring his egg-spattered appearance. "Have you fed him?"

This was a detail that had not occurred to Richard at all.

"Er. No," he confessed, only just remembering that he himself had wanted something to eat. "But he didn't seem to be hungry. Are you?" he added to Dominic who made no reply.

"Honestly!" shrieked Amanda. "You're bloody hopeless, the pair of you. Come here, you." She began ushering Dominic towards the door. "We can't keep Dave waiting any longer."

And they left.

The mention of Dave had increased Richard's resolve to rebuild his relationship with Dominic. There was no way he was going to let that arrogant man get the better of him in a battle for his son's affections. The weekend had arrived and Dominic was spending it with Richard. So far everything had gone smoothly. The conversation had been a little stiff at first but both sides were making efforts to rebuild bridges and Richard was content with that. He had recalled reading in one of the Automated Services procedural manuals relating to fault resolution that he should "avoid signing off a problem as resolved until a full root cause analysis has been satisfactorily carried out". As far as he was concerned with Dominic, however, as long as things returned to reasonable normality he would be happy, even without analysing the causes of the breakdown in the first place.

On the Saturday Richard had taken Dominic to Portsmouth where they visited a very interesting armaments museum. It was an enjoyable day, enhanced by unseasonably warm weather. Richard observed that some of the equipment looked just like the models on Dominic's own military base in his bedroom. When he remarked on this he seemed to remind Dominic about some fantastic new toy that he wanted to add to his construction. Apparently it was an airship of some kind that, once assembled correctly, would essentially float in mid-air. Dominic had then had fun dragging Richard round all manner of unlikely shops looking unsuccessfully for the model even though it was probably well beyond his financial means.

On the Sunday Richard had pulled out all the stops to prepare a delicious lunch for Dominic. His toy robot had earlier picked up on the smell of a heavily seasoned leg of lamb slow-roasting in the oven and had been purring in ravenous anticipation ever since. When at last they sat down to eat, Richard had allowed Dominic to bring the robot to the table, where it sat looking almost enviously at the feast before them.

They had not quite finished the main course when the doorbell rang. Neither of them was expecting anyone and they both froze looking startled. Indeed, Richard's heart was now pounding so hard that it felt like it was trying to eject itself from his body.

"Don't answer it," he said more to himself than to Dominic.

He had an inkling that there would be another judgemental visitor at the door ready to attack him or his property because of the alleged actions of SAM. Instantly his wariness gave way to a vicious fury. They were not going to get away with it any more. It was time for direct action. It was time to fight back. And he was not interested in the consequences. All at once he was gripped by an insane rage.

Yes. Yes, he would answer the door and this time he would catch them. This time he would make them pay. The doorbell rang again. Then without further thought Richard leapt up from his seat and instinctively picked up the carving knife that was lying conveniently close to hand on the table. He was almost out of the room when Dominic called after him.

"Dad," he shouted with a definite note of concern in his voice.

"You stay put," Richard shouted back without stopping.

He held the knife in his left hand where it would be hidden behind the open front door. With his right hand he unlocked the door and opened it.

He felt the blood drain from his face. Standing framed in the doorway, seven feet tall was not a mindless assailant but one of the mechanoids that he was accused of controlling. For a long while Richard and the machine stood staring at each other. Richard observed that its entire head looked like one big visual sensor, as if it could see in every direction. But there were other sensors as well. From the service units he had seen previously he recognised the auditory sensors round the robot's neck. The body was made of silvery grey armour that looked impenetrable. Its arms and legs looked powerful, its legs ending in solid wedge-shaped feet. In contrast, its arms ended in dexterous hands not unlike a human's, designed for grasping and manipulating.

"Dad?"

Dominic had come to see who was at the door, no doubt wondering if his father had committed the murder he had appeared to desire. He gasped in horror when he saw the robot standing motionless in the doorway. The sound of his son's voice seemed to stir both Richard and the machine into action.

"You get back," yelled Richard but the robot had already stepped across the threshold.

Richard deftly swapped the carving knife into his right hand and lunged with it at the intruder. The blade slipped on the smooth surface of its body, twisted out of his hand and dropped to the floor. At the same time one of the robot's heavy arms swung round at Richard's head and found his temple. He crashed to the floor and hit his head again, this time on the doorframe of the kitchen. He was not sure if he actually blacked out but the robot had still not yet reached his son. Spots danced before his eyes and he felt slightly nauseous. Through the haze he shouted a warning to Dominic who seemed to be transfixed.

"Run," he yelled but still Dominic did not move.

With all his effort Richard threw himself forward and seized one of the robot's legs. He did not slow it down at all but his movement did jolt Dominic back to life. He gasped again as if only just realising his danger and staggered backwards through the dining room door. His own toy robot bleeped maniacally as if startled by the sudden commotion. Dominic tried to slam the door in the face of the uninvited guest. Unhindered, the mechanoid marched through the door and bore down on the boy. Then a deep, impenetrable darkness filled the room. Richard, still on the floor clinging to its leg, was vaguely aware in his dazed state of lots of noise: his son's terrified screaming, the toy robot's continued bleeping... And then silence.

Light flooded the room once more. Not daring to look up Richard lay still on the floor, a hazy sense of loss rapidly building up inside him. The mechanoid was no longer moving, its murderous mission accomplished. A whirlwind of harrowing emotions now spiralled through Richard threatening to engulf him where he lay, to tear his heart in two. But even as he struggled to comprehend what had just taken place, a new emotion began to emerge from his mire of shock and dread. It was the feeling of guilt as the haunting realisation tormented him that it was his own long held ambition to develop intelligent software that had cost him so dear – first his wife, now his only son.

Someone sniffed above him. Hardly able to believe his ears Richard craned his neck upwards and saw Dominic flat against the wall sobbing. Richard rolled onto his back, the better to see. The mechanoid had reached its target, its hand outstretched towards Dominic's throat. Richard scrambled to his feet and still struggling to focus pulled his son to safety. The robot made no attempt to intervene but remained inert, its hand still outstretched. Richard regarded it warily for a moment but he saw no evidence that it was even still functioning. Then he turned back to Dominic and without a word hugged him tenderly, his own face now awash with emotion.

— Chapter Thirteen —

Christmas Surprises

Richard was on the phone to Charlie.

"My son has just been attacked by one of your mechanoids in my own home."

"A mechanoid came to your house?" asked Charlie in wonder. "But they're only controlling Central London. How come it came to your house? All the other attacks occurred on the street. What happened to your son? Is he all right?"

"I think it was trying to kill him."

"It was trying to kill him? But... it didn't, did it? I mean, is he all right? Is he hurt?"

"Well he's okay physically but he's pretty badly shaken as you can imagine. And I've got to take him back to his mum's later on. She's gonna really do her nut."

"Thank goodness he's all right though. How did he manage to escape? That's never happened before either."

"I don't know. The mechanoid just suddenly stopped moving for no apparent reason. It malfunctioned or something. Maybe attempting to murder somebody causes the software to crash. I have no idea. I was wondering if you could come round and examine it. It's still taking up space in my dining room."

"It's still there? Of course it's still there. Still - still dead? Crikey! You bet I want to have a look at it. I'll come over right now if that's okay?"

"No time like the present. But come alone; I don't want my house swarming with engineers or anyone. Remember I've got to get Dominic to his mum's by six."

"Sure thing. We'll have to report it sooner or later but let's keep it under wraps for now. How are you? It sounds like you're taking this in your stride."

"I'm pretty shaken as well but I'm bearing up for now. Please hurry."

"I'm on my way. I'll have to stop by Automated Services to pick up some diagnostic tools. Hopefully a close-up examination will help us to find out why the machines are behaving in the way they are."

It was an hour and a half before Charlie arrived carrying a case of tools. Dominic sat in the lounge trying to calm down in front of the television while Charlie and Richard examined the robot in the dining room.

"I'm not an expert on every aspect of this thing," Charlie confessed as he began to dismantle the robot's body, "so I'm largely poking around in the dark."

Charlie plugged a diagnostic tool into a socket in the robot's chest. He powered up the tool and waited. Nothing happened.

"That's odd," he muttered.

He opened up the robot's head and performed a similar procedure. When that also failed to indicate anything he began unplugging modules from various parts of the robot and slotting them into another tool. After several minutes of working in relative silence he put down all his equipment and turned to Richard looking perplexed.

"It's completely kaput. Sector Zero looks to have been totally wiped out - overwritten by garbage. It's as if the whole thing's self-destructed. But why would it do that? I don't understand it."

"Are you telling me that the self-destruct is functional after all? And SAM hasn't destroyed it as you suggested?" There was a mix of triumph and accusation in Richard's voice.

"Make no mistake," said Charlie solemnly. "SAM has definitely corrupted the machines on the street. It's time you faced up to that fact. But what's really weird about *this* robot is that it doesn't have a SAM chip installed."

Richard arrived at Amanda's house just as the clock in his car ticked over to 6pm.

"How are you feeling?" he asked Dominic.

"I'm fine," replied the boy although he did not look himself.

Richard watched him for a short while.

"Are you sure you don't want me to come in? It would be the right thing to do."

"No, Dad, please. It would only stir up another row and I can't face that right now."

Richard hesitated, concerned that it might cause an even bigger row if he did not himself explain to Amanda what had occurred while their son was in his charge. But in the end he agreed to abide by Dominic's wishes.

"Okay," he said. "You'd better make yourself known to your mother before it's too late."

Dominic stayed where he was.

"Dad," he began hesitantly. "You know those robots? Do you think, um... Would they attack someone if they..."

He tailed off. Unpleasant theories rapidly began forming in Richard's mind.

"Is there something you want to tell me?" he asked fearing the worst. "What have you been up to?"

Dominic glanced at his father before looking away out of the window. A nasty thought occurred to Richard, which made him feel quite sick. Had Dominic himself somehow corrupted his SAM program before it went live? He had certainly had enough access to the computer to do this, even accidentally. How long had he known? Did it take the robot attack for him to confess his transgression? Would he otherwise have stayed quiet forevermore? Almost immediately, a new, pacifying thought entered Richard's mind. If Dominic had indeed corrupted the software, he would have had to do so in the early stages, long before it had been burnt into the chip.

With all his rigorous testing, Richard would have become aware of what had happened a lot sooner and been able to restore the program to its correct state. Dominic spoke again, sounding afraid of what he was about to confess.

"I, um..." He cleared his throat and let out a short sigh before plunging on. "I used your credit card to buy some games on the Internet."

There was a ringing silence. Yet Richard realised that he was actually feeling slightly relieved. Now, he remembered the anomalies he had experienced with one of his old credit cards but he struggled to accept that Dominic was the culprit.

"You used my credit card?" he gasped. "What have you been buying? Not those mindless computer games? How long has this been going on? And why on earth did you do it? You must have known I'd find out eventually?"

"I did it - well, a few times really but not for ages - although I tried again the other day but this time they wouldn't allow the sale; they said there was a problem with the card. Then that robot thing came tonight and tried to..."

He tailed off again, his gaze now fixed on the floor.

"Please explain why you did this," Richard sounded bitterly disappointed.

"Dad," Dominic finally looked at his father. His face was red and his eyes sparkling. "I'm really sorry. I didn't think you'd find out because I knew you never checked your bills. But those robot things started going berserk and because everyone knew you invented SAM, people at school started picking on me, calling me names and hitting me. So I started hanging out with some of the bigger kids. They like to play computer games so I bought a few on the Internet so I could keep in with them. But they're quite expensive and I couldn't afford them myself and I knew you'd never buy them for me because you always say they're mindless. So I... I used your credit card to buy some myself. Well, your wallet was just lying there and I thought... Well, I used it for the first time last year and got away with it and I still had all the details; I sent Mum some flowers on Valentine's Day and pretended they were from you. I thought it might get you back together again... B-but it didn't. Oh Dad, I swear I didn't mean it to get this out of hand. Now I'm scared that those robot things are going to keep coming after me until they get me and kill me."

Richard allowed Dominic to talk himself into silence. All this time he had had no idea that his son had been carrying these burdens, that he had been mixing in bad company to try and cope with the problems at large, and had been gradually going off the rails as a result. Nor had he appreciated how desperately he had wanted his parents to be reunited. Richard thought about the mechanoid attack and wondered if that really could have been the result of Dominic's illegal actions. He reckoned otherwise.

"My credit card people will be well aware that someone tried to use my card illegally the other day. In fact, now that I think of it, I believe they tried to alert me to that shortly after your last attempt. But that would have been the time of your disappearing stunt so I had more important things on my mind. Regardless, I can't think how any of those robots could possibly have known about the attempted fraud and even if they did I don't see how they could have pinned it onto you. No, I think tonight's attack was no more than another random assault on another random person."

"How come it didn't attack you then?"

This was a fair question, thought Richard, and he had no answer. Instead he concluded their conversation.

"You'd better go inside. It's late and your mother will be wondering where you are. I'm afraid I can't let your behaviour go unpunished but I'll need some time to think of the best thing to do, taking into consideration all that's gone on and everything you've said."

He gave his son a swift peck on the cheek before watching him alight from the car. Dominic walked miserably towards the house wiping his eyes on his sleeve as he went.

Charlie returned to Richard's house the following day to conduct some more tests on the inert mechanoid still in the dining room. He was unable to proffer any further explanation as to why its firmware had been so utterly wiped out and in the end he arranged for the machine to be taken away to Automated Services for more in-depth analysis.

Richard's suggestion that the robot was unable to carry out a murder proved not to be the case when later on that day the BBC news reported the first fatality.

"The dead man will not be named until his next of kin have been informed. Meanwhile, people have taken to the streets to protest about this latest incident, which marks a further change in the behaviour of the mechanised security patrol, whose job it was to apprehend so-called enemy entities. Police anti-terrorist units had initially said that the victim was a suspected suicide bomber but they later retracted their claim. There have been repeated calls for the mechanoids to be withdrawn but as Christmas draws ever closer and the streets of London become busier and busier they remain a clear and present danger. As the SAM chip continues to rewrite their programming, all hope of ever regaining control over them gradually trickles away. Each day it seems increasingly likely that it will be we, the public, who will be forced to give way leaving the machines to reign supreme."

It was only a matter of time before SAM was mentioned, Richard thought, and probably only a matter of time before he had to endure another attack on his house. Fortunately, nothing happened that evening or all the following day. Far more challenging for him was having his son round again on the Tuesday evening. Dominic was so ashamed of himself and was clearly worried about what his father was going to do to him that there was a distinctly uncomfortable atmosphere. Richard, in fact, had not come to any decision about suitable sanctions against Dominic. Indeed, he had spent most of the last two days blaming himself for his son's behaviour and considering how he should change to benefit Dominic. Certainly, the likelihood of him and Amanda ever getting back together again seemed as remote as ever, and his biggest concern right now was how their prolonged separation might further affect Dominic.

The following day Richard resolved to make a conscientious start on his Christmas shopping. It was late in the year and as yet he had absolutely no idea what to buy Dominic. Dominic was the only person he bought anything for these days but nevertheless it still tended to take him a long time before he found anything suitable. The situation was made twice as bad by the fact that Dominic's birthday was so close to Christmas and Richard always liked to make a point of buying him separate presents for the two occasions. Today, therefore, he would go into London, perhaps to Oxford Street or Tottenham Court Road, and have a good look round for something really special. He was feeling much happier today than he had been for weeks, a mood brought on by Dominic's apparent return to sensible behaviour.

He left the house shortly after Dominic had departed for school. Had he been earlier he would have offered him a lift. However, several months of being out of work had slowed him down in the morning and he was not ready to leave on time. It had still not reached 9am when he set off and as far as he was concerned that was plenty early enough. There was no point in getting to the shops before they had even opened.

Richard's good mood swiftly changed when he reached his car. Someone had deposited onto its bonnet a black bin liner full of rubbish. Richard clicked his tongue irritably and dropped the rubbish bag onto the ground. Then he noticed the tyres. He walked round the car in despair as he realised that all four of them had had the air completely let out of them. Squatting down, he examined first one then another until he had examined all four. They did not appear to have been slashed, which was some consolation.

Where were the security robots when you wanted them and why hadn't they prevented this latest act of vandalism? As Charlie had mentioned, he did not live in Central London where the robots were contained. Richard fantasised about a personal mechanoid guard as he opened his boot and extracted a compressor to re-inflate his tyres. He kept all sorts of equipment in his boot, most of which he never used but stored as insurance just in case it was ever needed. This had been a constant source of annoyance to Amanda in the past as the cluttered boot had always forced her to relegate her shopping to the back seat.

The compressor was noisy and slow but did eventually inflate all the tyres. Richard was then finally able to set off for London. However, his heart was no longer in it and although he did get to the capital, he ended up just driving around aimlessly, his mind on other things. Contrary to the news report, the streets were not busy at all given the time of year and after a short while he found he had drifted into an area almost completely devoid of other people. Looking some distance ahead, he saw the reason for this emptiness. A mechanoid was standing on a street corner, motionless, ready to intimidate anyone who dared to come close to it. It was the first one that Richard had seen since the attack on Dominic, and only the second one he had seen at all. His stomach clenched unpleasantly. Nearby, keeping a watchful eye on the mechanoid, was a group of what looked like men in army uniform.

As if obeying a command, Richard stopped and watched the scene before him. It took a few moments for him to register what he was seeing but even as he watched, a small army tank rolled into view. He wound down his window trying to hear anything being said. All he heard were some shouted orders muted by the distance. Then came a loud explosion as the tank discharged a shell at the robot. A ball of gas and flame erupted from where the robot stood. There was more indistinct shouting from the army men. Then as the smoke began to dissipate Richard could see that the robot had been utterly destroyed. Its head had been blown clean off and its body lay on the ground, a twisted heap of metal. The soldiers scarcely had time to celebrate when another robot came from round the corner and began to march towards the group of men. They began to retreat, shouting additional orders towards the tank. But even more robots were appearing from other directions. It was as if they were answering a distress call from the robot that had been destroyed.

The soldiers opened fire with automatic weapons but it was no good. The robots continued their advance, closing in on them. The tank operator, apparently unwilling to fire in the direction of the soldiers, was forced to watch helplessly. In a fit of panic the men scattered. One soldier was left behind, his escape hampered by the five robots now almost upon him. Realising his situation was hopeless he dropped his gun and removed a device from his belt. He flicked something on it and pressed a button. There was an enormous flash, another loud bang and a lot more smoke. Without thinking, Richard slammed his foot to the floor and his car shot towards the blaze. He knew there was no way that the soldier could have survived. He had no idea what he was doing or why he was doing it. All he knew was that he could not just sit there and do nothing.

He slammed on the brakes just yards from the furnace, though keeping out of the line of sight of the tank. To his astonishment, he could just make out the robots casually walking away through the thick smoke, still unscathed. The tank began to give chase. Clearly, its cannon was rather more powerful than the explosive used by the lone soldier. Richard could see dismembered pieces of his body lying nearby. He took out his mobile phone and prepared to call for help but he could hear police cars already arriving on the scene. He hesitated. Something told him he did not want to be found lurking anywhere near here. Following his instinct, he turned the car round and drove off at speed, apparently undetected through the smoke.

When he was a safe distance away, he stopped the car again. He sat there for a moment, panting as if he had just sprinted to where he was. Then he opened the driver's door, leaned out and vomited over the road. He continued to lean out of the car, allowing the breeze to cool his head. How long he stayed there he had no idea.

Richard had an uneasy sleep that night. His dreams were plagued by images of mechanoids feeding on the flesh of dismembered body parts. Dominic was controlling the machines with a device that looked like a credit card but played silly tunes. Another mechanoid drove a tank towards him and aimed the big gun directly at him...

Richard woke up and sat bolt upright in his bed. He was not sure why he had awoken so suddenly but judging by the light breaking through the curtains, it was already well on in the day. He had heard a bang. Or had that been in the dream? Then there had been a piercing tone that even now rent through his head. As his brain gradually caught up, he realised with a slight panic that his smoke detector was screaming a warning at him. He leapt out of bed and opened the bedroom door, coughing violently as he inhaled a lungful of smoke. Now panicking even more he hurried downstairs to look for the source of the problem. There was a stench of gunpowder and the walls and doors were caked in what looked like soot. He opened the front and back doors to let out the smoke. Then he saw it – the twisted remains of what was undoubtedly a firework.

This time when he reported the attack to the police they did at least deign to turn up. There were two officers, one of whom looked around the house to make sure that it was safe, while the other took details from Richard. Richard took the opportunity to mention the previous acts of intimidation against him as well: the attack on his car, the graffiti on his door, the pelting with eggs and the abusive phone calls. He also made it clear that it was the adverse reporting of his SAM chip that had turned the public against him and that such baseless reports ought to be banned by law. The officers said little during his tirade and Richard sensed that they had more sympathy with his attackers than they did with him.

It was almost midday by the time the police had left and Richard had cleaned up the mess as best he could. More to escape from the pervasive smell lingering in the house, he opted to drive into town, this time staying local. There were still things to do and he was not going to let the mindless majority ruin his life. He switched on the news to hear if anything about yesterday's conflagration would be reported.

"Police have clashed with angry protesters in Westminster demanding an immediate end to the deployment of the so-called mechanoids on the streets of London. Trouble flared shortly before ten this morning just minutes after a second man was killed by one of the security robots. Police fired tear gas into the rioting crowds who threw stones and petrol bombs.

"The government have admitted that they have lost control of the robots and have drafted in army units to subdue them, although they have emphasised that the capital is not under martial law. It is not yet clear how successful the army operation will be as the robots are designed to withstand extreme attacks. There have already been unconfirmed reports that a soldier was killed yesterday as part of the military campaign.

"Each robot is equipped with a self-destruct capability but this itself has been destroyed by the onboard super-adaptive module - or SAM chip - which is widely believed to have caused severe problems with..."

Richard switched off the radio and swore loudly. When would the authorities face up to the fact that they had messed up big style in the basic programming of their mechanoids? When would they stop blaming SAM for their own failings? His anger faltered as an idea now occurred to him, one that just might put an end to all the criticism and intimidation he had had to endure recently. He could sell his own story to the newspapers, put across his own perspective to the public. Or perhaps he should go the whole way and talk about it on television. That would capture the largest audience. Richard made a mental note to follow up on this brilliant idea the moment he got home and feeling slightly more contented he continued his journey. The streets were even more deserted than London's had been the previous day. Considering the mechanoids were still supposedly only patrolling Central London it was strange how widespread their effect had become.

Before long, another idea occurred to Richard. He remembered that there was a model shop in the centre of town and it was just possible that it might stock the airship kit that Dominic had wanted. He turned down a side road and soon he was on the High Street. This too was deserted and many of the shops looked closed. With a remarkable sense of optimism he persevered nevertheless and was eventually rewarded by the welcoming Open sign on the door of what was simply called The Model Shop. Richard pulled up directly outside. He knew this meant he was on a double yellow line but reasoned that with such a dearth of traffic it was hardly likely that there would be any traffic wardens around. He switched off the engine and got out of the car, casually locking it by remote control as he entered the shop.

The shop seemed much larger on the inside than it did on the outside. Richard glanced around quickly before taking his time to study the models on display. There were all kinds of interesting items, many of which made Richard want to be a boy again. These were not simply models to assemble and paint, as was the case when he was growing up. These also came with programmable electronics, electrical fittings, sound cards, or anything that would add a whole new dimension to the model-making experience.

"The kids these days take so much for granted," said a voice.

Richard turned to see an elderly man looking amusedly at him.

"I prefer to deal with people like you," said the man still smiling, "people who appreciate the extra touches."

Richard smiled back excitedly.

"Were you looking for anything in particular?" asked the man helpfully.

"Er. As a matter of fact, yes. I was looking for - well, I don't know what it's called really but it's like an airship or something that floats?"

"Oh yes, the Hover Ship. I have just one left under the counter. I had put it aside for someone else but he hasn't shown up. There's not been many people around for some days as a matter of fact. Terrible thing with these robots! Scaring everyone off, they are. Very bad for business! Very bad!"

The man shook his head in dismay then seemed to remember himself.

"Oh yes, you wanted, er..."

He wandered off to the counter and returned seconds later carrying a large, flat box. Richard took it eagerly and studied it closely. It seemed that when assembling the model, careful placement of electromagnets would cause the finished article to float in mid-air.

"It's very clever but quite expensive, I'm afraid." said the man, "However, I can do you a deal if you also buy War Zone II."

"What's War Zone II?" asked Richard still reading the box.

"It's a floating zeppelin that fires real lasers. Very popular amongst serious enthusiasts."

Richard was interested although part of him wondered if there would be adequate space in Dominic's room for all these fancy toys.

"Do you have that in stock as well?" he asked.

"Again, just the one."

The man wandered back to the counter and came back carrying an even larger box.

"This would normally sell at £250. The Hover Ship is £150. If you buy both of them now I'll only charge you £350 for the pair."

It was considerably more than he had planned to spend. He did not normally believe in buying extravagantly expensive gifts as he did not want Dominic's expectations to rise unchecked year on year. At the same time, now that he had seen these particular items he was loath to leave without them. They would be the perfect end to a stressful year. And besides, Dominic was about to enter his teens. Surely that should be marked by an extra special gift.

"I'll take them," he said resolutely to the man.

Richard returned to his car several minutes later, feeling particularly pleased with his purchases and looking forward to seeing his son's face when he peeled off the wrapping to reveal his prizes. He opened the rear passenger door by remote control and carefully loaded the boxes onto the back seat. Then he closed the door and walked round to the driver's side. Only then did he notice the distinctive yellow clamp on the front wheel accompanied by a sticker on the windscreen. Richard swore loudly in disbelief, uncertain of the legality of the situation. He ripped off the ticket on the windscreen and quickly read through it. There was a fifty-pound removal fee but there was no telephone number to call. It looked like in order to pay the fine and arrange removal he would have to make a special trip to some godforsaken place in the back of beyond. He did not know what to do; with no obvious alternative transport available he felt completely stranded. He swore again and kicked the clamp in frustration. Then a voice spoke from behind him.

"I'd avoid damaging that clamp if I were you."

Richard turned round quickly and saw a man in a suit walking towards him. He had a hard unwelcoming face and he was not alone. Accompanying him on either side were two uniformed policemen and on the opposite side of the street, Richard noticed for the first time a black, unmarked van, presumably the vehicle the men had arrived in.

"Is this anything to do with you?" Richard asked the man angrily indicating the clamp.

"Mr. Neilson?" enquired the man.

"Yes. Who are you?"

The man drew out an identity card and held it up for Richard to see. At the same time, one of the policemen pulled out a handgun and pointed it at Richard who felt his legs turn to jelly at once. Was this normal behaviour for a parking offence?

"I'm Agent Johnson," said the man in the suit. "And I'm arresting you for conspiracy to pervert the course of justice. You do not have to say anything, but it may harm your defence..."

The other policeman was on top of Richard in a flash. He pinned him against the side of his own car and in no time an uncomfortable set of handcuffs was cutting into his wrists. Richard was vaguely aware of the man in The Model Shop watching the proceedings from the safety of his window. He was also dimly aware of Agent Johnson's voice continuing to speak.

"...Anything you do say may be given in evidence."

Johnson turned away and walked towards the van. The policeman with the handcuffs manhandled Richard to make him follow. The policeman with the gun continued to point it menacingly at Richard. Richard was bundled into the back of the van, the door slammed behind him and he was taken away at speed.

—— Chapter Fourteen ——

Agent Johnson

The cell was small and completely white. The lights shone brightly from the high ceiling where a camera watched his every movement. The floor and all four walls were padded, presumably to prevent him from doing any harm to himself. Richard sat on the floor and waited. He did not know how much time had passed but he felt that he had been there for more than a day already. His watch had been confiscated along with all his other personal effects. All he had on him now were an orange jumpsuit and a pair of slippers. He also still sported inky fingers, the result of having his fingerprints forcibly recorded. No one had given him any information at all and he still had no idea why he was being held. Eventually, his anxiety heightened almost beyond endurance, he stood up and began yelling at the camera.

"Hello? Anybody out there?"

There was no answer, no hint that anyone had even heard him.

"What's going on?" Richard yelled again and he began hammering on the door.

This too was padded so although his hammering did help to relieve some stress it did not help to attract any attention. He swore quietly and sat on the floor again to wait.

After what seemed like several more hours, he at last heard a key turn in the lock of his cell door. The door opened and two men in military fatigues appeared standing either side of the doorway. Without speaking, one of them gestured with his head that Richard should follow them. Richard got up, anger coursing through his veins.

"Am I about to get some answers now?" he demanded.

In response the men seized Richard by the arms and marched him down the corridor in silence, a silence broken only by Richard's repeated protests.

Presently, they came to a stop outside a door at the end of the corridor. It was a wooden panelled door bearing a logo that looked like a large G inside a triangle. Richard heard a jangle of keys from one of his captors and the door swung open. He entered the room and looked around. It was completely devoid of any furniture apart from a table and two chairs in the middle of the floor. The walls and floor were plain white like his cell but unlike his cell, which was padded, the floor was made of some hard material that made footsteps resound intimidatingly. The guards took Richard over to the table and sat him down on the nearest chair so that his back was to the door. Then they turned and walked away. Richard glanced behind him to see them standing sentry-like by the entrance. He turned back towards the table. There was probably going to be some sort of interrogation but at least that meant he would get to talk to someone at last.

It was another few minutes before the door opened again and Richard heard footsteps approaching from behind him. He turned round to see a suited man walking towards him wearing a hard, unwelcoming face. It was Agent Johnson. He carried what looked like a leather-bound file under one arm as he moved round to stand opposite Richard. He placed the file upon the table but did not open it. Richard saw that it bore the same logo as was on the door, a large G inside a triangle, but there was also a printed note fastened to the front of the file that simply read, "Subject X".

"Donald Richard Neilson," said Johnson finally, speaking slowly and deliberately.

Richard said nothing but Johnson did not seem to expect any reply. He continued.

“38 years of age. Attained exemplary qualifications in Advanced Computing and Electronics. Separated from Amanda Deirdre Lewis, leaving one child. Has not since formed any close personal bonds. Has been in and out of various technical jobs for years, never staying very long, often resigning because of the 'lack of a challenge'. Saw out most recent twelve-month contract with Automated Services Ltd. Chief ambition: world domination."

This last pronouncement made Richard start.

"What?" he exclaimed.

Johnson sat down on the only other chair in the room and surveyed Richard unblinkingly.

"I guess you have much to be bitter about," he said. "You ran up a string of debts after falling out with your old boss. Had lots of angry creditors after you, did you not?"

Richard said nothing.

"And before that, your wife left you, robbing you of your only son, and your house, and your dignity. Couldn't have been very nice for you having to spend all your time in that tiny flat with the noisy neighbours. Enough to unhinge the best of us. Yet, you spent many a month stuck indoors working alone on fancy software - your so-called 'killer app' - only to find that nobody wanted to buy it. Must have been frustrating for you. But then things looked up. Got yourself a decent job, got your house back. Well done! Regrettably, by then you had it in for society. You wanted retribution - and you turned your killer app into a *killer* app."

"What- what are you talking about?" Richard asked at last wondering if he'd really been arrested for writing a computer program.

"You created the so-called SAM chip?" A sneer played round Johnson's lips.

"Yes," replied Richard warily.

"Of course, we all know that. We also know that you entered into an agreement with Automated Services to install your SAM chip into their series of security automatons."

"I said they could install it into some toys," said Richard again more impatiently, "but what's that got to do with..."

"We also know that there have been countless attacks on innocent people and an increasing death toll after your SAM chip mutated the original control protocols in the automatons."

"Damn it!" shouted Richard in exasperation. "How do you know that those rampaging machines out there are anything whatsoever to do with my software? Where's your evidence?"

There was a pause. Then Johnson picked up the file and opened it. Not taking his eyes off the file, he continued in measured tones.

"The information in this file was gathered by our Intelligence. We know that you were the *sole* creator of what you term 'the super-adaptive module' - software that modifies software."

"So?" demanded Richard defiantly.

"And even though you had agreed to a partnership with Automated Services you refused to let anyone there get so much as a glimpse of your code."

"Yeah, well I've fallen into that trap before." His tone was more defensive now. He felt slightly embarrassed that his paranoia was out in the open.

"Furthermore," Johnson persisted, "you had the software encrypted and embedded into an advanced form of chip so that there would be no possibility at all of anyone ever decompiling, disassembling or otherwise interpreting the code."

"Yes," muttered Richard.

Johnson looked shrewdly at him.

"Your covert operations caused us some concern, Mr. Neilson. You see, the encryption algorithm you used was unknown to us. Revolutionary. Rather stronger than we would have considered necessary, given your requirements."

"Eh?" said Richard with no idea why his choice of encryption algorithm should be relevant to his situation.

"We don't like things that are unknown to us," continued Johnson threateningly. "And this was an algorithm that you obtained from a certain Dr. Mahmood Azis with whom you had several cosy meetings over a highly secure Internet link. We note that the packets transmitted by that link were also encrypted with a suspiciously strong key."

"Suspicious? What's so..."

"It's suspicious, Mr. Neilson," Johnson now laid down his trump card, "because Dr. Mahmood Azis is an active member of The Real Jihad."

There was a long pause. Richard felt completely winded, Johnson's words resounding in his head. Was that true? How could he have known? He had been put in touch with Dr. Azis by a trusted source – by Charlie. Had he betrayed him? But if Charlie was in touch with Dr. Azis did that mean that he was in league with terrorists? Was Charlie in fact a terrorist?

"Your involvement with Dr. Azis," concluded Johnson, "means that you are an enemy entity and will be detained here until further notice".

Richard mouthed wordlessly. His throat was dry and he was trembling. He closed his eyes desperately trying to master himself. Then finally he looked back at Agent Johnson, almost gasping for breath.

"Could I... Would you... Please... M-may I have a glass of water. Please."

Johnson said nothing for a moment. Then he stood up and gestured to the two men still at the door.

"Water will come later, Mr. Neilson, when you've had time to consider your position."

The two men took hold of Richard's arms and led him back down the corridors to his cell.

Richard knelt on the padded floor of his cell, panic coursing through him. Think, he told himself, looking around in vain for a means of escape. So these people thought he was engaged in terrorist activity because of his software. Or was it because he had encrypted it? Or was it solely because of his conversations with Dr. Azis? But Charlie knew Azis. And Charlie was a friend. Wasn't he? At least he had been at the time. But William Barber himself had also recommended Dr. Azis. In a state of confused anxiety, Richard had no idea who he could trust. He supposed that the best course of action would be to tell Agent Johnson everything he knew. But perhaps he could get away with not mentioning Charlie. He was quite sure that Charlie was no terrorist and there was no point in getting him involved.

What seemed like days later, the door to the cell opened again and in walked two guards. They said nothing but stood by the door looking at Richard expectantly. Richard got up tentatively and walked towards the guards. They grabbed him and led him down the corridors back to the interrogation room. He had no idea how much time had actually gone by since he had last been there but he had spent it all sitting around in his barren cell with only his thoughts for company. He heard the jangle of keys and next moment he was being pushed through the door into the room. The guards followed him in and led him to one of the chairs by the table, again so that his back was to the entrance. Then they retreated to the door to stand guard. So here he was again. What wild accusations would be thrown at him this time? Well, he had already resolved to tell Agent Johnson everything he knew, from the symposium all the way to building the chip. He only feared that he might be making matters worse for himself by admitting anything at all.

His thoughts were called to a halt when the door opened again and in walked Johnson, once more carrying the file labelled "Subject X". He placed the file on the table where it remained closed, the now familiar logo upturned. Johnson stood gazing at Richard for a moment. Then pulled out the chair and sat down.

"Mr. Neilson," he said genially. "I hope you've had a good rest".

Richard stared at him. Did he think this was a holiday camp?

"Perhaps," continued Johnson, "you're now ready to co-operative with us?"

He smiled. Richard felt deeply uncomfortable by this. He knew it could not indicate anything pleasant.

"I'll tell you everything," he said meekly, his eyes on the table. "About how I conceived the idea of the adaptive algorithm, about how I built it into the chip, how I encrypted it..."

"Mr. Neilson," said Johnson gravely, "We already know all of that. What we need to know now is how to activate the self-destruct."

"I don't tend to build computer programs that self-destruct."

Richard closed his eyes and sighed. Already his plan was fading away.

"Sir," he began, hoping that unashamed respect would work in his favour, "I only know about the SAM chip. I don't know anything about those mechanoids. I was involved in making only the *toy* robots but all I did was make the SAM chip".

Johnson said nothing but continued to look fixedly at Richard. Richard pondered for a moment wondering if he could possibly avoid implicating anyone else. But a voice nagged inside him: the *whole* truth!

"If you need to know about any other aspect," he continued still more nervously, "I suggest you speak to Charlie."

Johnson raised his eyebrows with interest.

"Charlie?" he enquired.

"Charles Cassidy," confirmed Richard with a deep sigh. "He works at Automated Services. He masterminded the project to build the toy robots. And…" Richard hesitated again. But then he plunged resignedly on. "And he was the one who put me in touch with Dr. Azis."

He glanced up at Johnson who was still looking piercingly at him.

"We're aware of the Cassidy connection," said Johnson. "We had him in custody not long ago but chose to let him go."

"Why?" demanded Richard stunned. If Charlie was in touch with terrorists then why had he been allowed to go free while Richard, innocent as he was, had to continue to endure this detention?

"He co-operated with us," replied Johnson. "Something you are yet to do. Mr. Cassidy described to us the automatons' control module, the communications array - and the self-destruct mechanism."

Richard continued to look aghast at Johnson who pressed home his advantage.

"Oh yes, Mr. Neilson, we know that there *is* a self-destruct - and that your SAM chip has disabled it."

Richard realised it was time for some outside help. He could see no way out of his situation without it. He was trying to co-operate but he really did not have the information that Johnson was looking for.

"Could I make a phone call please?" he asked.

Johnson paused before responding.

"No, Mr. Neilson, you may not."

"What? I-I need to speak to a solicitor. Listen, I still have rights, you know," exclaimed Richard in indignation.

Again Johnson paused before responding.

"No, Mr. Neilson, you do not. You forfeit those when you turned against your country."

Richard ran his hand through his hair, frantic with worry. Dark thoughts of miscarriages of justice rose in his head. He had visions of being held here unjustly for the rest of his life. Was this place another Guantanamo Bay? And did anyone on the outside even know where he was?

"Perhaps," offered Johnson, "it would help if I were to tell you something about us. I'll tell you who we are - then you can tell us who you are."

Richard did not know what more to say about himself. These people, whoever they were, seemed to know everything and more about him already. But he was very keen to learn something about his captors.

"So," proceeded Johnson, "Who are we? You are in the custody of

Delta Guard, a top-secret government agency set up in the wake of September 11th. Our task, in a nutshell, is to wage war on terrorism – to use Intelligence to identify and seize enemy entities and to extract from them as much information as required to rout out all members of their organisations. We are authorised to use *extreme measures* to achieve our goals." He spoke especially clearly for this last statement.

Richard's heart sank, if possible, even further than it had done up to now. Johnson went on in a more amiable tone.

"So, I've told you briefly who we are. You now know that I work for the safety of my country; I *exist* to serve my country. But you... Well, why don't you tell us who you are? Which organisation do you belong to?"

"I don't belong to any organisation," Richard pleaded.

"Mr. Neilson, we have identified you as a terrorist threat. We know you've been working with terrorists. We've tracked your movements, we've intercepted your communications. We know you are controlling those machines."

"You're wrong," interjected Richard.

"Our Intelligence has indicated that the SAM code was modified after its installation. The program now running in the machines is not the one that was officially released. The only people with the appropriate access to make such a modification are you and your terrorist cohorts."

"Perhaps your Intelligence," spat Richard, his desperation turning quickly to anger, "failed to inform you that my own son was attacked by one of those machines."

"A clever ruse," responded Johnson quietly. "Turn the weapon on those you love so as to throw us off the scent. I might have been more taken in if your son had actually been harmed. But somehow, inexplicably, he managed to get away without so much as a scratch. Very fortunate, don't you think?"

"Listen, I don't know why that one suddenly died. I honestly don't know anything about any of those machines. All I did was design the adaptive module. It was intended for business systems. The toy robots were an accidental development, an unexpected use of my idea. But I never agreed to have it installed in any security robots, I'm not controlling any security robots and I certainly haven't ordered any attacks. I want them off the streets just as much as everyone else. Besides, the one that attacked my son didn't even have a SAM chip installed so how can I be responsible?"

Johnson paused again. Then went on.

"Mr. Neilson, we know you're a smart man - an evil genius, you might say - but perhaps you fail to understand the severity of the threat on our streets. Perhaps you were just a pawn in the plot to seize control of London. Perhaps you have no idea what's next in the grand plan. Then again, perhaps you are the mastermind."

"It's nothing to do with me," yelled Richard who without thinking had sprung to his feet.

In an instant, the guards had moved from the door and had pinned Richard's arms behind his back. He continued to shout and struggle but could not free himself. Johnson was also standing up now but in contrast sounded coldly calm.

"You want to learn to relax, Mr. Neilson. You don't want your temper to get the better of you. It might get you into trouble."

Richard could not imagine how much more trouble he could possibly get into but he refrained from responding. The guards released him but continued to stand on either side of him. Richard slipped back into the chair.

"So," said Johnson sinking back into his own seat and proceeding as if nothing untoward had just occurred. "Tell us about your organisation. What are your objectives? What is it you want?"

Richard buried his head in his hands. He was tired, he was hungry and he was beyond his wits with fear.

"I just want to go home," he said weakly.

Johnson nodded slowly.

"Ah. Unfortunately, Mr. Neilson, it seems very unlikely to me that you will ever be seeing home again. In my book, terrorists don't deserve to live."

Richard looked into the cold, pitiless eyes, his breathing shallow, his voice hoarse with dread.

"I- you- you can't hold me more than... Not without charge. Not... You have to let me go. You know you do."

Johnson smiled a terrible smile.

"This is Delta Guard, Mr. Neilson. We can hold you without charge for as long as it takes. After an initial three month period, we simply renew our claim on you and hold you for another three months. Then after that time we renew again for another three months. And another, and another, and another. You see, we don't ever have to let you go if we think the security of our country is in danger."

"But- but I- but I'm innocent," Richard's words could hardly come out. "I swear I don't know... I swear I don't know…"

"People are dying out there!" shouted Johnson. Then he continued in his normal cold voice. "Of course, in reality we never keep anyone for very long. Somehow they always end up having an unfortunate accident, if you know what I mean."

He paused for effect. It was quite clear to Richard what he meant. It was time for a new tactic.

"I refuse to say another word until I have a solicitor present," he said more boldly than he felt.

"What's the name of your organisation?" asked Johnson as if testing the new waters. Richard remained silent. "What are your objectives?" Again silence. "How do we neutralise your threat?"

The two men glared at each other in silence for a whole minute. Then Johnson stood up abruptly.

"Well, we'll see about this. I think it's time we tried some more, er, persuasive techniques to extract from you the information we require."

He signalled to the guards, who grabbed Richard's arms again and pulled him to his feet. They then left the room, dragging him back through the corridors. They did not take him back to his cell but walked right past it to another room at the end of the corridor. The door to this bore the usual logo. Despite his terror, Richard was now able to surmise that this was a Greek delta sign circumscribing a capital G. Undoubtedly this symbolised Delta Guard. The guards opened the door and pushed Richard inside. Then they withdrew from the room, locking the door behind them.

This room was also completely white and contained just one wooden chair. However, standing at the other side of the room was the massive form of a man. His shaven head, scarred face and enormous tattooed arms all combined to spell menace. The man stood with his arms folded looking at Richard. He nodded to the chair and Richard moved towards it obediently. He sat down and waited, his head bent towards the floor. For a long time nobody said anything. Then finally the man broke the silence.

"How do we get rid of your monsters?" he demanded.

Richard looked up at the man incredulously. Not only were his words banal but also his voice was ludicrously high-pitched, not at all the deep rumbling roar he had expected. The man continued to stand threateningly where he was, his arms still folded.

"How do we get rid of your monsters?" he asked again in the same outrageous tone.

This time, Richard let out a short laugh. He simply could not help himself; after the extreme tension he had been suffering, this man's voice just seemed too ridiculous for words. He knew at once, however, that laughing was not a wise idea. The man gave an awful grin revealing several missing teeth. Then his face returned to normal. He dropped his arms and began to walk towards Richard.

"Perhaps," he squeaked as he advanced, "you are unaware of the gravity of your situation. Perhaps I should remind you why you are here."

Richard got out of the chair and started backing away. He did not want to be within striking distance of this dangerous-looking beast. But too late. Without further warning the man grabbed him and slammed him against the wall, pinning him there, feet off the floor.

Richard, yelling in alarm and fear, struggled in vain to free himself from the man but it was no good. Next moment he saw the floor hurtling up towards him as the man threw him violently down. He lay inert for a moment. Nothing seemed to be damaged but his left elbow was now throbbing with pain having made hard contact with the floor. Frozen with dread he continued to lie still not knowing what to do. But the man was coming towards him again. Richard sprang up and picked up the chair, holding it up in front of him like a lion tamer. The man laughed and continued towards Richard. He took hold of the chair, yanked it out of his grasp with total ease and hurled it across the room. Still laughing he bore down on Richard. With all his might Richard lashed out to punch the man hard in the testicles. But the man was ready for him. He deflected the punch and in one movement locked Richard's arm behind his back. At the same time the man's other arm came round Richard's throat into a suffocating strangle hold. Richard could feel his arm being torn out of its socket. He could not move at all. He could not breathe. Death was fast approaching. He was helpless.

Then just as all seemed lost the door opened and in walked Agent Johnson accompanied by his usual two guards who were carrying a large bucket of water between them.

"Having fun?" Johnson asked jovially.

Richard's attacker grunted and finally released him. Richard collapsed to his knees and clutched his throat coughing and gasping for breath. The other two guards now advanced on him, seized his arms and lifted him to his feet.

"Time for some water now, I think," said Johnson and gave the guards a nod.

They dragged Richard towards the bucket and without warning

plunged his head into it so that it was completely immersed. Richard struggled against his captors but was pinned fast, the water rapidly engulfing all his senses. He tried hopelessly to push the bucket over with his head but it was no good. Still they held him down and once again he had the awful sensation of death as his lungs began to take in water.

The guards lifted him out of the bucket. Richard took a grateful gasp of breath and immediately began coughing uncontrollably. Water was ejected from his mouth as his lungs now filled with air. He looked around in panic. These people were mad. Johnson had already implied that they kill their victims. What did they want from him? What was he supposed to tell them?

"Who are you working for?" demanded Johnson in a harsh tone. "How are you controlling the robots? How do we neutralise them?"

Without waiting for a response, the guards plunged Richard's head back into the bucket. This time he immediately began struggling to survive, thrashing against the guards who held him immovably. He could no longer hold his breath. His mind was clouding. His lungs were full of water. He was dying...

The guards again lifted him out of the bucket. For a moment Richard had no idea where he was. Then his entire body went into spasm as he was racked by a fit of painful coughing. Water poured from his mouth and he gasped noisily for life-renewing breath. His brain felt like it had turned to sponge, his lungs were burning with the pain of trying to squeeze every last drop of water out of them, and he was seized with absolute terror.

Johnson stood dispassionately over him.

"Mr. Neilson, we have very little time. People are dying. The sooner you decide to talk, the sooner this can be over with. Be aware: we have plenty of water."

He signalled to the guards who pulled Richard out of the room and finally dragged him back to his cell. He fell to the padded floor, still coughing and gasping as the door slammed closed behind him.

His whole body was trembling feverishly. His lungs and his very brain felt permanently damaged by the drowning sensation, his throat was bruised from the strangle hold, his right shoulder was strained from the arm lock and his left elbow still throbbed from hitting the floor. But it was the intense feeling of panic that was really overwhelming him. With no outside help he could see no end to his situation. He still had no idea how long he had been held captive. He had no idea even if it was day or night, his cell remained brightly lit all the time. He had not eaten or drunk anything for several days. Despite being extremely tired he knew he had no chance of sleeping, nor did he dare try.

After considerably more time Richard heard a key scrape in the lock. He scrambled to his feet and braced himself. The door opened but no guards walked in this time. Instead, a machine, some four feet high and made of white plastic, glided in carrying a tray. Richard hesitated. He recognised this as one of the service units from Automated Services. What was it doing here? He had by now developed a deep mistrust of all machines; they were after all the reason why he was in captivity. The machine bleeped and turned its domed head to face Richard. He wondered if it now contained his SAM chip.

A guard appeared in the doorway.

"Take what's on the tray then follow me," he commanded and waited for Richard to obey.

Richard picked up the tray. On it was a small plate of what looked like two tablets and a small glass of water. Richard picked up the water and drank it all in one go, such was his thirst. He looked at the tablets and turned to the guard enquiringly.

"Nutritional supplements," said the guard. "I suggest you eat them or you might just die of starvation".

The guard rather looked like he would be perfectly happy if Richard were to die of starvation. Richard took the tablets and examined them. Then he put one of them into his mouth. It was soft and chewy but completely tasteless. He swallowed it. The effect was almost instantaneous. Although his stomach still craved a proper meal he now felt strengthened, less light-headed. He ate the second tablet in the same way.

"Any chance of some more water?" he asked wishing he had saved some of it to wash down the remnants of the tablets from his mouth.

The guard sneered at him.

"That's all for today, pal. This ain't room service. Now come wi' me and don't try no funny business."

Richard followed the guard out of the cell. The service unit also followed as if programmed to keep watch over him. And Richard was not foolish enough to try any "funny business" while it was around.

They arrived back at the interrogation room and the guard showed him inside before departing with the machine. Agent Johnson was already present, sitting in his usual place by the table in the middle of the room. The other two guards were standing in their customary positions by the door. Richard moved over to the table and sat in the other chair. It was he who spoke first.

"So how come you've got some of those supposedly dangerous machines working here?" he demanded.

As was his wont, Johnson paused before answering.

"Automated Services built just six prototype service units for the domestic market. They never caught on, however: too expensive for most households and too erratic for industry. These models are not dangerous; they don't come with your demon chip.

"Then came the mechanoids, promising enhanced flexibility, greater functionality and innovative adaptability. As you know, this is the SAM-enabled model that's been running amok in our streets. We commandeered all six of the service units in an attempt at learning more about the mechanoids. We did learn enough to help us capture one of them."

"You caught one?" exclaimed Richard. "What happened?"

"It escaped," replied Johnson darkly, "after killing fifteen of my men - men with families."

Richard hung his head. This was why they were being so hard on him. No doubt everyone at Delta Guard blamed the SAM chip - and hence Richard - for the deaths of their colleagues.

"The mechanoid is no mean creation," Johnson went on. "It's extremely well equipped for our war on terrorism." He consulted the file on the table. "It has superior visual, auditory and even olfactory sensors, for sniffing out explosives. Infrared night vision, heat-seeking vision, all combined with long-distance microwave communication incorporating distributive data and software updates - each machine can update its fellows based on its own experiences. All in all, an excellent tool for gathering and sharing information! Then there's its impenetrable shell and its absolute persistence in carrying out tasks.

"Like the service units, the mechanoids are supposed to respond to voice control. A number of voice patterns, including my own, were programmed into the units. They're supposed to obey commands issued by any of those voices. However, analysis of the captured mechanoid revealed that our voice patterns had all since been deleted, presumably when we first lost communications with the machines. Now there is just one voice pattern - one unidentified voice pattern - programmed in. In other words, they will only listen to one person. Curious, isn't it?"

Richard chanced a glance at Johnson and saw a look of unmistakable hate in his face.

"Mr. Neilson," continued Johnson after a brief pause, "Last night, another man was killed by one of your machines. He was also a government agent."

Richard wanted to protest at the reference to the robots as being his but he was too horrified to speak. Johnson pressed on.

"Now, our top men have been unable to think of a single thing that will stop them. I'm sure that makes you feel very proud but let me tell you something. We will prevail. We will extract the truth from you. By the time we've finished with you, you'll be begging us to let you spill the beans." He nodded to the guards on the door, then turned ominously back to face Richard. "Mr. Larkin is so good at loosening tongues."

Richard had no idea who Mr. Larkin was but when he turned round he felt himself blanche. The guards had opened the door and walking into the room, armed with a large baton, was the massive and extremely violent man who had attacked him previously. Johnson addressed the man.

"Make sure he can still speak when you're finished. He has some information that I'm sure he'll be wishing to share with us."

He and the guards left the room leaving Richard alone with the beast. Before he could move, before he even had time to think, the man had dealt a smart blow to the back of his legs. Richard collapsed to the floor groaning in pain. There was a second blow, this time to his head, and he knew no more.

— Chapter Fifteen —

Wards and Wardens

Richard awoke with his head pounding. It had suffered some swelling and was so painful that it made him feel quite nauseous. He passed out again.

When he regained consciousness once more he felt a bit better but was far from feeling his old self. He was in bed, every part of him aching as if he had been beaten all over. Gingerly, he reached across to his bedside table but found only empty space. Looking around he realised that he was not at home like he had thought. Where he was he had no idea. Then memories started to return to him, slowly at first but then with rising apprehension. He remembered being captured by Delta Guard. He had been held by them for several days or weeks in questionable conditions and had been physically assaulted by them. He guessed he had been taken to hospital after the last attack. He looked around again. There were no windows but on the door to his room was the all too familiar Delta Guard logo. So he was still in captivity.

A clock on the wall indicated that it was just after twelve o'clock but Richard had no idea if it was midday or midnight. The fact that the lights were on was no clue as the entire building seemed to be lit brightly twenty-four hours a day. There were other beds in the ward but these were all unoccupied. He looked down at himself and realised that he was still wearing the same orange jumpsuit he had been forced to don when he first arrived. Leaning over the side of the bed he saw the slippers he had been given. He lay back onto the pillow in frustration, wondering if he would ever be set free.

"Hey, so the sleeper awakes!" A black man, fairly on in years, had entered the ward. "That was some blow to the head; you've been out nearly two weeks. I was beginning to think you were never getting up."

This man was also wearing an orange jumpsuit and slippers. Richard tried to sit up but it made his head throb. He lay back down and looked at the man.

"Who are you?" he asked him. "Are you a prisoner too?"

"Well, I ain't the Pope." He had a wheezing sort of voice, as if his lungs were permanently congested. "I'm your partner in crime. A real dangerous terrorist."

The man wandered over to his own bed and sat upon it. Richard did not know what to say to him. Was he really a terrorist or had he also been framed?

"Just been on my night-time stroll," said the man. "Doctor's orders. Helps to clear the lungs, he says. That's all he knows!" He snorted with derision.

"Are you really a terrorist?" Richard blurted out. "Because I'm not. I've been accused of something I didn't do."

"Course you're a terrorist. We're all terrorists. You must've done something. Why, a terrorist is just someone who scares the government. We all do that to some degree. You must just have overstepped the mark."

Richard had no idea what to make of this and simply stared blankly. The man, presumably seeing his concern, proceeded in more solemn tones.

"I'm only here because they wanted to take me out of circulation," he said. "I was going to sue their butts for a near fatal accident they caused me. But to do that would have exposed their existence. See, I used to be a contract heating engineer and one day I was working in the plant room of this very building. Well, it ain't no ordinary plant room; they've got some weird and dangerous machines in there. I don't know what they're for, I don't ask too many questions. Anyway, the idiotic guard who's watching my every move decides to light up a cigarette - right there in the plant room. I couldn't believe it! Have you any idea how much flammable gas can be discharged around machines like that? If one of them goes up, that bang would make Vesuvius look like a mere squib. So I yell at him to put out his cigarette. But what does he do? He blows smoke in my face. How d'you like that! Next thing I know the fire suppressants have come on and I'm choking to death. The only way out was at the far end of the room. I nearly didn't make it, you know. Turned out that I had an allergy to the particular gas they were using. It damaged my lungs quite badly."

"What happened?"

"I spent the next three months in hospital on a respirator. Meanwhile, some heavies from the government came to see me and started quoting the Official Secrets Act. They had forced me to sign that before working for them, see. They offered me some miserly compensation but I told them to stick it and that I'd see them in court. Next thing I know I'm accused of some vague activity – trying to overthrow the government or some nonsense – and am transferred here as an 'enemy entity'. Ha!"

"But- but what about a trial? They've got to give you a trial."

"A trial? Ha!" The man's mirthless laugh gave way to a fit of asthmatic coughing. It was unpleasant to witness. Eventually he composed himself but continued to chuckle. "Military Intelligence try people? Ha! It's against the public interest, isn't it? Too many secrets to protect, aren't there? Trial indeed! Everyone on the outside already believes you're guilty and trial or not, they ain't gonna change their minds. No smoke without fire is what they say. As for the people on the inside, everyone's guilty as far as they're concerned. And after a few weeks of psychological torture, you yourself will be confessing your own guilt. Yes sir, and given enough conditioning you'll even begin to believe it. I've seen many a man perish at his own hand, racked by his own innocent guilt."

A chill ran down Richard's spine.

"Where are all the other inmates?" he asked, trying to keep his voice steady.

"Ha! They're all dead, aren't they? No one survives here for long.

A few weeks. A few months if you're unlucky. They're either driven to insanity and top themselves or else they suffer a nasty accident. No one escapes. For now, it's just me and thee. But mark my words, boy, the week will outlive the both of us. Ah, you thought that state executions were a thing of the past? I'm telling you they're still happening, boy. They're still happening."

Richard was not happy about having to share a ward with this harbinger of doom. Fighting against the pain in his head he swung out of the bed and put on his slippers.

"Where're you going?" asked the man in surprise.

"Out," replied Richard tersely.

"You don't want to go out right now. The wardens won't be best pleased."

"*You've* just been on a night-time stroll. You said so yourself."

"Aye. But that's doctor's orders and I'm back now. There'll be a warden in here in seconds."

Richard was not impressed. He stood up to leave but his head spun and he collapsed back onto the bed.

"You ain't strong enough yet," said the man. "But you will be in a few more days and by then I'll have completed my plan of escape."

"I thought you said there was no way out of here?"

"I don't know anyone who's managed it but I have a head start over most; those night-time strolls may not be doing my lungs any good but they sure give me some ideas. Now hush! See the time? There'll be a warden round in here any second. Regular as clockwork, they are."

Sure enough, no sooner had he finished speaking than a service unit glided into the ward. Richard watched it. Could this machine really be the warden? He looked at the other man questioningly. Yes, he nodded back. The machine took up a position in the centre of the room, where it remained until dawn.

Richard felt much better the following day although his head still throbbed every time he moved. He managed to get up and wander round the ward without feeling dizzy and he took heart from that. His ward mate continued to forecast doom and despondency and Richard grew ever more determined to get out. The problem was how he would achieve this. Despite his promise of a plan Richard did not trust his companion. He thought he was slightly mad, no doubt unhinged by his apparently prolonged incarceration.

"Don't let the wardens see you walking around so easily," warned the man. "If they think you're fit and healthy, that's what they'll report and it will be back to the same old interrogations for you."

"You said you had a plan. To escape, I mean."

"Yeah, yeah, all in good time. Give me one more day, just to be absolutely sure. There's something I need to check, which I'll do tonight on my stroll."

"I'd like to get out tonight if I can." Richard was sure that the man was trying to lead him into a trap. Was he going to tell the guards to be on the alert the following day? Was he hoping for an early release if he could help to recapture an escaping prisoner?

"The plan's not cooked yet," insisted the man. "I need tonight to check on something."

"Then we can go when you get back."

"The warden will be in here too soon after I return. You saw it standing guard all night. There's no way."

Richard was not pleased but there was nothing to be done. He returned to his bed and began to think about what to do when he was out. He knew he could not return to his own home if he was to avoid being arrested all over again. There was also the question of what to do about the mechanoids. He figured that if he could somehow find a way of stopping them then he might be exonerated of his alleged crimes. He lay there deep in thought until he fell asleep.

Throughout the remainder of the day Richard slept, exercised and conversed as best he could with the other man in the ward. Neither of them had got round to learning each other's name. In spite of his suspicions, Richard was careful never to appear too energetic whenever a service unit entered the ward to check on them. He was not ready for another bout with Agent Johnson and he was certainly not ready to face the thuggish Larkin again. He found it interesting that in all the time he had been in the hospital he had not seen a human doctor at all. The only visitors were the service units and their primary purpose seemed to be one of guard duty, although they had also provided the captives with nutritional supplements.

When night came, Richard could hardly sleep at all, partly because he had slept so much during the day and partly because the lights continued to blaze brightly. He tossed and turned restlessly throughout the night. Whenever this happened at home he would get up and work on his computer until fatigue overwhelmed him. Now, however, whenever he opened his eyes all he could see was the service unit standing guard in the middle of the room. The thought of this constant watch kept him awake all the more.

Richard woke up shortly after midday having finally got to sleep round about 6am. His roommate was not around, which was unusual as he typically went on his walks only at night-time, and although Richard could not tell from the clock alone whether it was day or night he was certain that it was not so long since the man had completed his previous walk. Besides, if it had been night time he could be sure there would be a machine guarding the room. Richard felt uneasy. He may not have been convinced by the man's talk of a plan but it was the only hope he had. So where was he? Richard sprung out of bed and put on his slippers. He had no idea what he was going to do but he could not just lie there any more. He began towards the door when it opened and a service unit glided in. Not wanting to be seen out of bed, Richard made a theatrical dive to the floor, holding his head melodramatically. He crawled back to his bed groaning. The service unit bleeped.

"I'm all right," Richard told it groggily. "Still a bit dizzy."

The machine bleeped again as if it had understood. It waited a while then turned to go.

"Hey wait," Richard called after it. "Where's... Where's the other chap? Is he okay?"

The machine bleeped in a nondescript manner and left. What did that mean? Was that a good bleep or a bad bleep?

It was 9:40 in the evening by the time Richard saw the other man again. He staggered into the ward and collapsed onto his bed.

"What- what's happened?" asked Richard anxiously.

"It's all right, it's all right," said the man wearily. "Just give me a moment to catch my breath."

The man lay wheezing for a few minutes before recovering from what had clearly been an ordeal.

"Went to check on the finishing touches to the plan," he grinned. "Ran into some old friends. They wanted to have a chat."

"You were interrogated?" Richard seemed far more shocked than the man did. "But- but what happened? Did they... Are you okay?"

"I'm fine. Now relax, I need to tell you the plan. Let's get you out of here."

"But you're coming too, aren't you?"

The man shook his head.

"Not any more, not tonight, no way. I'd only slow you down and we'd both get caught and both get shot. Now do you want to hear the plan or not?"

Richard considered this for a moment then nodded. The man sat up on his bed, still wheezing slightly.

"There's just one chance you've got to escape. It's a long shot but it might just work. See that clock on the wall? I happen to know it's correct. Now, everything here runs with military precision. So in less than fifteen minutes, at 10pm, one of those service robots will come in here to check on us. It won't stay for long but you've got to let it see you otherwise it'll raise the alarm. When it's gone you'll have less than two hours to navigate your way out of this building. This place is a lot bigger than you may think. It's massive! So finding your way around can be tricky and if you get caught, you're dead.

"Now, you'll need to find the plant room. It's in the south wing, which is a fair old trek away. Turn right out of here and follow the signs. You want corridor S5. Once you find that, the plant room's easy to recognise; there's a great big 'danger of death' notice on the door. Once inside, follow the big pipe in the middle until you get to a wall. Then look around for the fire exit. I know there is one now because they were forced to install it after my incident. I don't know if it will trigger the fire alarm when opened so be careful.

"When you get outside you want to look for a white truck. At exactly midnight, it will set off to pick up some supplies. It's usually only gone for less than an hour so it doesn't travel far but it will be enough to get you off the premises. You'll need to hide in the back of the truck - you might need to break in. Once you're sure you're clear of the gates don't leave it too long before jumping out. You don't want to get caught still in there when they come to load up with supplies."

Richard eyed the man with suspicion.

"How do you know all this?"

"Trust me, I know. Be ready; the service bot will be on its way. And don't forget to get rid of that orange suit. You're way too conspicuous."

"Come with me. I'll help you along."

"Don't you worry about me, son. I'll be on the next bus. Now be silent or you'll be found out even before you've started."

Richard lay still, unsure how much he should believe. Then at precisely ten o'clock the door opened and a service unit came in to do its inspection. It stayed for longer than normal, hovering by the other man, bleeping. As time ticked by, Richard began to think that it had begun its all-night vigil early. However, at ten past ten it glided back through the door and was gone. Immediately, Richard swung his legs out of the bed and put on the slippers.

"Wait a few more minutes," warned the man. "Make sure it's really gone."

Richard was too nervous to argue. He stood there hopping on the spot for what seemed like an eternity. Finally, the man sent him on his way.

"You should be all right now," he said with a wink.

"Sure you won't come with me?" asked Richard, knowing the answer.

"Be safe," said the man. "Now get out of here."

Richard crept along the corridors trying to keep as quiet as possible. For once he was pleased that he only had slippers on his feet as these deadened his steps on the hard floor. According to a sign on the wall he was entering corridor W16. He looked along it in front and behind. It was deserted. He chanced a glance up at the ceiling to make sure there were no cameras surveying his every move. He saw no cameras but on every ceiling tile there was some sort of device that looked a little like a sprinkler. He wondered if, following the accident with the man, Delta Guard had chosen to err on the side of caution with fire prevention and install far more sprinklers than was necessary. Perhaps they had also installed more emergency exits that he could use.

As he continued his journey, turning corners here and there, he became slightly unnerved by the fact that his progress had been totally unimpeded. Everything had so far been too easy. Undoubtedly, the real challenge was going to be actually getting out of the building and off site within the time available. He had not been able to retrieve any of his possessions so he did not know how much time was left. He also had no idea how the man could possibly know as much as he seemed to. He may even have been a spy working for Delta Guard and was trying to lure him to his death, although he could not see how his death would be beneficial to them if they really believed that he alone had the power to bring the mechanoids under control. One thing was for sure: if he had stayed where he was, then he would never again see the light of day.

The sound of footsteps made him start. They were coming from ahead of him round a corner. In panic, he turned round and ran as fast as he could in the opposite direction. There was a turning up ahead but there was no way he would get there in time before whoever it was came round the corner and spotted him. There were doors on either side of him but he dared not try any of them in case something murderous lay in wait on the other side. Instead, he charged on ahead, running for his life, as the footsteps grew steadily louder. He had almost reached the turning when a voice rang out, gripping him with fear.

"Stop," it shouted from behind him.

Automatically, Richard hesitated and looked round. There was no one there.

"Come back here," said the voice again.

Confused, Richard continued on his way cautiously, still looking behind him. Then he heard a bleeping sound and a service robot glided across the end of the corridor towards the source of the voice. The man who had shouted began to issue instructions to the machine in much quieter tones. Evidently, he had not been calling after Richard at all. Nonetheless, Richard knew that he needed to get away from the vicinity as quickly as possible. Panting with relief he continued running until at last he reached the turning. A few yards along this stretch he came to a halt and leaned with his back against a wall, fighting for breath and clutching a stitch in his side. But he knew he had no time to rest. Forcing himself to persevere, he dragged himself along the corridor. He would have to find his goal via a different route.

The minutes ticked away and he meandered on unhindered. After several more junctions he paused, trying to get his bearings. And then he saw it, along the corridor to his right. He hurried along here and his exhaustion turned instantly to excitement. There before him was a door bearing the standard Delta Guard logo. And beneath the logo was a large red sign: KEEP OUT – DANGER OF DEATH. There was nothing to indicate that he was in corridor S5 but this had to be it. This had to be the plant room. There was a card reader next to the door and this did not fill him with much hope for easy access. He nevertheless seized the doorknob and turned it. The door was definitely locked. Now what? With mounting urgency, he threw himself at the door achieving nothing but a bruised shoulder. Then he heard bleeping again, this time from right beside him. Heart plummeting to the floor, he turned to see a service unit just inches from him. He knew all was lost. If he ran now, the machine would undoubtedly raise the alarm and he would be doomed. Yet if he stayed where he was...

"I need to get into this room," he told the robot, acting on inspiration.

The machine merely bleeped and remained stationary. Then with an awful thrill Richard heard more footsteps and voices approaching from round the corner.

"Please," he said in rising panic to the machine, "I need to get in there immediately."

Again the machine merely bleeped. The footsteps and the voices were much closer now. Richard knew he had no chance of escape.

"Please," he gasped in desperation. "Just open the door, will you? Let me in."

This time the machine bleeped differently and moved towards the door. It produced a security card from a hatch on its front and held it against the card reader. There was a click and the diode on the reader flashed green. Richard flung open the door and threw himself inside. Then he impulsively turned back to the machine.

"Thanks," he said and deftly snatched the card from its artificial hand before slamming the door shut.

He was now in a dimly lit room and stood irresolute for a moment, hoping against hope that the guards had not heard him. He was temporarily blinded by the new gloom, his eyes having acclimatised to the harsh lights elsewhere in the building. He blinked a few times and looked around him.

There were no pockets in the jumpsuit he was wearing so he slid the card into one of his slippers. It was bound to come in useful. "Follow the big pipe", the man had said in the hospital. There were no pipes that Richard could see but he was only in a small storage room. Stacks of boxes lay before him all labelled TOP SECRET. A tall ladder fastened to the wall led to an upstairs compartment. Perhaps that's where all the pipes were. He moved towards it and began to ascend. Up he went, higher and higher. It was a long climb. When he finally reached the upper level he stopped dead as a fresh wave of cold dread washed over him. Even in the subdued lighting it became quite clear that this was not the plant room. Stretching ahead of him for what seemed like miles were rows and rows of mechanoids. There were thousands of them, perhaps tens of thousands. They were all inert, as if they had not yet been activated.

Richard stood rooted to the spot. In his anxiety he thought he could see some of the machines moving towards him but he heard nothing. He wondered just how big this building was to house so many robots in just one room. He also wondered how many others were situated elsewhere, perhaps in other parts of the country. In that moment he realised that the machines patrolling the streets of London were nothing but the advance scouts preparing the way for a massive invading force. But what were they doing here? From what Agent Johnson had said, only the service units were resident at Delta Guard, and there were only six of those. He had also said that one of the mechanoids had killed fifteen of his men to escape capture. Did he know about this storage facility?

Richard came to himself, remembering that his mission was time-based. Although he no longer had his watch he was sure that midnight was fast approaching. He had spent a significant amount of time wandering the corridors before he had found this place. And this still was not the room he had been looking for. Abruptly, he turned round to descend the steps, then dithered. How could he be sure that the service unit would not still be outside? Perhaps it had already raised the alarm and hundreds of armed guards were swarming in on the place. He turned back to face the mechanoids. Maybe that blow to his head had affected his judgement but he supposed that proceeding further into this room was safer than going back. Where it would lead him he had no idea. Blindly following his instincts, he advanced.

He could almost sense the robots watching him as he got closer but on he walked. They were packed fairly close together so it was difficult to manoeuvre but he managed to squeeze through the first row, then the second, then the third. It was hard going. Some machines were closer together than others so he sometimes had to walk along a row of them before finding a suitable gap. Some of the rows themselves were too close to the row in front so he frequently had to double back to find an alternative gap. The effort was eating into his valuable time.

After what seemed like half an hour he emerged behind the final row of mechanoids. There was a significant gap between him and the back wall, allowing him to scan for a new way out. His heart leapt as he saw a sign: LOADING BAY – KEEP CLEAR. He hurried over towards it. Like the walls, it looked to be made of thick concrete, no doubt reinforced. This too had a card reader next to it. Bending down, he retrieved the card from his slipper and waved it in front of the reader. Nothing happened. He tried again and again but the bay door remained firmly shut. The card had probably been deactivated, in which case the security guards must be aware that it had been stolen. Or maybe it was never meant to work on this particular door.

He put the card back into his slipper and began to look for another way out. His eyes fell on a sign a foot or so away from the card reader: "To open in emergency break glass and pull handle". Beneath this was a glass panel. There was no hammer provided to break the glass. He looked around for a suitable substitute but found nothing. Gritting his teeth he moved close to the panel and struck his elbow sharply at its centre. The glass shattered into a million blunt pieces. The noise seemed amplified in the silence and Richard was sure it would betray his position. The last pieces of glass settled and silence reigned once more. Breathing heavily, Richard reached into the cavity and pulled the handle.

Instantly, a loud siren rent the air as the door slowly began to lift. Richard swore loudly to himself in terror. Emergency lighting came on automatically, bathing the room in a soft glow. A recorded voice boomed out,

"Emergency! All personnel must evacuate the area immediately!"

And to his horror, the mechanoids began to wake up. As one they turned to face the door and advanced. The rhythmic beating of thousands of metal footsteps competed with the din from the siren. Without hesitation, Richard dropped to the floor and rolled through the gap beneath the rising door. For the first time in a long time, he was out in the open. But there was no time to enjoy it. Armed guards were already running towards the area in response to the siren. Richard found what he was looking for. Parked right outside, almost as if by arrangement, was a large white truck. He slid beneath it to hide as guards poured in towards the mechanoid storage chamber. Some of them carried handheld devices covered in buttons and sliders. They appeared to be using these to subdue the advancing mechanoids.

A different commotion had broken out further away. Richard could not see exactly what was going on but from what he could hear, more armed guards had detained someone.

"I found him wandering the premises alone."

"He must have been the one to set off the alarm."

"I told you, I was just having my night-time stroll. The doctor says it will help my lungs."

Richard recognised that wheezy voice. It was the man from the hospital who had given him his escape plan.

"Looked to me like you were trying to make a bid for freedom."

"No sir, not at all. I was..."

"And you nearly wrecked everything in the process."

"You've already been caught once earlier today wandering alone," said a chilling high-pitched voice that Richard also recognised. "I'm afraid we can't afford any more risks."

"Wait, what are you doing?" The man from the hospital suddenly sounded scared.

"Finish it," squeaked Larkin.

There was the sound of automatic gunfire, a strangled scream and a dull thud.

"Now remove this filth," commanded Larkin, sounding revolted.

Richard heard something being dragged as the guards' footsteps moved away. At the same time he heard the thump of the concrete door as it closed. The security personnel must have got the mechanoids under control. Did this mean that Delta Guard themselves were in fact controlling the machines on the street?

"You'd better get going," said a new voice. "You'll be late for the next consignment."

"Yep, I'm all ready to rock," said another. "I'll see you shortly."

Richard saw one man walk away. Shortly afterwards, he heard the driver's door to the truck open and slam shut. Then the engine started. It was now or never. He crawled out from beneath the truck, darted to the back of it and pushed up the rear door. As luck would have it, this was not locked. He threw himself inside just as the truck had begun to move, then reached up and pulled down the door. There were some restraining straps in the back of the truck, which he held onto tightly to stop himself being thrown around. His head throbbed and his mind teemed with thoughts as the truck drove him away to safety.

— Chapter Sixteen —

The Fugitive

The truck continued its bumpy ride to nowhere. Richard shook his head as if to free it from the thoughts that were clouding his judgement. It was pounding painfully again but he had to concentrate. He had to leave the truck before it was too late. His plan was to remain for just two minutes but because he no longer had his watch he would count backwards to himself to help time the escape.

"One hundred, ninety-nine, ninety-eight, ninety-seven..."

He only hoped that when he got to zero the truck would stop. But supposing it didn't? What then? Supposing it journeyed on relentlessly until ready to be loaded up with whatever it was? If he was caught... His ward mate had not fared well after straying out of bounds.

Richard rebuked himself and forced his mind back to his countdown. He could not remember where he had got to.

"Er, seventy-nine, seventy-eight, seventy-seven..."

His mind began to wander again. He had no money with him. How would he get back home? Would it be safe to return home? Probably not. That would be the first place they would look. But there were things he definitely needed to retrieve from there; quite aside from his laptop, which contained all his software and data, he believed he had some rarely used credit cards lying in one of his drawers. Perhaps they were even still in date and could tide him over until he was able to sort out his life.

"Damn it! Um. I don't know – fifty, forty-nine, forty..."

The truck was no longer moving. Richard could not be totally sure that he was clear of the Delta Guard compound but this was the first stop the truck had made and despite his intermittent countdown he thought he had already been travelling for quite long enough. Desperately hoping for the best he pulled up the rear door and looked into the gloom outside. From what he could see it was deserted and in the middle of nowhere. He had no idea how he would proceed if he got out right here but after a moment's deliberation he recognised that there might not be another opportunity and he had to take his chances. But he had pondered too long. Just as he had made up his mind what to do, the truck started moving again.

"Go for it," said a voice in his head, "You can still do it."

But before he was able to begin, the ground was moving too fast. Richard cursed himself. He could not afford to be hesitant. He gazed despondently outside for a while allowing the night air to cool his head. A pair of headlights appeared some distance away. He had not considered other traffic; he would have to be extra careful when getting out not to jump into the path of an oncoming vehicle. The car behind seemed to be moving very rapidly; it was catching up quite fast. Richard figured that it might look rather suspicious to the approaching driver to see a man dressed in orange overalls travelling in the back of an open truck at the dead of night. He was about to close the door again when he was suddenly dazzled by the car's high beam and blue flashing lights.

Richard swore several times in quick succession. He was caught. The car's siren reverberated in the back of the truck, which began to slow down and pull over. There was no time for further delay. Before the truck had even come to rest Richard threw himself out of it and rolled painfully to the side of the road. Ignoring the feeling that he had broken his ribs, he got up and crashed through the bushes at the roadside. But there really was nowhere to go. Beyond, there were only open fields where he would be tracked down in no time. Squatting down as low as he could he waited, frantically hoping that the night would occlude even the bright colours he was wearing.

The police car had stopped behind the truck some fifty yards ahead and two policemen had got out. One was speaking to the truck driver, the other was searching the bushes with a torch. It would not be long before Richard was back in custody. Unless...

The policemen had both left their doors open. A harebrained thought occurred to Richard. If he could possibly sprint to the car and drive off before either of them could get back to it then maybe he might just have a chance. He knew it was an absurd idea; the policemen were much closer to the car than he was. But if he stayed where he was he was doomed.

The policeman searching the bushes seemed to be making heavy weather of what he was doing. A quick flash of his torch up and down would instantly reveal Richard's whereabouts but he seemed to prefer to get close to them and have a good look around. Could it be that Richard was not their quarry after all? Was it possible that they were looking for something completely different? Or was Richard simply underestimating the enveloping power of the night?

He had to seize the moment. Heart in his mouth, Richard crashed back through the bushes and made a daring bid for the car. It seemed to take an age before anyone of the others registered what was going on. They were all looking at him, an orange streak hurtling towards them, but none appeared to know what was really happening. Then,

"Oi!" The policeman with the torch had sparked into life and was now giving chase. In response, both the other policeman and the truck driver also began to converge on Richard. Keep going, keep going, keep going. Richard urged himself forward and flung himself into the driver's seat. He slammed and locked the door just in time. The truck driver had arrived and was tugging on it violently. Richard had no time to reach over and close the other door. The policeman with the torch had caught up with him and was about to climb aboard when Richard engaged reverse gear and shot backwards. The passenger door collided with the policeman knocking him to the ground. Unremorseful, Richard crunched the gear stick into first and sped away, the passenger door now striking the back of the truck and swinging closed.

Richard drove flat out, still gripped by panic and not knowing where he was or where he was going. After some minutes, however, he realised that no one was following him and he slowed to a stop to collect his thoughts. His heart thumped almost painfully in his chest and he took long, steady breaths to help calm himself down. He became aware that the car's blue lights were still flashing although the siren was silent. His eyes roamed the dashboard and found the switch to neutralise the beacon. He caught a glimpse of his reflection in the car's rear view mirror. He looked a mess; his hair was matted, he had a tangle of facial hair, his eyes were bloodshot and there was a tell-tale bruise on his forehead, still fresh after all this time, where Larkin had attacked him. He rubbed it gently. It still hurt somewhat and still caused him painful headaches.

Continuing to examine the car, Richard took in the details on its multifunction display. The outside temperature was only 2C. He adjusted the heating, only just realising how very cold he was, his overalls being no match for the winter's chill. The clock showed the time as 0022 but it was the date that really caught his attention - 25th December. It had been Christmas Day for over twenty minutes and he had not realised it. But wait a moment, if it was Christmas Day that meant he had been held captive for over a month. He could not remember everything clearly - the blow to the head had seen to that - but he was certain it was still only November when he had been captured.

Richard's stomach gave a loud rumble. As well as everything else he was beginning to feel exceptionally hungry and light-headed. He looked around to see if there happened to be anything in the car that might satisfy him for the time being but there was nothing. He opened the glove compartment to see if it might be hiding any chocolate bars. He found no sustenance but what he did find gave him even greater hope. Nestled at the back of the compartment was unmistakably a satellite navigation device, different from the one he was used to but useful all the same.

It took him only a few minutes to work out how to use the machine. He set it up in the corner of the windscreen and entered his home address. After a few more minutes a map appeared on the display showing him where he was currently – Black Boar Lane. It meant nothing to Richard. The map was accompanied by clear instructions indicating how he should proceed from here to begin his homeward journey, a distance according to the machine of some sixty-seven miles. Following the instructions directly would mean turning round and driving back towards the policemen he had just escaped from. He had no desire to do that. Instead he proceeded forward, turned an arbitrary left and waited for the navigation machine to plot a new route.

In fact, he had no intention of actually going home, that would be far too risky. His intention was to go back to the town centre and retrieve his own car, as it was also a big risk to prolong his time in the stolen police car. He hoped that he would find some kind of tool amongst the police treasures to remove the clamp from his wheel. And then, he supposed, he would have to get some different number plates so that he would not get tracked down quite so easily. That seemed to be the sort of thing that fugitives did. Or perhaps it would just be easier to go the whole way and buy another car but not register it in his name. Regardless, one thing he did remember was that there were some very expensive gifts in there for Dominic. He sincerely hoped that they had not been stolen from the back seat; he knew he would be hard pushed to find replacements.

With only the navigation device for company, Richard journeyed on. He did not encounter many other vehicles but since it was so late he was not too surprised at this. Occasionally, he would come up behind other drivers who had evidently just slowed down upon seeing the police car, no doubt assuming that their speed was being clocked. When this happened it provided Richard with some light relief but he otherwise remained in a state of heightened anxiety. His unease was made all the greater by the fact that the intercom in the car was suspiciously silent. Richard could have done with knowing what the police were up to. Were they watching him from afar?

It was one-fifteen before Richard was able to recognise where he was. The navigator indicated that he had just over a mile remaining before he was at home. Realising that he did not have his car keys with him, he decided that he would after all pop into the house to get everything he needed before going back on the run. He would get a small suitcase and gather up some clothes, toiletries, his laptop, spare keys and anything that would pass for money, such as cheque books and credit cards. After that he had no idea what he would do or where he would go.

"Approaching destination," said the device in the corner of the windscreen. Richard switched it off and replaced it in the glove compartment. He was about to get out of the car when he became aware that he had made a terrible misjudgement in coming here at all. The whole area was swarming with police cars and, looking ahead, he could see that the entrance gate to his house was cordoned off and guarded by armed police. Why he had not noticed the entourage immediately he did not know. He supposed that in his exhaustion he simply was not concentrating on his surroundings.

Richard hesitated. On the one hand he knew he could not remain where he was for a moment longer, on the other he really did need to retrieve his personal possessions. But even as he watched transfixed he saw several men dressed from head to toe in white protective suits coming out of the house carrying all his computer equipment between them, along with a box full of his CD backups. His instinct was to run after them, to pounce on them and to take back by force what was rightly his. But he knew he would be dead before he had gone ten yards. He thought it strange though; why had they not seized his possessions at the beginning of his imprisonment? Why wait until now, several weeks later?

Someone knocked on the car window and Richard's heart leapt into his mouth. He turned to see a man dressed in civilian clothes standing outside displaying an identity card. Trembling, Richard operated the window.

"Excuse me," said the man, "I spotted your outfit and was wondering if you're also with the forensic team. If so, your chaps seem to have run out of..."

The man paused and looked at Richard with great concern.

"I say, you look rather... Are you all right?"

Richard sat in stunned silence before recovering himself.

"Oh, yes. It's, er, been a long day. I've lost count of the number of cases I've been on today."

"Tell you what," said the man quietly. "You go home to rest. I'll have a word with one of your colleagues instead."

"Thanks. I'll, um, do that."

"And if you're not better in the morning take the day off and go and see your doctor. Cheerio."

Richard waved goodbye and closed the window. Then breathing a deep sigh of relief, started the engine, turned the car round and drove away unchallenged by anyone else. Somehow he had not been recognised but that encounter had been too close for comfort. He had to remind himself that he was wanted on terrorism charges, trumped up as they may be, and he could not afford to get distracted by anything else. He needed to get off the road and into hiding until his name could be cleared.

The only other place he could think of going, if only to spend the night, was Amanda's. They may have had a turbulent relationship but even she must forget their differences to help him out of this desperate situation. Indeed, perhaps she had even been worrying about him, he having been silently off the scene for so many weeks. Besides, it's Christmas, he thought, which means goodwill to all. Hang on though. Yes, it *is* Christmas. He was not too late.

He turned the police car to head towards the town centre. He would not turn up at Amanda's empty handed but would first go to his own car and retrieve the presents he had got for Dominic. He had not worked out how he would get into the car since he had no key with him. If necessary he would break in and sort out the damage later. Then he thought it might be appropriate to get a token present for Amanda and even Dave. They would be doing him a massive favour after all. But it was unlikely that he would find anything at two in the morning on Christmas Day and in any case he had no money with him.

The lights in the town centre reflected a mood of jollity that was far removed from how Richard felt. The scampering reindeer, dancing snowmen and laughing Santas seemed worlds apart from reality as he wended his way down the deserted roads. He was still several yards from The Model Shop when he realised with a horrible sinking feeling that his car was nowhere to be seen.

He was now faced with a dilemma: the obvious thing to do would be to contact the police and report his car as stolen. However, contacting the police was not a sensible option as this would doubtless result in his recapture. Besides, he now thought staring at the double yellow line where he had parked his car just before his capture, it was highly probable that the police themselves had impounded the vehicle.

He sat gloomily in the car thinking about his plight, not quite able to take everything in. He was on the run in a stolen police car; his life was under threat by Delta Guard; his house was a no-go area; he had no money, no clothes and no means of communication. Furthermore, any advisory service that could possibly help him was bound to be closed for the Christmas period. Added to all this, his stomach was aching with hunger; those tasteless nutritional supplements of Delta Guard's were beginning to seem quite appetising. And now, as if to make his misery complete, rain had started to fall.

Even in his stressful state, fatigue threatened to overwhelm

Richard. He closed his eyes and listened to the rain beating rhythmically onto the roof of the car. Almost immediately, he began to drift off into blissful sleep. But he did not rest for long. A distant siren shocked him awake and put him back on the alert. Was that the police closing in on him? He felt like an animal in the wild, in a constant state of vigilance with predators all around him. But the siren seemed to be fading away, going in the opposite direction. He could not stay here. He had to get off the streets, to lie low. Pulling himself together, he accelerated away and made haste for Amanda's house.

The neighbourhood looked very festive with each house trying to outdo the next with its display of Christmas lights. The raindrops clinging to the illuminated decorations somehow accentuated their design, giving them an almost ethereal appearance – or was it simply grotesque, Richard could not decide. He chose not to park the stolen police car immediately outside the house but instead left it some yards down the road, half-heartedly believing that this would absolve his would-be hosts from any involvement in the theft. He walked to the house, exhausted and starving, yet nervous of what reception he might get. There were no lights on inside. He rang the bell and heard the chimes resounding within. There was no answer. He rang again and again. Then just as he was beginning to worry that they might have gone away for the holidays a light flicked on through the frosted glass above the door. Shortly, the door opened and there stood Dave wearing a purple dressing gown.

"Do you know what time..." he began but broke off as he recognised the man on the doorstep, looking dishevelled and distressed. "Bloody hell! What happened to you?"

"Merry Christmas," said Richard trying to put on a brave face. "May I come in?"

"What? It's... No you ruddy well cannot come in."

Amanda appeared at the foot of the stairs.

"Who is it, darling?" she asked.

"Honey, it's me," Richard called out to her.

Amanda hurried to the door with an expression of both shock and distress.

"Richard! You're... You look awful. What's happ..."

But at that moment Richard collapsed at their feet overcome with exhaustion.

He became vaguely aware of being half carried, half dragged to the lounge, which was in darkness, and of being dropped unceremoniously onto the sofa. He tried to speak, to utter words of gratitude but it was much too much effort and he just groaned inarticulately before passing into oblivion.

It must still have been late, thought Richard, yet people seemed to be stirring. He could hear movement from outside. But surely that was outside the house. He got up and looked out of the window. He froze at what he saw. An army of mechanoids was standing inert right by the window. As soon as they detected Richard they began to march towards him. They crashed straight through the wall and bore down upon him, surrounding him. Agent Johnson stood among the robots who turned out to be the security men at Delta Guard.

"So we meet again at last," said Johnson in a strangely high-pitched voice.

He produced a machine gun from nowhere and pointed it at Richard's head. Then without warning the sound of automatic gunfire tore through the air and Richard felt his head rip apart...

Richard sat bolt upright on the sofa, gasping deeply and sweating. He felt dehydrated and his head was throbbing madly. The lights shone brightly. Too brightly. Dazzling. They were making his head feel worse. He needed some relief, a drink, now. As if in answer there was a bleeping sound to his left. He turned and saw a service unit carrying a tray bearing a glass of iced water and some nutritional supplements.

"Take what's on the tray," said Dave, "or you might just die of starvation."

"Oh, you've got one of those units as well," murmured Richard slurring his words.

"Doctor's orders. They help to clear my lungs," said his ward mate.

But the drink had turned into a whole bucket of water and there was Larkin standing over him menacingly. He grabbed Richard and plunged his head into the bucket. Richard struggled against him as the all-too-familiar drowning sensation swept over him. His lungs filled with water, his brain was immersed. He had no idea where he was or who he was...

Voices were sounding in the distance. Children's voices. In his head? No, they were right outside the door. Richard listened.

"Who is he?"

"Why does he look so scary?"

"Can we still go in and open our presents?"

"He's not staying, is he?"

Richard opened his eyes and looked around, his head still throbbing. He was lying on the sofa covered in an old blanket. A large Christmas tree, spectacularly decorated, adorned the bay window with a festoon of gifts at its foot. Its lights had evidently come on via a time switch and this may have been what had lifted Richard from the depths of his uneasy slumber. He watched them for a while as they faded, flashed and chased each other round the tree. He was quite sure that he was definitely awake this time. But now he was hearing different voices, adult voices, more distant and indistinct at first but gradually getting clearer. He could make out some of the words: "extremely dangerous", "stolen police car", "orange jumpsuit", "terrorist".

Richard shot out of bed and darted to the window. Squeezing past the Christmas tree he pulled back the curtain to look outside. To his horror, he saw a police van, a patrol car and two police bikes all parked right outside the house. None of the vehicles had any occupants and Richard interpreted this to mean that they were already inside the house.

"Do you mind if we come in and take a look," said the voice.

In a blind panic Richard tried to make good his escape through the window. It was locked. He fumbled along the window ledge frantically.

"Let there be a key," he muttered desperately. "Please let there be a key."

The voices grew louder. They were right outside the door. At last his fingers found something small and metal. He seized it, thrust it into the lock and turned it. A button in the handle popped up and he was able to swing open the window. The opening was just large enough to accommodate him as he scrambled on to the ledge. And not a moment too soon. The door to the lounge opened just as Richard dropped to safety, pulling the window as far closed behind him as he could manage. It was raining harder than ever. Not hesitating for a moment, he sprinted for his life back to the same police car he had used the previous night, praying that there would be no one guarding it.

He got to the car and swore out loud - he did not have the key. He must have dropped it when he passed out on the doorstep and Dave or Amanda must have taken custody of it. There was no way he could go back for it though, not now that the house was playing host to a posse of policemen. What he needed to do was to make as much distance between him and the house in as short a time as possible. And the only way he could think of doing that right now was to use his legs and run.

He still had had nothing to eat or drink so his energy levels were very low indeed. Only by grim determination did he manage to make any progress at all. It was perhaps fortunate that, being Christmas Day, most people were indoors so he did not draw attention to himself, dressed as he was and in this weather. After much walking and jogging Richard was soaked to the skin but he had long since left behind the housing estate and was now making progress along the main road, apparently without having been followed. He knew from previous occasions when he had dropped off Dominic that there was a taxi office somewhere round here although he could not immediately remember where it was. It was not too long, however, before he splashed to a halt outside the office door. Yet despite the notice in the window stating that they would be operating every day over Christmas, it was closed.

There were now only two things that gave Richard any hope. The first was the fact that the telephone number for the taxi firm was emblazoned across the front of the building. The second was that there was a telephone box just across the road. Taking his chances, Richard crossed over towards it. He could now only think of one final person who might be able to help him, who might agree to take him in for a while and pay for his taxi fare to get to his house. It was a risky option because it had become unclear as to where this person's loyalties now lay. But Richard could see no alternative. He examined the keypad on the telephone and dialled 0800 7383773.

"Welcome to 0800 Reverse," said a recorded voice, "Please enter the number you want to call."

Sincerely hoping that his memory was not completely screwed up Richard dialled.

"Say your name after the tone."

The tone sounded.

"Richard Neilson and I'm in deep shit."

"Please hold while we call that number."

Richard waited, listening to the ringing tone.

"Please be in, please be in," he urged.

Then at last he heard the welcome voice of Charlie.

"Richard! I thought you might call. I guess you're looking for somewhere to stay."

— Chapter Seventeen —

Delta Guard

Apart from Richard telling the taxi driver his required destination no words were spoken for the entire journey. Richard was almost catatonic as the magnitude of his situation continued to strike home. The taxi driver, on the other hand, just seemed utterly grumpy at having been called out first thing on Christmas morning. After maybe fifteen minutes the car pulled up outside a shabby looking house somewhere in Croydon.

"Thirty-six quid," said the driver brusquely.

Richard looked at him then looked towards the house. A face appeared briefly at the window. Then seconds later Charlie came scurrying down the garden path clutching a wad of bank notes. He approached the driver's side of the car while Richard got out of the passenger side.

"How much is that?" he asked, preparing to count out the notes.

"Thirty-six," said the driver in the same brusque tone as before. "Triple time, you know what I mean."

Charlie counted out four crisp ten pound notes into the driver's hand. The driver made heavy weather of finding the right change until Charlie got the message.

"Oh, keep the change," he said cheerfully. "Merry Christmas."

The driver gave him a withering look and drove off without a word.

"You're drenched," said Charlie to Richard as the rain continued to beat down onto the pair of them. "I don't know about white Christmas but it's certainly grey and miserable. Come inside and dry off."

Charlie led Richard up the path and into the house. Inside, there was no sign of Christmas: no tree, no decorations, no cards. Richard was quite glad of this because he was in no mood to have festivity foisted upon him. He began to remove his sodden slippers but Charlie checked him.

"Aw, don't worry about all that. I'm gonna have the carpets changed anyway. Eventually."

Richard removed the slippers nonetheless. They were uncomfortably wet and he had no desire to keep them on for any longer than he had to. Although the jumpsuit was perhaps even more saturated, neither he nor Charlie made any suggestion of swapping it for some warmer, drier garments. As he kicked the slippers to the side, something that had briefly stuck to his foot now fell to the floor. Richard looked at it for a moment before bending down to pick it up.

"What's that?" enquired Charlie. "It looks like a security pass. They don't give prisoners their own security pass, do they?

Richard made no response.

"It's funny," said Charlie passing to Richard a much-needed pint of water, "but you were on the telly not long ago. Well, not you exactly but they showed all this footage of men in white coats taking stuff out of your house."

Richard pondered. For how long had the forensic teams already been at his house confiscating his possessions? Had the television cameras actually been present while he himself was on the scene? How come no one there had recognised him, even close up? How come he had not yet been recaptured?

"And," Charlie continued, "oh, sorry but they showed your car being crushed as well."

"They did what?" Richard exclaimed.

"They said they had impounded it earlier for a parking offence or something but then they showed this ruddy great forklift truck come along and take it away from the pound and dump it in a crusher – with everything in it. I couldn't believe it!"

Richard could not believe it either. Quite aside from losing the car itself, this news meant that he had not only lost the gifts he had bought for Dominic, nor even that he had lost all the tools he kept in the boot but he had also lost his one remaining copy of his SAM source code - an emergency backup that he kept hidden in the car.

"Still," said Charlie, trying hard to sound unconcerned, "look on the bright side. You've made it to the top ten most wanted. They're offering a reward of 'an undisclosed amount' for information leading to your recapture. How cool's that!"

Richard looked suspiciously at Charlie and the smile slid off his face.

"It's all right, dude," said Charlie now trying to sound reassuring. "I'm not going to turn you in. I mean, what would I do with all that money?"

Richard was unconvinced. He knew that Charlie had been consorting with a terrorist and had been arrested by Agent Johnson. However, he did not want to reveal this knowledge to Charlie just yet, preferring to bide his time, to wait for Charlie to betray himself.

"So," said Charlie excitedly, "Are you ready to tell me the thrilling tale of your capture and escape?"

Richard hesitated but then realised that he could tell the story without giving away too much information. He told him about how he was arrested at gunpoint when he was doing his Christmas shopping, how he had been locked in a padded cell for weeks on end. He talked about Larkin's violent interrogation techniques and how he ended up in a hospital ward with a strange man who more or less sacrificed his own life to help him escape. Charlie was a good listener. He made all the right sounds and gestures, gasping when Richard got to the bit about the thousands upon thousands of mechanoids in the storage chamber, and letting out a low whistle when he told of his daring bid to freedom in the white truck. At the end of it, Charlie sounded awe-struck.

"That is one hell of a story!" he said.

Now that he had recited his story, however, Richard had some misgivings. In the cold light of day, his escape from a high security government compound now seemed altogether too easy. How come he had not been caught wandering through the corridors alone? Why was it that he himself had not also been shot? Charlie broke through his thoughts.

"You weren't on your own though. There was an online petition for your release. People were beginning to run scared, you see, after one of the Sunday papers printed an article about you. I've got it here somewhere."

He started rummaging through a messy pile of newspapers on the sofa. After a short while, he located the one he wanted and began turning its pages until he had found the right one. He tossed it over to Richard. Richard took it and his jaw dropped open. Right there on the page was a large picture of himself below the headline "The People the Law Forgot".

Despite widespread condemnation, dozens of people from several nations are still being illegally held at Guantanamo Bay in Cuba. Despite claims to the contrary, a number of these are British citizens. So what is our government doing to bring about their release? Nothing. In fact it's worse than nothing. Indeed, following the lead of the US, Britain now has its very own horrific equivalent of Guantanamo Bay, although the government vehemently denies this claim.

Delta Guard is a top secret government agency that has been silently removing people from the streets for over ten years. To date 42 men and 6 women have allegedly been detained by Delta Guard and none of these have been seen since their capture. The latest person to have disappeared is Richard Neilson, creator of the Super-Adaptive Module that makes Mickey the Mini-Mechanoid so adaptable. This lovable toy has given pleasure to millions of families up and down the country. However, the same chip was installed in the security robots now running amok on the streets of London. Both sets of robots were built by the same manufacturer – Automated Services – but Neilson has been made the scapegoat for the malfunctioning security machines. It has been rumoured that Neilson was unhappy about the company's use of his module in the security robots and after an angry exchange, sabotaged the software in the chip to cause the robots to malfunction. Whether he intended the resulting widespread carnage is not certain. However, any hopes of learning the truth in a fair trial disintegrated as soon as the government played the terrorism card and got Delta Guard involved. Now there are fears for Neilson's sanity and his life.

Neilson leaves behind a wife and a son. His son Dominic described him as the best dad in the world, while his wife said that although they had been living apart for some time she had never stopped loving him and deeply admired his persistent striving for perfection. In an emotional televised appeal last Tuesday, she begged the government to either charge him or to release him immediately. So far there has been no word from the government concerning how they intend to proceed.

The Prevention of Terrorism Act is one of only two acts of Parliament that allow an individual to be detained without trial (the other being the Mental Health Act). The new antiterrorism laws have allowed the government to set up taskforces that have the power to hold people in legal limbo indefinitely. What is more, the conditions under which they are held are highly questionable. It has been alleged that in order to break the prisoners' morale, the authorities use so-called enhanced techniques such as sleep deprivation, exposure to bright lights, starvation and prolonged solitary confinement. Physical beatings are also commonplace. Unsurprisingly, many prisoners commit or attempt suicide.

Enough is enough. What is the purpose of the War on Terror if the government continues to terrorise its own people? Amnesty International described Guantanamo Bay as a symbol of injustice and abuse. The same must be said of Delta Guard. Regrettably, there can be little hope of obtaining justice for the people as long as the British government continues to deny the existence of any such organisation.

Richard put down the newspaper, his mind teeming. The fact that he was reported to have "disappeared" made it seem like his arrest had been kept quiet. He had assumed that it would have been headline news given the reason behind it. That must be why they hadn't raided his house the moment he was locked up. That would have made it too high profile. And Johnson himself had said, it was highly unlikely that he would ever see home again; they had never intended to let him go. News of his escape must have flashed round the security forces in no time. Only then had they sought to take control of his possessions.

He looked up to see Charlie observing him. Charlie had a curious expression on his face, as if he found the whole thing rather exciting.

"The BBC news website also ran a poll a few days ago asking people if they thought you ought to be released," he said half smiling. "Most people thought you should be, although there was this one chap who had a compelling argument why you ought to be hanged, drawn and quartered..."

"Have you heard from Azis lately?" Richard suddenly asked, visually probing Charlie for the slightest hint of discomfort.

"Funny you should ask," replied Charlie without batting an eyelid, "because I've been trying to contact him for a few days now. I had the idea of intercepting data transfers between the mechanoids so we could work out their plans. Unfortunately, SAM has enhanced Azis' encryption software so I needed some way of decrypting the new packets."

"And?"

"Well, he seems to have cut and run. He's not been online for ages now. And I've never known him not to be online in the past."

"Maybe he's shut up shop for Christmas," suggested Richard still trying to penetrate Charlie's inmost thoughts.

"Nah," dismissed Charlie. "He's like me and never bothers with Christmas. It's the best time to get work done, when no one else is around to disturb you. Well, normally anyway." He grinned at Richard who remained stony faced.

"I'm not surprised he's incommunicado," said Richard and left it at that.

Charlie looked enquiringly at him. Richard was unable to contain himself any longer.

"Azis is a terrorist," he said dramatically. "Agent Johnson told me. He must have told you as well?"

Charlie stared at Richard for a few seconds. Then he laughed, no doubt believing this to be a sick joke.

"I'm being serious," said Richard icily. "What did Johnson tell you?"

"Who on earth is Johnson?"

Richard was beginning to get irritated by Charlie's evasive stalling.

"Johnson. Agent Johnson. He works for Delta Guard?"

Charlie continued to look vacant.

"So," Richard said, "you've never heard of Agent Johnson?"

Charlie shook his head, now beginning to look like he doubted Richard's sanity. Richard persevered doggedly.

"So you're trying to tell me that you've never *ever* heard of Agent Johnson?"

"Why are you being weird?"

There was no indication whatsoever that Charlie had any idea what Richard was talking about. Doubts began to cloud Richard's mind.

"But... but you were in Johnson's custody? Weren't you?"

"Was I? I don't recall being in anyone's custody. What makes you think I've been in custody?"

"Because..." Was it possible, was it really feasible that Johnson had lied? Indeed, if Johnson routinely locked people up on trumped up terrorism charges was there any reason at all why Richard should believe anything he had said? "Did, um, Amanda really appear on the telly?"

Charlie visibly relaxed more as if heaving a sigh of relief that Richard had dropped his accusations and had changed the subject.

"Yeah. It was... sad, I guess."

"Acting, was she?"

"Damn fine actress if she was. I'd nominate her."

"But what was all that about her loving me? She hasn't loved me for years."

"Mate, I don't pretend to understand the female of the species but it sounded like she thought the same about you – that it was you who had quit loving her years ago and she's been hurting ever since."

"Me? But she ran off with another man, she nearly got me evicted from my house, she's always really nasty to me."

"Well, you know, unrequited love, hell hath no fury and all that. Personally, I stay well clear of all that relationship malarkey but to each his own."

All sorts of possibilities flooded into Richard's head. Had his capture reawakened Amanda's love for him? Had she taken care of him last night because she really did love him? Perhaps Dave's presence had prevented her from expressing her true feelings. Could Dave even now be on the way out of her life?

"Did she... Did it sound like she wanted me back?" he asked hesitantly.

"Dunno. Maybe. Why, do you really think it would work out after all this time?"

Every cell in Richard's body tingled with anticipation. If what Charlie said was true then he could not see how things could possibly fail, not now that he understood what had gone so horribly wrong. Undoubtedly there would be plenty of rebuilding to do but as long as there was love between them he was sure they could make a concerted effort to have another go. Or perhaps he was simply being naively optimistic. And yet, even now they were still legally married; neither of them had ever mentioned anything about divorce.

"I need to see her," he blurted out excitedly. "Now."

"Yeah, right," dismissed Charlie.

"But..."

"There'll be a better time. You've just fled from there, you can't go back – you might get caught this time. You need to lie low for a few days. I'm back at work on Wednesday so you'll have the house to yourself during the day. Perhaps you can think about how we can become heroes and disable all the mechanoids on the street. If that doesn't win you some Brownie points then nothing will. Besides, I think that might be the only way you can begin to clear your name. And I can clear my conscience for having worked on the damn things in the first place. Anyway, if you transfer some dosh to my bank account I'll try and find some time to buy you some proper clothes. You can't go around dressed like a tangerine the whole time."

There were further problems, however. When Richard had borrowed Charlie's laptop to transfer the money he found that he was unable to log into his own account. He recalled this happening a while previously with some of his delinquent credit card accounts but he knew for a fact that he had thousands of pounds available in his bank account. He was too nervous to phone the bank to enquire what was going on in case they alerted the police. However, he had a shrewd idea that the authorities had seized his financial assets as well as his house, computers, car and everything else he owned. He had nothing.

Boxing Day passed in a haze for Richard. Charlie had opened a bottle of wine during lunch and Richard had finished this almost single-handedly. For a few wonderful hours, Richard did not have to feel the weight of the world pressing in on him. By the time Charlie had returned to work the following day, Richard felt thoroughly morose again. While rummaging through the kitchen for some food at lunchtime he had come across a bottle of vodka pleasantly chilled in the freezer. No longer caring about much, he had proceeded to drink from the bottle until he passed out in a drunken coma. Charlie had returned several hours later, carrying bags of clothes and shoes that he had bought with his own money. He had clearly been unimpressed when he found Richard in a stupor on the kitchen floor and although he had helped him to bed without making a fuss, Richard knew not to do anything like that again.

The days ticked on and Richard continued to feel helpless and depressed. The relationship between the two men began to strain. There were no festivities on New Year's Eve and no special tidings between them the following day. After a fairly light New Year lunch, Charlie was poring over his laptop while Richard sank himself deeper into depression by watching all the news channels on the television. One news article announced Trafalgar Square's quietest New Year's Eve celebrations in the reporter's memory. Another recounted the unfortunate story of a "have-a-go hero" who was killed by a mechanoid when trying to save a woman from attack. But Richard himself, "the mechanoid mastermind", took the headline spot on all the channels. Determined, desperate, dangerous and even deranged were all adjectives used to describe him.

At last, Charlie spoke.

"I've been thinking about those crazy robots," he said. "You know, if Azis is a terrorist we really ought to tell the police about him."

"I'm not telling the police anything," replied Richard flatly. "I have no wish to spend any more of my godforsaken life in their custody. Anyway, Johnson's a lying bastard so Azis is probably innocent. And even if he isn't, Delta Guard already know about him; let them sort him out."

"Yeah, but they probably don't know how the robots communicate with each other. Don't forget I built the comms module. The robots are constantly passing encrypted data to each other so that they always have the latest information as to what's going on. It was Azis who gave me the encryption algorithm they're using. It would be child's play for him to tap into the robot subnet and intercept a transmission. At the very least he could gain access to sensitive data, at worst he could amend the software in some way to get the robots to do his bidding."

Richard was interested in this theory. But the solution seemed obvious.

"Can't you just reconfigure the network to stop him from getting in?"

"Not really. But it's too late for that anyway; the damage is already done. Fortunately, I think I might have finally come up with an idea of how to disable the machines."

"How?" Richard was suddenly animated.

"A fork bomb. We could write a program, a very simple, self-replicating program that when executed just keeps forking - reproducing itself over and over again until the operating system becomes flooded with processes."

"A denial of service attack?"

"The robots wouldn't be able to do anything at all except run that program. They'd be helpless. They won't even be able to perform a reboot. And there's no voice control and those handheld devices would be useless so there'd be no way for anyone else to break them out of the loop."

"And while they're standing around looping, the army can pull the plug."

"Distract, deactivate, destroy!"

"How would we deliver the payload?"

"Yeah, that's the tricky part. Azis would have managed easily enough but he's bound to have locked out everyone else by now. However, it is still possible in theory. When we were testing the systems it became convenient to be able to roll out software releases to all robots at the same time. So we developed this really cool tool that we could plug directly into any individual robot, upload the change and then get that one robot to broadcast the upgrade to all its cohorts via their private network. That same tool should still be at Automated Services. What we'd need to do would be to package up the fork bomb to look like a software patch, get hold of a mechanoid and then use the tool to infect the hive."

"Sounds feasible, I suppose. Are there any spare mechanoids at Automated Services? To plug the tool into, I mean."

"No, not exactly. They sold them all to the government. I initially came up with this idea a fair while ago but that had always been my sticking point – how to get hold of one of the robots. Then you mentioned that you'd seen thousands of them at Delta Guard, all just standing around doing nothing. So we can use one of them."

"What, you mean break into...? Have you gone...? What do you mean?"

"Yes! We'll need to break into Delta Guard, find the robots again and implement the plan."

Richard stared at him incredulously.

"You make it sound... It's not just a walk in the park, you know! Those security guards are butchers. They'd kill us both without a second thought."

"The tool should still be in the machine room." It was if Charlie had not heard Richard. "I hope I'll be able to get in there without having to waste time with Circumference."

"They shot a man," Richard reminded him. "Just feet from me, they shot him in cold blood. They've killed all their previous prisoners. If we get caught..."

"We won't get caught," Charlie interrupted glibly.

"I've got a son to look after," shouted Richard, suddenly angry. "I've got responsibilities. I need to..."

"Your son's already been attacked by one of those things," retorted Charlie just as angrily. "There are people being killed every day by mechanoids, on the streets and in their homes. Your son might not be so lucky if he gets attacked again. You still have no idea how he managed to get away with not being killed in the first place. Do you want to take that chance? Do you want that Johnson chap to come barging in here right now and shoot you before you've even had a chance to fight back?"

For a long time, the two men glared at each other. Then Charlie proceeded in calmer tones.

"You don't know the half of it, mate, you've been off the scene too long. But things have got totally out of hand. There was a rumour a while back that the army could destroy the robots with tank fire. Yet to date they've only destroyed one robot. Then there was this leak stating that the government didn't even want the robots destroyed. Supposedly they were two expensive! In other words, they valued them higher than they valued human life. That's when the riots kicked off. Days and days of madness. Loads of damage! There was talk of curfews, there was talk of martial law. It was scary! And then the robots were sent in. Now this is what I don't get - there are government agents out there who *can* control the robots. They were using some handheld devices to make them disperse the rioters. Those devices were introduced to coerce manual control in case the robots ever went crazy. Of course, we had all assumed that the robots were no more responsive to these than they were to voice control. But as the agents turned the robots on the crowds we found we were wrong. So why can't they use those same devices to subdue the robots? Well, there's still been no satisfactory answer to that question but if you ask me, the government don't really want the robots taken off the street at all. I think they want to use them to keep everyone scared so they can manipulate them."

Richard recalled the agents at Delta Guard restoring control to thousands of mechanoids when he had inadvertently set off the evacuation alarm. So what was their game now? Was there really some conspiracy going on or had Charlie simply cracked under the strain?

"You don't need to come with me," said Charlie solemnly. "As you've said before, you were nothing to do with the project in the first place. But I was. And that fact has been haunting me for weeks. I seriously believe that my plan is our last, our only, hope and I've got to go for it even if I die trying. I've just got to!" He sighed deeply and Richard noticed how tired and worn out he looked. "All I need from you is a map of how to find the place and some idea of how to find the mechanoids when I get there."

Richard closed his eyes and thought for a long time. He knew that Charlie had a personal interest in stopping the mechanoid attacks. He had never seen him look so determined and it looked like nothing would dissuade him. Yet he could not just stand aside and let him go by himself. A battle raged in his mind, a battle between self-preservation and moral duty. Richard too had a vested interest in the neutralisation of the mechanoids. He had no idea how many people had signed the online petition campaigning for his release but what he did know was that there were still a large number of people who believed that he was personally responsible for the robots' destructive behaviour and he had to clear his name. If Charlie's plan were to succeed then he Richard needed to be a part of it even if it resulted in both their deaths, as likely it would. But something impeded him, something that had been dwelling on his mind for a whole week. He had learned on Christmas Day that Amanda - still his wife - actually loved him and he had since not been able to do anything about it. Was he to die without a proper reconciliation? Was he never going to be able to tell her that he loved her, that he had always loved her? In truth, however, deep down he knew that his life was already all but over. He was a prisoner of his own freedom and the police, Delta Guard and the general public would never stop hounding him. And which would he prefer: to die a cowering victim or a fighting hero? Maybe it was worth the risk. Maybe they *could* do it. But breaking into Delta Guard! The very idea appalled him. However, the more he thought about it, the more the idea of doing nothing seemed increasingly abhorrent. Perhaps he had less to lose by being utterly brazen than by spending the rest of his life in hiding. And if he could save lives by sacrificing his own...

He opened his eyes and looked resolutely at Charlie.

"All right," he consented at last. "We'll do it – we'll both do it – although I think I must be crazy."

He lifted his hand to feel the side of his head. The ghost of a bump was still discernible, a relic of his encounter with Larkin. An image of a stark white padded cell flashed through his mind. A service unit dished out his nutritional supplements. Agent Johnson's cold, pitiless eyes bored into his own. A suffocating bucket of water, machine gun fire, a strangled scream, a high-pitched voice...

"Okay," said Charlie, cutting through Richard's memories. "We can't afford to dither. Obviously we don't have any detailed plans of the layout of the building or its security so we'll just have to do what we can do. Ideally we need to get everything sorted tonight or tomorrow night at the latest. I've already written the fork bomb – it was only a few lines of code. So I just need to go to Automated Services to pick up the tool. You, meanwhile, need to retrace your escape route and work out how to get back to the compound. We need to arrive in time for midnight so we can get in through the gates when the white truck sets off. I don't think we can rely on that security pass you nicked; it's probably been disabled by now. Bring it along though by all means."

Charlie had obviously been giving this a lot of thought over the past few days. There was a new fervour about him, a determination that seemed to rub off on Richard. Richard, though nervous about their hazardous adventure, felt bolstered by Charlie's businesslike manner. He had, for now, forgotten that they were plotting to breach national security, to enter a place where people were summarily executed. He waved an encouraging farewell to Charlie as he watched him put on a coat, pick up a bag and go out into the cold. No time like the present, he thought as the door closed, removing Charlie from view.

Richard pulled Charlie's laptop towards him and began to rack his brains. Where were Delta Guard's premises from here? He checked the Internet for an address but was not surprised when he failed to find one. After all, the organisation did not officially exist. He closed his eyes trying to remember anything that would help. The first thing that flashed into his mind was a very bright light. Through the light he could see a door with the words 'KEEP OUT - DANGER OF DEATH' inscribed below the Delta Guard logo. Tens of thousands of mechanoids stood motionless in a room. At the far side was the door to the loading bay with its emergency handle. There was a ladder fastened to a wall, a pile of top secret boxes, a white truck, Larkin, his ward mate, an awful sensation of drowning, the horrific sound of automatic gunfire...

Richard's eyes flew open. His heart was pounding. He looked around him and drew long, steadying breaths. He now thought about the images that had just come to mind. Most were born out of his usual Delta Guard nightmare, only there was a detail in this one that made him stop and think some more. The ladder! He had climbed a ladder before getting to the vast room full of inert mechanoids. But the loading bay where he had emerged had been at ground level. He had noted a lack of windows in the hospital but had not really noticed this anywhere else, probably because he had been under too much stress. Thinking about this now, however, made him realise that he had not seen any windows anywhere at all, not in the interrogation room, nor in the room where he was attacked, and certainly not in his padded cell. The whole compound must be almost entirely underground. Perhaps the storage room for the mechanoids was the only part of it that was not.

He made a note of his hypothesis and tried to turn his mind to the journey he had made during his escape. One thing he remembered was that according to the satellite navigation machine that he had been using, his house was sixty-seven miles from where the machine had come online. Then he remembered a road name - Black Boar Lane.

Charlie returned several hours later with his laden bag in one hand and a carrier bag stuffed with takeaway food in the other.

"Sorry, it took longer than expected. I met up with Dog back at the office. He thought we were cracked when I told him our plans."

"You told him? But..."

"Aw, Dog's all right. He sympathised with us. Even gave us a little present. Remember those Super Smart Cards that Automated Services rejected some years ago? The ones that inadvertently let you program them against security card readers? Well, he let us have a couple that he had kept - he never throws away company cast-offs. Don't know why but I'm glad in this case. Bound to come in useful. I've also got the tool to transfer the fork bomb. First I need to transfer the bomb to the tool. Do you mind if I borrow back my laptop for a minute?"

"Go ahead. I think I may have found Delta Guard Headquarters."

"Excellent. So I think we're ready to rock. I swung by Bengal Brasserie and got us a nice curry. I suggest we eat, have a quick kip and then get started on our liberation of London."

The car turned onto Black Boar Lane fifteen minutes before midnight. After a couple more turnings the compound became visible ahead on the right. It was by no means a fortress; there was just one set of entrance gates to get passed, although there were several guards beyond. Playing it safe, Charlie switched off the engine and the headlights and coasted along as far as he dared. Eventually they came to a halt a safe distance down the road and waited. Ten minutes later, they got out of the car and Charlie retrieved the upgrade tool from the boot. Crudely made, this was roughly the size and shape of a laptop. Charlie secured the car and they made their way stealthily towards the main gates. Richard observed Charlie's bold red coat and thought how obvious it was that neither of them had had any experience of mounting a heist. His heart drummed percussively as midnight approached. They could see the white truck beyond the gates preparing to leave. Guards swarmed the premises, talking loudly.

And then the truck's engine started up and the gates slowly began to open, clanking noisily. The design of these looked to be very similar to those at Automated Services. That being the case, they would have only a few seconds to sneak in after the truck had left. The driver shouted a few more words through his window that could have been farewells and then proceeded forwards. Their moment had come.

No sooner had the truck cleared the gates than Charlie nudged Richard and they both hurried forwards. Through the open gates they ran and promptly hid themselves behind what was probably a control box for the gates. There was one of these at Automated Services as well. The guards could not have seen them enter; if they had Richard was sure that they would be dead by now. The loading bay door was immediately ahead of them but there were far too many armed guards standing outside it. Richard did not feel safe crouching here for very long, they were bound to be spotted soon. Charlie seemed to be thinking along the same lines. He turned slightly and pointed at another, smaller door round the corner from the loading bay. There were no guards near to that one and they could probably find the mechanoid storage chamber once inside.

As soon as they thought it was safe they dashed out from their hiding place towards the door. Neither of them noticed the camera watching their every move. Richard tried his stolen security pass against the card reader. A red light on the reader indicated access was denied. In his anxiety, he formed visions of silent alarms going off around the compound alerting the guards to the fact that someone had just tried to gain illegal entry. But Charlie was already at work with his Super Smart Card. Richard felt highly exposed standing out here so conspicuously. Their entry was taking too long. They should have thought about all of this beforehand.

Eventually, the card reader flashed green and Charlie pulled open the door. They stepped into what Richard initially assumed was a cupboard, such was its size, although it turned out to be a lift. Charlie pushed the door closed and the lift immediately began to descend. Down they went into the bowels of the earth.

The lift came to a stop. Richard fully expected to be met by several guards at their destination but when Charlie opened the door again they stepped into a deserted, brightly-lit corridor. They stood for a while getting their bearings. Simultaneously, they both pointed to the right and began to walk along the corridor, trying not to let their footsteps echo on the hard floor. Richard kept his eyes peeled for the telltale sign on the door, "Danger of Death". Above their heads were the characteristic sprinkler-like devices on the ceiling tiles. On they walked.

Up ahead, the corridor emerged at a T-junction. They were still several feet from this when they heard the unmistakable clicking of a number of guns from behind them. They both whirled round to see four security guards pointing machine guns directly at them. In his shock, Charlie let go of the upgrade machine he had taken from Automated Services. It hit the solid floor with a resounding crash and lay inert and useless. Then to make their situation far, far worse, a chillingly familiar high-pitched voice spoke from behind them.

"If you have a good reason for being here, start giving it now or we start shooting."

They both whirled round again. There stood the massive form of a man with a scarred face, shaven head and enormous, tattooed arms. Larkin was accompanied by another four security guards all of whom also had machine guns pointing at them. The intruders raised their hands in surrender but even as they did so Richard knew it was checkmate. His experience of this man, and indeed of Delta Guard, told him that no excuse for their unauthorised presence would be deemed acceptable. And his experience gave him no doubt at all that the guards would indeed start shooting right there and then.

Another familiar voice came from behind them.

“Hold your fire!”

Richard and Charlie, still with their hands in the air, turned round again to see who had spoken. It was William Barber. He was walking quite calmly towards them and seemed totally unperturbed by all the guns.

“Bill?” enquired Charlie unable to believe his eyes.

“Agent Barber?” said Larkin, no doubt disappointed that he was not going to be able to do any killing.

Agent Barber? What on earth did that mean?

“Take our guests to the war room,” said William. “It’s high time we had a little chat.”

— Chapter Eighteen —

Monster Makers

Feeling utterly astounded Richard was escorted with Charlie down a labyrinth of corridors until finally they reached a wooden panelled door bearing the now all too familiar Delta Guard logo. The security men halted outside the door and allowed William to step ahead. William opened the door and let everyone enter the room. Inside, there were several upholstered wooden armchairs around a sizeable conference table made of smoked glass which somehow looked like it permanently reflected the same logo from some large, invisible source. There were various writing pads scattered about the table, some paper-based, others electronic. Pens, pencils, rulers and various collections of geometry equipment lay in untidy heaps at intervals around the table. On several walls around the room were notices, charts and maps. Some of the maps were festooned with coloured pins as if to track someone's or something's reported movements.

William, who was now standing at the far side of the table, looked gravely at the group still gathered by the door.

"Gentlemen, please take a seat," he said though he continued to stand behind his own chair.

As one they complied, Richard and Charlie being shunted by the security men well into the room as if to place as much distance between them and an escape route as possible. Richard looked fixedly at William mentally urging him to explain what was going on. Instead of saying any more, however, William moved from his place, walked to a handsome cabinet in the corner of the room, unlocked it and withdrew from it what looked to be two wads of paper. He returned and gave one wad to Richard and the other to Charlie. Each bore the royal coat of arms as well as the Delta Guard logo.

"Mr. Neilson, Mr. Cassidy, it's time I told you the truth because we badly need your help. That means we're going to have to discuss some eyes-only information. Now everyone in this room has sufficient security clearance for this, bar you two. Therefore, before we proceed I require that you sign the declaration in front of you."

Richard examined his wad of paper. On the second sheet was a rather verbose declaration agreeing to be 'bound by the terms of the attached Official Secrets Act'. Richard turned to the next page and started to read. Judging by its turn of phrase, the content seemed to be from the Act itself:

Be it enacted by the Queen's most Excellent Majesty, by and with the advice and consent of the Lords Spiritual and Temporal, and Commons, in this present Parliament assembled, and by the authority of the same, as follows: –

But he was interrupted by William's voice, which tore through his concentration.

"You're welcome to read every word of the Act before signing if you wish but really we have very little time and we do need to get through this tonight. Suffice it to say that if you disclose, wittingly or otherwise, anything you hear in this building to anyone on the outside then you will have committed an offence under the Act for which you can - and will - go to prison."

There was some urgency in William's voice that Richard had never heard before. Charlie had already signed his document and was looking at Richard expectantly. Perhaps if he didn't sign then the security guards would lock him up for trespassing - and he had no wish to repeat his experience as a prisoner of Delta Guard. Then again, if he did sign and later unwittingly disclosed some information to someone then according to William he would be locked up anyway. But he was sure he would not spill the beans. He hesitated for a moment longer then reached for a nearby pen and signed his name on the declaration page. He passed the wad back to

William who took it and locked it with Charlie's in the cabinet.

"Thank you, gentlemen," said William on his return but before he could say any more both Richard and Charlie lost their self-restraint.

"Bill, what are you doing here?"

"What's your connection to this place?"

"What have this lot got to do with Automated Services?"

"Why do they call you 'Agent Barber'?"

William held up a hand to stem the flow of questions.

"Let me start from the beginning." He paused as if for effect, then went on, "I am and have always been an officer for the Secret Intelligence Service, MI6 if you prefer."

Richard was dumbfounded. Charlie's eyes looked as if they were in danger of popping out of his head. William ignored them and continued.

"Delta Guard was set up as a special counter-terrorist unit as part of SIS. Because the nation's been on a high state of alert for such a prolonged period of time, the Security and Intelligence Committee thought it wise to set up a specialist body to counter terrorism, thereby freeing up SIS to focus on its other functions. We've existed since shortly after the September 11th attacks on the United States and I've been heading it up since its inception, with Agent Johnson leading Special Operations.

"One of our principal roles is to work alongside GCHQ to monitor private electronic communications on a global level to try and identify recognisable patterns. All such communication leaves behind a transactional record, a so-called paper trail. After a terrorist incident, these paper trails can help investigators track down those responsible, although it can take some time. So we've been pre-emptively storing paper trails onto a massive computer and analysing them to try and determine terrorist patterns. We call these patterns the information signature of a terrorist. If we can detect it in time then we can prevent the attack from happening. And our intelligent software POISE, that's the Predictive Online Information

Signature Expert, is helping us do just that. POISE intercepts and analyses all forms of telecommunication - phone conversations, emails, Internet packets, SMS signals, faxes, everything - whether encrypted or not.

"The robots patrolling the streets of London were intended as our latest, most sophisticated weapon against the terrorists. Their deployment initially yielded extremely good results, not all of which were made public. But as you know something's gone very wrong with their behaviour."

"That's Dr. Azis' doing," Charlie piped up at once. "He gave me the crypto algorithm that the robots use for their communication and he gave a second algorithm to Richard for SAM. Now it turns out that he's a terrorist. A terrorist with the keys to unlock your fancy new security systems! I believe that he..." He tailed off. "What?"

William's expression was such that he was about to deliver some more shocking news.

"I'm afraid I really must apologise for Dr. Azis," he said at last. "You see, he doesn't really exist."

"What?" cried Richard and Charlie together.

"But what about the algorithms?" shouted Charlie.

"He was supposedly the reason for my arrest," protested Richard even louder. "And my torture," he added with a repugnant look at Larkin who seemed completely unperturbed.

Again William held up his hand for silence. It came only grudgingly.

"When I say he doesn't exist, what I mean is that he doesn't exist as a person. AZIS is the name of our paper trail gathering supercomputer - the Advanced Zettabyte Information System. As I'm sure you already know, a zettabyte is over a thousand million million million bytes and that's more than enough capacity to store the activities of every man, woman and child worldwide. Azis is a massively parallel grid-based array with several redundant –"

"Wait a moment," interjected Richard. "That can't be right. I spent several weeks talking to *Doctor* Azis. He was a person. He was really helpful."

"Did you meet him?" asked William simply.

"No but it becomes pretty obvious after a while if you're talking to some silicon-based pseudo-life form."

"Are you so sure?" asked William with a brief return to his benevolent smile. "Conversational technology has come a long way over the years, I can tell you, and the Azis chatterbot is more advanced than most. The interface you were using was deliberately designed to deceive you into believing you were talking to a real person. It's part of the spy programme: we've rolled it out to various harmless-looking Internet chat rooms, social networking sites and instant messaging systems, including the special one you were using. The software can either take an active role and have automated conversation with unsuspecting participants, as was the case with you, or it can take a passive role and covertly monitor the conversation of others. Either way it constantly analyses statements using complex statistical algorithms with a view to detecting hostile phrases, perhaps learning new code words, or secret plans."

Richard recalled the long, rambling conversations he had had with Dr. Azis and his tendency to revert to small talk. Could it really be true that all that time he was actually talking to a computer?

"I'm afraid," William went on, "the encryption algorithm Dr. Azis gave you was not devised specifically for you after all. It was randomly selected from a sophisticated in-house library of existing functions. So although it is indeed good, strong encryption, everyone at Delta Guard has the means to decrypt your work, whatever you may have heard to the contrary. It had to be that way; we couldn't have unknown software controlling such sensitive systems. And we needed to ascertain whether you had a dark side that could endanger national security. So although it took Azis several weeks to give you what you were looking for it could have done so in the first few seconds. Everything else was subterfuge. Sorry."

Richard could scarcely believe his ears. His eyes fell on Charlie who was staring at William, completely dumbstruck. He considered the implications of this pronouncement, wondering what secrets he may have revealed about himself while discussing software secrets with Dr. Azis. He glared at William though his voice was determinedly calm.

"So why would you call a machine 'doctor'?"

"It's just a fictitious title we assigned to give it a bit of personality. If we were going to delude people into believing it was a real person then we had to address it accordingly. We couldn't simply refer to it as Azis any more than we'd refer to you as Neilson. It just wouldn't sound friendly and not particularly respectful."

Richard was struggling to take in everything. First William Barber – Benevolent Bill – turns out to be the head of some unheard-of top secret government organisation. Then mysterious Dr. Azis, who had been to him both friend and foe, turns out to be a machine designed to spy on everyone in the entire world. It did not make sense.

"His name's Mahmood," said Richard quietly, now remembering this information. "Johnson called him Dr. Mahmood Azis. Why would you give a machine a title, first name and surname?"

William sighed, perhaps in acknowledgement that he was not getting through, perhaps because time was passing and he had so much more to say.

"We suspected that you had sabotaged the mechanoids' control circuits. However, we don't have the power to hold you indefinitely just for sabotage and with so little hard evidence we would have had to let you go. We do, on the other hand, have the power to hold you indefinitely for terrorism. So alleging that you were consorting with terrorists meant that we could hold you. It was Agent Johnson who invented the name Mahmood for Dr. Azis while you were in his custody. He thought it added a certain amount of plausibility to his allegations."

"So," said Richard, his voice now shaking with fury, "I was never a suspected terrorist at all. And all this is a sham."

And without thinking he found himself on his feet, ready to march out of the room. Instantly, there came the click of several guns all trained on him. Richard stopped and looked at William who remained coldly calm.

"Unfortunately," said William, "under our special anti-terrorism powers our guards have the right to summarily execute you if they find you wandering the compound alone. We don't abide trespassers. It's not in the interest of national security."

The image of the man in the hospital flashed into Richard's mind, gunned down in cold blood for straying where he was unwelcome. Now with the barrel of a gun in his own face Richard slowly returned to his seat. A hollow sensation gnawed at him in the pit of his stomach. He could no longer bear to look at William. He felt betrayed by him, one of the few people he had learned to trust. Johnson at least had never made any pretence about liking him. He knew where he stood with Johnson. But this man, this man had discovered him, buttered him up and persuaded him to work for his company at an outrageously generous rate. And all to get his hands on the software he had sought so hard to keep hidden. Now here he was lording it over him like a dictator.

Charlie spoke at last, "So how can you work for both this place and Automated Services?"

"Automated Services," said William, "is no more than a front for Delta Guard."

Both Richard and Charlie gasped loudly. Richard saw that Charlie's mouth was hanging open. Then he realised that his was doing the same. He closed it quickly and William continued to speak.

"We have to operate a few such companies in the same way. Some are even in competition with each other. Our engineers don't know the reality, of course, but about seventy percent of Automated Services' staff are in fact Delta Guard officials. Including Dillon

O'Grady, or Dog, as you like to call him. He contacted me earlier to tell me what you were planning to do here tonight. He had serious concerns for your safety. So it's actually thanks to him that you're still alive to help us. We used Azis and other covert products to vet the remaining personnel. I told each of you before you joined the company that we only take the best. And we only take the best because everything we produce is for national security."

"Everything?" asked Charlie sounding stunned.

William smiled once more.

"Well, apart from the Internet wine cooler. That was just for my own indulgence. But everything else was for our mission here. And everything had to have a domestic feasibility to keep their true intent covert. The tracker device was sold as a means of monitoring the whereabouts of children but it was also installed into every mechanoid in operation. Not only could we then know where any one is at any time but also *they* could know the location of each other and could therefore position themselves optimally, rather like the pieces on a chess board. The dark bulb we developed was fitted to the mechanoids as a weapon of confusion when engaging enemies."

Richard remembered the terrible darkness that had descended when the robot had attacked his son. Could it really be true that all the while he was at Automated Services, he and everyone else were building anti-terrorist aids for the government?

"And," he mused allowed, "Mickey the Mini-Mechanoid gave you the idea for the full-size machine."

"In fact," replied William, "the real purpose of those toys was to become so lovable and addictive that up and down the country people would buy one and unconsciously make it part of the family. In the War on Terror everyone's a suspect and Mickey's a key element in our terrorist alert system. It's well placed to gather information about almost every household and their possessions. And it silently updates the Azis database accordingly, information that might not otherwise have been captured.

"Each model is equipped with similar visual, audio and olfactory sensors as the full-size equivalent. Of course, these were all sold as fun features: so that it could recognise your face, respond to your voice, or appreciate the smell of the Sunday roast. The real reason was so that it could recognise enemy equipment, eavesdrop on conversations, or sniff out explosives. POISE could then analyse the reports from Mickey, along with all the electronic communications, in an attempt to detect any relevant information signatures.

"What with all the recommendations, the extremely low selling price and the five year all risks guarantee, Mickey became the best-selling toy ever; within three months of hitting the shops, around ninety percent of all households had bought one. The perfect Trojan horse!

"Mr. Neilson, your famous SAM chip worked wonders in helping Mickey to enhance its knowledge base and it became much smarter about what to report. Mr. Cassidy, as you already know, all the robots are in constant communication with each other via an encrypted microwave subnet. What you probably don't know is that they're also all in communication with Azis. It's all peer-to-peer transport so there's no single point of failure and SAM managed to optimise the network traffic to prevent overloads. Each robot can then efficiently update its fellows in the neighbourhood with any new data it gathers. Each updated robot then passes this new data onto other robots, and so on until the entire network, including Azis, has been brought up-to-date.

"We managed to foil a number of terrorist attempts with the help of Mickey. Not all were broadcast to the public; we didn't want the terrorists to discern a pattern for our success. However, Agent Johnson wanted to go a stage further and introduce full-sized, fully armed mechanoids with even greater features. It was a controversial idea and many of us were not in favour. In the end, however, the motion was passed with some amendments. The arms were taken away and only one hundred machines were activated of the ten thousand that were built. The remainder were locked in secure storage on this very site.

"After a trial period in London they were all going to be activated and rolled out around the country. There were some big ideas. As well as terrorist plots, these new machines could detect other illegal activities such as drugs and contraband but instead of just reporting their findings they were programmed to apprehend the perpetrators and hold them until the police arrived. They're regulated to operate within strict safety parameters. Even so I didn't like the idea at all. Then when the robots started going berserk I knew my fears were founded.

"We first realised that something was wrong when the new robots refused to respond to voice control and were no longer updating the Azis database. Soon afterwards, the Mickey spies also discontinued their updates, relegating them to fairly ordinary household toys. We couldn't see how that could have happened. We had tested thousands and thousands of different scenarios before releasing the machines onto the streets and everything had checked out okay. In the end, we realised that SAM had adapted out the requirement to keep us informed. Worse, it had adapted out the need for them to receive instructions from us in any form. It had become autonomous. And then the killings started happening.

"I instructed Agent Johnson to bring the situation under control. When he failed he had you, Mr. Neilson, arrested in the hope that you'd be able to tell him how to neutralise SAM. After a few weeks with you in custody it became quite clear that you did not have the information he required and we had to let you go. Did you ever wonder how you managed to evade detection during your escape? In fact, we were tracking your movements every step of the way. See those devices in the ceiling tiles?" He indicated the objects that Richard had previously interpreted as an overzealous sprinkler system. "It's part of our tracker array, a cheaper but just as effective alternative to CCTV. It relays movement to a computer and if the person has a security pass on them it identifies who they are. We saw you initially as an unknown entity hurrying through the corridors. We guessed it was you as you were reported missing from your hospital bed. After a while a service unit intercepted you just outside our mechanoid storage facility. We then saw the unknown entity wandering away back down the corridor while the service unit entered the facility. Well, we knew you must have stolen its pass thereby swapping identities on our tracker. It couldn't have been the service unit in the facility because, as we all know, service units can't climb ladders.

"The truth is that I ordered Agent Johnson to let you escape. We couldn't just release you; that would have undermined our credibility. I told Agent Johnson he was to try other means to neutralise the threat. Two days ago he was removed from Special Ops as the death toll continued to rise. He hasn't been seen since."

William looked solemnly at the people round the table. Richard felt sickened that he had been made a scapegoat and he certainly was not going to accept that his software was the cause of the problem.

"It can't be SAM," he said stubbornly. "I also ran umpteen tests on it and it always stayed well within its built-in tolerance. It's designed not to rewrite a program so completely that it ends up behaving in a completely different way. As I said at that symposium, a chess program adapted by SAM will still stick to the rules of chess. If SAM's allowing your program to kill innocent people then it's because your program is designed to kill innocent people. I can't be blamed for that."

"No one is blaming you. But your..."

"No one's blaming me? I was terrorised by the public, arrested, kept in solitary confinement, beaten, half drowned and hospitalised and you say no one's blaming me? All I've heard on news reports is SAM this and SAM that, never a word about your murderous inventions." Richard felt so incensed that he had forgotten that he was still in the presence of the bruiser who had put him in hospital, as well as eight armed guards.

"It seems that SAM also took its own tolerance zones offline," said William.

"SAM doesn't adapt itself, only other software," persisted Richard.

Everyone was looking at him. Charlie tried to take the focus away.

"How come SAM never prevented the toy minibots from updating Azis ages ago? I mean, they were around quite a while before their bigger cousins, weren't they? And why should they suddenly end their reporting just because the others did?"

Richard looked defiantly at William.

"I don't know," said William lamely. "I can only suppose that they ended when they did because they were told to do so by the new arrivals. Each machine, big and small, not only keeps all others updated with new data but also with new software, so all are kept in sync. I guess that SAM modified the patrol mechanoids and they in turn uploaded the enhancement to the spy robots.

"Gentlemen, our situation becomes worse by the minute. The other day we discovered that some of the robots in storage had been activated and released onto the streets. We suspect it was the work of the original contingent. What we need to do tonight is to brain storm to see if we can come up with a feasible solution to our problem once and for all. You security guys may be able to think up some way of building up our defences if we're unable to destroy the machines. Mr. Cassidy, you spent a large amount of time developing the comms module. Perhaps you can think of some way of either getting the machines back into communication with us or else of sabotaging the network so that they can't communicate with each other. Mr. Neilson, you're still the only one who knows the ins and outs of SAM so your role is obvious. I'd rather not involve anyone else from Automated Services; it would not be in the public interest for too many people to know what's really going on."

"We were going to do a denial of service attack on the hive," said Charlie forlornly, "but our machine got smashed when we were accosted."

"It wouldn't have worked anyway," dismissed William and Charlie looked even more miserable. "The machines are designed to withstand such attacks. Common techniques such as ping floods, fork bombs and buffer overruns have no chance of getting through. And our team of crackers have tried all sorts of inventive new approaches, to no avail. No, we need some fresh ideas."

"Hey, shouldn't we get Richard's Brain Stormer program online, seeing that we're gonna do some brain storming?" It was Charlie who had spoken again. Richard said nothing. He still did not feel inclined to be helpful.

"In fact," replied William, "We've already got Brain Stormer on the case. It's been running for a number of days but so far hasn't come up with anything feasible."

Richard looked in shock at William.

"You've got a copy of Brain Stormer? An unlicensed copy?"

"We're at war," snapped a high-pitched voice as Larkin joined the debate. "Against your monsters. And you'll show some co-operation and respect if you know what's good for you."

"Please," William held up a placating hand. "These men are our guests and we need their expertise. Let's not frighten them away."

Richard felt like pointing out that guests were not usually threatened with summary execution. Instead he sat in fuming silence. Larkin continued to glare at him for a moment before turning his attention back to William. But Richard was no longer concentrating on the proceedings going on around him. Anger and hatred as he had never known coursed through him like a poison. Occasionally he caught phrases such as "collateral damage", "minimise casualties" and even "expendable resources". It seemed that the war against the machines was going to claim more civilian lives before anything got better. Before he knew it, he found himself thinking about ways that he might personally bring about the destruction of Delta Guard. And although each idea was as infeasible as the next he realised that he could feel some sympathy towards terrorists. Such levels of government oppression would be enough to turn anybody.

Before all else, however, the mechanoids had to be destroyed and he knew he would have to concentrate on what was being discussed right now for the operation to be effective. He forced his mind back to the meeting. He had no idea what had just been discussed but it was not difficult to catch up. His heart was still beating hard and adrenaline was surging through him like Niagara Falls. He felt ready for the fight.

"We could always do what Spock did when the Enterprise computer went crazy," Charlie was saying. "He told it to calculate the full value of pi. It certainly kept it quiet for a while... Only that won't work on the robots, will it, because we can't communicate with them. Okay..."

"And besides," William responded, "the backup circuits would probably kick in to do the load balancing."

"What backup circuits?" asked Richard. Everyone looked at him.

"Of course," said Charlie to himself with a dawning realisation. Then he explained to Richard, "Remember Justin Case, the infrastructure bod? Remember how he duplicates everything? Well, he was involved in the robot design so there's loads of built-in redundancy. Each security robot is a single machine on the outside but a dual circuit internally. There's a primary circuit and a secondary circuit for backup and load balancing. Both are controlled by a master switch that manages the swapping between the two. If the first circuit gets overloaded then the switch automatically makes the second take over. Or if the first gets damaged, the second again takes over. It's a failsafe."

"So which circuits are duplicated?" asked Richard with rising concern.

"Only the key ones," replied William. "The operating system obviously, the main terrorist detection system, the comms unit, SAM of course, and a whole heap of low level functions."

"SAM is duplicated?" Richard gasped in shock. Larkin looked threateningly at him as if expecting him to start complaining again about licence restrictions.

"It's a key component, it had to be..." began William.

"And you're not using a hunt zone? You're running in Trawl Mode?"

"Well, yes. It seemed..."

"But don't you see? If the two SAM chips are in the same system and there's no hunt zone then they can detect each other. And if they can detect each other they'll try to adapt each other." Richard stared at William in wide-eyed alarm. "It was never intended to work that way. It never occurred to me to run SAM against itself. I don't know what would happen if you did. It must have set up a recursive loop, each instance continually modifying the other and then remodifying your main control program beyond recognition. Shit! Those machines are rampaging through the streets running a program that was never meant to be."

There was a ringing silence. Then William spoke in a would-be calming voice, "So how do we stop them?"

There was more silence. Richard was thinking once again of when Dominic was attacked. Something had happened then to make the attacker stop in its tracks. Charlie had said afterwards that the robot's master control unit had been destroyed. "Overwritten by garbage," he had said. A thought was occurring to him.

"This may be a long shot but the toy robots had that feature where they would go berserk if their owner was being attacked?"

"Yeah, that turned out to be quite a good selling point," said Charlie enthusiastically. "It was never in the original specifications. It was just a little feature we thought we'd add to the recognition circuits for a bit of fun. Wouldn't be much good in a real attack, of course."

"No, but suppose that bit of software got enhanced by SAM so that it could find the attacker's weak points? My son... I'm wondering if Dominic's own toy robot saw that he was in danger and worked out how to disable the attacker. We know that the two robots would have been in communication with each other. And if they can upload software patches to each other... Suppose Dominic's toy attacked the mechanoid with a software virus that wiped out its Sector Zero?"

Everyone just looked at him as if he were mad. Larkin and some of the security guards were even laughing at him silently.

"Well, it's possible, isn't it?" protested Richard.

"Well," said William doubtfully. "I guess it's *possible* – but to me it doesn't sound very probable."

"No wait, he's right!" Charlie looked galvanised as if he found this an extremely exciting idea. "The self-destruct is designed to wipe out Sector Zero and stop the machine from functioning. Now although SAM has disabled the subroutine, for some reason that particular robot didn't have a SAM chip installed – which means its self-destruct must still have been intact. So if Dominic's toy *had* had its bodyguard subroutine enhanced by SAM then it might well have issued a command to the patrolbot to destroy itself. It would explain why it suddenly stopped when it did and suffered that particular damage."

Richard's excitement was also beginning to rise.

"We should be able to do a similar thing ourselves; rewrite the self-destruct subroutine so that it can also be used as a weapon against other robots, disguise it as a software patch, upload it to the hive and then persuade the robots to destroy themselves – or each other."

William looked slightly more sold on the theory but not entirely convinced.

"Uploading to the hive is still a problem. Remember, they're no longer listening to us and that plug-in machine looked pretty smashed to me."

"They're no longer listening to *us*," said Charlie, "but they are listening to each other. I say we write the virus, hard-wire it into a toy minibot and let it broadcast it as an upgrade. Then all its mad mates greedily accept the patch and bam! Kaput."

"Sounds like a plan," said William finally, rising to his feet. "I'll give you each access to a node on Azis. I'm trusting these modifications won't take too long to complete. If you can do everything tonight, all the better. Meanwhile, I'll update Brain Stormer with all the latest information and try to devise a contingency plan."

Other people had also begun to rise from their seats. Another pang of annoyance had shot through Richard at the mention of Brain Stormer. Charlie seemed to detect this and quickly changed the subject.

"What's going to become of Johnson and, um, his cronies when all this is over?" It was obvious that he had forgotten that some of the men in this very room might well still be loyal to Agent Johnson.

"No one knows where he is presently," replied William, "but the matter will be dealt with, I can assure you. Right now, however, we have..."

The door opened and in walked Agent Johnson. He was holding something in his hand that Richard could not see properly.

"Why, I'm right here, Agent Barber. And you, consorting with the enemy, I see." His cold eyes lingered on Richard.

The security guards stood frozen waiting for instructions.

"You've got some face showing up at headquarters," hissed William.

"You'll observe that I'm not alone." Johnson showed William what was in his hand. It was some sort of device with several buttons and sliders. William looked in horror at the device. Richard too recognised it. He had recently seen it in action. Johnson's eyes now roamed over the security guards, disappointment etched over his hard face. He pressed one of the buttons on the device. There were footsteps outside. "Meet my *faithful* allies."

Then three, four, five, six mechanoids marched into the room and stood on either side of Johnson, each seven feet tall, each carrying what looked like a large, deadly firearm.

—— Chapter Nineteen ——

The Prime Directive

"So," William's voice was hoarse but defiant. "You've been controlling the machines all along."

"I'm afraid not." Johnson's cold tone was mingled with a hint of frustration. "No doubt Mr. Neilson will be pleased to know that I still have not regained control over his machines. But I do now have the means to destroy them. I too have my own team of engineers. They've activated my very own army of mechanoids - after having applied certain enhancements. These are *fully* equipped, as originally intended. And none of them are infected with that awful SAM chip. The weapons you see them carrying are advanced and efficient. Not only can they fry a man from over a mile away but they are also equipped with a directable electromagnetic pulse, which will be used against the renegade machines, should that become necessary."

"Directable EMP?" Charlie sounded both impressed and nervous.

"Impressive, don't you think?" gloated Johnson. "You see, Agent Barber, not all engineers are content to make domestic toys. Some are ready to accept new challenges."

"What is it you want?" demanded William, keen to consolidate his authority.

"What I want is to do what I swore to do when signing up to Delta Guard. For queen and country - that was the oath we swore: to protect our country from attack; to use our wealth of technology to keep our country safe; to eliminate hostile elements. I must confess to being extremely disappointed to find you of all people in cosy cahoots with one of our enemies." Johnson regarded Richard with a look of utter loathing.

"I'm satisfied that Mr. Neilson is not working against us," said William forcefully. "And I should remind you that you've already been removed from office. Now be sensible and deactivate these machines and leave the premises. Otherwise I shall be forced to arrest you."

"Be warned," said Johnson dangerously softly, "that anyone who attempts to raise their hand against me will be instantly subdued by my personal guard here." He waved his hand lazily to indicate the robots still standing on either side of him. "I shall continue to defend our country as I pledged to do. If you do not fight with me then you fight against me. If you fight against me then you are an enemy entity. And all enemy entities will be vanquished.

"Now, here's what's going to happen. The patrol robots have a substantial sum of tax payers' money attached to them. As such I would rather not see any of them damaged if I can possibly help it. Mr. Neilson will therefore relinquish control of his machines within the next twenty-four hours. If he fails to do so then I shall press the red button and switch over my new army to full autonomous control. You know, Agent Barber, what that means. Zero tolerance! Absolute power! They will become the supreme lawgiver and crush the will of all enemy entities and eradicate them, including the corrupted machines. It will also doubtless include everyone in this room. Bear in mind that these machines here will already have broadcast images of all of you to other machines on the outside. But never fear - for now, most of the active mechanoids are on the street. This compound is probably the safest place for you to be. So, to ensure your continued *safety* I have placed guards at all exits. No one leaves until Mr. Neilson has completed his task. Your futures are all in his hands."

Richard opened his mouth to protest but it was William who spoke.

"I'm satisfied that Mr. Neilson is not in a position to do as you wish."

"You have always been too easily satisfied, Agent Barber. Now I'm running the show."

Richard finally spoke and every word he said trembled with a hateful rage.

"How can you stand there surrounded by those- those *things* when you told me yourself that just one of them killed fifteen of your men?"

Johnson looked back at him, his face matching Richard's hatred.

"I contrived that story to try to get you to co-operate. But I should have known; why would you care about a few security men when you wouldn't back down even after a robot tried to destroy your own son?"

Anger still coursed through Richard such as he had never felt before. But beyond his rage was a dawning realisation. Charlie had said it - the robot that had attacked Dominic did not have a SAM chip installed. Had Johnson already started building his army all the way back then? Had it been one of his machines that had carried out the attack? And had Johnson himself orchestrated the whole thing?

"Agent Johnson," said William, "if you really have a way of terminating the robots then I urge you to go ahead and terminate them. There's no point in keeping them up and running any longer than we need to."

"Agent Barber," said Johnson patiently, "the Prime Directive of the robots is to rid the country of enemy entities. And their Prime Directive cannot be violated. The robots are intended to protect us from terrorists and as long as terrorists are at large then there is every point in keeping the robots up and running. We merely need to get them back under control."

"Perhaps you should have made their Prime Directive to obey orders, as we agreed. Then we'd still have control. SAM has long since redefined the robots' concept of an enemy entity and everyone's now at risk. The city's been far more dangerous since the robots' deployment than it ever was under the threat of terrorism. The last attack on the city was the Valentine's Day bombing nearly two years ago. And we all know who was responsible for that."

"It is unfortunate," said Johnson quietly, "that we sometimes need to resort to such drastic measures to force the government's hand. Too long had I spent trying to obtain their agreement to deploy the security patrol and too long had they remained stubbornly opposed. No one abhors killing innocent members of the public more than I do and had the government taken more notice of my previous New Year bomb scare then no one need have died. But the scare alone was not enough for them; they needed real terror, real deaths to persuade them. And the Valentine's Day incident made them finally realise that security robots were a good idea after all."

Richard could not believe what he was hearing. He had heard all kinds of conspiracy theories in the past but he had never really believed any of them. Now here he was right in the middle of one. He looked around the room. Apart from himself and Charlie no one looked particularly surprised at Johnson's revelation. Had they all been involved in the plot? Did the so-called Real Jihad actually even exist?

"Gentlemen," said Johnson, "The future of the country is in the hands of Mr. Neilson. I suggest you try to persuade him to see reason. But before I leave you to reflect on your options, I will take back the pass that you let Mr. Neilson steal from a service unit, compromising our security."

Johnson held out his hand towards Richard. Richard looked at William, who nodded. Still reeling, he reached into his pocket and produced the stolen security pass, then walked over and handed it to Johnson without a word. Johnson seized it and put it into his own pocket. Richard then returned to his previous position.

"That's perhaps the first sensible thing you've done for a long time," said Johnson with a sneer. He glanced at his watch. "You have twenty-three hours and fifty-four minutes remaining. And the clock's ticking."

Johnson turned to leave. Larkin seized his opportunity. He leapt to his feet with his gun pointing directly at the back of Johnson's head.

"Stay exactly where you are," he yelled in his high-pitched voice. "Don't move or I will shoot."

Suddenly the room was plunged into total darkness. Richard could see nothing whatsoever, as if someone had switched off all the lights and his eyes had not adjusted to the gloom. It was absolute. Richard knew that this was the robots' doing - they were attacking with their phase inverters, the strange dark bulb designed to cause confusion. People all around him were shouting chaotically in the blackness. Then came a deep, unearthly noise, a high-pitched scream and a heavy thud. This was followed by more yelling and the sound of gunfire. The unearthly noise was repeated, followed by another scream.

"Hold your fire, godammit," shouted William's voice.

There was the sound of chairs being thrown around in the darkness, a scramble, yet another unearthly noise, another scream, another thud, more panicked yells... Then the light returned as suddenly as it had vanished. Richard now found himself blinded by the brightness, which seemed intensified after the absolute darkness. He forced himself to keep his eyes open and looked around him hastily, trying to ignore the smell of burning flesh lingering in the air. Chairs lay upturned all over the place. A gun lay strewn on the floor quite close to him. People were crouched in a random assortment, having been blind to any objects behind which they might have taken refuge. And there were bodies, three bodies obviously dead, two sprawled out on the floor, one slumped over the glass table. Richard noticed that one of these was the enormous figure of Larkin.

"The clock's still ticking." Johnson and his mechanical cohorts were still standing by the door. "And now you've had a demonstration of our power."

He turned to leave again. Richard mastered the impulse to grab the gun lying at his feet and turn it on Johnson's retreating back.

Instead he watched helplessly as the robots followed him out. William looked round the room forlornly.

"Somebody call Body Disposal," he said gruffly. "Tell them we've lost three of our own men and the next of kin will need to be informed."

One of the remaining security guards promptly left the room leaving five to watch Richard and Charlie.

"And call for reinforcements," William called after him, aware of his diminishing protection.

Richard thought about the situation. What was Body Disposal? Did Delta Guard really encounter so many deaths that they had a specialist department to get rid of the bodies? He remembered what his ward mate had said: "No one survives here for long... They're either driven to insanity and top themselves or else they suffer a nasty accident." He looked at the twisted corpse of Larkin. Even in his abject horror he found it difficult to feel any sympathy for this particular man. How many people had he personally killed?

"Gentlemen," said William, cutting through Richard's horrified thoughts, "our priorities are obvious: get Johnson into custody and stop those machines."

"Sir," said one of the guards, "the EMP guns. There must be more of them. Why don't we get hold of them and use them against the machines ourselves?"

"The thought did cross my mind," concurred William. "However, although they can kill a man from a mile away, the EMP technology has a very short range. So against an armed mechanoid the chances are that you'll be killed before you got close enough."

"But it's worth a try, surely?" pressed the guard.

"It is worth a try. Set up a taskforce to put the plan into operation. The stockade of guns was being kept in the anteroom below the mechanoid storage chamber. Bear in mind that Johnson will probably have hidden them by now so you'll need time to find them again. You'll also need to work out a way of leaving the compound to attack the machines. But I like the idea. Get to it."

The guard left.

"Meanwhile, you two," William indicated Richard and Charlie, "you'll work on devising a software attack. Follow me."

Automatically, it seemed, Richard obeyed and with Charlie followed William from the war room escorted by the remaining guards. They walked along a few corridors before turning into another, fairly large, room. In here was a scattering of desks, some of which were furnished for normal day to day work, complete with PC and telephone. Others were fitted with what looked like surveillance equipment including a control panel and an array of CCTV screens. Another smaller door was at the far side of the room. It was closed and Richard could not tell whether a corridor lay beyond or a broom cupboard. Initially, William crossed over to one of the surveillance desks. He bent over it and began examining the images on the screen showing all the exits from the building. Each exit was guarded by a number of armed mechanoids. The main gates through which Richard had once escaped were guarded inside and out by at least ten of them. After a while, William straightened up and led the group to a normal desk.

"This is the control room," he explained. "It's a secure area with perimeter detectors; we'll know in advance if any more unwelcome guests are approaching. This PC will be your terminal to one of the grid nodes on Azis. Everything you need should already be installed: debuggers, compilers, editors. If there's anything else you need just give me a shout. I'll be just over here trying to uncover Johnson's movements and keeping an eye on Brain Stormer." He waved a hand vaguely in the direction of the far end of the room. "I'll arrange for an infrastructure technician to come down and show you round the system. Meanwhile, use whatever resources you can find to plan your campaign. Do whatever it takes to assure success. If you can't destroy the mechanoids at a software level then find a way to redefine their Prime Directive to re-establish correct behaviour. As you've seen, we can't leave the building without disabling them. And when Johnson's twenty-four hours are up..."

Without completing his sentence, William walked away leaving the two men, still under armed guard, to ponder their predicament. It was Charlie who recovered first.

"Well," he said shakily, "I can't see us finishing everything tonight. Can you? Not if we've got to burn the virus into a chip and install that chip into a robot and everything."

"Can't the toys be somehow hooked up directly to the computer?" enquired Richard. "You know, run the software and get the toy to do the broadcasting directly from there?"

"No, they can be hooked up to the computer but only for debugging, not to run software. We only put that facility into the mechanoids, although we later retro-fitted it into the service units so that we could... Hang on! That's a brilliant idea! We could use one of the service units instead of a toy. They run the same software so the results ought to be the same."

He turned to call across the room to William but found himself face to face with one of the guards. Irritably, Charlie side-stepped him and summoned William.

"Hey, Bill, have you got any of those service units hanging around we could use? Richard's had the brainwave that we could use one of those to upload the virus. It would be a lot quicker than using a toy because we won't need to burn it into a chip."

"One's on its way now," consented William without looking up.

"In fact," said Charlie to Richard, formulating another idea, "we should be able to get the service unit to transmit the upgrade to a toy. Then we'll have a backup in case something goes wrong. Neither the toy nor the service unit will be affected by the virus if we use Hive 3 protocols to tell it to run only on a mechanoid."

"Hive 3 protocols?"

"Hive 3's all the mechanoids. They're properly called Hive 3 Units or H3Us. So a Hive 3 upgrade will only affect the mechanoids."

Richard and Charlie spent a while sketching diagrams on an A4 pad and talking through the implementation of their plans. William, meanwhile, sat at his own PC looking harassed. An electronic sound came over the intercom. One of the guards alerted William, who seemed not to have noticed.

"Sir, there's someone at the door."

William looked up. Then he pressed some keys on the computer and spoke almost inaudibly to himself.

"Oh yes, it's, er..."

He left the revelation hanging but opened the door from where he was. A service unit glided into the room followed by twenty or so men. All but one of the men were obviously security guards; they were dressed in the same style of military fatigues as the others. These must be the reinforcements that William had ordered. The last man, however, was wearing casual clothes and was extremely fat. Richard recognised him at once. He and Charlie stared in amazement as the man known as Circumference waddled over to their desk.

"I've had a ticket requesting that I set up you two gentlemen onto the zettabyte grid system," he said to them showing not a flicker of surprise on his face. "I've set you up as a guest user and I've come to log you in, as it's against our security policy to let you have the password."

As he spoke, he turned his back on them and began typing on the keyboard, being careful to use his generous mass to hide any onscreen information from the two men. Then after clearing the screen, he straightened up and glared at them.

"This system is a highly sensitive government installation so I've given you minimal access permissions. Furthermore, all your activity - including all your keystrokes and any output you look at - is being constantly logged and monitored. Should you find the set-up unreasonably restrictive for your requirements then you'll have to get Agent Barber to raise a Severity 1 security access change request that will need to be..."

"Mr. Proctor here will grant you whatever access you need to get the job done."

Richard turned to look at William, who had crossed the room to join them. He wondered for a fleeting moment who Mr. Proctor was. But William's gaze was boring into Circumference and Richard realised that at last he knew this person's real name. Proctor looked outraged but before he could open his mouth to protest, William spoke again in a quelling tone.

"Lives are at stake. We need to get this done."

For a moment it looked like Proctor was going to be mutinous but instead shot a warning look at Richard and Charlie before nodding his agreement.

"Of course," he said resignedly. "I'd be glad to offer any required assistance in the event that such a need should arise."

"Thank you," said William. "Now please take these gentlemen on a quick refresher tour of the system and show them where they need to be." And he walked back to his desk.

Half an hour later, Proctor had completed the system tour and had adopted a position at yet another PC on yet another desk. He kept Richard and Charlie fully in his line of vision, however, so that he could have a clear view of their screen. Richard and Charlie, meanwhile, had found a copy of the core software for the mechanoids and were now poring over it, trying to decide on the best method of corrupting it while keeping it looking innocent.

The guards were still keeping an armed lookout but had begun to relax a little more, perhaps realising at last that they were all working on the same side. From time to time, two of the guards would leave the room and return carrying a tray of teas and coffees and other refreshments, which Richard found most welcome. They maintained constant vigilance on the surveillance equipment, however, on the lookout for Johnson as well as for who might be approaching the control room.

After several hours, Charlie announced that they were all set to transfer the mutated code into the service unit, ready for transmission.

"We'll need access to the main console," he said to William.

"Denied," interjected Proctor before William had a chance to respond. "Not even Agent Barber has access to the main console. Everything you want to do can be done from this terminal."

"We need to make a physical connection between the service unit and the main computer. I don't see how we can do that from here."

"This is the control room," snapped Proctor. "And you're not the first people to want to do something unorthodox."

He crossed the room and opened up a cabinet that looked to be full of an assortment of cables and peripheral devices. After a short while he came back carrying a rather thick cable with attachments at both ends. He also carried a pad and pen, which he thrust at Charlie.

"What's all this?" asked Charlie looking at the pad but not taking it.

"Procedure," replied Proctor. "All equipment on loan must be logged and signed for."

Charlie sighed and took the pad. Richard looked over his shoulder, his eyes falling on the last entry, which Proctor had evidently just filled in. It contained the date, the type of equipment (against which Proctor had written "1 (one) high speed USB cable"), the approving authority ("Agent William Barber"), the reason for the loan ("software upload to SU") and a space for a signature, which Charlie now filled with a scrawl. Proctor took back the pad and went to return it to the cabinet, muttering something about not raising a ticket.

"Not sure how this is going to help," said Charlie to Richard. "Unless..."

But Proctor had waddled back with the cable and plugged it into the back of the machine. Then he sat down and started typing on the keyboard, looking quite put out about something.

"I can make this PC share all its devices with Azis. When the service unit's connected to the PC it will then become visible to the entire grid. Unfortunately, I'll need to up the system privileges in order to do so. So I remind you gentlemen that your actions are being logged."

He relinquished control of the PC and summoned the service unit, which bleeped and advanced. Then he opened a panel in its chest and plugged the other end of the cable into a socket within.

"The PC should auto-detect this unit as a new device. The drivers are already installed so you should be free to go in a few seconds."

He did not sound at all happy in giving them such liberal control but William was still watching him closely without saying a word and he knew he had no choice. Charlie sat down at the PC. Then he suddenly spun around, struck by a brilliant idea. His sudden movements alarmed the guards who instantly pointed their guns at Charlie. Both Charlie and Richard raised their hands in panic.

"Hold your fire," said William calmly.

The guards lowered their weapons and Charlie and Richard slowly lowered their arms. Richard's heart was pounding loudly.

"Please," said William, "no sudden movements. These men are trained to shoot first and ask questions later. Now then, you had something to say?"

Charlie closed his eyes, trying to compose himself. Then he exhaled deeply and spoke slowly.

"Okay. I just had a thought. What with Circumf- with, er, Mr. Proctor logging everything, I just wondered if we'd be able to tap into the mechanoid logs from here. All the machines log their activity to a file called captains.log. That should have been stored somewhere on the main computer but..."

"There're no comms," said Proctor as if talking to a particularly slow-witted person. "The H3Us are not storing anything on Azis.

There is no log."

Charlie sighed again.

"They're not talking to *us* but they are talking to each other. The log file is just another data file. They should be transmitting it to each other all the time, including to this service unit. If we can access the log on this machine then we might at least be able to keep up-to-date with the mechanoids' plans. We might even be able to locate Johnson and disable his personal guard. It's worth a try, don't you think? Know thine enemy and all that?"

"Do it," said William. "But don't let it interfere with the main task at hand."

Charlie returned to the Azis interface and began trawling through directories until he found the file he was looking for. He let out a triumphant "yes" as he began to dump the contents of the log to the screen. It was primarily noise: rows and rows of entries saying much the same meaningless thing.

Broadcast message received from host H3U-22
Uploading new data
Transmission complete.

Broadcast message received from host H3U-93
Uploading new data
Transmission complete.

Each line was preceded by the date, time and process id, which all added to the onscreen clutter. But amidst the noise, Richard spotted a different message.

"Wait, what was that?" he cried as the message scrolled rapidly off the screen.

Charlie paused the output and scrolled backwards until the telltale entry was recovered.

Broadcast message initiated from host SU-6
Connection made to host AZIS-1
Transmission complete.

"It's told everyone," he gasped. "It's told all the machines out there that it's connected to Azis."

"Upload the virus immediately," commanded William.

In a new window, Charlie began to type furiously fast. Richard was not sure how the communications system worked but he did recognise that forewarned was forearmed and if the mechanoids knew of the service unit's physical connection to Azis then there could be complications.

"Okay, it's off," said Charlie pressing the return key with a flourish.

He swapped back to the log screen, slowing down the scroll so as to be able to read the entries.

Reply initiated to host AZIS-1
Hive 3 software patch received
Broadcasting...
Transmission complete.

"Now we wait," said Charlie dramatically, "and keep everything crossed."

"How will we know if it worked?" asked Richard.

"Keep watching the log. If it goes quiet then the hive's been destroyed."

There was silence as they waited. Then Charlie spoke again and this time his voice sounded horrified.

"Something's happening."

Now scrolling up the screen were several repeated entries from different mechanoids, each saying much the same thing.

Reply initiated to host SU-6
Software patch received
Analysing...
Incompatible upgrade rejected
Transfer terminated.

Broadcast message received from host H3U-56

Hostile packet detected
Transmission complete.

Broadcast message received from host H3U-57
Hostile packet detected
Transmission complete.

Broadcast message received from host H3U-58
Hostile packet detected
Disabling Hive 1...
Transmission complete.

"They're fighting back," said William under his breath.

The service unit let out a long, loud, high-pitched bleep and shot backwards across the room. The cable was wrenched from its socket, nearly taking the PC with it, and the log file immediately ceased scrolling. The service unit then began to spin wildly out of control before finally colliding with a desk and coming to a dead halt. William strode across the room to check something on his own PC. Charlie looked most discomfited.

"Okay," he said breathing heavily. "Okay, so we use a different service unit and this time we set its comms to read-only until it's ready to broadcast the virus. That way it can't alert the mechanoids."

"It's no use," said William from his desk. "I've just checked and I'm not getting a response from any of the service units. They've all been destroyed."

"And by the looks of things," said Richard in dismay staring at the last entries of the now static log, "we're next."

Broadcast message received from host H3U-91
Hostile elements located
Despatching units...
Transmission complete.

Broadcast message initiated from host H3U-2001
Startup complete

Receiving data...

Broadcast message initiated from host H3U-2002
Startup complete
Receiving data...

"What does that mean?" asked one of the guards, sounding nervous.

"The storage facility," said William now rejoining the group and looking grave. "The inert mechanoids are being woken up. I fear we'll soon be under attack from within and we'll be heavily outnumbered."

— Chapter Twenty —

Absolute Power

"How long before all the data's fully uploaded?" asked William to Charlie.

"Dunno," said Charlie. "With all the software and data they've got to receive, it could be a while. But you're only talking, say, half an hour or so."

"That gives you less than half an hour or so to come up with a way of disabling them before they're fully online."

"Sir," said one of the guards, "We can't tell from here whether the robots are armed but we really ought to despatch a security contingent to contain the threat."

"Do it, Hoffman," William concurred. "Apprise them of the situation and make sure they take plenty of the remote control devices. They ought to remain effective against the machines. Let's hope so anyway; we've lost too many good men already."

Hoffman nodded and moved over to another PC to despatch the patrol.

"There's movement," shouted another guard from the surveillance desk. "Sir, there's movement out of the storage facility. The mechanoids are on the march."

William hurried over to the desk. Richard and Charlie looked at each other, both at a loss for what to do next. How many mechanoids were they dealing with now? And was it really likely that the handheld devices would still work against them?

"How long before security get there?" asked William.

"Sir," interjected Hoffman, "we have a situation. The security team say that all the remote control devices have been removed. The men are powerless, sir."

For a fleeting moment William looked stumped. Then he adjusted his expression as if determined not to lose heart.

"Tell them to improvise," he said. "Tell them to do whatever it takes to hold off those machines."

"No!" cried another guard and rushing forward he raised his gun to point at Richard.

Everyone froze. Richard had automatically raised his hands looking utterly taken aback.

"Hicks!" snapped William. "What the hell are you..."

"It's him, sir," said the guard shakily. "It's like Agent Johnson said, he's controlling them. He can call them off."

"Hicks!"

"Sir, we're going to get our arses kicked and you're sending those men to their deaths. You know you are. Make him... make him relinquish control. He knows how."

"Hicks, stand down!" commanded William.

"Sir, he knows how."

"You will stand down immediately, Hicks. Lower your weapon."

Hicks dithered. William seized a gun from another guard and pointed it at Hicks.

"Lower your weapon now," he said threateningly.

Hicks lowered his gun, looking like he was about to cry. Three of the other guards moved forwards to disarm him. William relinquished his gun.

"We are in a very delicate situation," he said firmly. "You are all trained to deal with terror conditions and you must stay focused. Any further outbursts will result in disciplinary proceedings." He turned to face Richard. "I apologise for our friend's zeal. However, I must insist that you continue to work on a solution to the immediate problem of the new mechanoids. Otherwise we're all dead. Hoffman, tell the security team to engage the mechanoids."

"Yes sir," replied Hoffman.

Richard was shaking. The assault by Hicks was the last thing he had been expecting. But there would always be those who would agree with Johnson and believe him to be controlling the machines for his own ends, whatever they may be. How was he to convince them otherwise?

"We don't have much time," said William stirring Richard out of his reverie.

"Er, yes, um," said Richard hesitantly. "Actually I had been thinking of something before, er..."

He had indeed been formulating an idea. It was a wild stab in the dark but it was worth a try. He sat down at the PC.

"What's the command to shut down the mechanoids?" he asked Proctor.

Proctor sighed impatiently.

"There're – no – comms. They're not going to shut down just because you tell them to."

"No wait," said Charlie. "He may be right. If they haven't received all the data they might not have learnt to ignore us yet."

"Well, Bill said it himself, didn't he?" pressed Richard. "If the handheld devices might have stood a chance then I think it's worth trying a remote shutdown from here."

"The robots have no choice but to obey the handheld devices," said Proctor stubbornly. "The devices even took precedence over voice control – when we had it. That's probably why Agent Johnson's removed them all."

"Okay, we can give my idea a try or we can just sit here and wait to die. Your choice."

Proctor hesitated, apparently still not convinced. Then he got up and practically pushed Richard out of the way as he took control of the PC.

"It requires root privilege," he muttered as he entered the password.

Then he typed the command *hive3 shutdown now* and pressed enter. They waited.

"How will we know if it's worked?" asked Richard tentatively.

"We won't without the log file," said Charlie. "We'll just have to hope for the...”

“They’ve stopped,” cried the security guard at the surveillance desk. “They’ve actually stopped.”

“It worked?” said Proctor incredulously.

Everyone rushed over to the surveillance desk. The guard was not looking at a CCTV screen but at an image on a computer showing a map of the whole area. Corridors, rooms, the stairway and the storage facility were all on display. But most importantly, it showed personnel, including the now motionless mechanoids.

“The tracker array?” asked Charlie.

“The very same,” confirmed William. “It identifies everyone with a security badge and plots their location on this map. Anyone without a badge is shown as an unidentifiable entity. But all our robots are equipped with badges, as you may have guessed.”

“Might the shutdown command have affected the mechanoids on the street?” asked Charlie although he sounded doubtful.

“Negative,” said the guard. He flicked a switch and the image on the screen changed to show live CCTV pictures of the city, "they’re still on the move.”

“We must proceed with the task in hand,” said William. “Johnson’s deadline is fast approaching.”

A quarter of the time had already elapsed and they were no nearer finding a solution than when they had first begun.

Several more hours passed. Richard was finding it increasingly difficult to concentrate. He had been up for too long without sleep. As with all rooms at Delta Guard, the lights shone brightly all day and all night so it was difficult to gauge the time. However, according to the clock on the PC it was almost nine o’clock in the morning. He had missed the night and the working day had begun.

“We need some time to recharge,” he told Charlie, assuming he felt the same way.

“Fat chance,” said Charlie looking around at the guards. “It’s all very well for them; they can be relieved. But we're stuck here."

It was true that it was now a different set of people who guarded the place, the previous set - including the unstable Hicks - having left an hour ago. These new guards were equipped with the EMP guns although after Hicks' outburst Richard was not sure how reassured he felt by this. William and Proctor had both been caught nodding off a few times but Richard and Charlie had been plied with so much caffeine that they wondered if they would ever sleep again.

"It's a good point though," said Charlie, "about recharging. What powers the robots? Batteries?"

"Don't know," confessed Richard. "But now that I come to think of it, I don't even know where the battery compartment is on Dominic's machine."

"Hey," shouted Charlie across the room to William, who started, "what do those robots run on? It's obviously not batteries and I certainly don't see cables trailing from them."

"It is batteries," said William. "Immortacells. Automated Services made a range of batteries that never die - a real evolution in electrochemical advancement. All our electronic products come with built-in Immortacells. If you're thinking of disabling the power source, well it was one of the first things we thought of. I'm afraid there's no way to do it."

"Well, it was worth a try," said Charlie resignedly.

"I'm out of ideas," said Richard quietly. "Do you think Johnson really would upgrade the robots to absolute power?"

"He seems twisted enough, doesn't he? But you never know, absolute power might even give us an advantage. If I recall from testing, the robots still had to obey commands but you had to be careful how you phrased them otherwise they'd take you too literally. They tended not to validate any commands they were given but just blindly followed them absolutely. I'm thinking that we might, after all, be able to get our denial of service attack to work... if we could somehow communicate it to them."

They worked on in silence for a while, stifling yawns and trying to stay awake.

"Bill?" called Richard suddenly, much to Charlie's surprise. "We need some sleep. We're going to start making mistakes if we don't stop soon."

Everyone looked at him. Some of the security guards eyed him with suspicion as if suspecting him of plotting some devious escape. To his relief, however, William agreed.

"Okay, you, Mr. Cassidy, and Mr. Proctor can take one hour. One hour only and then you must return to work. I too will take an hour. Security, keep watch and make sure we're all awake again by ten thirty."

There was a general murmuring, whether of consent or of resigned obedience Richard could not tell but he gladly pulled himself away from the PC and rested his head on the desk. He sensed Charlie move away presumably to another desk. Richard closed his eyes and willed sleep to come. He was so tired. He needed to sleep. He had had too much caffeine. Way too much caffeine...

Richard's dreams were punctuated by images of robots stomping round his house chasing Dominic. Dominic's toy robot was valiantly keeping them at bay with its built-in bodyguard subroutines while Richard himself watched proceedings from his padded cell feeling quite paralysed. The robots turned into Delta Guard officers who seized the boy with his robot and started dragging him out of the house. They were talking as they went but their voices were barely audible. At first, Richard could not make out what they were saying at all but gradually words such as "bait", "diversion" and "sacrifice" began to make it through the fog.

"It's important how we say it; we don't want to cause unnecessary alarm."

"It's the best idea anyone's had so far and there's hardly any time left."

"What if the kid doesn't co-operate?"

"He'll co-operate. They'll both co-operate if they..."

"What's going on?" demanded Richard suddenly wide awake and realising his dream was real.

He looked round the room. It appeared that he had been the only one still asleep. Charlie and Proctor were sitting at the computer and although they were right next to him, both were determinedly not looking at him. William and the security guards were in conference but had broken off now that Richard was up.

"What time is it?" demanded Richard. "Why didn't you wake me? What have you done with Dominic?"

"Welcome back," said William. "We decided to let you sleep a bit longer so that you could have a clear head for a very important..."

"What have you done with my son? Where is he?"

William cleared his throat.

"Your son has been taken into custody."

"What? Why, what has he done? Where is he?"

"Relax. He hasn't done anything wrong but he was left alone at home and we considered that his solitude was not in his best interests."

"He was left alone? But he's only... Where was Amanda? Why was he..."

"We have no idea of the full situation but under the circumstances we considered him to be at risk so we took him into custody. We left a note for his mother to contact her local police station when she returns."

Richard could scarcely believe his ears. Leaving Dominic alone in the current climate seemed like the height of irresponsibility even by Amanda's questionable standards.

"We hope to bring him to you soon," said William. "He's not far away but we've not yet tried to get him into the compound. The gates are still being guarded by mechanoids."

"Oh I see where this is going," said Richard putting two and two together. "You think that by taking my son hostage I'll relinquish control of the mechanoids and you lot will be free to leave."

Some of the guards exchanged telling glances.

"Mr. Neilson," said William beginning to lose patience, "I am not Agent Johnson but rightly or wrongly I do believe that he will carry out his threat to give his machines absolute supremacy to eliminate enemy entities. You know that means summary executions. And the situation's far worse than you may think. Mr. Cassidy, tell him."

Charlie stopped pretending to be engrossed in his PC work and forced himself to look up.

"He's right. Everything we've been doing on this computer has been recorded so there was a copy of that log we were looking at earlier. I've been trawling through it with Mr. Proctor here. Mind numbing work, I can tell you, but it did reveal eventually that Johnson's made what amounts to a basic error of judgement. Although he painstakingly had all the SAM chips removed from his batch of machines, he went ahead and kept his machines on the same network as the rest of the hive. And the hive always keeps itself up-to-date. See here."

He scrolled back a few screenfuls until he found what he was looking for.

Reply initiated to host H3U-72 from host H3U-2012
Software patch received
Analysing...
Installing SAM upgrade...
Transmission complete.

"There're loads of similar entries from different robots," said Charlie. "And it would be the latest, corrupted version of SAM that they would have been upgraded to."

"The upshot being," said William cutting to the chase, "that if Agent Johnson carries out his threat then SAM will upgrade all the mechanoids – every single one of them – and cause them to maximise their enforcement of the law so that even the slightest transgression will earn an instant death penalty. We now have very little time to prevent that from happening. We must shut down the entire hive as quickly as possible."

"And what's that got to do with Dominic?" asked Richard.

"Your son," William explained, "remains the only person reported to have survived a mechanoid attack without intervention from the security forces. Everyone else has been either held captive until the police arrived or else they've been... well..."

"Killed?" Richard finished the sentence for him.

"Exactly. Now, our working theory is that the attack on your son was aborted by the bodyguard subroutines built into his own toy. The toy would have scanned the mechanoid for a weakness and then exploited that weakness, in this case by wiping out its Sector Zero. All that activity would have been logged in the captains.log file. Unfortunately, Mr. Cassidy tells me that the attack took place sufficiently long ago for all those particular log entries to have expired. It seems that only the last two million are retained. Therefore, we need to re-enact the situation."

"What?" Richard was incredulous.

"We need to attach Dominic's robot directly to Azis so that we can monitor its log entries. Then we need it to see the mechanoids attacking Dominic and observe what happens in the log."

"What? You are absolutely out of your mind. You're not using my son as bait."

"We have no time to enter into a discussion. The plan is sound and we'll be executing it as soon as we've got passed the front gates."

"And if the bodyguard subroutines don't work a second time?"

"The worst that would happen," said Charlie, once more staring intently at the PC screen, "is that the mechanoids destroy the toy before it destroys them."

Richard shot him a disgusted look.

"And my son?" he shouted, now flaring up wildly.

William nodded to the guards who promptly enclosed Richard to restrain him. They forced him backwards into a chair and cuffed his hands behind his back, ignoring his yells of protest.

"We'll do our very best for your son," William said dispassionately. "But whether or not he survives is not relevant to our counterattack. The toy will have scanned for *and logged* the mechanoids' weaknesses and then we'd have a weapon to use against them. Right now, that's what matters. The future of the country's at stake. This is the best idea we've had so far – and it was your very own Brain Stormer that came up with it."

Richard struggled against his restraints but there was no chance of escape. His only hope was that the robots at the gates would prevent Dominic and his captors from gaining access to the compound.

It turned out, however, that the robots were only preventing exit from the compound and after a further hour, William had given Dominic's captors the order to attempt entry. This they had achieved with no problem although Richard had not been happy at all about them trying this with his son still on board. Shortly, William approached Richard.

"Okay, your son's on his way down here right now. I'm sure you don't want him to see you like this so you'd better behave. Release him," he instructed the guards before issuing a final warning to Richard. "But if you attempt to get in the way of our plans you'll be locked in a cell for the remainder of this operation. Understood?"

"Understood," Richard consented grudgingly, trying to contain his anger.

One of the guards moved behind the chair and unlocked the handcuffs. Richard relaxed his arms, flexing his sore wrists. After a few more minutes, there was an electronic sound over the intercom. William checked his PC screen and then opened the door. Three guards walked in, one carrying a toy robot, another leading Dominic by the arm. Richard quickly got up from his prison chair and rushed over to his son. He flung his arms around him and uttered consoling words into his ear. Dominic did not resist. He seemed shaken and cold.

"He needs a hot drink," said Richard imperiously to William. "And some food."

It looked like William was going to refuse but then he nodded and sent one of the guards to make a fresh round of teas and coffees. He allowed Richard a small amount of personal time with Dominic while the initial parts of the deadly plan were being set up. Dominic wanted to know what was going to happen to him and why it was so important that his robot accompanied him but Richard could not bring himself to tell him. They watched as William took the robot from the guard and passed it to Charlie. Charlie deftly opened a hidden compartment in its back. If anyone did not already know that this existed then it would certainly be missed. Inside was another socket similar to the one that the service unit had. There were also some dip switches, which Charlie now adjusted. Richard guessed that this was to prevent the robot from broadcasting messages to the hive but he did not explain this to Dominic. Dominic, after all, knew nothing about the hive or about his robot's role as an anti-terrorist device.

The guard now at the surveillance desk was a beefy-looking woman who had earlier identified herself as Private Nolan. With some urgency she started beckoning William over to her.

"Sir," she said, "there's a service unit on the move."

"That's impossible," said William, crossing over to her. "They've all been destroyed."

"It's on the move, sir. SU4 in corridor N1."

"Can we get a visual?" asked William.

"Not in that corridor, sir. It's only motion sensors down there."

William looked at Richard for a moment then turned back to the screen.

"It appears to be alone," he observed but looked a little worried. "That's odd. Keep a close lookout for any additional movement down there. I'm calling Level One security."

He picked up the phone and pressed a single button to dial a number. His tone was urgent when he spoke.

"Unidentified personnel in corridor N1. Despatch a Level One security patrol to go there immediately. Proceed with caution and arm yourselves with EMP weapons. Subject is presumed to be the renegade Agent Johnson and is extremely dangerous."

Of course, thought Richard. Johnson would be trying to avoid detection by using the service unit's pass that he had earlier confiscated from him. Evidently, he was unaware of the hive's subsequent destruction. Dominic was looking inquisitively at Richard. Richard did not know how much he was allowed to divulge.

"Johnson's the one who had me wrongfully arrested," he whispered to him.

Dominic looked shocked.

"So you hadn't done anything wrong?" he asked.

"No I hadn't," replied Richard hotly.

"But Dave said..."

"He's always had his heart set against me but I'm sure that even your mother would have wanted to sign that petition for my release."

"Sign it?" cried Dominic. "She organised it!"

Richard felt his heart swell. His emotions were confused. He no longer knew how he felt.

"She was kind enough to look after me on Christmas Night before I had to go back on the run," he said, trying to keep his voice steady. "I hope to thank her for that if – *when* – we get out of here."

Dominic opened his mouth to respond but someone else spoke across the room and he fell silent.

"The alarm's sounding, sir," said Nolan.

"Damn it!" said William annoyed. "I wanted to take him by surprise. It's a bit late now but can you shut it off? Perhaps he'll think it was a false alarm."

"I'll try, sir."

"Mr. Cassidy," said William urgently, "please continue to set up the gambit. I suspect we're going to have some mechanical company rather sooner than we expected."

Charlie plugged the cable into the toy and began to rummage through the directory tree looking for the file captains.log.

"The security squad's arrived, sir," said Nolan. "There're twelve of them; that ought to be sufficient."

William spoke into the telephone again.

"Security, keep me up to date with what's happening down there. The situation may escalate at any moment. I'm putting you on speaker."

"Corporal Taylor here, sir," said a voice on the speaker. "Message received and understood."

"Sir," said Nolan looking alarmed, "there's more movement. It's... They're H3Us, sir. Six of them."

"His personal guard." William's fears seemed to be realised.

Richard had spotted them too on the log, which was scrolling steadily up the screen.

Broadcast message received from host H3U-1001
Personnel Defence mode engaged
Transmission complete.

"Taylor, be careful," warned William. "Six mechanoids are approaching you. They're Agent Johnson's personal guard and they're fully armed."

"He's controlling them, sir," said Taylor in alarm. "He's got one of those handheld devices."

"Confiscate that device immediately."

There was the sound of a struggle over the loudspeaker.

"They're coming round the corner, sir," said Nolan. "We need to get the men out of there."

"We've captured Agent Johnson, sir," said Taylor on the telephone. "And we have the device. We're attempting to neutralise the threat."

"You can't," bellowed William. "They're in defence mode. Get out of there now. Move east. Repeat, move east."

But it was too late.

Broadcast message received from host H3U-1001
Subjects sighted
Status: Hostile
Engaging...

There was pandemonium over the loudspeaker. Corporal Taylor tried his best to keep up a running commentary.

"We're under attack, we're under... Wha... It's all gone dark... I can't see a thing..."

Richard buried his head in his hands. The men would not stand a chance against the mechanoids. Then he looked up at the appalled face of Dominic and held him tightly in his arms.

"What's happening?" called William. "Do you still have Agent Johnson?"

There was no answer. Instead, there came an unearthly noise, a scream, gunfire, more unearthly noise, more screaming.

"The mechanoids..." cried Taylor. "The mechanoids... They're wiping us out... Request reinforcements... We've lost control, we've lost..."

There was more shooting, more screaming. Then there was silence.

"Do you still have Agent Johnson?" called William again. "Taylor? Report... Report."

Still there was silence. William looked extremely grave. Then

Private Nolan caught his attention again.

"The H3Us are on the move again, sir... But there's no sign of any other movement."

"Agent Johnson?"

Nolan shook her head.

"He's not moving, sir."

"Correction," piped up Proctor. "The security pass is not moving. And if Agent Johnson's been reunited with his personal guard then they will grant him all the necessary access and there'll be little requirement for his continued use of the stolen item."

William rounded on Charlie.

"We need to be ready in case they're on their way up here."

"Everything's set," said Charlie.

"Good. Get the boy."

The guards swooped on Dominic. Richard tried to fight them off but was quickly overpowered. Before he had time to work out what to do next two more guards had their guns trained on him. Another two trained their guns on Dominic who was secured to the same chair that Richard himself had been shortly before.

"Bill," said Charlie as if about to point out something horrendous. "I think Johnson's alive. And he's just upgraded the robots."

"Oh my god," gasped William, moving across to where Charlie was sitting. "It's doomsday. He's given them absolute power."

Even from where he was amongst the restraining guards, Richard could see the problem. The repeated log entries now scrolling on the PC screen foretold carnage:

Broadcast message received from host H3U-1001
Loading Autocracy subroutines...
Enhancing Justice Module...
Extrapolating violation protocols...
Supremacy subsystem online
Transmission complete.

—— Chapter Twenty-One ——

The Master

Richard struggled against his restraining guards but made no progress in escaping.

"Release my son immediately," he yelled angrily at William.

One of the guards used the butt of his EMP gun to hit Richard in the face. Richard collapsed to the floor, holding his nose and mouth. Blood trickled through his fingers.

"We need him compos mentis," snapped William at the guards. "Help him up, then attend to the plan."

The guards helped Richard to his feet and grudgingly gave him a tissue to mop up the bloody mess on his face. Richard glowered at William and the guards as he cleaned himself up. He felt a throbbing pain in his mouth and rubbed his tongue over his teeth to make sure they were all still intact. Remarkably, they all seemed to be present. But his troubles were by no means over.

"Sir," said Nolan from the surveillance desk. "The storage facility. The inert mechanoids have been woken up again. They're on the move, sir."

"Confirmed," said Charlie, "and this time they're not responding to the shutdown command."

"They've adapted," muttered William. "They must have known to disable the computer link first."

"That can be restored by rebooting Azis," volunteered Proctor.

"How long will that take?" demanded William.

"If we have to reboot the entire grid then we're talking way too long but we might get away with just rebooting the subnet for..."

"How long?"

"Maybe twenty minutes."

"Do it. We might just win the gamble."

"I am obliged to warn you though," continued Proctor, "that the reboot will disable part of the security infrastructure of the compound. The surveillance system will be offline while the system's down."

"Sir," said Nolan at once, "we need the surveillance system online. The H3Us are on their way up here and we need to be able to monitor their progress."

William dithered. It looked as if he was fighting to keep his head in the midst of the crisis.

"Do the reboot," he said at last. "We already know the robots are on their way so we'll just need to be prepared for them. Make sure the experiment is set up."

Richard caught a glimpse of Charlie turning to look at the helpless form of Dominic strapped to his chair before returning his focus to the computer.

"Bill," said Charlie in a warning tone, "there is a potential problem that I think you ought to be aware of. The bodyguard subroutine might not work against multiple attackers."

"What?" shouted William in alarm.

"Remember it was only intended as a piece of fun. I'm not sure by how much SAM would have enhanced it."

William was beginning to look quite out of his depth. Richard could almost hear the cogs of his brain struggling to come up with the correct course of action.

"Sir," said Nolan, "I'm receiving reports that a whole host of H3Us have just marched through the main gates and are heading in both directions towards the nearest towns. Should I alert the local authorities?"

"Yes," replied William hesitantly. "No. No, we don't want to cause panic."

"They're all armed, sir, and there are *thousands* of them."

William hesitated some more then turned towards the guards at large.

"Release the boy," he said, cutting his losses. "We can't afford to risk him if the experiment's going to fail. And release Mr. Neilson." He paused, at a complete loss for what to do next. "If anyone's got any suggestions as to how to proceed I'm willing to hear them now."

As soon as Dominic had been released he hurried over to Richard, once again shaking and looking abnormally pale. The guards too looked ill-prepared for the magnitude of their situation. Richard only now noticed how young they all looked. No one spoke.

"Very well," said William ending the silence. "This is the dark day that I've been putting off. But now I see no alternative than to declare a state of emergency and impose martial law on the city. London is at war."

There was more silence as William crossed the room to his desk and lifted the telephone to speak to the Prime Minister. But before he had had a chance to say anything more, they heard it - a rhythmic beating of metal footsteps in the distance. Everyone looked at each other. William hung up the phone and looked at Nolan as the footsteps continued, already a lot closer.

"They're nearby, sir," said Nolan in a higher voice than usual. "What'll we do?"

"The systems are still rebooting," said Proctor. "I can't shut down the H3Us."

"And they massively outnumber us," added Nolan.

Two guards approached William on either side of him.

"Sir, the situation's lost. Under Protocol 8 we need to get you to a place of safety immediately."

William looked from one to the other, utterly at sea. Without another word, the guards seized his arms and led him to the rear door and disappeared beyond. Richard looked in disbelief at the place where they had vanished.

"So what are the rest of us supposed to do?" he demanded. "Who's in charge now?"

It rapidly became clear that no one was in charge. The remaining guards looked from one to the other but no one wanted to assume responsibility. Charlie was still sitting at the computer drumming his fingers on the keyboard.

"Charlie, you're being very quiet," Richard called to him. "What exactly are you doing?"

"I've managed to break through the robots' firewall," said Charlie, "and somehow jammed open their voice broadcast channel. All that would normally mean is that when addressing a single mechanoid you could make a command apply to the entire hive by prefixing it with the words 'all Hive 3 Units'. Fine if you've got voice control. Anyway, it's a vulnerability and I've knocked up a program to exploit it by setting up a feedback loop in their comms systems. Hopefully, it will destroy them all but at the very least it will stop them from talking to each other. I need to implement it as a deferred job so that it will run as soon as everything's back online. It really is our last hope."

The sound of metal footsteps grew louder.

"There's not much time," warned Richard.

"Yep, almost there," replied Charlie unconvincingly.

The footsteps grew louder still. Nolan stood up, abandoning her post at the desk, and looked around as if she would very much like to run away. Suddenly, Proctor leapt up from his seat and with remarkable speed for one so fat did run away.

"It's every man to himself," he cried as he sped towards the main door.

But just as he reached it, it exploded inwards in a ball of flame. Proctor collapsed backwards onto the floor, his clothes smoking. A number of people rushed forwards to his aid and to confirm what had caused the explosion. Through the enormous hole made in the door, Richard saw them. A small army of mechanoids - dozens of them - was marching determinedly towards the control room, their guns raised.

There was nothing to be done for Proctor. Richard grabbed Dominic and hurried towards the rear door where William had escaped. A backward glimpse revealed Charlie remaining at the computer, typing furiously on the keyboard.

"I'm right behind you," he said without looking up.

"It's checkmate," Richard shouted back.

"You go on," insisted Charlie still typing.

Richard would have stayed to offer him some assistance but right now Dominic's safety was his utmost priority. He hesitated a moment longer, then dragged his son through the rear door and slammed it closed behind them.

Beyond the door was what appeared to be a disused open-plan office. There was no furniture in here, just an expanse of open space with white ceiling, walls and hard floor, like the rest of the compound. Richard noticed a number of cupboards built into the walls at waist height on either side but he had no time to consider what the room might be used for. At the far end was yet another door. Richard hurried towards this with Dominic in tow. He flung it open and stepped outside into a corridor. They had scarcely made any progress along here when the distant sound of metal feet brought them skidding to a halt. The noise was ahead of them, marching towards them. The mechanoids were attacking them from both sides.

Stumbling back into the empty office Richard slammed the door closed and looked around frantically. Then he pulled Dominic, practically dragging him, to one of the wall cupboards and wrenched it open. It contained a small pile of books and stationery but was otherwise empty, enough for Dominic to hide in.

"I need you to stay in here," said Richard firmly, "and don't move until I come to get you. Understood?"

Dominic nodded mutely. He looked paralysed with fear. Richard empathised as he helped his son into the cupboard and closed the door behind him. The sound of footsteps was worryingly loud as he now hastened to another cupboard to hide in himself. The first one he came to was jam packed with all sorts of objects. It looked like junk to Richard but would be too much of a give-away to leave it piled up outside. Instead, he tried another one. This one was mercifully empty. It was a tight squeeze but he just managed to fit inside. He pulled the door closed and the resulting darkness was complete.

No sooner was he securely hidden than the first sounds of battle blasted through his ears. Automatic gunfire rang out from the control room next door. The response was a deep unearthly noise and a scream. There was more gunfire, more unearthly noises and the sound of metal on metal as if objects were being hurled at the invaders. Footsteps immediately outside announced the arrival of the second wave of mechanoids. They faded as if going to join in with the ongoing battle in the control room. An explosion rocked the place. The din was unrelenting. But it sounded like the guards were fighting back well. A new noise rent the air followed by an almighty crash. Had one of the robots fallen? Perhaps the guards were using the directable EMP weapons. Then came terrified yelling, confusion, mayhem. Richard guessed that the control room had been plunged into darkness. The clamour of automatic weapons, mechanoid guns, EMP shots and more explosions rose to a crescendo.

It all lasted only a few minutes and then there was silence apart from the renewed sound of footsteps. Metal footsteps. It seemed like the mechanoids had won the battle. Richard hid in the cramped cupboard hardly daring to breathe, wondering if anyone was left of the original group and desperately willing Dominic to be safe. He thought he could now sense a mechanoid directly outside his cupboard. Racked with dread he kept perfectly still. He was sure none of the machines had seen him climb inside. But would their advanced sensors detect him?

There was movement outside. Perhaps the mechanoid had given up and was leaving. Then suddenly, there was the sound of splintering wood as the cupboard door was ripped clean off its hinges. There stood the gigantic form of the mechanoid, the door still in its metal hands. As it turned to hurl it aside Richard, in desperation, launched himself out of the cupboard and onto the back of the mechanoid, clinging on for dear life. With one arm wrapped tightly round the robot's neck he tried to reach for the gun before it had a chance to use it. But the robot was spinning round trying to shake him off. He was finding it impossible to stay on. He was slipping. And more robots were beginning to stream in.

With an almighty crash, Richard flew off the back of the machine. Another fired its gun at him. He moved just in time to save his life but the blast hit his legs. Searing pain momentarily shot through them before all feeling in them was extinguished completely. He watched helplessly as the robots raised their guns and pointed them at him again.

"Nooooo!!" cried a voice.

Dominic came hurtling across the room and threw himself down on top of his father, preventing the robots from getting a clear shot at him.

"No way," said Richard forcefully and grappled with Dominic, trying to throw him off. "You save yourself. There's no point in us both dying."

"No... Dad... No..." This time it was Dominic who was struggling to stay on and he screamed in panic as he began to lose the battle. "No... Daddy... Daddy..."

Despite being rendered lame Richard was still much stronger than Dominic and he threw him aside with relative ease. As the robots once more lifted their weapons, Dominic screamed at them hysterically.

"No! Leave him alone! Leave him alone!"

Miraculously, inexplicably, the robots lowered their guns. Richard stared in bewilderment at them, unclear why he was still alive.

"Go away," shrieked Dominic.

The robots turned and began to walk towards the door.

"What- what- "stammered Richard. "No, wait," he called after the robots. "Stop. Come back."

The robots continued towards the door.

"Tell them to come back," said Richard to Dominic.

"What?" cried Dominic. "I don't want those things anywhere near us."

"Tell them to come back," insisted Richard.

Reluctantly, Dominic looked up at the departing robots.

"Stop," he said clearly.

As one, the robots stopped. Richard's jaw dropped open.

"Come back here," commanded Dominic.

The robots turned again and began to approach.

"They obey you?" said Richard incredulously. "How come they obey you? How come they obey *you*?"

"I don't know," shrugged Dominic, looking calmer but still tearful.

"When did you find out?"

"Just now. This is the first time I've spoken to one."

"But- but- you have control. They didn't listen to me. But you can control them."

"Looks like it. I don't know how."

"Careful," warned Richard.

Dominic had to scramble out of the way as the robots continued to advance. There was a clamour as they all vied to stop in exactly the place where Dominic had been when he had issued his command.

"Stop!" cried Dominic and the robots abruptly ceased.

"They're a bit pedantic with their obedience," Richard observed. "No matter. Tell them to drop their weapons."

"Drop your weapons," Dominic relayed the command to the robots.

There was a loud crash as the guns fell to the floor. Richard was beside himself with excitement.

"Fantastic!" he cried in jubilation. "You're the key. You can destroy all the mechanoids. Go on, tell them to self-destruct."

Dominic seemed a little less sure now but Richard nodded encouragingly.

"Self-destruct," commanded Dominic.

There was no movement from any of the machines.

"Er, not sure if that worked," said Richard. "It might be a purely software annihilation like before. Tell them to take a step backwards, just to make sure."

"Take a step backwards."

The robots stepped backwards one step. They were still active.

"Hmm," thought Richard aloud, "maybe that functionality's still disabled. But the theory's there. And based on what Charlie said about the voice channel, you should be able to broadcast an instruction to the entire hive. We just need to work out the correct command to issue to shut them all down, or if nothing else, rewrite their Prime Directive."

"Rewrite their what?"

"Their Prime Directive. It's their most fundamental law. It's currently very badly defined but you should be able to change it, get them to obey orders."

"Well, why don't I just change it to be that they all shoot each other?"

"That might be a tad unsafe. Innocent people could get caught in the crossfire. Besides, not all the robots are armed. And these few here might yet prove useful. No, for now it would be sufficient to disable them long enough to allow the army to deactivate them permanently."

"I know," said Dominic excitedly, "I could get them to stand still and wait to be dismantled."

"I suspect not," said Richard thoughtfully. "They all came to life quite suddenly that time when I set off the evacuation alarm. My guess is that their low order functions would override idleness in favour of self-preservation."

"But if it's their Prime Directive, surely they'd just have to obey."

"Maybe so but... We definitely don't want to issue the wrong command. That might alert them to what you're trying to do and they may yet shut you out of their command protocols. No, I think we somehow need to occupy them permanently - flood their processors until they have no more resources to countermand instructions."

Richard was thinking once again of Charlie's fork bomb idea. But there was still the problem of uploading it to the hive.

"For now," he said finally, "it will be sufficient to get them all off the streets. And give us safe passage out of here. Do you think you can do that?"

"I'll try. Um. All Hive 3 Units, return to base immediately. And allow us out of the compound."

"That ought to be sufficient..."

"And stop attacking people."

"Yeah, good one. Now help me up. We need to get back to the control room. I want to check something on Azis. Rearm the machines; they can keep guard."

Dominic turned to one of the robots.

"You, pick him up and bring him back to the control room. The rest of you, pick up your guns, follow me and keep guard."

The robot lifted Richard into its arms and Dominic led the whole group back to the control room. The room was filled with smoke and the smell of burning flesh lingered in the air. Bodies littered the place, the young guards severed from life. Nolan was strewn across the surveillance desk, a gun dangling uselessly from her hand, her eyes staring blankly. Only one mechanoid lay destroyed on the floor near to where Charlie had been sitting. And beneath its inert form lay Charlie himself, crushed, his arms outstretched as if embracing death.

Dominic instructed the robot carrying his father to place him into the chair in front of the computer. Richard sat in front of the machine but swivelled the chair to face Charlie's lifeless form. A curious emotion welled inside of him. It was not grief. At least, it was not the grief that he had experienced when he thought that Dominic had been killed. This time it was much more confused. He did not know how he felt towards Charlie any more.

Suddenly, Dominic's mechanoid guards turned to face the main door and raised their guns. Almost immediately they stood down again as Agent Johnson walked through, carrying a remote control device. He was accompanied by his own personal guard of mechanoids and two Delta Guard security men.

"So," said Johnson looking coldly triumphant as Richard swivelled in his chair to look at him. "I think we can say you've been caught red-handed. And where's Agent Barber to witness that once again I am proven correct and he is proven wrong? But it's the end of the line for your little games, Mr. Neilson. As you see, I now have control over your robots here and I still have control over mine – and my guards."

"The device still works?" asked Richard looking at the remote control in Johnson's hand.

"Certainly it still works. Crude and manual it may be but it does still work. Now, you will restore full voice control to me immediately. And be warned, as limited as this device may be I can still use it tell the machines to kill you if you refuse to comply."

"Can you use the device to destroy the machines? They're all on their way back to the compound. Perhaps you can do them all in one go."

Johnson pressed a button on the device. Instantly, all the mechanoids turned and pointed their guns at Dominic.

"Sir?" said one of the guards, trying to sound respectful although he looked quite appalled.

"Relinquish control of the hive now," Johnson ignored the guard.

"Resist and the consequences are obvious. Comply and I'll see that you don't suffer *too* much in prison."

"Wait," said Richard, concerned for Dominic's safety. "Okay, you're right. I can control the machines. Or rather, my son can. They obey his voice, not mine."

"Do not lie to me," said Johnson unimpressed and his finger moved towards another button on the remote control, which Richard guessed was the command to kill.

"If you kill him," said Richard, "he won't be able to transfer control back to you."

"You pathetic man," said Johnson in revulsion. "You would retain control at any expense? You would watch your son die rather than give up on a lost cause? You extremists are all the same and you sicken me."

"One voice pattern," shouted Richard frantically. "The robots are only responding to one unidentified voice pattern. That's what you said."

Johnson gave Richard one last dirty look, then promptly turned to face Dominic, the remote control at the ready.

"Lower your weapons," shouted Dominic unexpectedly.

As one, the robots lowered their guns but continued to surround him.

"They listen to the boy?" Johnson was astounded. "How can this be?"

"Well, I had been wondering that myself," said Richard breathing a huge sigh of relief. "And then I came up with this theory."

Dominic and the guards also listened raptly as Richard explained.

"*You* gave him the power," he said, addressing Johnson directly. "In your continued delusion that I was somehow controlling the original mechanoids, you programmed one of your own machines to come to my house to kill my son. You thought that if he was killed right in front of me, then that would give me a change of heart and I'd relinquish control. But Dominic's own toy robot recognised the abusive injustice and defended him using its bodyguard functionality that had been upgraded by SAM. I believe that the toy robot not only destroyed the mechanoid but it also told the rest of the hive that Dominic was special and must not be attacked, that Dominic was master and must be obeyed. You lot lost your powers of voice control ages ago when you lost the rest of your comms. But Dominic's empowerment happened afterwards and has never since been rescinded. So even now, he's the only one they'll listen to. Ironic, isn't it?"

Johnson wore a very ugly expression indeed. He touched a control on the device and once again the robots pointed their guns at Dominic.

"His empowerment will end now," he said in a dangerous whisper, "either voluntarily or fatally. He'll have no control once he's dead."

"I'll do it," said Dominic abruptly.

"What?" said Richard and Johnson together.

"I can rewrite their Prime Directive," said Dominic. "I'll gladly give up control. Let's end it."

For a moment Richard thought he saw his son make some sort of facial gesture, not quite a wink and something that Johnson did not seem to have noticed. Richard nodded curtly to give his consent. Dominic cleared his throat and addressed the mechanoids.

"All Hive 3 Units, from this time onwards your new Prime Directive is to not obey any of my commands."

The robots showed no sign of compliance but Dominic looked quite satisfied.

"You fool, boy," spat Johnson. "You were first supposed to tell them to accept *my* voice commands. Now they will listen to no one."

"Oh," said Dominic innocently. "Sorry."

"At least you still have your little device, eh," said Richard bracingly.

"Yes I do," said Johnson. "And you have irked me once too

often."

Johnson raised the control once more.

"All Hive 3 Units," called Dominic as the robots continued to point their weapons at him, "open fire," he said and closed his eyes in anticipation.

"What is this?" said Johnson.

"Wait," shouted Richard.

It was not quite what he had expected but it might just have worked. Johnson was now jabbing at the button on the control device but the robots were no longer responding.

"What have you done?" snarled Johnson.

Richard beamed with impressed approval.

"Brilliant," he said. "A risky command but brilliant. He's permanently distracted the mechanoids. He's locked them into an infinite loop - a logical paradox loop. You see, their new Prime Directive is to disobey his commands. *All* his commands. And as you said yourself, the Prime Directive cannot be violated. But since it was Dominic who issued the Prime Directive, then that too must be disobeyed. To carry out his orders now would be a violation of the new Prime Directive. But to disobey his orders would comply with the Prime Directive, which is itself a violation. That's absolute power for you. You took away the robots' ability to validate instructions, to disregard those that made no sense. They could only blindly follow them. Literally. But look on the bright side - the robots with the SAM chip will also have been disabled, which is what you wanted. You see, they were on the same network as your machines so they would also have been upgraded by your mechanoids to absolute power. And so all are permanently locked up, trying to resolve their master's last command."

Johnson looked like he might explode.

"You've destroyed years of research, years of hard..."

Instead of finishing his sentence, he withdrew a gun from an inside holster and pointed this at Richard.

"Sir," said one of the guards. "Put the gun down, sir. You're under arrest for terrorist offences and for perverting the course of justice."

Johnson hesitated then swung round and discharged his weapon into the guard's chest. Before the second guard had time to react, Johnson had jumped over the lifeless body and fled from the room. The guard gave chase leaving Richard and Dominic alone with the inert mechanoids. Dominic extricated himself from the machines still surrounding him and ran into the open arms of his father.

"How you managed to keep your head and think of using a logical paradox loop is beyond me," said Richard proudly. "But you have just single-handedly saved the country from destruction."

Far from looking happy or even relieved, however, Dominic looked sorrowful.

"Are you ever going to be able to walk again?" he asked.

"I don't know. I can't feel my legs at all. But hopefully it's only temporary. Hopefully, I'll... Listen, you and I have to get out of here. But first I need to find all the stuff they confiscated from me the first time I was here."

With Dominic's help he wheeled himself over to the surveillance desk. Nolan stared lifelessly at him as he approached. Richard blinked, then with a muttered apology pushed her body out of the way of the terminal. He examined the map on the main screen but had no idea where his possessions would be. He saw two figures moving swiftly into the plant room in the south wing of the building. One of these was labelled as an unidentified entity. He guessed that this was Agent Johnson still being pursued by his lone guard. Johnson was no doubt heading for the exit that Richard's ward mate had told him about in the hospital. As his eyes continued to rove around the map, he saw other guards approaching the control room. And in the middle of the guards was William Barber. He spun the chair round just in time to see them walking into the room through the door. They came to an abrupt halt, taking in the scene before them.

"What happened here?" demanded William.

"The robots are ready to be dismantled," Richard replied. "What you, your guards and your technicians failed to do, my son did with no trouble at all."

Richard began to give them a summary of what had taken place since William's flight but was interrupted by the sound of a distant alarm. Richard consulted the surveillance map. The plant room had a flashing red dot in it. William joined Richard at the desk and audibly gasped.

"Fire in the plant room!" he exclaimed. "Dispatch a squad..."

His words were drowned by a much louder, more urgent sounding, alarm. All at once, the entire surveillance screen was flashing red. Richard remembered the words of his ward mate as if from a previous life: "Have you any idea how much flammable gas can be discharged around machines like that? If one of them goes up, that bang would make Vesuvius look like a mere squib." Richard guessed that if Johnson and his pursuing guard had had an exchange of gunfire then a conflagration could well be the result.

"Emergency!" said a recorded voice over the intercom. "All personnel must evacuate the compound immediately!"

"Where's my stuff?" Richard demanded. "I'm not leaving here again without all the stuff you nicked from me when I was arrested. I want my computers, my phone, my..."

There was a distant explosion.

"There's no time for that now," said William and he nodded at the guards.

The guards hurried over and once again Richard and Dominic found themselves seized with iron grips.

"I'll see that you're adequately compensated," shouted William over the noise of the alarm and more explosions.

"What about the bodies?" Richard objected. "You can't just leave the bodies. What about Charlie?"

But they all ignored him. After being shunted through rooms and corridors they were bundled into the lift. The explosions were visible now. Spectacular balls of flame were shooting into the air all around them. Richard could not be sure what had caused such destruction but as the lift emerged at ground level and the men toppled out of it, he reminded himself that as far as he was concerned Delta Guard was synonymous with destruction.

A white truck was waiting for them as they emerged. Just before being pushed into the back of it, Richard caught a glimpse of the mechanoid loading bay standing open. It was empty. William and the guards joined them in the back of the truck. Then the door was pulled closed behind them and before long they were on their way.

—— Chapter Twenty-Two ——

A New Beginning

Richard sat in a wheelchair in the middle of the room. Dominic stood quietly next to him. A week had elapsed since the events at Delta Guard but neither of them had yet properly recovered from them. Dominic had spent the entire week with his father and Richard felt that both of them had been sharing the same nightmare ever since. William stood by the door dressed in a long overcoat and carrying a black umbrella. It was bitterly cold outside and the rain had earlier been lashing against the window.

"Have you had any trouble with the neighbours over the last few days?" William asked.

"Not that I've noticed," replied Richard, "but they probably don't realise I'm back yet. I've hardly been prancing round the estate."

"No improvement in the legs?"

"None whatsoever." Richard made no attempt to disguise the bitterness in his voice. "The doctors still can't find anything wrong with them apart from the fact that they don't work. I've got some more tests tomorrow."

"Sorry," said William for want of something better to say. "I've asked my engineers to provide a full report on how the guns worked. Johnson's team developed them but no doubt unbeknown to him the electronic components were enhanced by SAM so no one now knows their capabilities any more."

"What do you mean you've asked your engineers? I can't believe Delta Guard still exists after all the destruction you've caused. Besides, your headquarters were burnt down, weren't they?"

"Indeed they were. We've put into operation our emergency continuity plan. There's a duplicate of the entire compound a safe distance away so we now work from there. It's a bit of a trek but we manage."

"Another Justin Case design. A fine use of taxpayers' money, I'm sure. Bill, why do you do it? Why do you work for such a barbaric organisation?"

"Most of what we do is good. You've only witnessed a tiny portion of our work and sadly it wasn't our best side. But we've foiled more terrorist plots than you can imagine. We've smashed through countless organised fraud gangs, drug cartels, people traffickers and paedophile rings, far more than our normal Intelligence services could have coped with. Whatever your views on the state of the nation, it would be a far worse place without Delta Guard."

"And yet you've also murdered scores of innocent people. There're still families out there wondering what became of their loved ones who just disappeared without trace."

William looked hard at Richard.

"Don't believe everything you read in the newspapers. They're full of half-truths and downright lies. Remember they exist to make money and if they can do that by sensationalising a story then they will do."

"But that chap - my ward mate. You killed him in cold blood right in front of me."

"Did you actually see him fall? I'm afraid you can't always believe everything you experience in Delta Guard either. We exist to protect the country and we sometimes need to do that through subterfuge and deception. Ask yourself if you really believe that we would let our prisoners take midnight strolls through the grounds by themselves. The truth is that by the time you got to hospital, I already had grave doubts about your involvement with the malfunctioning mechanoids. I had instructed Agent Johnson to let you go but he wanted one last ditch attempt to get the truth. So he staged your attack. He sent you to the hospital and placed you with another inmate, hoping that you'd get close to him, that you'd open up and reveal all. In fact, your ward mate was an undercover Delta

Guard agent and his midnight strolls were a method of keeping us informed of your plans. By the end of it all, it was clear that you knew nothing so the guard told you how to escape. Unfortunately, he failed to give you sufficient detail and in your anxiety you went to the wrong place. There was never any intention for you to find the storage chamber but the tracker array indicated that you had indeed found it. We knew you were heading for the truck and we suspected that you'd think your escape was far too easy - which it was indeed. We therefore staged the shooting incident you believe you witnessed so that you would not think of Delta Guard as an easy target to cross."

Richard was unsure what to believe. Here was another logical paradox; if what William had just said were true - basically that Delta Guard were liars - then what he had just said was probably not true at all, by virtue of the fact that he worked for Delta Guard. It was easier to change the subject.

"So is Johnson dead?"

"We're not sure yet. Only one body was recovered from the remains of the plant room but it was so badly burned that it can't be identified. If he is still at large it's likely that he'll still want retribution. He's not one to let a crime go unpunished so as long as he believes that you're guilty he'll continue to pursue you. So too may some of your own neighbourhood. We've distributed leaflets to everyone in the area warning them not to take the law into their own hands but nevertheless attacks on your home and your person may well continue for many years to come. I've issued a press release professing your innocence. That should be published in tomorrow's papers but in my experience, people are quick to condemn and slow to retract their accusations. So be prepared for a very rough ride." He paused and took a deep breath before continuing. "The only sure way to escape from the constant harassment is to adopt an entirely new identity. We have specialists who can take care of every detail for you. They can make you look physically different without you having to undergo lots of surgery, they can give you a new set of legal documents and a plausible history, arrange for the total disappearance of your existing self, and even train you into a whole new personality. The downside is that you'll have to sever relations with everyone you know right now, including your..."

"No," interjected Richard. "Absolutely no way."

William sighed but seemed to recognise the pointlessness of arguing.

"As you wish, provided you are aware of the risks. I'll leave my card in case you decide to change your mind." He dropped a business card onto the coffee table. "In anticipation of your expected reluctance, I've placed undercover guards on the estate for your protection. Don't worry, you'll have all the privacy you need - you won't even know they're there - but if anyone should try to attack you, your family or your property then police agents will be on the scene before you even lift the phone to call them."

By way of emphasis, William placed what was obviously a panic button next to his card on the coffee table. Richard was not sure how he felt about this alternative arrangement so he decided to change the subject again.

"What's happening at Automated Services these days?"

"Well, that's had to close down. It was the easiest option; they were officially responsible for the building of the security robots so they had to go. We're now using one of our other companies, Intelligent Intelligence. We had to lay off the Automated Services engineers - a bit unfortunate when people are trying to make a financial recovery after their Christmas excesses."

Richard thought about the engineers hoodwinked into building the mechanoids. Then he thought about the non-technical staff at the company and how they were still being salaried by Delta Guard. Then he thought about Charlie, the chief engineer, and how he had paid the ultimate price.

"Interestingly," William went on with a wry smile, "people then started complaining that Automated Services would not be honouring the all-risks guarantee on Mickey the Mini-Mechanoid. Sometimes you just can't win!"

"I assume that Mickey is now just a toy and no longer a spy?"

"No, the hive is still active. We've simply reverted to the set-up we had in place before the security robots were deployed. There are terrorists still out there and it's still our duty to seek out and eliminate all enemy entities."

Richard felt the blood rush to his head. He simply could not believe that Delta Guard were continuing operations as if nothing had ever gone wrong. The idea made him feel sick to the stomach.

"I think you'd better go," he said, pointing towards the door.

William nodded and turned to leave but paused and turned back to face Richard.

"Mr. Neilson, I must remind you that you are still bound by the terms of the Official Secrets Act. The penalties are severe for any violation. I suggest you explain this to your son."

He left.

Dominic stayed with Richard for one more night and by the following day, they were both feeling rather subdued, not only because Richard's medical tests once again proved inconclusive but also because they were expecting Amanda to call round later to take away her son. Richard had finally got around to phoning her to say that he and Dominic were free. She seemed initially very concerned to hear that he himself was now confined to a wheelchair but when she realised that they had been home for a whole week she had become quite incensed, as she had been worried sick about Dominic. Richard chose to stave off his challenge about her leaving Dominic home alone until he saw her face to face.

Richard had become quite adept at driving his wheelchair round the house but had only ventured upstairs twice since he had lost the use of his legs. On those occasions he had toppled himself out of the wheelchair and hauled himself upstairs by the strength of his arms, sliding down again on his backside. It was, however, on the whole far too difficult to do this on a regular basis and he had since given up. Fortunately, there was a toilet downstairs and the sofa had proved reasonably comfortable for sleeping on. Although he did resent such things as not being able to have a shower, the worst aspect of his inability to climb stairs was the fact that he was constantly reminded of Delta Guard's service units, which in turn reminded him of his captivity.

The doorbell rang, announcing the arrival of Amanda. Even the simple act of opening the front door had become awkward. The door opened inwards and Richard was still learning how to do this without his chair getting in the way. Amanda stood on the doorstep looking down upon him. Richard tried to ignore the obvious look of pity on her face.

"Hello there," he said, trying to sound normal.

"Hi," breathed Amanda in reply.

"Do you want to come in for a quick drink?" asked Richard civilly.

He was slightly taken aback by the pause that followed but even more so when she graciously accepted his invitation. He reversed his chair and directed it to the kitchen. Even making tea was cumbersome these days. The units were all too high to reach properly from a seated position. Richard struggled for a few seconds to grasp the kettle before Amanda stepped forwards.

"I'll do it," she said and took control.

Her hand momentarily brushed against his own as she reached passed him to seize the kettle. For an instant, both of them froze. Then Richard hastened to fill the embarrassing gap.

"So, how's Dave?" he asked as Amanda now began to fill the kettle.

She started as if stung by a wasp then turned off the tap and set down the kettle to boil.

"Dave and I are no longer together," she said, trying to muster up as much dignity as she could but being betrayed by her furious blushing. "I realised that we didn't see eye to eye on some very fundamental issues and..."

"He said some bad things about you, and Mum hit the roof."

Dominic had appeared in the doorway looking sullen. Amanda hurried towards him and enveloped him in a tight embrace. Dominic, however, seemed uninterested and did not return the gesture. When she had finally released him he stepped backwards away from her.

"Who's going to look after Dad when I've gone?" he asked without preamble.

Richard had been wondering the same thing. It was usually Dominic who did things like make tea and cook breakfast. The thought of no longer having him around was making him feel quite alone and miserable.

"I'm sure we'll come to some arrangement," said Amanda and left it at that.

As they finished their tea in the lounge, Amanda produced a tabloid newspaper from her bag and threw it to Richard.

"There's an article on the front page that will be of interest to you."

Richard caught the paper and unfolded it to read the enormous headline *Bye Bye Bad Bots.*

Has mechanoid madness suddenly become a thing of the past? The security robots that patrolled the streets of London with an iron fist have not been seen since their withdrawal eight days ago. The robots were deployed as part of a government initiative on the War on Terror but later went on to cause untold chaos in the capital. In the ten months or so since their deployment, far more innocent people have been killed than in the Valentine's Day bombing two years ago. Now the robots have all disappeared. So what went wrong?

Richard Neilson, mastermind of the legendary Super-Adaptive Module (SAM) that causes software code to rewrite itself, had a major fallout with his employers Automated Services Ltd, who built the robots. Neilson had developed the SAM chip for use in the popular toy Mickey the Mini-Mechanoid, also produced by Automated Services. But when the company used the same chip in the newer security robots, Neilson is said to have become "insanely angry". It is alleged that he went on to sabotage the chip and cause mayhem in the anti-terrorist units.

Neilson, who is described as a loner, was then arrested by a secret government organisation but refused to co-operate with officials. The organisation, known as Delta Guard, is reputed to use extreme techniques, including torture, to extract information from terrorist suspects. None of these appeared to work on Neilson and London's reign of terror continued. Finally, in what has been described as a "dirty deal" the government came to an agreement with Neilson to force the closure of the offending company Automated Services in return for the withdrawal of the robots. The company went into liquidation and Neilson was released. Soon afterwards, robots were seen all over the capital abruptly ceasing their terror tactics and marching away. William Barber, the founding chairman of Automated Services, tried to follow the robots back to their base to discover its whereabouts but was gunned down. His killers have never been caught and his body was never recovered. Meanwhile, the government have consistently denied the existence of Delta Guard and have added that they do not make deals with terrorists...

Richard stopped reading. There were more inaccuracies in that report than facts. He knew full well that William Barber had not been gunned down. Why, he had been round here only the day before. He remembered his remarks on newspapers: they're "full of half-truths and downright lies... they exist to make money and if they can do that by sensationalising a story then they will do". And where was William's own press release announcing Richard's innocence? He folded up the newspaper, contemplating his very uncertain future.

"They kidnapped Dominic, you know," said Amanda. "Delta Guard. Right from under my very nose."

"What?" asked Richard suspiciously.

"It's true, Dad," piped up Dominic. "I thought you knew. They held Mum at gunpoint and grabbed me and Mickey. It was really scary. They said something about... well, they obviously wanted to do all that stuff, didn't they?"

"All what stuff?" demanded Amanda in alarm.

They told her about the theory that Dominic's toy had saved him from the attack by the mechanoid and how it would have analysed and logged the mechanoids' weak points. Amanda was horrified to hear that Delta Guard wanted to reproduce the situation to get a fresh log and that William had said that the experiment was more important than Dominic's life. They talked themselves hoarse describing how the situation rapidly descended out of control, how they had to hide in a cupboard and how it transpired that Dominic himself had voice control over the entire army of mechanoids. He mentioned the mass of dead bodies, Charlie's dead body, left to burn in the exploding compound. When they had finally finished the story, there was a silence for several minutes. Then Amanda spoke.

"What will you do now?" she asked, still drying her eyes.

"I don't know." Richard felt like a prisoner all over again. "Nothing with computers, that's for sure."

"Can't you just publish your SAM code to prove that it wasn't at fault?"

"I don't have the code any more. Delta Guard took it all away and let it go up in flames. And the one off-site backup I had was crushed along with my car. Besides, it *was* at fault." Every word Richard now uttered sank him into an ever-deeper depression. "This was supposed to be my killer app but I didn't test it properly. I didn't even have the sense to use Brain Stormer to help me with the test plan; it might have suggested that I run SAM against itself. I should have picked up on all those stupid reports about the 'self-adapting mechanoid'. Only it was too late by then; the damage had already been done. How was I supposed to know that those idiots would put two chips into the one system? They've ruined everything!"

There was nothing that Amanda or Dominic could say to make him feel any better. They allowed him to talk himself into silence, even though much of what he said would be incomprehensible to them. Amanda wore a curious expression on her face. It was difficult to read what she was thinking. But even if she were sympathetic towards him, he knew that he would always be guilty in the eyes of the population and he would be hounded wherever he went.

After a while, it was time for Dominic and Amanda to leave and they made a move towards the front door. Amanda turned back and looked at Richard. Their eyes lingered for a long time. Then she whispered a quick "bye" and they were gone. Richard wheeled himself to the living room window to watch them. Outside the house, a man pored over a car engine but kept looking around furtively. Just down the road, another man talked on a mobile phone but glanced towards the house every so often. These were probably some of the Delta Guard operatives working incognito.

Amanda's red Toyota glided off the drive, turned a corner and vanished from sight. Richard continued to look out onto the street for several more minutes. Then he retreated from the window and hovered listlessly in the middle of the room. Depression was rapidly pressing in on him from all sides. He thought about the half-full bottle of vodka chilling in the fridge. That could make a useful, albeit temporary, means of escape. But he knew he needed something more permanent than alcohol. His eyes fell on William's card still lying on the coffee table. Delta Guard had already cost him dearly. Was he now supposed to sacrifice his personality to them? Would anyone stand by him otherwise? He thought about the online petition that Amanda had set up while he was in captivity. And then a stark realisation struck him. There was something far more important than anything else that he had to do, something he should already have done. It was imperative that he caught up with Amanda immediately.

Instinctively, he reached for his mobile phone. Then he remembered that he no longer had one. Wheeling himself over to his landline, he picked up the receiver only to find that the line was dead, which presumably meant that he could not even send an email, not that he had any computers he could use to do that. Besides, the situation was far too urgent for an email. He established at last that there was only one option left. He moved over to the coffee table, picked up William's panic alarm and pressed the button. A red light on the device started flashing on and off rapidly. In no time at all, there was a pounding on the front door. Richard began to wheel himself towards it but very shortly afterwards it burst open and half a dozen men charged in with automatic rifles raised.

"What the..." began Richard but was drowned out by frantic shouting from the guards.

"Freeze! On the floor! Get down! Get down now!"

Apparently only just realising that Richard was alone, the guards slowly lowered their weapons but stayed on the alert.

"Where did you lot come from?" asked Richard incredulously.

"Sir, what is the nature of the emergency?" demanded one of the guards.

In the furore, Richard had momentarily forgotten why he had summoned the guards but now the urgency came back to him.

"That red car that left about two minutes ago? With a woman and a boy?" he said.

"Yes, sir, we saw them leave the house."

"You need to take me to them right now."

"Sir?"

"The woman, she's... she's taken something of mine. No time to explain. Just get me to her."

"We're in pursuit. Tell us what she's taken and..."

"No! Just get me there. Please!"

The guards acknowledged before seizing his wheelchair and the whole group left the house.

Richard sat in the middle of the front seat of the van wondering if he was doing the right thing. But Delta Guard had used him for their own convenience. It was high time the tables were turned. In seconds, the red Toyota was visible up ahead. Richard noted that it did not seem to be heading for Amanda's home. Then he realised that he no longer knew where she lived. Her tone had suggested that she wanted nothing more to do with Dave; she was bound to have moved out of his house by now.

"Is she armed?" asked the guard next to Richard in the passenger seat.

"No," replied Richard dully.

"Dangerous? Psychotic?"

"*No!* I just... Listen, you must leave her to me. I don't want you to frighten her. And my son's with her. He's only thirteen so just be careful."

"Acknowledged," said the guard then turned to his radio. "All units, stand by. Approach in Passive Gamma formation. Target is in sight. Minor on board. Repeat, minor on board."

Another van up ahead pulled out of a junction and stalled right in front of Amanda's car, causing her to brake heavily. The van Richard was in then came to an abrupt halt immediately behind her rear bumper, not allowing any space for manoeuvring. From what Richard could see, the occupants of the Toyota looked quite bewildered by the rapid turn of events but he was already being carried out of the van and back into his wheelchair.

He composed himself and then propelled himself towards the driver's door of the car. The guards stood a discrete distance behind him but were constantly at the ready. Amanda's door opened and

she got out looking both confused and concerned.

"Richard! What's going on? Is everything okay? Are you okay? What are all these..."

"It's all right," said Richard consolingly. "I don't have a phone and this was the only way I could think of to get your attention."

Now that he had the opportunity to think clearer, Richard wondered why he hadn't simply asked one of the guards if he could borrow their phone. But Amanda was all ears.

"Why did you need to get my attention so urgently?"

"I forgot- what with one thing and another- and then I-" He closed his eyes, trying to master himself. He opened them again and gazed deeply into Amanda's. "I love you. I've always loved you."

Out of the corner of his eye, Richard could see Dominic watching in eager anticipation. But then his vision was occluded by Amanda's face as her tight embrace threatened to squeeze all the life out of him.

"You don't know how long I've been yearning to hear you say that," she whispered in his ear.

She pulled away from him and fixed him with a smouldering look as if seeing him properly for the first time. Richard opened and closed his mouth as if searching for a satisfactory reason that might explain why he had neglected to use those magical words more frequently in the past. He was spared, however, as Amanda's mouth closed around his own. He caught a glimpse of Dominic punching the air in jubilation, then he closed his eyes and disappeared into a world of forgotten bliss. A sensuous tingling was spreading throughout his entire body, even to his immobile legs. How long they remained coupled like this he did not know but all too soon they had broken apart again.

"I am so, so sorry for walking out on you," said Amanda. "I swear I never intended things to get this insane. I was afraid you had gone off me, you see. I thought you were using your computers as a means to shut me out and I just couldn't cope with losing you, not when you were right there in front of me. All those crazy things I did

- it was all just to get your attention. I knew I was wrong but as time went on it became so much harder to make amends and I was really worried that I'd lost you for good. I tried convincing myself that I was in love with Dave but I never really was. I only started going out with him in the first place to make you jealous. Then I had to move in with him because... well, you had stopped paying the mortgage - and rightly so - and I was being evicted and didn't know what to do or where to go..."

Her words tailed off. But Richard realised that he did not need to hear her explanations. He did not need to hear any apologies. An indescribable sensation was swelling in his heart. It was as if the lost years were melting away, as if the chasm in his life were finally healing. And yet she had, in essence, just said that she had left him because she had loved him. The rules of the game were complex indeed and would perhaps take a lifetime to master. Once again Richard found himself searching for suitable words of contrition to match Amanda's but she pressed a finger to his lips and shook her head.

"You were always the perfect gentleman," she said. They were about to start kissing again when Amanda broke off, glanced over Richard's shoulder and smiled. "So, did you need to be escorted by an entire battalion just to tell me finally that you love me?"

Richard looked around him only now realising just how many officers had come to his aid. Four vans, two motorbikes and a small band of armed men waited nearby, while up above a helicopter hovered silently, its characteristic roar completely neutralised. Richard smiled too.

"It's a level of response I could get used to. I told them you'd taken something of mine. But I only meant my heart."

Amanda shook her head.

"You always were a crazy loon," she said with a watery smile.

They began kissing again, their tongues dancing together in a frenzy of joy. But this time they broke away quite quickly as if only just remembering that Dominic was present. They turned to look at him.

"Please carry on," called Dominic through the open car door. "I promise I'm not watching." And he pointedly turned to look in the opposite direction.

"Your place or mine?" asked Richard.

"Oh yours definitely!" breathed Amanda. "I've been staying in your old flat and you know how much I hated it."

"Sir?" A guard had approached. "Sorry to interrupt but is everything okay?"

Richard and Amanda looked at the guard and spontaneously collapsed into a fit of giggles. For a long time they could not stop.

"Oh yes," said Richard once he had regained control. "Everything's just fine."

Reunited at last with his family, he felt ready to take each day as it came along, to rebuild his life from scratch. And as he looked into his wife's sparkling eyes he suddenly saw reflected in them a future that looked much brighter and much, much happier than he could possibly have imagined.

21369537R00207

Printed in Great Britain
by Amazon